Such Things May Be
Collected Writings

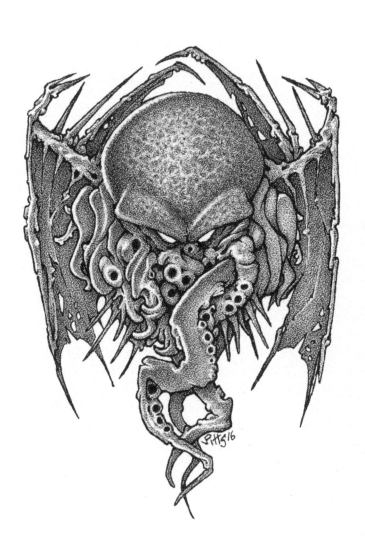

Such Things May Be Collected Writings

James Wade

Edited by Edward P. Berglund

Shadow Publishing

SUCH THINGS MAY BE
COLLECTED WRITINGS

ISBN: 978-0-9572962-6-8

Shadow Publishing
david.sutton986@btinternet.com
19 Awdry Court
15 St Nicolas Gardens
Kings Norton
Birmingham B38 8BH
UK

Acknowledgements

All pieces by James Wade published here for the first time are
© The Estate of James Wade 2017
'Preface' by Edward P. Berglund © 2017
'Foreword' by Fritz Leiber, published here for the first time,
and is © 2017 by The Estate of Fritz Leiber.
'Introduction' by James Wade, © 2017,
published here for the first time.

'Full Cycle' © 1955. Originally published in *The Stylus*, (April issue,
edited by Sotireos Vlahopoulos).
'Final Decree' © 2017. Published here for the first time.
'The Elevator' © 1971. Originally published in *Dark Things*, edited by
August Derleth; Arkham House, 1971; © 2017. Restored version
published here for the first time.
'Snow in the City' © 1970. Originally published in *The Eleventh Pan
Book of Horror Stories*, edited by Herbert van Thal; Pan Books, 1970.
'The Pursuer' © 1980. Originally published in *New Terrors 1*,
edited by Ramsey Campbell. Pan Books, 1980.
'Grooley' © 1972. Originally published in *New Writings in Horror
and the Supernatural, Volume 2*, edited by David A. Sutton.
Sphere Books, 1972.
'Something for Grooley' © 2017. Published here for the first time.
'Grooley' © 2017. Adapted by Terence Staples,
published here for the first time.
'Time After Time' © 1966. Originally published in
Korea Times, March 6th.
'Temple of the Fox' © 1965. Originally published in
Korea Times, October 31st.
'The Deep Ones' © 1969. Originally published in *Tales of the Cthulhu
Mythos*, edited by August Derleth, Arkham House, 1969; restored ver-
sion originally appeared in *Tales of the Cthulhu Mythos, Volume 2*,
edited by August Derleth, Beagle Books, 1971.
'The Nightingale Floors' © 1975. Originally published in *The Satyr's
Head & Other Tales of Terror* edited by David A. Sutton.
Corgi Books, 1975.
'The Facts in the Case' © 2017, published here for the first time.
'Who's Got the Button?' © 2017, published here for the first time.
'Medium Without Message' © 2017, published here for the first time.
'The Silence of Erika Zann' © 1976. Originally published in
The Disciples of Cthulhu, edited by Edward P. Berglund.
DAW Books, 1976.

To Fritz Leiber

who showed a lot of us

how it was done

Contents

Realistic Stories:

Music Scores:

Essays & Reviews:

"Enough to think such things may be;
To say they are not or they are
Were folly ..."

—Sir Richard Burton,
The Kasidah

PREFACE

Edward P. Berglund

JAMES WADE
(January 5, 1930 (Granite City, Ill.) to Aug 1, 1983 (Seoul, Korea)

I FIND IN looking back that there are interesting "moments" (not necessarily mine alone) that eventually combine with other "moments" to produce something worthwhile, such as the collection you are now holding.

Moments:

March 1971 – David Sutton, the publisher for Shadow Publishing, accepted and published my first story outside of the United States in his fanzine *Weird Window*.

September 1971 – I started correspondence with James Wade in Seoul, Korea. His wife, Lee, had worked as the librarian for the 8th Army Library since 1959. They had two sons, Adam and John. As well as writing fiction and composing and playing music, James also wrote for the *Korea Times* (an English-language newspaper in Korea) and the Overseas Section of the ROK Ministry of Public Information. Lee later died from a brain tumor on January 20, 1973.

April 1973 – I started correspondence with Fritz Leiber, who lived in San Francisco. When he lived in Chicago, he and James were friends and continued their friendship through correspondence.

April 1974 – I invited Fritz Leiber to contribute a story for an anthology that I was trying to put together.

June 1974 – I received James Wade's contribution for my anthology.

November 1974 – Lew Cabos, Randall Larson, and I visited with

Fritz Leiber at a restaurant in downtown San Francisco.

May 1975 – I received Fritz Leiber's contribution for my anthology.

Jul 1975 – James said that Arkham House was interested in doing a collection of his work, but that he could not include "The Deep Ones" or "The Elevator", as they had previously been included in Arkham House anthologies. James felt that this would be his only fiction collection and did not want it to be a truncated edition. Thus James declined their offer.

October 1976 – My anthology *The Disciples of Cthulhu* was published by DAW Books.

March 1977 – I mentioned to James that I had started a literary agency. James became one of my clients the following month.

June 1977 – James mentioned that David Sutton was interested in doing a paperback edition of his unpublished collection. James said this was the only lead he had for the collection, but he would rather it be a British reprint of an existing hardcover.

December 1977 – I visited with James Wade and his sons at his home in Seoul, Korea. He provided me with a copy of the manuscript for his collection to be entitled SUCH THINGS MAY BE. James said that he had the collection out for consideration at various places, but if those submissions fell through, the collection would be mine to place.

February 1979 – When James' "various places" (to which he submitted the manuscript) proved unfruitful, I submitted SUCH THINGS MAY BE to Lancaster-Miller Publishers, Berkeley, California, for consideration for publication. Lancaster-Miller had been recommended by Fritz Leiber to both James and myself.

December 1979 – Although Lancaster-Miller were interested in publishing James' collection, their anticipated financing fell through and they returned the manuscript.

April 2013 – I learned that David Sutton, through Shadow Publishing, was planning on issuing a collection of James Wade's work entitled as THE TEMPLE OF THE FOX. I wrote to David and provided him with James' contents for his collection, and David asked me to edit the collection. We decided we would use the title James wanted for the collection. Naturally, I accepted David's offer.

Edward P. Berglund
Jacksonville NC, USA
May 21, 2017

FOREWORD

Fritz Leiber

I AM WRITING this in an ocean-girt city of hills and high rooftops
that are blown clear of smog nine days out of ten by the prevailing
westerlies that stream out the flags and bring cool moisture from the
vast Pacific. But when I first met the author of this book more than
quarter century ago I lived, worked and wrote in a larger, darker city
almost two thousand miles east, a gray industrial metropolis at the
foot of a dying lake and mostly trailing a smoky pall. Yes indeed,
Chicago was very different from San Francisco, a more ominous and
energetic clumping of humanity altogether, and for a dozen years I
had been writing supernatural horror stories set in its gloomy street-
canyons and grim industrial wastelands, or at least taking their mood
from its strange and exciting black electricity.

Throughout my youth Chicago teased my sense of beauty and
wonder as well as frightening and depressing me—there was always
mystery around, one felt sure. A chief focus of this fascination was
the city's great elevated electric system, the all-encompassing "El"
with its shining gunmetal rails stretching all ways like serried knives
drawn across the brick-and-concrete wilderness, its richly dark and
odorous stations hidden in the shadows below or else slung beside or
just beneath the tracks like ships' cabins or the gondolas of fabulous
Victorian dirigibles. (In my young days the El was all above ground;
it had not yet turned half subway and burrowed through the muck
beneath the city's central Loop.)

It was from the El's lurching cars and through their grimy
windows that I first became aware of Chicago's filthy back yards and
of the mysterious black world of the unending roofs, an untenanted

checkerboard expanse unsuspected by most of the city's inhabitants, a spawning ground for sinister wonders.

While I type I watch them fitting out across the street a marvelous tiny second-storey park—Irene's, it's called—with sturdy small trees, flowerbeds, trellises, sunken lights, an arabesque of walks, tiled pools and fountains like a Persian garden; deeper downtown a bank has won permission to erect an over-high skyscraper by promising there will be around its base a larger such fourth-story park in miniature. I imagine a wonder-city with greenery sprouting from every building-top, even the high-rises—the hanging gardens of Babylon reborn. But that's in the future, even for San Francisco. Midcentury Chicago's roof-world was another matter altogether, a sinister lonely immensity shooting out beautiful dark rays.

I spent my boyhood on the north side, my young manhood on the south near the university I attended, whose imaginative gray gothic-to-modern architecture added a baroque intellectual element to the all-over darkly strange picture.

For me, the chief element in Chicago's climate was the smoke that is the industrial world's banner (my first modern-set supernatural horror story of any account was "Smoke Ghost"), making the summers acrid and in winter creating "thin, ugly, runny snow that made gray and brown chunks in the gutter."

That quote is from James Wade's "Snow in the City," one of the stories he showed me the evening we first met in my small house at 5447 Ridgewood Court, midway between the University and the Illinois Central tracks (electric although no part of the El system) beside the huge sullen lake. I recall him then as an unassuming but communicative slender young man, somewhat drably clad, slightly seedy. He may have told me he was a music student, but I soon forgot that in my delight at having discovered a kindred spirit.

Here was someone who shared my notion that Chicago was a place of darkly supernatural terrors and infernal miracles, the ideal setting for dramas of the weird and the unknown. Although a relative newcomer to the city, he knew it well. He had not only read and liked my stores, he had himself written tales that, although wholly his own in style and content, mined the same general Chicago veins that mine did.

His darkly atmospheric "The Nightingale Floors" with its clouds of echoing footsteps confirmed these impressions in a special way. We both knew the grotesque old privately-owned Harding Museum where (under another name) the story is set. It was only a few blocks north and lake-ward of where I lived. (Near the Harding and fronting the Illinois Central right-of-way was another strange structure reared by an eccentric millionaire with an Eiffel tower, a sunken room-girt garden and a third-storey glass dome, all guarded by a high wire fence and savage dogs. But a story is yet to be set in the purlieus of the Kiosk-Sphinx.) The drug problems of the narrator of the Harding Museum story also seemed to me a convincing modern touch.

"The Pursuer," which flirts with paranoia, was another tale of Wade's that gripped me. Chicago is not the nicest city in which to fear you're being followed. And if you're never quite sure your pursuer is that, and if you cannot find a pretext for (or nerve yourself into) confronting him, what then? What then?

For the writer of weird tales, there are always the problems of how much physical horror and eerie monstrousness to show the reader and visit on the protagonist-victim, and of how much to explain and reveal at the end about the underlying forces that made it all happen. If too little of both, you are left with only a mood piece. The reader feels he has been led on enticingly and then cheated. If too much, the reader is apt to feel that his imagination has been thrillingly, even deliciously stirred, and then a bucket of blood and offal dumped on his head, leaving him nauseated and with imagination thoroughly quenched.

Also, if the reader is at the end left completely in the dark as to how many of the events in the story really happened and how many were the narrator's hallucinations and faulty impressions, the result is apt to be irritating—though, of course, some uncertainties must probably always remain. For if the story is told with too much of an air of laying down the law, the reader will be left with the feeling that he has just been lectured to by some occult fanatic, and who wants that? Too many of those spoon-bending, UFO-contacting, white-witchcraft working authoritarians around as it is! No, the narrator of a terror tale must always manage to win, or almost win, our trust.

One thing I'm sure of: the reader's imagination must be left alive at the end, not horror-sated or mired in a sane—insane uncertainty. Vibrantly alive, even, and with an expanding cosmic horizon left to quest through, not a contracting one. The feeling of, My God, if such things can possibly be thought of for a moment as true, what other weird wonders may not be lurking out there in the unfathomed universe? To achieve this, the writer must tell just enough. Nice judgment is required.

An outstanding example of the terror tale that tells just enough is provided by another Chicago story Wade showed me more than a quarter century ago. "The Elevator" is set in a department store just before closing time. The events are puzzling, suggestive, faintly disturbing—no outright horrors. But near the end we glimpse—by our own deductions, not by being clumsily told so—the workings of a supernatural organization that is not hell although surely related to it, a sort of supernal mafia, a granter of ill wishes for a price, which froze this reader's marrow. ("If such things can be, what else may not be true? Just think—")

The same story also has toward the end a short paragraph which chillingly exemplifies the value of understatement: (The female narrator has just seen the elevator operator—a dark, smiling girl—beneath her window standing at her door) "I do not know if it is wise, but I am going down to let her in. I must know the solution to this whole affair, whatever the price. And besides, I am not at all sure that there would be any way of keeping her out."

After that quietly momentous evening meeting, Wade and I kept sporadically in touch by letter, exchanging news, observations, stories and comments on them. I was patchily aware of his Korean adventure and of the gradual transfer there of his life and many of his interests as he became a leading journalist in the large English-speaking colony, chief literary figure and musical composer, so that when I next met him in the flesh only three years ago he had become a half-oriental gentleman with a faint exotic music in his voice and eyes that, to me, definitely slanted.

But regarding the weird tales we both love, the next news of note came in the later 1960s when I learned that August Derleth had taken a novella of his for *Tales of the Cthulhu Mythos*, a collection which Arkham House seemed to take forever in getting published. I was distinctly in two states of mind about this news. I was happy for Wade getting this acceptance and I knew he admired Lovecraft as a writer as much as I did, but at the time I was dubious about the worth or wisdom of writing stories imitative of Lovecraft's tales—yes, even the ones Derleth himself wrote—and making use of Lovecraft's pantheon of grotesque extraterrestrial gods and monsters. Later my view mellowed somewhat, to the point where I wrote a couple of Lovecraft pastiches myself and decided I had nothing against such stories provided they were written with care, inventiveness, and complete seriousness, but at the time I felt strongly and adversely about the practice, so that I hate to confess how long it was before I did more than skim Wade's "The Deep Ones"—or carefully read any imitation Lovecraft, for that matter, except for the purpose of putting it down. Let me hasten to say that when I finally read "The Deep Ones" with an open mind I found it a quite stimulating and well realized Lovecraft pastiche. It takes off from a very modern area of research, the language of dolphins—an area that would have interested Lovecraft mightily had he lived to learn of it—and adds to that the imagined and equally modern notion of a scientific attempt to penetrate such marine creatures' minds telepathically. The setting is novel for such a tale—the Pacific coast—while the tale explores human pairing and sexual relationships (and also human-animal ones) in a way that Lovecraft himself was beginning to do in his nearly last story, 'The Thing on the Doorstep.' I must not give away too much of the plot, I will only say that when one finishes the story, one discovers that new depth and dimension have been given to the familiar romantic image of a young human riding through the waves astride a dolphin.

The same sorts of things, I had discovered somewhat earlier, were also true of the other Lovecraft pastiche Wade has included in this book, the short story, "The Silence of Erika Zann." Again there is a Pacific coast setting—San Francisco. This time the new area of experience tapped and explored is that of rock music compounded with diabolism, drugs, and a hypnotic use of lights—one thinks of Lovecraft's "The Horror at Red Hook" with its leering youths "playing eerily on cheap instruments of music"—while the story presses on toward its horrific climax.

Reading these stories and thinking of my own too that move in the same direction ("The Terror from the Depths" and "To Arkham and the Stars") it seems to me now that they are chiefly tributes to the magic Lovecraft's tales worked on us in earlier times, the precious glimpses his stories gave us of the world as a weird and wonderful place. They are attempts to create the same sorts of moods and experiences for ourselves and others from contemporary materials, to see if it can still be done, validate the Lovecraftian magic as it were— a minor yet fascinating area of story-telling.

During the first part of the present decade of the 1970s I lost touch with Wade for several years—it was a time of grief and troubles for us both, a cloudy time—and when we began to correspond again I found that a few of my memories about him and past topics had grown uncertain (some of the cloudiness had lingered in my mind, you see). For one thing, he seemed an older and more strangely worldly person than I recalled, so I asked him his age. He responded in his next letter that it was the same as Jack Benny's. I did not catch his joke—in his radio programs Benny always claimed to be 39—but dutifully looked up Benny's age in my *World Almanac* and for the next few months visualized Wade as a silver-haired, rather frail yet still remarkably vigorous 76. (If only I'd have as carefully visualized our first meeting I'd have known this couldn't be so—there was cloudiness in my top storey, all right!)

All too soon, however, I had to erase this rather touching picture of my correspondent. I think now that what I sensed as age was probably his eastern experience, the deepening of his character coming from life in a second world. At any rate, the stories he occasionally passed on to me now, along with items from the newspaper column he conducted in Seoul, all bore the imprint of his knowledge of Korea and Korean weirdities: "The Temple of the Fox," "Time After Time," and "Among the Sand Dunes at Crane Rock Point." That last story he classifies as "realistic," but it is a haunting tale for all that with a cachet all its own, very Korean. And something of the same is true of the two stories reflecting his army experiences: "Foreign Policy" and "The Scowler." Like his poetry ("Cotton Mather's Vision" is my personal favorite), like his pointed and ironic briefer tales ("Grooley" and "Medium Without Message" are particularly memorable to me), they go to make up and shade the complex entity, the multi-faceted point of view that is James Wade. He has more than one thinking cap, and in his writing he wears several hats—one is Midwest American and one is indubitably Korean.

—San Francisco 1979

INTRODUCTION

James Wade

INTEREST IN MACABRE fiction, fitful at best in the 20th century English-speaking world, has been stimulated by the recent revival of occultism. Output of weird tales has increased, and the severely limited markets have expanded somewhat, without producing much noticeable upgrading in either quality or originality of the product.

There is indeed little in modern macabre literature that can be called really original. Offhand I would tentatively cite Jorge Luis Borges. With his cryptic allegories; the wild zaniness of Donald Barthelme and Bruce Jay Friedman; the sinister black comedy of Thomas Pynchon; and the drug-dream nastiness of William Burroughs. But these writers are not consciously working the macabre vein: their varied visions of the world simply strike most readers as weird or fantastic.

The rest of us are attempting only further variations on ever more familiar, and archaic, themes.

Even H. P. Lovecraft's celebrated Mythos was more novel than original; its sources have been exhaustively traced down, and it is admired—if at all—for the individual blend he made of his borrowings.

Fear of the unknown, as has often been said, is the key to the fascination of this kind of writing, and today much less remains unknown (or so we prefer to believe). What remains hidden seems susceptible of eventual explanation, and therefore no longer projects an aura of dread.

Nowadays we fear ourselves and each other, all too well known, if not really understood—not the nebulous traditional terrors. (The occult revival is a reaction to this attitude, but probably not a very potent or permanent one.)

As a traditionalist I am quite clearly aware, then, that much of the fiction in this book is derivative at one or more removes from some of the basic plots, or even myth-patterns, of world visionary literature; that my effects echo or build upon those of earlier and more nearly original, if not better, writers. This is unavoidable and perhaps no disadvantage. True originality is much rarer than some critics suppose, and in many places for long periods it was looked upon as unnecessary, presumptuous, and highly suspect. Appropriate manipulation of traditional materials was considered sufficient indication of a writer's gift, and this is all I have tried to achieve here.

Sometimes my stories are consciously pastiche, as in "The Silence of Erika Zann"; at other times I became aware of what I had been doing only after I had finished. I differ from most modern writers of the genre only in cheerfully admitting these facts.

Though my strongest influence as a fantasiste came from the work of Lovecraft, encountered in 1945, this was not my first inspiration. My earliest story was written in 1937, when I was in the second grade: an imitation of part of a book called *The Cat in Grandfather's House* by Carl Grabo (Laidlaw, 1929), which still seems to me the best juvenile Gothic since George MacDonald's unforgettable *Princess and the Goblin* (1872). (I recommend it to the attention of reprint houses.)

As I grew up, I read and occasionally imitated the usual standard fare; Poe (discovered at nine in my grandfather's library), Bierce, Machen, Blackwood, Chambers, Dunsany, Collier and especially Lovecraft.

August Derleth was understandably unimpressed with a Mythos novella I sent him at 15 (though he later published work nearly as inept), and this discouraged my weird writing until college days in

Chicago, when I wrote half a dozen tales that were to some degree under a new influence, that of the urban horror stories in Fritz Leiber's *Night's Black Agents*. Leiber was a fairly near neighbor, and though I met him only once for an evening-long talkfest on macabre fiction, he proved most sympathetic and encouraging, and has remained so to this day as a correspondent. The dedication of this book to him is a belated gesture of gratitude.

The stories from my "Chicago period" were at the time submitted only to the moribund *Weird Tales* and the new *Magazine of Fantasy*, and they did not sell. I wrote little more in the next ten years. During the late 1960's I sent the same stories to other markets in England and America, where most of them were readily accepted. A few years before this I had begun writing again in a desultory fashion. (My available time for fiction is strictly limited, since I am basically a composer—a time-consuming habit!—who makes his living as a free-lance editor and journalist, in South Korea of all places.)

The first of my later stories to appear commercially was the Mythos novella "The Deep Ones", written with Derleth's projected *Tales of the Cthulhu Mythos* in mind, and published there in 1969 (later in paperbacks, in English, French and Italian). This tale was suggested by an item in *Time* about experiments with dolphins, including the photo of a pretty girl being suggestively nuzzled by one purposeful porpoise. (Commentators have not, so far as I am aware, noted that this story was a modest attempt to write a contribution to the Mythos involving both romantic interest and plausible character development germane to the theme, as was Lovecraft's late work "The Thing on the Doorstep", and none before or since that I know of.)

Derleth then bought my 20-year-old Chicago story "The Elevator" for the Arkham anthology *Dark Things* (1971), but insisted on a rewrite for clarification that I always felt was awkward and needless. On the advice of Leiber and others, and with all due respect to Derleth, I have restored my original, more sharply focused version in this volume, so specialists may if they wish compare the two. (There was a third, intermediary draft that nobody liked.)

Other sales followed of material new and old, though I stopped writing again for nearly five years after my wife's illness in 1972 and subsequent death in 1973. At length I found that from a 30-year hobbyist I had been thrust into a position I had never expected to attain: that of a "published author" in the genre, even a senior one in terms of years if not experience, whose opinion and advocacy were sought by unwitting neophytes. The next step was obvious: I had published half a dozen books consisting of poetry, material on Korea, and a grand opera: why not a volume of macabre fiction?

That took some doing, but the result is before you.

A few more comments about the contents, to conclude. Two stories originated from my travels in the Orient since 1960: "Temple of the Fox" and "Time After Time". The latter, written on shipboard in 1963, I soon realized was a variation on Conrad Aiken's "Mr. Arcularis", which had already inspired many other imitations. I sent it to Aiken for his judgment; he liked the story, and remarked that if I didn't mind the similarity, he certainly had no objection.

More obviously, "The Facts in the Case" projects Poe's "M. Valdemar" into the future, and of course both end in precisely the same words.

Probably the closest I have ever come to originality is in "Medium Without Message", which resulted from my intermittent inattention to a 1970 news broadcast. The resulting jumbled "double exposure" might not have been set down, though, if I had not been reading

Donald Barthelme at the time.

The museum in "The Nightingale Floors" is real: The old Harper Museum on Chicago's south side, long since demolished. The Korean temple in "Temple of the Fox" is an actual one. Not much else in these stories has ever concretely existed, since when I write fiction I tend to make it up out of whole cloth, setting and all; just as when I write non-fiction, I usually stick strictly to actual fact.

All these stories were written to entertain, to be entertaining, and—I think the phrase is Lovecraft's—to "crystallize a mood". I am sure the first purpose was achieved; and for me the third has been at least partially fulfilled. As for the second, the vital link of communication between author and reader, that is up to such of the unwary as this collection may manage to attract.

I hope it is not entirely unworthy of its wide-ranging and freely acknowledged progenitors.

—J. W.
Seoul, S. Korea

FULL CYCLE

L IFE HAD GROWN old. In the ten billion years since the advent of man on the planet, the protoplasmic material in the cells of all earth life had become stagnant, flaccid, and weak.

From the mightiest and most glittering pinnacles of civilization, human society had sunk back slowly, until now men lived little better than the pitiful, degenerate beasts that were left. Towering cities of half a billion population lay wrecked and deserted, strewn with the debris of geologic time spans.

Forgotten were the planet-mastering pioneers of the race, who had once brought to these crumbling towers all the riches of the remote solar system. The eyes of men, weary with gazing at the stars, turned inward again, this time to a great emptiness. Even as plant life grew pale and unproductive, and whole species of animals came to senile extinction, so the spark of creative reason in man's confused mind flared and faded into darkness and silence.

In the thin watery sunlight of an almost deserted village of stone huts, an old man was feebly instructing his young son in the vestiges of belief and custom remaining to the clan. Both were dressed in the flimsy pelts of beasts grown almost denuded of fur, and their thin forms crouched close together as if to ward off the ever-present spectre of hunger, or the eternal sharpness of the chill morning air.

The old man spoke in the jumbled remnants of a dozen once-great languages that had risen and fallen in past eons, employing only the most crude images and diction in his communication of the world's knowledge to the next—and perhaps last—generation. What he said might be rendered approximately thus:

"My son, when life began in the far-off times, our Great Destroyer was already working for simplicity and peace. But the evil principle of Complexity corrupted the spirits of the first innocent creations, causing a multitude of complicated and useless developments which carried life further and further from its goal of primal peace.

"But we know this universe to be primarily a place of beauty and good, and so we can see and gladly believe that the Great Destroyer is bringing our race and our world nearer and nearer the goal of beauty and peace. Soon the harsh and needless complication of life will de-evolve itself, passing through simpler and simpler forms, until at last, as our sun and planet grow colder, the single cell of life's fevered origin will be gathered back to its inorganic sources.

"With our hope and faith fixed on total oblivion, eternal sleep, we wickedly complex creatures of this futile earthly existence can find courage to live through our lives. We know that, joyfully, as time passes, life sinks lower and lower toward the undifferentiated chemical formation of utter peace."

The old man ceased speaking, but still the cold sun mounted wearily above the desolate village.

FINAL DECREE

I LOOKED AT her.

"Do you mean it?"

Her smile was defiant.

"I meant it."

"But when?"

"Any time. There's lots of time. It can't be too soon for me, though."

"But why, actually? What reason? You can't be serious about it!"

I was stalling along; the idea had caught me off balance.

"Must there be a reason for everything, in your thinking? Of course I'm serious. I wanted to, I did the ceremony, I'm sealed and delivered to Him. He may come for me whenever He wishes."

"I'm an intelligent man, I always assumed; and I thought you were an intelligent woman, Velma. But when you talk utter, disgusting nonsense like this—"

Her smile now seemed a little nervous.

"Why is it nonsense? You see a lot and learn a lot in L.A. these days, if you keep your eyes open. I met the group. I liked the idea, and I swore the oath. You never suspected a thing, but I'm his now. No one else can ever touch me; it's like being a nun."

"The divorce isn't final, Velma. We're still married."

"Don't get any ideas. It would be dangerous—for both of us."

Her smile was suddenly mocking.

I became disgusted with her for her silly credulity, her naive affectations, her superior attitude—but mostly because she was my wife and she was divorcing me, and I still loved her.

23

My disgust and my love mingled, producing a somewhat shame-faced and sadistic blend of lust. I snapped the latch of the hotel room door and stood with my back to it. I'd come after her to Reno to persuade her to give me one last chance. Maybe this was the way to go about it.

"We're still married," I repeated.

She saw my face and her smile vanished. I reached out quickly and grabbed her.

She struggled in silence and I began to make love to her savagely. After I had roughed her up a little, she stopped fighting, but it was almost as if fear had paralyzed her. She craned her neck over the edge of the bed, staring white-faced at the locked door.

It was only a few seconds after I heard the screams echoing down the hall that the door-frame exploded free of the wall.

Then He entered.

THE ELEVATOR

I

"GOING DOWN!"

Charles Dexter hurried deviously across the crowded main floor of the department store, and, breathless, bundled himself into the packed elevator. He sidled around a little, brushing against adjacent passengers, as if to assert his claim to the small space he occupied. The elevator began to descend with hesitant jerkiness. Rather stifled by the stuffy atmosphere, he gasped out an unnecessary, "basement, please."

Immediately he felt foolish. Where else was there to go? The elevator operator—was she smiling at his *faux pas*? It was hard to tell. She was a dark, swarthy girl (of Mediterranean origin, he supposed.), whose face seemed frozen in a smile no doubt meant to be ingratiating, but which impressed Charles as sinister and mocking. He had once seen something like that smile; that face. Yes, it resembled the mask of a Maenad which he had seen in a museum years ago, when he had been younger and addicted to going to museums. He looked around at the other passengers apologetically.

His mind returned to the business of the moment. What color curtain material was it that Edith wanted? Pink? Yes, he was sure it was pink. He smiled to himself, bitterly. Time was when he'd thought it was fun to run his wife's errands for her. Now, when these shopping expeditions had become a humiliating custom, he wondered why he kept on. Why didn't Edith, if she were ill (she was always ill), write or phone in her orders? Or have a friend (a female one) do the shopping? What kind of a Milquetoast was he supposed

25

to be, anyway? Just because he was little didn't mean that he could be imposed upon forever. He shot out his weak chin in mock aggressiveness.

This morning, over the breakfast table, when she'd put down the paper (it was she, not he, who read the paper at breakfast) and said, "Dear, I'd like you to pick up some curtain material at Feldman's on the way home tonight. It's on sale and I'm really too sick to go down. Five yards of the pink will do nicely."—why hadn't he stormed, struck her, left the house? Not over the curtain material (ridiculous symbol), but over the calculated, placid insult to his manhood, repeated over fifteen years until its ritual was taken for granted?

Instead, he'd merely muttered assent, got upset about it internally, thus forgetting his overcoat when he left. An annoying mistake on such a chilly day, which illogically strengthened his resentment.

No, he'd never objected, never broken the pattern, perhaps for the same reasons that he was still in the same job, living in the same apartment, thinking the same thoughts after twenty years. There was just no use trying to change, not any more.

The elevator, sinking abruptly, came level with the basement floor. Through the glass outer doors, the passengers could see the thronged, garishly lit aisles, the tricked-out cases of merchandise on display. A middle-aged woman stood near the shaft, probably waiting for an up elevator. Then Charles noticed that they were not slowing up, that the floor of the basement was rising to knee-level, to chest-height, and then disappearing, leaving them a view of absolute darkness.

The other passengers noticed, too. "Hey," protested a brash, big man in a brown hat and suit, "why are we heading for the bottom of the shaft?" An old woman next to Charles clutched the flowers on her ancient straw hat and looked confused.

Whatever shaft they were descending was a deep one, for the speed of the elevator had increased greatly, also its rattling. All eyes turned to the imperturbably grinning face of the operator. In the back of the car, a child began to cry. But the Maenad mask of the swarthy, uniformed woman did not change ...

II

My name is Dorothy Welker. I am an English teacher. I have just had the most unnerving, the most frightening experience of my life, and I am going to set it down here, hoping that a later, dispassionate examination of what I have written may lead me to discover a logical natural explanation for what I observed. At the worst, I can convince myself that what I think I saw was a dream or an hallucination, and use this account in an attempt to diagnose the cause and nature of my delusion.

Late this afternoon, after school, I went to the Feldman Department Store on North Grand Avenue, to buy a birthday gift for my brother. This errand took me to the basement, where I was somewhat shaken up by the typical sale-hungry crowds which thronged the place. The lights, the noises made the place seem a fantastic and rather grotesque mirage after a time and I remember thinking that the hubbub was almost hypnotic. I was not, however, ill, or even unduly tired. My purchase made, I was standing by the elevators, waiting for one to take me up to street level. As service was inadequate at this rush hour, I occupied my mind by idly observing the passing crowds, speculating upon their origin, background, and occupations. With an aloof detachment which is, I suppose, typical of school teachers.

Something—a light or noise—caused me to glance at the elevator shaft nearest me, and I saw that a full car was descending. As it drew

27

level with the floor, lit like a display case for mannequins, I distinctly saw and observed a number of the passengers: an old woman in a flowery bonnet, a short middle-aged man, a heavy youngish man in brown, a mother with a small child in her arms, and the strangely-smiling operator, an odd, dark-skinned girl.

But then my idly complacent attitude received a jolt. Instead of coming to rest and discharging its occupants, the elevator continued to sink past the floor level. Peering through the bottom pane of the glass door, I glimpsed the faces of the passengers, who seemed to be staring up in astonishment.

For a moment I was speechless and a little shaken. I quickly reassured myself, however, by postulating a sub-basement; a boiler room or office facilities down there. Stepping nearer the door, I tried to fathom the darkness of the shaft, but could see nothing.

Intrigued by the mystery, I allowed another elevator to go up without me. I was determined to wait for the one I had seen disappear, see who came up in it, and ask the operator what was in the sub-basement. I was oddly anxious to be reassured as to the existence of that hypothetical sub-basement.

My heart beating with inexplicable rapidity, I waited, peering into the dark shaft. I could not have waited long, no more than thirty seconds, yet it seemed very long. The noise and glare behind me had passed from my notice almost entirely, remaining on the periphery of consciousness, like an endless surf on a distant shore.

Then the cables in the shaft reversed direction, and the car swiftly climbed into view. It was still crowded, but I was more than ever shocked to discover that in none of the passengers would I recognize a remembered form. Could the car have descended, emptied, refilled, and ascended so quickly? Impossible. Yet there were no little man nor large man, no old woman nor young mother. I saw a tall figure

28

muffled in a black overcoat, a hennaed harridan in a purple dress, a midget with baleful eyes, a blonde girl whose thin face shone with an agonized, innocent martyrdom ...

Astounded (and more than a little frightened), I fell back a few paces. As the brightly lit cage vanished up the shaft, I saw that the weirdly smiling operator was still at the controls, sole remnant of the group I had first seen. It seemed to me that her glance sought me out, and that her strange smile deepened.

Almost in terror, I plunged into the crowd, searching for a floor-walker. I soon spotted an immaculate suit, a gardenia, and the aura of omniscience I craved. I approached him, calming and steadying myself with an effort.

"Could you tell, me, is there a sub-basement to this building? Some lower floor that the elevators run to?"

"No, ma'am. This is the rock-bottom. The foundations begin under this floor." His smile was wider even than his moustache.

"But I'm sure I saw an elevator, full of passengers, go down past this level."

"There's nothing down in the bottom of the shafts. Where exactly did you see this?"

I led him to the elevators and pointed out the place.

"It couldn't have been that one," he said. "That elevator's been out of commission all day. The gates in the car jammed yesterday after-noon. You must have seen some other car overshoot the mark a little. We have two new operators, and that happens."

I opened my mouth to protest, but said nothing. His assurance told me that I would find no car in service in that shaft, no lower level in the building.

Flourishing his smile at me, the floorwalker strode away. I stood alone by the shaft, confused and uneasy. By now, the passengers in the strange elevator would have melted elusively into the crowd; with no operator and no car, I was helpless to investigate further.

I stood by the shaft for perhaps fifteen minutes. No car descended, although the crowds, dispersing homeward now as closing time approached, kept the three others in service constantly. For the first time I noticed that there was a small, typed placard under the call button for the empty shaft: OUT OF ORDER.

I decided to take the stairs to the main floor.

As I headed dazedly for the door, I thought I caught sight of the woman in the purple dress who I had seen in the vanished elevator. I tried to break through the cordon around a perfume counter, but by the time I fought clear, her red curls had disappeared among the hundreds of bobbing heads.

I came straight home to my room, too upset even to eat, and began writing this statement.

Later. The bell has just rung downstairs. Curious to discover who might be calling so late, I went to the window. There I saw in the glare of the porch light, looking up at me, the set smiling face of the girl who ran that elevator past the rim of the known.

I do not know if it is wise, but I am going down to let her in. I must know the solution to this whole affair, whatever the price. And besides, I am not at all sure that there would be any way of keeping her out.

III

The tall man in the dark overcoat, carrying a package under his arm, stalked purposefully through the crowded corridors of the store. Soft chiming notes from a public address system rippled the surface of clamorous noise, warning of the store's imminent closing. Already, in far corners, lights were being snapped off, counters covered, tired salesgirls were primping for the parade home.

The man left the store through a revolving door and took a street car on the corner of Grand and Ontario. He rode several miles, to a shabby-genteel residential district of brick streets and brick flats. When he left the car, dusk had fallen ahead of him. Refracted rays of the invisible sun still shone on the flats and stores to the left, but gloom gathered in the narrow street he entered.

For several blocks he walked with the odd, clumsily purposeful gait of an automaton, still clutching his package, still keeping his coat hunched around his ears. Finally he turned in at a three-story flat and mounted the stairs to the top landing.

There he paused, produced a key-ring from an inner pocket, and examined several keys carefully. Subdued radio music eddied around him; from below came cooking-smells and evening laughter. Selecting a key he fitted it to the lock of the door before him. After some difficulty, perhaps occasioned by the unwieldy package under his arm, he swung the door open, away from him.

He entered a dim hallway, shut the door, and stood still, as if awaiting something. From an inner room a woman's voice whined weakly, "Is that you, Charles, dear?"

Another door opened and a middle-aged woman emerged, silhouetted in the stronger light from within. She wore a soiled white dressing gown, but was heavily made up and vigorous in her movements. As she entered the hall. her eyes must have first sought the package he held, for she walked forward, exclaiming, "So you did get the curtain material. But did you get enough? That package is so small I—"

Then her face grew pale and she started back, gathering the folds of the dressing gown about her throat.

"You're not Charlie! Who are you? What do you want?"

But the tall, determined man in the black overcoat had begun unwrapping the package he held. Slowly he advanced, approaching the woman, who clutched weakly at the door-frame beside her. From the package he drew a bright new carving knife, which shimmered liquidly in the bright glare of the bedroom light ...

SNOW IN THE CITY

W HEN I CAME out of the building, it was snowing.
Thin, ugly, runny snow that made grey and brown chunks in the gutter.

White in the air, showing up in the dusk; a pasty mud on the side-walk.

Snow in the country is beautiful; snow in the city is wretched.

It was cold.

"Buy a flower, mister. Nice flower for yah girlfriend, huh?"

The old flower woman accosted me as I stood on the wet curb waiting for a light to change. She thrust toward me her meager basket of wilted violets, crisp carnations, gardenia corsages with their sick-sweet reek.

"Buy a flower for yah girlfriend."

I looked at her: thin, wispy grey hair under frayed, dark shawl; mute, tired eyes; a slack mouth twisted with the fatigue of the past day. Her coat was an old, patched relic, her stockings of cheap cotton, her shoes split at the seams and with the edges of the soles worn away.

I smiled at her.

"What if I don't have a girl friend, mother?"

"Ah, mister, a young feller like you is sure to have some lady-friend. You're young and good-looking, you got money, why not make some gal happy with a nice bouquet?"

"I'm new in the city," I lied. "I don't have a girl."

"Then buy a carnation for yah lapel. Give me a break, mister. I been selling here all day and only took in a dollar an' a half."

"It's late, mother," I said, raising my voice to cover the traffic nois-es, "and, I have no place to wear a boutonnière. I'm just going home, to my room, and read a book." I prepared to cross the street, as the light had by that time changed.

"Jeez, can't cha give me a break, mister? I'm tired and hungry, been selling here all day."

"I know, I saw you when I went in. That was four hours ago, and it's a cold day. Are you cold, mother?"

Suspicion and anger gleamed in her eyes. "Hey, what you giving me? If you ain't going to buy, say so. Why you wanta string a poor old woman along?"

I prepared to step off the curb. "I really don't care to buy anything, but I was about to suggest that you might like to take supper with me. There's a very good cafeteria down the block, and I'm sure you must be hungry after selling here all day."

I peered ahead to make sure that the light was still green. I saw its bluish glow refracted among the scurrying snowflakes.

I stepped off the curb. It had now become swiftly quite dark. I seemed to be ambulating in an island of blackness, fringed by a remote surf of headlights.

When I reached the middle of the street, I noticed that the old flower woman was with me, mincing hurriedly to keep up with my long strides.

"Did you mean that, mister? About the meal?"

"Certainly," I replied. "Be careful of the slush, mother. It's begin-ning to freeze."

After the meal, I inquired where she lived. She gave an address in the slum district to the west. The distance would have required a long ride by bus and street car, and, since it was snowing anew even harder, I hinted that something warming, which I had in my room might not be amiss before she commenced her journey. She had been friendly, even garrulous, during the meal, but now her wary eyes narrowed to suspicion again.

"Where do you live, mister?"

"Down the street: a walk-up hotel. Nothing luxurious, but a nice-size room. Do step up for a moment."

She followed me in silence, still clutching the wicker basket of flowers. A few hundred feet further on, we turned into the entry of my hotel. As we climbed the dingy stairs to the third floor, I held the old woman's arm and helped her hobble clumsily up, step by step.

Out of the corner of my eye, I watched her impassive face and wondered what she was thinking. Did she really accept me as a charitable, lonely young man who had taken pity on her wretchedness, or was she alert for any possible, hypothetical danger?

At supper, she had told me quite a bit about herself; she had been a widow for thirty-two years, she had no close relatives, her father's family had come from Rumania, business was not good this time of year, you ran into all kinds being on the downtown streets every day. But had she really trusted me at all? Surely her slum-born cunning would stay instinctively alert longer than this? I must be cautious.

On the third floor, I hurried her down the hall and quickly unlocked the door of my room. Hustling her inside, I took her ragged old coat and shawl, seated her ceremoniously in an easy chair, and produced a half-full bottle of whiskey. Her eyes lit up. I poured her some in a tumbler and she downed it straight. I took a few drops and murmured, "To your health, mother."

She seemed not to notice, but glanced covertly around the room, the absolutely nondescript walls, the absolutely nondescript furniture. Her gaze rested for a moment on the blank window, before which a few snowflakes swirled like a stage illusion.

I refilled her glass, while she cooed and murmured inarticulately in an attempt to limit the quantity I was pouring. Nevertheless, I was most generous.

When she was well along with that drink, she looked around again and said deliberately. "Nice place you got here, mister. Nice of you to have me up."

"The pleasure will be all mine," I replied, graciously from my seat on the bed (the room had but one chair).

"You know, I can't help but think," she mumbled, apparently a little woozy already, "you're just about the age my son Charlie would have been if he hadn't died of croup. Just about the age."

"Perhaps the age," I admitted, "but it is very likely that I am quite a different person than your Charlie would have been."

She tried again, futilely, to wave away the bottle.

"I got to get home tonight," she said thickly.

"Never mind." I reassured. "We'll get you home."

She drank in silence for a few moments and then said with a return of the shrewd gleam to her eyes, "You know, mister, you're a funny guy. What you wanta help me out for is more than I can see. You buys me food, gives me liquor, treats me like a lady, and I don't even know your name."

"Have I asked yours?" I countered. "As for mine, even the stars in the furthest spaces would hush their writhing fires to hear it."

She was still engrossed in her own thoughts, now lapsed into the maudlinly drunken.

"My Charlie, he liked the stars. He tried to touch the big one on the Christmas tree the night before he died, just reached out his little hands for it, and next day he was dead, with his father not two months in the ground. Charlie ..."

36

I saw that the time was right.

I lifted the old woman from where she sat, almost drowsing in the chair. She was quite heavy, but I managed to place her gently at full length on the bed. She seemed to become aroused by the motion, for she blinked and moved her arms and legs incoherently.

"What? ... What?" she murmured.

"Never mind, mother." I soothed her, "just lie quietly."

I took off my jacket, rolled up my shirt sleeves past the elbow, and removed my wrist watch and signet ring. Reaching into a drawer of the bedside table, I took out the razor-sharp carving knife.

When I began to rip off her clothes, she struggled feebly, so I stunned her slightly with the bedside lamp. Then I finished removing the clothing from her wrinkled, old body. She recovered conscious-ness and began to scream faintly in a low, throaty voice. I stuffed my handkerchief into her mouth, but her wildly rolling eyes continued screaming at me.

With the knife I opened a long, deep slit in her abdomen, extend-ing lengthwise down her body. By dint of patient enlargement, I opened this incision to a width of some inches.

There were many interesting things in there.

By this time the old woman had ceased all movement, and the blood was flowing much less freely. I looked around, chuckling rather pointlessly, as if to receive the plaudits of some cosmic audience. Then, turning again to the work in progress, I made a number of com-plex excisions and alterations in my new treasure chest.

When I was perfectly satisfied with the job, I turned to leave. As I turned, I noticed the basketful of wilted violets, carnations, and gardenias sitting on the floor. As a final, decorative touch, I filled the old woman's abdomen with the limp, flaccid flowers. They seemed to be springing from her as if in some monstrous birth: here and there a green leaf or blossom was spotted with blood.

I removed the handkerchief from her mouth and surveyed the general effect.

I was well pleased.

I wiped my hands carefully on the handkerchief, gathered up my belongings, and left the room. Nobody saw me pass the desk, of that I am sure. The name under which I had registered that morning was false, of course.

Outside, it was still snowing. Traffic was less heavy and now the flakes had been able to unite, forming a smooth, white blanket over the cement.

It was beautiful, like in the country.

THE PURSUER

H E HAS BEEN following me for longer than I dare to remember. And it scares me to think how long he may have been following me before I noticed him.

He follows me when I go to work in the morning, and when I come home at night. He follows me when I am alone, and when I date a girl or go out with friends—although I've almost stopped doing those things because it's no fun to be with people while he's around.

I can't say to my friends, or to the police or anyone, "That man there—he's following me! He's been following me for months!" They'd think I was crazy. And if I tried to point him out to them another time, somewhere else far away from the first place, to prove it, why—he just wouldn't be there. I'm sure of that.

I think I know now what he wants.

I remember when I first noticed him—noticed that he was following me, that is. I was down in the loop on a Saturday night, just messing around, planning to take in a few of the cheaper bars and lounges. Saturday night is a pretty big night in Chicago.

I was getting some cigarettes in a drug store, and when I turned around he was there standing right next to me: small and seedy-looking, in a long brown overcoat and a brown hat pulled low. His face was long and leathery, with a thin nose and wide, wet lips. He didn't seem to be looking at me or at anything in particular.

I recognized him as the little guy I'd seen around my neighborhood a lot, in stores and on the street. I didn't know who he was, and I'd never talked to him, but I started to open my mouth and say something in a conversational way about running into him down here. Then I looked closer at his face and for some reason I didn't say anything. I just edged past him and left the store. He followed.

Every bar. Every lounge. Every joint.

As I fled from him, one spot to another, I kept remembering other unlikely times and places I'd seen him in the last few days, and longer ago than that, it seemed to me. Maybe I imagined a few of them, but there were plenty I could be pretty sure about.

And I began to get scared. I didn't know what he wanted; I thought he might be planning to rob me or kill me (why, I didn't know; I had little enough)—I couldn't face him, I couldn't look at him.

He would come into a place like he always does, just a little after me—very quiet, very unnoticeable—and stay just a medium distance away from me. Nothing suspicious. And he wouldn't leave just when I did, he was too clever for that; but soon after I'd know that he was coming on behind me.

I have never heard him speak.

The last place I went to that night, I must have been pretty shook up. I couldn't stand to keep looking at it, either. The barkeep, a big bald-headed guy, leaned forward and squinted at me through the foggy neon-light.

"'S matter, buddy, you expecting somebody?"

I got up and went out.

It took a lot of courage to go through that door; I was deadly afraid of meeting him coming in.

I didn't, and I didn't see him on the street, either, but right away I knew he was behind me.

I was pretty drunk by that time, with all the doubles I had knocked back in the bars I'd visited, and it was like some crazy nightmare, staggering along Randolph Street under all the glaring neon signs, with the loudspeakers blaring music from inside the lounges, and the crowds pushing in every direction. I felt sick and soared enough almost to cry. People looked at me, but I guess they thought I was just drunk. Naturally, no one ever noticed him.

After a while I threw up in an alley, and then I felt a little calmer and headed for home. I knew he was on the streetcar with me, and I knew he got off at my stop. I went down the street as fast as I could, hardly able to tell my rooming house from all the others just like it.

At last I found it and staggered upstairs, groped open my door, and threw the bolt behind me. I went to the window and looked down, peering intently through the darkness toward the splashes of light from the street lamps, but I didn't see him below on the street, it was dark and quiet and empty. (I never do see him down there, in fact, but somehow he's always after me as soon as I come out.)

I went over to the mirror and stood there, as if for company. If only I'd had some family, or anyone that cared enough to believe such a crazy story! But there was no one.

I was very scared; at that time I believed he wanted to hurt me. I know better now.

I went over and lay down on the bed, trembling. After a while I fell asleep, and slept all the next day.

When I went out that evening, he was standing on the corner.

That's how it's been ever since: day or night, anywhere, everywhere, I can always spot him if I dare look. I've tried every way to dodge or elude him, even made a sort of grim game out of it, but nothing is any good.

All this time I couldn't think of anything to do about him. I knew that I couldn't prove a thing, that there was no way to get any witnesses without making people think I was crazy. I knew that even if I took a train or plane and went a thousand miles, he'd be there, if he wanted to be, as soon as I was there or sooner, and it would start all over.

After a while I began almost to get used to it. I became convinced he wouldn't try to hurt me; he'd had too many chances to do that already. The only thing I could think of to do was to keep working, to act as if nothing was the matter, and to ignore him, maybe someday he wouldn't be there.

I started staying in, not seeing anyone, pretending to be sick if friends called. Gradually they stopped calling. I tried to read magazines all the time I was off work.

Lately I find that I can't stand that any more. I can't sit in my room and do nothing, and not know where he is. As bad as it is, it's better to know that he's walking behind me, or standing at the end of the bar, or waiting on the corner outside—better than imagining all sorts of things.

So I walk.

I walk in all kinds of weather, in all kinds of places. I walk at any time of the day or night. I walk for hours and if I get tired I get on a streetcar or a bus, and when I get off I walk some more.

I walk along shabby streets of lined-up flats and brownstones where the prostitutes stand under the street lights after dark and writhe their bodies when you pass by. I walk in the park during afternoon rains, when no one is there but us and the thunder. I walk on the lake-front breakwater at midnight, while the cold wind sends waves slithering inland to shatter into nets of spray.

I walk in suburban neighborhoods, the sun bakes the brick and concrete, cars are parked in neat rows under shade trees. I walk in the snow and slush along skid row, where legless beggars and awful cripples and drunks and degenerates sprawl on the sidewalks. I walk through market day on Maxwell Street, with all the million-and-one things in stalls and booths, with the spicy food-smells and the crazy sales-spiels and the jabbering crowds of every kind of people on earth.

I walk by the university campuses, and the churches, and the blocks and blocks of stores and bars, stores and bars. And I know that whenever I look behind, I'll be able to see his small, shuffling form, that brown hat and overcoat, that long, expressionless face— never looking at me, but knowing I'm there.

And I know what he wants.

He wants me, some night on a dark street (or in the neon-glow outside a tavern, or in a park at noon, or by a church while they're holding service inside and you can hear the hymn singing)—he wants me to turn around and wait for him. No—he wants me to walk back and come up to him.

He wants more than that. He doesn't expect me to ask what he's doing, why he's following me. The time is long past for that. He wants me—he is inviting me to come up to him in blind rage and attack him; to try to kill him in any way I'm able.

And that I must not do. I don't know why, but the thought of doing that—as satisfying as it should be after all I've been through— makes me run cold with a sweat of horror beyond any revulsion I felt for him up to now.

I must not, I dare not approach him. Above all, I must not touch him, or try to injure him in any way. I can't imagine what would happen if I did, but it would be very awful.

I must continue not to pay him any heed at all.

And yet I know, if he keeps on following me, sometime, some-where, I'll not be able to help myself; I will turn back on him with insane fury and try to kill him. And then ...

GROOLEY

W HEN TIMMY FIRST started doing it, we thought it was a usual four-to-six gambit: an only child, too young even for kindergarten, living in an apartment house where the other kids are all younger or older than he, imagines a playmate for himself—some fanciful wish-projection that provides companionship and a shared private world adults can't enter. It's all in the books. We didn't pay much attention when Timmy started talking about Grooley.

"I played with Grooley today a while. He's funny looking and all wet."

"That sounds like some of the guys I work with," Roger said. He can't resist making jokes that are over Timmy's head, though he knows what the psychology books say about that. "Who's Grooley?"

"Oh, he lives in the other room. Not really there, but someplace else. Down below."

The TV was on and neither of us took the trouble to try to analyze Timmy's answer. Ignored, he toddled away.

"Where do you suppose he got that name—Grooley, was it?" Roger asked presently.

"Maybe from TV. He wanders around in here a lot while we watch, and he can hear even if he isn't looking," I suggested. Timmy seldom sat still long enough to watch television.

"Is it good, this business of making up playmates? And wet ones at that! I forget what the book says."

"Perfectly normal, no matter how far-out their attributes. Gives a healthy release to the imagination."

"I wish he had some kids his own age to play with, Babs."

45

"I know, I do too. But he won't be going to school for almost two years."

"We may move before then. Someplace where there are kids and yard space. Apartments aren't good for children."

Roger has been talking about a place of our own ever since Timmy was born. But the apartment is close to his work, and it is my guarded private opinion that he likes it here.

The next phase was a difficult one, but again scarcely unique. One morning while he was dressing Roger yelled into the kitchen, "Where's my tie-clasp, Babs? You know, the one with the turquoise setting?"

I left off preparing breakfast and went to help him hunt, confident that it would turn up in some perfectly obvious place. "Just like Blondie in the funny papers," I said to myself, which is one of those things you don't say aloud.

It didn't turn up. As we rummaged the drawers, Roger growled, "Do you think that maid might have—?" Roger chronically distrusts all domestics, though we have never yet lost anything through pilfering.

"She hasn't been here since last Thursday, and I distinctly remember your wearing it Monday. With that blue tie."

"Timmy likes to play with it. Ask him."

Timmy, still tousle-headed and blinky from sleep, remembered playing with the clasp on some vague past occasion that might have been the day before, but didn't remember where he might have left it. He was padding around the kitchen in his blue bunny-pajamas, more interested in breakfast than tie-clasps.

I abandoned the latter for the former, but Roger continued his futile search, the unsuccessful outcome of which probably spoiled his whole day, as little things have a habit of doing with him.

That afternoon I opened the bathroom door and caught Timmy in the act of tossing something into the john. A flash of pink and a plangent plop brought my new shell earrings to mind. He had pulled the handle before I could reach him.

Timmy in tow, I lurched into the bedroom to confirm my suspicions: the little jewel box was open and the earrings, which had fascinated Timmy, were missing. I lost my temper in a way that the Book would never condone and paddled the child soundly.

"I think I know where your tie-clasp went." I told Roger grimly when he got home. "Timmy flushed it down the john, as I caught him doing with my shell earrings this afternoon."

Roger seemed more concerned than angry. I'll give him credit for that. "I know this is just a phase but, damn it, why good stuff like that? Can't we give him some toothpicks or something and let him get the urge out of his system?"

"I don't know. I didn't try to talk with him. He wouldn't stop crying, so I shut him in his room."

We went to the nursery and found Timmy dry-eyed but sullen. His father tried to be patient and reasonable, I kept in the background, as I always try to do during such confrontations.

"Timmy, why in the world did you want to throw away those nice things in the john?"

His answer was a double puzzle. "For Grooley."

"My God, Grooley again! What's he got to do with it?"

"Grooley lives down there, and sometimes he comes up to play with me. I showed him some of my things and he said he likes nice things, and showed me what to do with them."

"This is worse than I expected. Somebody comes out of the toilet bowl and persuades you to throw things in there? What does this Grooley look like, for God's sake?"

"He's kind of long and thin and he's wet, 'cause he lives down there. He's a orange color, and he doesn't have any head, but he talks anyway, or I know what he means without talking. Maybe his head is down below, he never comes all the way out."

"That child is seriously disturbed," said Roger apprehensively in the living room a few minutes later. "There's nothing in the child guidance literature that I know of about orange-colored monsters without any head that comes out of the john! Are you sure he hasn't been seeing any of those science fiction horror movies on TV?"

"They always come on long after he's asleep, dear; and anyway, we never watch them."

"We'll have to take him to a psychologist if this goes on."

"Let's watch what happens for a few days more. You certainly laid down the law strongly enough there at the end. Maybe he'll forget the whole thing."

Roger was worried and uncertain, but two days passed with no further misdemeanors. Indeed, Timmy seemed chastened and thoughtful. Then on the evening of the second day, as we were getting ready for bed, Roger pointed rather melodramatically at the dresser top.

"Where's that money I put down there when I changed clothes? I broke a ten at the news stand and had the change in my suit pocket.

"I don't know, dear," I answered. "I'm not in the market for a new hat." Just like Blondie and Dagwood.

Then we heard the toilet flush.

Roger beat me to the bathroom and Timmy was already howling before his father shook him by the shoulder. "I had to do it," he sobbed. "Grooley wants things. He says I have to give him things or he'll do something real bad!"

"Nine dollars and thirty-seven cents," Roger was muttering to himself as he dragged the child past me out of the bathroom. As I turned to follow them, my eye fell on the polished porcelain fixture, which was sighing contentedly as it refilled, and I felt a little involuntary pang that was hard to analyze.

This time Roger administered the spanking and, after Timmy had cried himself to sleep, he went into the utility room for his tool chest. Working with furious silent concentration, he screwed a hook-and-eye high up on the bathroom door frame out of Timmy's reach.

"This door is to be kept hooked at all times," he announced rhetorically. "He'll just have to ask when he wants in. And I want you to make an appointment with Dr. Steingruber first thing tomorrow morning."

His eyes were bewildered as he went back into the bedroom.

Dr. Steingruber couldn't give us an appointment till the end of the week, but when I told him the situation over the phone, he minimized it. "No cause for alarm. Common pattern at that age. A nuisance, no more."

All that day Timmy and I went through the mutually humiliating ritual of the locked bathroom. I searched him before disengaging the hook, and stood in the doorway until he was finished, then locked up again. It was very embarrassing, with Timmy's hurt, accusing eyes on me.

In the evening, Roger said, "Maybe we'll have to move to the suburbs where they have yards." I said nothing, not wanting to arouse his opposition, which usually happens when I agree with him about anything.

At bedtime Timmy came up to Roger, wearing the blue bunny suit. His face was urgent. "Daddy, we have to give something to Grooley. We have to. You say what. If we don't he'll be awful mad. He'll do something terrible."

"I don't want to hear any more of this kind of talk," Roger snapped at him. "Get into bed."

Troubled and nearly tearful, Timmy went away, leaving the echo of a reproachful look.

"Damned foolishness. It's not normal," Roger said under his breath, as if to himself.

That night the plumbing was noisy, rumbling and vibrating fitfully. But it often does that up here on the fourth floor when there's a dry spell and city water pressure is down. It was certainly dry and deadly hot; this and the noise made sleeping difficult.

The next day was the same, the roaring in the pipes continuing. Timmy seemed almost afraid to go into the bathroom, but he wouldn't discuss his fears with me. I had the feeling we had failed him somehow.

Roger and I were both depressed all evening. We didn't refer to the bathroom situation, except for Roger saying, "You see the doctor tomorrow? Try to get something settled, Babs. I think he needs an appointment with a specialist."

We went to bed early and slept at once, tired out by the wakeful night before. I had no idea what time it was when Roger woke me by sitting up. He was out of bed by the time I was fully awake, and in response to my mumbled question he hissed, "I think I hear him." I heard nothing but the breeze rising outside, a welcome relief from the still heat of the evening.

Roger opened the door softly and crept down the hall. I followed. The bathroom door was ajar and the light was on. I was just behind Roger as he went in—over his shoulder I could see Timmy in his pajamas crouched on the tile floor, feeding pennies and trinkets from his toy box into the toilet bowl. I noticed, lying at the threshold, the long ruler he had used to dislodge the door hook.

"All right, young man," Roger shouted, angrily, lunging inside and grabbing Timmy's arm. "That will be enough of that!" He yanked the child roughly to his feet and shoved him through the door at me, then turned. "Let's get those things out of there."

At that moment a strong breeze billowed through the open window and slammed the door shut in my face. Simultaneously the rumbling of the plumbing commenced anew, louder this time. Roger began shouting incoherently, his voice muffled by the intervening door, and Timmy pulled at my hand: "It's Grooley! He's hurting him!"

The shouts turned into screams, and I felt again that strange pang, mingled with rising terror—of what, I didn't know. The roars were now mingled with splashing and loud, unidentifiable noises.

I rattled the door knob in panic; somehow the door had jammed itself. The noises got louder and louder, and there were violent, churning concussions. It seemed hours before I discovered that the door, in slamming, had jolted that high hook into place; I had only to release it.

As l did so, the noise died down and ceased.

I threw open the door, desperate with terror, Timmy weeping behind me. The room was blindingly white in the fluorescent glare, and empty. Nothing was changed, nothing added except the crimson splash inundating the bowl, staining the white tile floor, the white wall opposite.

The plumbing rumbled once more; it had a satisfied sound, the torpor of some great beast that has been fed.

SOMETHING FOR GROOLEY

I KNEW MOMMY would get mad, but I had to give Grooley some-thing or he might do awful things—flood the house or I don't know what. So while Mommy was in the kitchen I went into her room quiet like Freddy Fox in the story, and there on the dresser was the money left that she took out of her pocketbook when she gave some to the dry-cleaner man.

I took some of the green money in my hand—it was pretty and I thought Grooley would like it, probably. So I went out of Mommy's room and walked on tiptoe to the room where Grooley was, holding the money carefully so as not to crumple it.

Grooley was sitting there, white and quiet like always. I went up to him, not scared really but kind of excited and shivery, and I made the motions with my hand that Grooley wants me to make, the circle with two fingers and then the sharp corners with both hands. And I said his secret name very low, so that nobody could hear it even if they had been passing the door. After that I put the money into Grooley and pulled the little handle.

There was the big splashing noise like always, and the money was gone. I hoped Grooley liked it, at least better than the cookies I gave him last week. He didn't like those at all, I could tell. He almost did something awful then, but I promised to do better and he forgave me. He's not like people.

Later that day, Mommy couldn't find her money and right away she asked me where it was. But I couldn't tell, of course. She cried and said that child, you can't leave anything around. Then she got mad and shut me in my room, and I couldn't get out even to go to

Grooley all afternoon.

I don't know just when I first knew Grooley was there. It was a long, long time ago, before last summer even, before my birthday, so I was four then. Grooley never really said anything or did anything, but somehow I knew he was there—not in the white china or the box up above or the water, but inside kind of and down below. Daddy says that down below there are lots of pipes that run along and join other pipes and I guess that's where Grooley really lives, down there where it's all dark and wet and cold.

Some way I got to know that Grooley was there, and that that was his name, and what he wanted me to do. It was funny that I knew and nobody else, because everybody goes there to see him sometimes.

After I knew he was there, I would throw things in to see the splash and watch him take them; pieces of jigsaw puzzle and crusts of bread I put in my pocket so I wouldn't have to eat them at dinner. He liked those things and wanted better things and more and he wanted me to make the circle and all with my fingers, and whisper his name and bow down to him. I don't know how I knew all this, but I did. All day it was bad what happened to him and I thought he deserved to have what he wanted. Besides, when he wanted something he used to roar and gurgle in a scary way, I was afraid of what he might do. He was very old and very strong.

I started to take things from Mommy and Daddy—things they wouldn't miss, like pictures from the album and nails and pencils. Once I took Daddy's garters and gave them to Grooley, and once I gave him one of the goldfish. I could tell by the way he roared, but I didn't give him any more because I was afraid he might get to like things that were alive, and I didn't have many alive things I could give him. Mommy says that's why I can't have all the cookies I want, I might get so that was all I'd eat.

Grooley always wanted more things too—little things would do for a while, and then at other times he would roar for something better. Those times scared me, but I always did what he wanted, so he would like me and not do anything bad to me if he ever wanted to do bad things to people.

The day I gave the money to Grooley I had to stay in my room till Daddy came home. After a long time I heard the front door open and Mommy started to tell him how I took the money and wouldn't tell where it was. She sounded mad and excited. Daddy said this is too much, ten dollar bills don't grow on trees, and Mommy said we've never touched him but this calls for old-fashioned methods. You're right we've been too soft Daddy said.

He came in my room then sort of stiff and squinting and asked me where was the money that I took. I didn't say anything and his face got still redder and he said tell me or I will have to punish you.

I still didn't say anything and he grabbed my collar and shook me so that my head hurt and I bit my tongue. He hit me on the ear and I yelled don't you hit me, Grooley will do something bad to you, Grooley is my friend.

I tried to kick him.

He hit me some more and Mommy said go ahead we must find out where he hid the money. Daddy shoved me on the floor and said he probably burned it or threw it out on the street. I was crying and my head hurt and I began to whisper to myself, Grooley you're my friend, help me, help me because I do things for you.

After a while I quit crying, but I stayed on the floor by my bed where Daddy pushed me and kept quiet, like Freddy Fox.

Then I heard Daddy go into the room where Grooley is and shut the door. In a second I heard Grooley begin to roar and splash louder than he ever did before. I heard Daddy yell and say help the thing is pulling me in. The water roared and splashed more than ever.

I got up and went to the door of my room. I saw Mommy run down the hall and open the door of the room where the noise was coming from. The door swung shut as she went in.

Then I heard her screaming and both of them yelling, while Grooley just sang a song like a thunderstorm, the prayer he used to do when Daddy said this plumbing is bad, only louder.

After a while I went down the hall and opened the shut door. Nobody was in the room but Grooley.

I was very glad to know that Grooley had helped me when I asked him. I made the motion with my hand that Grooley wants me to make, the circle with two fingers and then the sharp corners with both hands. I made the motions a lot of times, and I said his secret name lots of times. I said it loud. because there was nobody in the house to hear.

That was yesterday. This morning when I got up I ate some bread from the table in the kitchen, and gave Grooley the raw steak that was on the cupboard. Then I gave Grooley the rest of the goldfish, and I gave him the kitty too. He roared his thank-you very loud.

I don't guess he really needed anything for a long time after what happened yesterday, but I wanted to show him I was grateful that he was my friend.

GROOLEY
A short film based on the story by James Wade

Adapted by Terence Staples

1. *Credits Over.* river flowing along dark, murky. full of garbage. ... Tilt down: to water bubbling up in the river from some underground source.	Noise of flush com-mences and carries through (2)	
2. *Dissolve to.* water whirling around in flushing lavatory pan.		
3. *Cut to CU* of child's face (Timmy) framed in the oval of the lavatory seat. He looks down intently at the camera, then deliberately stretches out his hand down through the seat.	... and fades away during (3)	

4. *Cut to BCU* of sausage on white plate. Tilt up and Pull Back as we see Timmy's hand fiddling with it, then his mother's hands entering the frame and vigorously cutting up the sausage ... then as Timmy's face appears we see that he has found a tube of mustard and is squeezing a long snake of it on to the plate ... PAN to mother, who is eating her breakfast and casting watchful glances at Timmy. Continue Pan: to father, who is obscured by the Daily Telegraph, from behind which his hand emerges to grope for his cup of coffee.		*MOTHER*: (talks informally to Timmy, e.g.) Don't mess about with that now Timmy, eat up your breakfast like a good boy ... that's enough! Mustard for goodness sake. ... Eat it up now ...
5. *Cut to Timmy*. looking out of frame towards mother as he speaks. He pauses, waiting for a response, but there is none.		*TIMMY*: I played with Grooley this morning. He's funny looking and all wet. He lives ... right down ... in the toilet!
6. *Cut to Mother*. who finds this sort of talk objectionable at the breakfast table, and fears father's reaction. Pan to: newspaper, which rustles dismissively; then father folds it up, gets up crossly, slurps up some coffee and rushes away from the table ...		*MOTHER*: That's enough now, Timmy, get on with your breakfast and let Daddy read the paper
7. *Cut to Mother*. piling up dishes, lightly smacking Timmy's hand as he fiddles with food again ...		
8. *Cut to CU* of food being scraped into waste disposal unit; then camera follows mother's hands as she turns to one side and wipes Timmy's hands ... and drops them as she goes to help look.	Churning of Waste Disposal	*FATHER*: (OS) Look, where the hell is my tiepin?

9. *Cut to Father* in foreground, searching dressing table angrily: table between him and camera, and bedroom door some distance behind him. Mother enters and starts to help.		*MOTHER*: You know, I'm getting a bit worried about Timmy. He keeps on about things down in the toilet—
10. *Father* gives up search and stomps off angrily—		*FATHER*: For God's sake stop niggling about that child. I'm trying to get to work and every damn thing I put down in this place disappears.
11. *Father* into hall to collect coat and hat and umbrella from stand, and some money, keys, etc. from hall table. As he does so mother follows him out of bedroom, and in the background we see Timmy crossing the hall from the kitchen and going into the bedroom. Neither parent notices this.		*MOTHER*: I'm not niggling! If he develops some sort of phobia about the toilet, it's a serious matter.
12. *Father* opens the front door and goes out; mother follows him. Timmy comes out of the bedroom again looking at something in his hand; the camera follows him as he goes purposefully towards the toilet door.		*FATHER*: Phobia, Phobia, do me a favour and stop pretending you're a psychologist or something, would you? Every morning it's the same thing, I'm trying to go and earn a living and all you can talk about is phobias ... and neuroses ... and rubbish like that.

13. *Cut to* view of outer hall of the flats: both parents walk towards lift/ camera, father presses the button to call lift and mother lags behind despondently.		*MOTHER:* How can you be so stupid and standoffish about your own child?
14. *Cut to Timmy* dropping an earring into the toilet pan. He pulls the flush handle.	Noise of flush which continues in background of 15 and to the beginning of 16	*FATHER:* (in mid-speech as 15 commences) ... just go on in and have a
15. *Cut to Father* disappearing downwards, his voice fading as the lift vanishes from sight.		Few more fantasies while some of us do some real work.
16. *Cut to* view of flat hall and front door from inside mother appears in doorway, walks down the hall and turns the corner to the toilet, camera panning with her. She looks round th toilet door, her back to camera ...		*MOTHER:* Timmy, what are you doing?
17. *Cut to Timmy* dropping the second earring into the toilet and pulling the handle. Mother advances into frame and yanks him out of the room. As we hear Timmy and his mother going away, the camera advances to the toilet pan and peers in to see the water whirling around. Fade Out A SERIES OF CLOSE-UPS	Noise of Flush again	*MOTHER:* Come out here this minute! How dare you just take our things and throw them away? *TIMMY:* (OS voice receding) I didn't throw it away, Mummy, it's for Grooley, he likes nice things ...

18. *Mother:* snatching soap from dish.		**_MOTHER_**: (Voice in background) ... and we're not going to take any more of Mummy's nice things tomorrow, are we?
19. *Timmy's* hands dabbling in the bathwater while an orange toy floats nearby.		**_TIMMY:_** Well, I might have to Mummy, because Grooley wants them. He lives down
20. *Mother* scrubbing dirty knees.		There and sometimes he comes up to play with me. He likes nice things.
21. *Mother* ... and dirty fingernails ...		**_MOTHER_**: Who is this Grooley, Timmy? What does he look like?
22. *Mother* rummaging with corner of flannel in Timmy's ear.		**_TIMMY:_** Well, he's sort of long and thin, and he's all wet ... and he's orange ... and he hasn't
23. *Mother* plunking soap down in the dish.		Got a head but he talks anyway, or I know what he means without talking.
24. *Timmy* submerging the orange toy		Maybe his head is down below. He never comes all the way out.
25. *Mother* pours a jug of water cascading over Timmy's head.		**_MOTHER_**: My goodness, that doesn't sound like a very nice friend

26. *Mother's* hand snatching a towel.		to me ... not the sort of friend for nice little boys to have.
27. *Mother.* ... pulling out the plug ...		*TIMMY:* He's my friend though Mummy. He likes me,
28. *Timmy:* being toweled vigor-ously.		especially when I give him things.
29. *Mother:* grabs dressing-gown.		*MOTHER:* But darling you mustn't throw mummy's nice things
30. *Mother:* Squeezing yellow toothpaste on to brush.		Down the toilet, must you? Now come along, into bed in one minute and Mummy will read you a nice story ...
31. *Mother and Timmy:* bustling along corridor.		
32. *Mother:* Turning back the bed-clothes.	Gurgles	*MOTHER:* (Voice, read-ing fades in over gurgles) ... Big-Ears rushed into the
33. *Cut to:* Water revolving down plug-hole. *Slow Zoom in:* as water dis-appears.		Sea at once, quite fright-ened. What was happen-ing to little Naddy? Who was under the water, clutching at his foot? Naddy fell over in the wa-ter when a big wave came. He screamed loudly. "Big-Ears,

34. *Cut to Timmy's* face, not very attentive, as he listens to story.		Big-Ears! Come quickly! Something has got me!" So ... now let's wait until tomorrow night, shall we,
35. *Cut to MS* of mother sitting by Timmy's bed. She shuts the book and gets up, turns out the light so that we see only a faint silhouette as she goes towards the door.		to see what happened to Naddy? Off to sleep now ...
36. *Cut to CU* of Timmy in bed, eyes shut—very dim light. As he hears the gurgle from the toilet his eyes open and he half sits up, looking anxiously in the direction of the door. *Fade out.*	Gurgle (OS)	
37. *(Next Morning.)* *CU* of meat being fed into mincer. Camera pulls back enough to show Timmy going by in the background, obviously avoiding mother's eye.		
38. *BCU* of small, shiny toy. Timmy's hand snatches it up.		
39. *Cut to* high angle behind Timmy's head as he drops the toy into the toilet and pulls the handle.	Noise of flush.	
40. *(That evening.)* *Father* comes in at front door, takes off coat and hat, puts umbrella in hall stand, and bits and pieces on hall table. Camera follows him ... ... as he takes off his jacket and hangs it on a chair, then goes into bedroom to change.	Gurgle (OS)	

41. *Cut to BCU* of the gleaming clip of a pen in the jacket pocket. Timmy's hand removes it: it's a ball-point, not too expensive, but nice and shiny.		
42. *Cut to Timmy* as in 17, drop-ping pen into toilet pan. He looks up out of frame, frightened, as he pulls the handle.	Loud noise of flush continues through shot 43.	
43. *Low angle of Timmy's* POV as father looms up in doorway, looking huge and angry. He stomps towards camera, stretching out his hand to grab Timmy.		
44. *Cut to similar angle* but in-cluding toilet bowl, as we see father yank Timmy out of the room.	(OS) Two speeches interrupt-ing each other.	*FATHER:* Right I've had just about enough of this—you'll go to your room and you'll bloody well stay there.
Toilet comes into sharper focus as we hear Timmy and his father shouting at each other, and the camera begins to tilt downwards so that we can see part way into the bowl. *Fade Out.*	Smacking and Weep-ing (OS)	*TIMMY:* I had to do it, Daddy. I had to: Grooley wants things, he says I'll have to get him things or he'll do something terrible!

45. *CU* of father fixing hook and eye high up on door jamb. Camera moves back and down and we see that Mother is standing nearby and Timmy is close to her. As the camera reaches him, he moves away from his parents, looking sad, and the camera tracks in front of him away from the door, which we now recognize as the toilet door.		*MOTHER:* I still think we ought to take him to the doctor. He really seems to be getting worked up about this. *FATHER:* It's *you* who's getting worked up, you know. It's a perfectly simple solution: we only let him go to the toilet when one of us is with him and he'll forget the whole thing in time. There that's fixed it. We won't get any more things stolen *now*.
46. *(Next Morning) Mother:* using the washing machine (we can see the water churning around); Timmy in the background picking his nose; he approaches and taps her arm; she looks down at him ... and takes off her rubber gloves.	Loud churning of washing machine fades into background in shot 47	*MOTHER:* What? Again?
47. *Cut to* Mother and Timmy outside the toilet door. She is searching him, patting his pockets, making him open his hands. Then she stands up and opens the toilet door, beckoning Timmy in.		
48. *Cut to* Mother in toilet doorway watching Timmy, unhappy about this undignified solution to the problem. As Timmy comes into frame, having finished, she reaches down to touch him in a gesture of reconciliation, but he shrugs away. Disconsolately she reaches over to pull the toilet handle.	Noise of Flush dissolves into noise of water in sink 49	

49. *Cut to CU* of mother's hand turning a tap. Water runs down into the sink which is spattered with Blue Vim. She scours it out busily.		
50. *Cut to* another angle, showing Timmy tugging at her skirt.		
51. *Cut to CU* of mother as she opens the hook-and-eye and gestures down to Timmy. We see her standing in the doorway looking beyond the camera into the toilet. She looks worried. *Fade Out.*		
52. *Night:* the parents' bedroom. High angle shot of the bed: father fast asleep, and mother lying wide awake, looking worried.	Gurgling, which continues through shots 52 thru 56, with other plumbing noises.	
53. *Timmy:* lying awake in bed. Suddenly he sits up, looking desperate.		
54. *Mother:* turns over and tries to sleep.		
55. *Timmy:* gets out of bed.		
56. *Camera:* tracks behind Timmy as he walks through the hall towards the table where his father habitually leaves his keys and change. He picks up a handful of change, and takes the umbrella out of its stand. He then approaches the toilet door and reaches up with umbrella. The camera follows the umbrella point up as it approaches and then neatly dislodges the hook. The door starts to swing open—	Sudden loud increase in gurgling.	

66

57. *Cut to* parent's bed, as in 52. Mother wakes and sits up terrified; father wakes more slowly.		
58. *Father:* Sits up—		
59. *Father:* —Swings his feet to the floor—		
60. *Father:* —dashes to the door.		
61. *Cut to Timmy* in toilet, feeding coins into the bowl. He looks up in a panic, towards camera and door, then terrified, tips in the whole lot.	Footsteps (barefoot but rapid and angry) heard through slightly softer gur-gling.	
62. *Cut to* very short shot of father in doorway, Timmy's POV, in pajam-as, furious, starting forward—		
63. *Cut to Timmy* as in 61, snatch-ing at the handle and pulling it just as his father's back looms up in the frame and he is thrust to one side, and father dives down towards the toilet pan.	Loud flush which con-tinues bois-terously through shots 63 and 64	
64. *Cut to LS* of toilet doorway down at the end of the hall. Timmy comes rushing out and slams door in fury/panic. He rushes towards his mother who appears at the side of the frame. She crouches down with arms open: he rushes to her and they hug.		

65. *Cut to Reverse Angle MCU* of mother looking over Timmy's head in sudden fright at the change in the noise. Camera pulls back as she pushes him aside and rushes towards the toilet door.	Flushing sounds merge into a loud gurgling noise which increased in volume. We here muffled shouts and violent churning concussions, extremely loud.	
66. *Cut to low angle* behind mother as she shakes handle and rattles at the toilet door. We can see the hook above her head has fallen into the eye.	The noise begins to fade and change into a new sort of quiet rhythmic gurgle as the door opens.	*TIMMY:* It's Grooley! He's hurting him.
67. *Cut to CU* of mother's face tearful and screaming, as she looks up—		
68. *Cut to CU* of hook being opened.		
69. *Cut to CU* of mother's face from within toilet as she opens door, her face suddenly freezing in total horror. The door opens wider as she staggers forward and to one side—	Gurgles become more and more resonant and satisfied in shot 70, fading to silence with fade-out.	

68

70. *Cut to tracking shot,* Timmy's POV rushing past her into toilet, seen as a brilliantly lit white cube, walls daubed with bright red blood. Track forward more slowly to look in the bowl where a red whirlpool is subsiding. Hold ... and ... *Fade Out.*	Very quiet belch.	

TIME AFTER TIME

THE VOYAGE BY freighter, was to be leisurely, without pressures or tensions of any kind. The vessel was a small one, and I was the only passenger booked for this off-season crossing. My doctors in Korea, including the Yale-trained specalist, had agreed that I needed a rest as much as I needed anything, so though the trip back to America was partly on business, yet it was very largely the prospect of that restful ocean voyage which made my doctors favor it.

"You Americans think too much of time. Forget there is such a thing as time," advised Dr. Kang, the Yale man. "Time will have no significance for you on this trip; it will be as if time does not exist." I determined to follow his advice fully; the several seizures I had experienced had frightened me, and convinced me that I would have to slow down. Accordingly, when I packed for the journey I placed all business papers and paraphernalia with the hold baggage, which I would not see until the end of the trip, taking with me for the cabin only a supply of paperback novels for light reading.

My secretary had booked me on a vessel that sailed from Pusan, to which city I went by rail on the day before the ship was due to leave. At my hotel I learned that there had been some last-minute delays that would postpone our departure for several days. At first I was somewhat upset to hear this since to my taste Pusan is an even more raw and raucous boom-town than Seoul. But my hotel was pleasantly quiet and secluded, so I determined to act as if the voyage had already begun, sticking to my own room and the dining room, bookshop, barber, and a few other peaceful, innocuous spots in the hotel itself. In this way I spent several fairly pleasant days without worrying at all

71

about the passage of time. I found that I was adjusting better than I had hoped to the complete absence of the urgent obligations and responsibilities which had been my life for so long in the Seoul export firm of which I was foreign operations manager. It was good to have a chance for some uninterrupted reading and rest.

The delay in departure was extended, once more without any uneasiness on my part; faithful to Dr. Kang's advice, I had ceased to reckon time, not even reading the English-language newspapers that were readily available in the hotel lobby. On the day of sailing I glanced over my ticket and noticed that the name of the vessel itself was SS Chronos. This seemed to me a strange coincidence, until I realized that several lines have named their ships for the various ancient deities, such as the Neptune, Jupiter, and so forth.

On checking over my hotel bill, I became aware of the date for the first time in several days: the charges terminated as of October 29, so that must be the present date.

The SS Chronos, as I have said, was a small ship on which I was the sole passenger. As she lay trussed alongside the pier in Pusan, she indeed looked small, but very clean and trim. I decided that I would enjoy this trip, the first ocean voyage for which I had had the leisure in many years.

I was shown to my cabin by the steward, Mr. Martin, a slight, unobtrusive man of middle years. The quarters were most pleasantly appointed, containing a large double bed, cushioned armchair anchored to the floor in usual nautical fashion, a desk and wardrobe. The bathroom, I was pleased to note, contained a tub as well as shower facilities. I find a hot bath very relaxing before slumber.

Mr. Martin gave me the meal hours and indicated his willingness to assist in any way he could. I fear I indulged myself a bit when I mentioned to him my heart condition, and indicated that I might occasionally find it desirable to dine in my quarters. His ready sympathy and agreement made me feel rather guilty; I am certainly perfectly able to make the short trip from my cabin to the dining saloon. But then the luxury of dining in bed is very relaxing and since I am the only passenger the occasional inconvenience to the staff will be slight.

As if to make amends for my self-indulgence, I was at pains to go down to the dining room for the first evening meal. There I met many of the officers of the ship, including Captain Danton, a rugged and capable-looking first officer. The food was plentiful if a bit too greasy, a circumstance I seemed to remember from previous voyages before the war.

I bathed and turned in early, since Mr. Martin had told me the ship would sail in the small hours of the morning, and I thought perhaps my rest would be disturbed or even terminated at that point. I did wake once during the night, feeling rather ill, due no doubt to the greasy food—but there was no motion to indicate the ship had cast off.

When I awoke in the morning, however, we were definitely under way. Looking out my porthole, all I could see was a churning mass of white fog. The swaying, weaving gait of the ship through the choppy waves, however, left no room for doubt. The motion was not very pleasant, and although I did not feel sick, I decided to breakfast lightly in the cabin, and accordingly rang for Mr. Martin by pressing a button which he had told me communicated with his quarters. When he arrived, I ordered dry toast and coffee, and told him I thought I would remain inside all day. (This day, it occurred to me, was the 30th.)

By selecting judiciously from the sparse menus of the two later meals, I was able to avoid a repetition of yesterday's indigestion, if that is what it was, and closely approximated Dr. Kang's recommended diet. I took my various medicines punctually and spent the day reading and napping. The fog did not clear.

By the next morning I was more accustomed to the regular, gentle motion of the ship, but since I still did not feel quite myself, I decided on another day of rest. The fog outside remained oppressively heavy, and I knew there was little I would be able to see from deck.

When the steward came in with the evening meal, I inquired, "Mr. Martin, shouldn't we be setting our watches back an hour every day during this trip East? I seem to remember doing so in the old days."

"I'll let you know when to do all that, Mr. Halbert," Martin replied, and continued setting out the dishes.

I was puzzled, because I clearly remembered and had subsequently often heard about the ritual loss of an hour daily, and the eventual repetition of one day, however illogical that sounds, on such trips. However, I reflected, they may have a different schedule for that sort of thing nowadays.

Next morning I felt almost normal, but quite weak. The eternal fog swirling outside the porthole had a definitely enervating effect, and I decreed myself another day in bed. Mr. Martin showed no signs of impatience at all; on the contrary, he exhibited a worried solicitude about my state of health. I laughingly informed him that I was probably not as sick as I acted, but needed rest even more than I had imagined.

I asked him about the ever-present fog, and he answered, "Well, sir, as you may know, we travel by the Great Circle Route, passing near the Aleutians, and this time of year you're likely to encounter quite a bit of fog. No way to tell how long we'll be having it."

"Well, no great matter," I responded. "By the way, what is the date today?"

"The date? October 30, Mr. Halbert."

"Oh, but that can't be. I boarded on the 29th, and this is the third day out."

"But it's the 30th. Mr. Halbert, I'm sure of it. If you want me to check and find out..."

"No, never mind—it doesn't matter what day it is, does it? They're all alike."

I decided I would press no further, in obedience to Dr. Kang's admonition. I thought of him saying. "Time will have no significance for you on this trip; it will be as if time does not exist," He was right about that, I thought wryly.

Nevertheless, after Mr. Martin left, I took the trouble of rummaging among my passport and personal papers to dig out the Pusan Hotel bill from which I was reckoning our date of departure. I checked thoroughly the length of my stay there, computing backward to a date I could definitely place, the day I left Seoul. Yes, it had certainly been the 29th on which I had boarded the Chronos. That was four days ago. Even with the loss of an hour a day—even with the repetition of an entire day—. My head began to ache; I would worry no more about the inaccurate Mr. Martin. A lifetime at sea had no doubt left him hazy about those simple facts that mean so much to landlubbers.

My sleep that night was not as sound as it might have been.

By next morning the fog seemed almost an old friend. Mr. Martin came in with my breakfast even before I had rung. As he was going out, I couldn't resist a little gibe about our contretemps of the day before.

"Well, Mr. Martin, have you found out yet what date it is?"

He paused, his hand on the knob, and turned a puzzled look on me. "Date, sir? Why, today is October 30th, a Thursday."

I caught myself before exclaiming whatever it was that came into my mind. Obviously the man was an eccentric, at least when it came to dates. No use arguing with him. Mr. Martin left the room.

Suddenly the fog outside didn't seem friendly any more, but sinister, even threatening.

I did not eat the breakfast.

That was twenty days ago—twenty, I know, because I have made a little pencil X in the margin of this book every day since. Twenty days, twenty-four days really, for a trip that ordinarily takes less than two weeks. (I must not think about time—Dr. Kang said, "Forget there is such a thing as time.") But twenty-four days of fog, of isolation! Since that first night I have seen no one, not a single member of the crew, save the steward Martin. I see him three times every day, at mealtime, and I am afraid to ask him that question again. I am afraid of the fog, and of the ship, and of Martin. But most of all I am afraid of that question, afraid of the answer it will receive.

Afraid—

(Excerpt from a report to the owners of SS Chronos by Captain E.J. Danton, first officer of the vessel, November 10, 1963)

> —The only untoward incident on the return voyage was the sudden death, apparently from a heart-ailment, of Mr. Frederick Halbert, our sole passenger. Mr. Halbert died sometime during the night of October 29, prior to our departure from Pusan, but his death was not discovered until next morning when the steward was unable to arouse him. Compounding the tragedy, our steward, Rudolph Martin, who had a long standing

cardiac condition, was so shocked by discovering Mr. Halbert's body that he himself was the victim of a heart attack that proved fatal within the hour. Since the vessel was well at sea, the bodies were crated and placed in an empty refrigeration compartment prior to being turned over to the coroner in Seattle. I am sending to your office the personal effects of both deceased for disposition in the customary manner...

TEMPLE OF THE FOX

"Who sees ghost foxes is not apt ever to see anything else. Dead souls ravenous for life, though always fastidious, they gathered in old temples and wayside shrines, demons attached to the maize goddess. Trouble is the only thing that thaws their icy courtesy."
David Stacton: *Segaki*

I

IT HAD BEEN a hard climb, up the pine-wooded slope where the long slanting rays of afternoon sun washed green thickets with a haze of gold, past the chattering little stream whose steep descent had worn a deep gulley among clumps of enduring rock. The sounds of the small village on the lower shelf of Song-Ni Mountain had long faded; the picnickers and tradesmen shuffling through the dust of the single street beside a widened, placid pooling of the same stream were inaudible, now, even in this dense hush. Martinson knew he must be near the gently domed peak he had glimpsed from the valley road far below, though the thick pine growth still prevented his seeing it. The temple must be near, then; though the villagers, indeed, had only gestured vaguely in this direction to confirm his supposition about its exact location.

Martinson stopped for a moment to try to orient himself. The cessation of his footsteps crackling in the undergrowth crystallized the silence. This was remote, certainly; about as remote as one can get, even in a remote corner of the world like southwest Korea. He mentally retraced his pilgrimage from its beginning: the crowded, noisy Victorian train station in Seoul; all night on the antique sleeper, alighting in the deserted early morning of a market town way-station, the long dusty bus ride ever higher into the mountains, then the broken-down jitney that staggered up winding, steeply sloped roads overlooking dizzy drops and a miniature landscape that seemed unrolled from some ancient oriental scroll. Finally he had gotten as far as modern conveniences could take him, and the all-afternoon hike up from the little village by the pond was nearing its end.

Far as the heat and dust of the journey, Martinson wasn't sorry about his decision to spend a week's vacation at a Buddhist temple. A Fulbright lecturer in Seoul couldn't say he had seen Korea properly without travelling to outlying districts and actually living there for a time. When his colleague Thorwald came back the month before with stories of this Song-Ni district and its dozens of tiny cloud-scraping temples set on the mountainsides far above the immense Popju-Sa Monastery, Martinson had resolved to spend time in the area, and to live at the particular hermitage glimpsed by Thorwald, the location of which he had sketched so painstakingly. After almost a year in Korea, Martinson was sure his knowledge of the spoken language, shaky though it was, would get him through everyday situations. And temples were traditionally ready to accept guests, especially paying guests who were willing and even eager to follow the temple regulations: vegetarian meals and early prayers at 3 A.M., announced by the clatter of wooden clappers and ringing of bells.

As Martinson glanced about; he was unaccountably startled to realize that he was not alone on the mountainside. Off to the left, near the concealed foaming of the stream, he glimpsed a patch of grey that moved; soon he made out a figure in monk's robe, bald brown head bowed over a staff with whose aid its owner was ascending slowly, laboriously. The American altered his course, plunging through the light undergrowth at right angles to his previous direction.

Martinson hailed the man politely, realizing as he did so that the monk was not as old as his shambling gait had suggested. If the man was surprised to hear his language spoken by a foreigner, he gave no evidence of it. On the other hand, his own responses were difficult for Martinson to grasp; his Korean must be very scholarly or very old-fashioned, perhaps both.

Yes, there was a temple at the head of this slope; he himself was a *bonze* attached to it, and was returning there now. Yes, they could entertain guests who might deign to accept their humble fare, though very few pilgrims ever got this far.

As he spoke, something about the hoarse, high voice suggested to Martinson what he had read of the eunuchs of the old royal palace. But the man couldn't be that old; almost nobody of that time was still alive. The monk peered at the intruder (Martinson expected to assume the role of intruder, for the first few days at least) less with curiosity than a son of disinterested appraisal. The man's mouth opened in a seemingly permanent, mirthless, canine grin, revealing broken and blackened teeth. The eyes told him nothing, though he had been in the Orient long enough to discard the cliché of inscrutability.

The monk was speaking again: If the young *yang-ban* would just follow him, they could reach the temple well before dusk, before the dinner hour. (They began to climb slowly, Martinson adjusting his strides to the deliberate pace of the other.) The dinner might seem very meager to a hungry traveler, since the monks did not often have meat. (But aren't Buddhist temples always strictly vegetarian? Perhaps he had misunderstood.) How many brothers lived at this temple? Six, ordinarily. They were poor, did their own farming on a few hillside plots, tended to their devotions and studies, had little to do with the outside world, even with the mountain village below. Right now, several of the brothers were off in the remote depths of the mountains, gathering edible mushrooms. The young gentleman must know that this Song-Ni district was famous for the quality of its mushrooms, and this was the time of year, autumn, when they were gathered. It was the one cash crop of the year, which provided money for clothing, upkeep of the temple, and any little amenities for the winter ahead. A very important time of year; everyone worked very hard.

They had continued to climb through the slanting sunset rays that gilded the tall pines. Now a distinct hint of dusk clung to the ground; the valley below was hazy with twilight, picked out by a few, a very few, remote, twinkling cook-fires. A smell of wood smoke drifted in the air; Martinson did not think it came from as far away as the valley. Sure enough, a steeper slope led suddenly to a crude, weathered set of stone steps. Climbing this precarious barrier, they alighted on a sort of broad ledge, whether leveled artificially in whole or part Martinson could not tell. There stood the temple compound, still surrounded on three sides by the encroaching pines, the trees flowing up behind it on a steep rocky slope that must have led to the summit of the mountain itself.

The temple was very small and quite ordinary from an architectural viewpoint, as he had expected. It consisted of four buildings, the unpretentious main temple and two tiny side-shrines devoted to propitiating the mountain gods from whom this land had been wrested, further up the slope a primitive straw-roofed farm house indicated the living quarters of the monks, the source of the wood-smoke smell.

Framing the temple buildings on three sides was a breast-high wall of mud bricks surmounted by clay roof-tiles. The main temple buildings, of weathered, painted wood, with high peaked roofs, also tile-covered, could be any age: they were probably late Yi-Dynasty, but might have been older if fire and warfare had spared them, as might well be the case in such a remote spot. Here, Martinson thought, was what he had been looking for; a chance to blend into the Korean countryside, to sit passively, not even trying to study or absorb, but letting the spirit of the place come to him. A chance for the aroma of ancient Korea to fill him in a way that could never happen in a less isolated, undisturbed spot.

They were walking now toward the temple. Perhaps, his companion inquired, he would like to glance at the buildings while there was still enough light? (Dusk had begun rapidly to fill the small courtyard, with its struggling, unkempt flower beds.) Yes, he would very much like to see them.

Peering through the elaborate and much-damaged carved wooden doors into the shallow sanctuary, Martinson could just see the solemn shape of the seated Buddha. Though he knew little of Buddhist art, this statue seemed to him rather untypical, and he wondered vaguely if it might be an artistic find of some interest. The pose of the figure was strange, less placid and serene than most. The hands were held differently, too. He could not see the face clearly.

They walked to one of the side chapels devoted to the mountain gods. Here the last rays of the setting sun fell upon a carved figure perhaps no more grotesque than most to be found in this strange blending of sophisticated religion and primitive animism. But he noticed in the tangled, gaudy paintings on the back wall one anomaly. The laughing, white-bearded old man, a nature-spirit carried over from Chinese tradition, was usually pictured astride a tiger. Here he was seated upon a fox, whose strange grin matched his own, and somehow reminded Martinson of the smile of his grey-clad guide.

"What is the name of this temple?" asked Martinson suddenly.

"The Temple of the Fox," replied his companion.

Odd! Shouldn't a temple have a more religious name? And weren't foxes in Korean folk-lore rather sinister, devilish creatures? How could this be called the Temple of the Fox?

The old man looked at him disinterestedly, still smiling his gap-toothed, broken grin. No, no, truly, this was the Temple of the Fox—.

II

It was deep night; the darkness matched the dense texture of the silence. Martinson lay on a straw mat, shivering under the thin blanket from his knapsack, the one luxury he had permitted himself to pack. Not much of a luxury at that, he reflected grimly. He had known that even October nights in the mountains could be cold, and suspected that frugal monks would not light the fires that ran through flues under the clay sleeping-floors until the first snowfall. Well, he had been determined to live as the monks lived, and he certainly wasn't going to begin by asking for extra heat.

He felt he had made a good initial impression. The four monks who gathered for the evening meal had smiled at him, darting quick appraising glances when they didn't think he was looking. He had answered their polite questions politely: he was from Seoul, he was a teacher, a *pak-sa*; he wished to live for a short while at the temple to share the wisdom and peace of those devoted to the Great Eightfold Way. They had smiled and nodded. In days to come he would try to speak to them in some detail, however lamely, about their temple and its peculiar name. He thought vaguely that here might be some hitherto unrecorded intrusion of pure animism into the Buddhist religion,

84

perhaps worth a tentative initial monograph for the *Transactions* of the Royal Asiatic Society's Korea branch, though religion was not his field. He had made out all right with the meal, too, eating his thin bean-sprout soup noisily enough to indicate approval, managing the rough wooden chopsticks with aplomb as he picked up bits of peppery pickled vegetables, lotus root, and mushrooms in vinegar (this was mushroom country, he remembered). Some meat would have been welcome, but at least there was rice, and that was filling.

Soon after the meal his initial guide, whose name was Chae, showed him to a small, stuffy private room that had been cleared for him, handed him a pile of old but clean straw mats and bade him goodnight.

His room, like all the rooms in the L-shaped house, opened onto a narrow, elevated porch of polished wood. Before he retired he glanced outside and noticed that the monks were still wakeful. Candle lights flickered behind the rice paper panes of the sliding door panels leading into their main room, used for sleeping and eating. He could hear their voices; all of them seemed to speak in the same high, sibilant tone and antique locutions that old Chae employed. He found their voices vaguely disquieting, and wondered if this were some kind of ritualized religious intonation. From this distance he couldn't make out any words, but they seemed to be laughing, and he caught inflections that sounded sarcastic and mocking. He wondered if they were talking about him.

Later he lay shivering under the light blanket and waiting for time to pass. Despite his tired muscles, he did not seem to be able to relax. Sounds had ceased in the other wing of the house around nine o'clock. He must have dozed intermittently, for when he next looked at his watch, the luminous dial registered close to two A.M. Since he did not seem able really to sleep, he thought he might get up for the prayer-service at three. But this was his first day here, and it might be resented as an intrusion. He would ask about attending services tomorrow; for tonight he would content himself with listening, seeing only as much as he might glimpse from his own doorway.

He may have partially dozed again, for he started violently when a clatter arose close at hand. The monks were evidently leaving their quarters in procession, beating on the hollow, round wooden *mok-t'ak*, which he had often seen and heard used for daytime prayer services at other temples. The dinning of a gong seemed added to the racket as well.

Gradually the noise passed by and Martinson stretched stiffly, stood up, and quietly slid his door aside. His room commanded an oblique view of the main sanctuary where the anomalous Buddha squatted in darkness. But to his surprise the procession had moved out of sight, around to the far side of this structure. He could see the flicker of torchlight and a steadier glow which might be a small bonfire. There was no question about it; the devotees had gathered around the little shrine to the mountain spirit, where he had seen the painted god astride a fox.

Voices were now raised in chant: a feeble, puling whine that was particularly unpleasant. Martinson even thought he heard furtive snorts and yelps of glee, degraded laughter and bestial mumbling under the flowing chanted line. It was certainly unlike any Buddhist service he had ever heard—but then was it directed at all toward the Lord Gautama? Apparently not. Suddenly the gongs and rattles sounded again, overwhelming a concerted human yell of surprise or triumph. The flickering glow visible above the peaked temple roof writhed and shifted, flaring momentarily enough for Martinson to spot a small moving shape that darted around the front of the building toward him. The animal froze for a second as if undecided which

86

way to run. Martinson saw, with an unthinking reflex of chill, that it was a large fox. The fox suddenly turned and scurried across the courtyard, disappearing into the black pine woods.

A few moments later the procession of monks paraded sedately around the corner of the temple. They were silent now. The leader carried a torch. Martinson noted that there were only three of them. One monk must be ill; or perhaps three were sufficient to carry out this distinctly unorthodox service. Before they got too near, Martinson stepped back discreetly into his room and slid the door panel shut. As they passed, he heard muttered words in that high-pitched bantering tone; he thought he caught the words for "change" and "surprise".

His thoughts and reactions were confused when night and silence had closed in on him again. Were these heretic monks, worshipping a fox spirit under the guise of Buddhism? He had never heard of such a thing in Korea, but he knew that primitive nature-religions died hard, even in advanced civilizations. Did the monks keep a tame fox or foxes at the temple as part of their wayward beliefs? For that matter, can a wild fox ever be tamed? He wasn't sure.

He wanted a cigarette badly, but had brought none along on what he had considered an ascetic as well as aesthetic retreat. That wasn't how it was turning out, was it? But why, no matter how unorthodox these religions might be, should he feel a strong misgiving, a sense of peril and repugnance mixed?

He settled back to wait for daylight.

III

While the monks were rousing and dressing themselves in the clear, white light of dawn, Martinson slipped out of his room and down the gentle slope to the temple compound. The harsh early rays of the sun made the center sanctuary look even older and more decrepit than it had the previous evening. Its wooden panels and door frames were mostly grey and weather-beaten; only a few flakes of faded paint in once-gaudy hues stuck to the wood, faintly outlining where the conventional pictures and rococo decorative patterns had been. When he glanced inside, he was shocked: the hard morning light fell full on the face of the seated image, and it was truly like no Buddha he had ever seen before. The face was grimacing and cruel: the carved aureole behind the figure seemed to represent writhing flames. Where had he seen that pose and expression before? Perhaps in prints of the Buddhist hell and its grim master. Later decadent Buddhism had spawned a hell as ingenious and depraved as medieval Europe's, ignoring completely the doctrines of Buddha himself. Yes, this image must be the terrible KANG-HEE, Lord of Hell and scourge of accursed souls.

But Martinson wanted especially to see the side temple where the ceremony had been held last night. Passing the main temple, he turned the corner and approached the small, closet-size structure, almost like a medieval European wayside shrine. Here was where they had gathered and chanted, where the fox had suddenly, terrifyingly dashed away into the forest. He would see the sodden ashes of a small bonfire, but no other sign of disturbance. He approached the building, glancing first at the malevolently painted figure on the back wall, the cruelly grinning old man astride a fox. Yes, he had been right about that, it was surely a fox, its grin as depraved as that of its rider. But then his eye fell on the carved idol enshrined on the central pedestal. Again he experienced shock. Why hadn't he noticed last evening? Though the statue now seemed more than customarily grotesque, its stylized distortions tended in one direction. The elongated jaw that was almost a muzzle, the cruel, tiny eyes, the tawny tint to the skin of the face: this figure, too, was the symbolic human, but unmistakably bestial, representation of a fox.

IV

Martinson felt an inexplicable repugnance at the thought of joining the monks for their morning meal. Besides, the drowsiness that had eluded him last night was now descending upon him. He went back to his room unnoticed, closed the door, and almost immediately fell asleep.

When he woke, his watch told him it was well after noon. Stepping outside, he saw that the entire temple area was deserted. The monks were probably at their fields, wherever these might be. Although he wasn't hungry, he unwrapped and ate several chocolate bars from his knapsack, which he had packed for emergencies. He decided, more from restlessness than any other reason, to take a hike around the area. Perhaps he would come upon the cleared patches of hillside that the monks farmed. Shouldering the knapsack, he struck off at an angle downhill, not retracing the route by which he had ascended.

The forest was as quiet as it had been the day before, but the silence did not seem as peaceful and secure as then. This was probably because the outlandish discoveries he had made at the temple had unaccountably unnerved him. Certainly the sun-striped glades of pines that shifted past him as he walked held no undertone of menace. Neither did the temple, really, if one thought about it logically. The full light of day was fast dispelling the unsettling fancies of darkness.

Then he became aware, just as on the previous afternoon, that he was not alone.

The man was standing still beneath a tall, somber pine, looking at him. This man was no monk, he wore the rough, dark work clothes of a peasant. His smile was uncertain and questioning, and his voice when he answered Martinson's hail was harsh and deep, not like the monks' feminine whine.

He carried a shapeless sack over one shoulder, and in response to questions explained that he was a gatherer of mushrooms and lived in the little village down at the foot of the mountain.

Martinson introduced himself and said that he was staying at a temple on this mountain.

The man glanced at him oddly. "Surely you mean a temple on the other mountain, down the slope and around the other side. There is no temple on this mountain."

Martinson, puzzled, checked his reply and rapidly substituted, "Yes, but there is a temple on this mountain, too. I caught a glimpse of it over there." He gestured in the direction from which he had come.

"No", insisted the man; "there is no temple there now, just some deserted buildings. Once it had been a temple, but no monks had lived there for a hundred years. No one lived there now."

"But it looked well cared for. There were no trees or plants grown up around the buildings," insisted Martinson.

"It is cared for, yes, but not by people. It is the home of—." The man used an unfamiliar phrase which seemed to contain the Korean word for fox.

"Foxes?" questioned Martinson, feeling a breath of chill, angry at himself for admitting it.

"Yes, the fox-spirits dwell there." In his earnestness the man spat out the harsh Korean consonants explosively. "No one comes near here, especially at night, because the fox-spirits are very dangerous and sometimes kill men. Everybody in the valley knows this and stays

90

away. Sometimes at night one can see lights shining up here, and echoes of strange noises reach the valley. When that happens, the monks of the great Popju-Sa Temple burn incense and chant sutras to avert the evil. But no one comes up here at night, ever."

"What do these fox-spirits do?"

"In our old stories we have many accounts of foxes who assume human form. Sometimes the fox is a beautiful girl who will entice a young man to her house. After they make love she becomes again a thousand year-old fox and devours him. Sometimes the foxes keep an inn and kill travellers who stop there. It is the way of fox-spirits, very dangerous and cunning, very ancient."

Martinson had heard stories like this before; the Koreans, like the Chinese, have many legends of tigers, foxes, even bears who assume human form, a reversal of western werewolf myths.

After he had left the mushroom-gatherer, who stared after him in some trepidation, as if he might be a fox-spirit himself instead of just another blundering "big-nose" foreigner, Martinson felt some of the cobwebs clear away. A natural thing, really, for renegade monks to take possession of an abandoned temple site and keep superstitious fears alive to protect their usurpation from exposure! Such persons might actually be rough customers indeed, highly desirable to avoid. He would certainly not spend the full week with them as he had planned. Tomorrow he would take off for that temple on the other mountain which the man had spoken of. But since the fox-worshipping monks had not molested him in any way last night, surely one more evening at their temple would be small risk. He wanted badly to see and take notes on the heretical ritual they were performing in the night. This might be an important anthropological find.

V

And yet when he returned to the temple for the evening meal it was hard to fight down the old repugnance. All six monks had assembled this time, and their jovially whining voices seemed latently sinister as they sat on the wooden porch awaiting the meal. One man especially had a high, yelping laugh that was not seemly. Another, stripped in the courtyard to bathe from a wooden bucket, revealed a mat of thick red-brown hair covering his body—Martinson had never seen an Oriental with so much body hair.

Finally the meal was served. It was the same as last night's and the old man Chae once again apologized sententiously that there was no meat today. One of the younger monks glanced at Martinson in mischievous glee as the American deflected the apology with gracious words. Why was he amused?

When the meal ended, Martinson addressed Chae, who seemed the eldest, though he had never ascertained what rank or authority existed in this place. He would very much like, if it were permitted, to attend the early morning prayer service here, part of which he had heard last night. Might this be possible?

Yes, replied Chae, widening his blackened smile, certainly. They would wake the young *yang-ban* some little time before the service. They would be honored by his participation.

The other monks seemed to glance carefully away from Martinson and each other. Conversation was silenced, and a tenuous feeling of tension, of anticipation, descended with the gathering darkness.

VI

He had thought that sleep would elude him again, but nervous tension can be as exhausting as physical exertion, and despite the unreasoning foreboding he felt, drowsiness overtook him as soon as he lay down in the little cubicle. He must have dozed intermittently a long time, for the warning rap on his door a little before three startled him as much as last night's musical outburst had done. He leaped to his feet and sprang through the sliding door almost too quickly to indicate a meditative frame of mind.

The six priests, in their grey outer robes and baggy knickerbockers, were assembling outside their quarters. As they formed a line for the procession, Chae, the one who had summoned Martinson, indicated that the American would come last in the line. He himself hobbled over rapidly to head it, carrying a stubby torch.

And now the procession paced slowly forward in the darkness, to the rattle of *mok-t'aks* and blurred whirring of gongs. Martinson couldn't help feeling that the idea of marching about so solemnly under the stars with none to witness was a bit ridiculous; but he thought of the pathos and dignity of the clergy in English backwaters who maintained the ritual of service with or without a congregation.

They were passing the central sanctuary; torchlight fell malevolently upon the crouched god—devil?—inside; the painted eyes seemed to glare, the carved flames to flicker. Now they were approaching the Fox-Shrine, forming a little semi-circle around the front of it. Martinson stood a bit to one side.

Old Chae touched his torch to a pile of brushwood that must have been prepared in advance, then placed the torch in an iron ring fastened to the shrine. The other monks put their musical implements aside.

The monk Chae addressed the others in a high, ritual tone. He was not speaking Korean, Martinson was sure, whether it was Chinese or another, perhaps older, language he could not guess. The monks whined a response in the same tongue, apparently. Then Chae let his eyes and gestures turn toward the stranger who stood almost outside the circle of firelight. He smiled with that black, gaping grimace that mirrored the unseen images in the shrine at his back. The monks turned toward Martinson, and they were smiling, too.

Suddenly the fire seemed to flare of its own accord, and a curious milling or stirring swept over the group of monks. They were bowing—genuflecting; no, they were actually prostrating themselves. They resembled—they had actually become—only heaps of garments scattered on the ground around the fire!

These heaps of garments stirred, shook. Martinson was rooted to the spot, bewildered, too uncomprehending to feel fear.

From each pile of discarded robes emerged a large, tawny fox eyeing him slyly, slowly advancing, jaws gaped in the shared grin of the shrine figures, of the monks.

Martinson tried to scream.

There was meat, the first in a long time, on the menu of the Temple of the Fox the next day.

(NOTE: The author knows of no recent or historical diabolist sect in Korean Buddhism; nor of any surviving belief in the were-fox legends of antiquity. But it is the privilege of the fantasiste to invent and aside from these matters, the customs and locales are rendered as accurately as possible. A real temple is described, with all apology to the worthy and no doubt thoroughly prosaic inmates.)

THE DEEP ONES

"Diviner than the dolphin is nothing yet
created; for indeed they were aforetime men,
and lived in cities along with mortals."
—Oppian: Halieutica (A.D. 200)

I

I HAD NEVER met Dr. Frederick Wilhelm before I went to work
at his Institute for Zoological Studies, situated in a remote cove on
the California coast some miles north of San Simeon and Piedras
Blancas, not far from the Big Sur area; but of course I had heard of his
studies. The Sunday supplements picked Wilhelm up years ago,
which was only natural: what more potentially sensational subject
could a journalist hope for than the idea that man shared the earth
with another, older, and perhaps more intelligent species overlooked
or ignored by modern science, but with which communication might
someday be established?

It wasn't a worn-out gambit like flying saucer people, or spiritual-
ism, or trolls hidden under the hills, of course, Wilhelm's subject was
the dolphin, that ocean mammal glimpsed centuries ago by
superstitious sailors and transmogrified into myths of mermaids,
sirens, all the fabulous sea-dwelling secret races of legend. Now, it
appeared, the superstitions might not be far wrong.

Preliminary tests had showed long ago that our ocean-going distant cousins harbored a high degree of pure intelligence and
potential for communication, unsuspected because of their watery

habitat and their lack of hands or early other prehensile apparatus for producing artifacts. Wilhelm's researches had not been the first, but his speculations were certainly the most daring, and he had parlayed his preoccupation into a career, attracting both government and private foundation funds to set up the institute toward which I found myself jogging in a rented jeep over rutted, sandy roads beside the sinuous green Pacific one starkly sunlit afternoon in April a year ago.

Although I knew of Frederick Wilhelm and his institute, I wasn't sure just how or what he knew of me. In a sense, I could easily see how my field, extrasensory perception and telepathy, might tie in with his work; but his initial letters and wires to me had never spelled out in any detail what he expected or projected of our collaboration. His messages, indeed, had seemed at once euphoric and evasive, confining themselves mostly to grandiloquent descriptions of his basic purposes and facilities, plus details on the financial aspects of our association.

I will admit that the amount of money Dr. Wilhelm offered was a strong factor in my accepting a job the exact nature of which remained unclear. As research co-ordinator of a small Eastern foundation devoted to para-psychological studies overlooked by the Rhine group at Duke, I had had my fill of skimped budgets and starvation wages.

Actually, the location of Wilhelm's experiments gave me more pause than any of the other doubtful aspects of his offer. I confess that I have always had an antipathy to California, despite the little time I recall having spent there. Perhaps I had read too much in the works of mordant satirists like Waugh and Nathanael West, but to me there has always seemed something decadent and even sinister about this self-eulogizing Pacific paradise.

The impression had not been allayed by my arrival via plane in gritty, galvanic Los Angeles, or by a stroll through that tiny down-town park where predatory homosexuals, drug derelicts, and demented fanatics of all kinds congregate under the bloated, twisted palms like so many patients in the garden of Dr. Caligari's madhouse. To some, Gothic battlements or New England backwaters represent the apex of spiritual horror and decay; for me, the neon-lit, screaming depravity of Los Angeles filled the bill.

These thoughts and others tangled in my mind as I guided my jeep over the rough beachside path, which I had been assured by the car rental agent in San Simeon, would take me unfailingly to the Institute for Zoological Studies. ("Ain't no place else the road goes, after you turn off left at the first orange juice stand—you know, the kind where the stand is built to look just like a great big orange. Jest keep on going, and don't stop for hippies or high water till the road ends!")

As I glanced rather nervously around, I could see on my left a sort of encampment of bleached white tents and dark, darting figures down by the wavering face of surf at water's edge. Were these the hippies my guide had referred to, those sardonic jesters on the periphery of our society, razzing and reviling all the standards and values of three thousand civilized years? Or had he been spoofing me; were these only a gaggle of middle-class youngsters out for an after-noon of beachside sun, sand, and sex as a respite from the abrasive grind of our precariously affluent society?

Even as these trite and puerile thoughts chased through my head, the vestigial road took a sharp turn over a rise and I found myself startlingly close up (a zoom-lens effect) to what could only be the famous Institute for Zoological Studies.

II

"What, actually, do you know about dolphins—or porpoises, as they are sometimes called?" queried Dr. Frederick Wilhelm, his eyes invisible behind thick lenses that caught the light from filtered globes under gold-tinted shades in his plush office. We had just settled down over a late afternoon cocktail, expertly crafted by Wilhelm himself, after my first rapid tour of the Institute, conducted by its director immediately after meeting my arriving jeep.

Wilhelm had been cordial and almost courtly, though it seemed a bit odd for him to start me off on a junket around his establishment before I had had a chance even to drop my luggage at my quarters and freshen up a bit after the long drive. I put it down to the vanity of a self-made scientific pioneer jockeying a cherished hobby horse down the home stretch in the big race.

The impression I'd received on the whirlwind tour was superficial and a bit bewildering, the long, low, white-plastered cement buildings straggling along the shoreline seemed crammed with more sound, lighting, recording, photographic, and less identifiable computerized equipment than would be needed to study the entire passenger list of Noah's ark, let alone one minor sub-species of marine mammal.

About Wilhelm himself there was nothing odd, though: a big, rumpled, greying penguin of a man, he moved and spoke with the disarming enthusiasm of a schoolboy just discovering that there is such a thing as science. As he hurried me from lab to lab at a breathless pace, he explained, "We'll see the dolphin pools tomorrow morning. Josephine—my research assistant, Josephine Gilman—is working there now; she'll join us later for drinks and dinner."

As I had learned from correspondence with Dr. Wilhelm, his senior staff (now totaling three, himself included, with my arrival) had quarters at the Institute, while the dozen or so technicians and laboratory assistants employed here made the trip to and from San Simeon billets in a Volkswagen micro-bus each day.

Now as I sat with Wilhelm in the dim richly decorated office over an acridly enticing martini, I heard the bus pull away, and realized that I was alone in the sprawling complex of buildings with its director and the un-surmised Josephine Gilman.

"What do you actually know about dolphins?" Wilhelm was saying.

"About what any layman knows," I found myself replying frankly. "I know that research started back in the 1950's, and indicated that dolphin brain size and specialized adaptations made probable a high degree of intelligence, along with sensory equipment suggesting a possibility of communication with man. So far as I recall, up to date nothing conclusive has come of it all, despite a lot of effort. I bought Dr. Lilly's books on his research in the Virgin Islands, but all this has happened so fast I haven't gone very far into them, though I have them with me in my suitcase."

"Don't bother with Lilly," Dr. Wilhelm broke in, refilling my glass from a crystal shaker with the etched classical design of a boy riding a dolphin. "I can show you things here that Lilly never even dreamed of."

"But the big mystery to me," I had the temerity to interject, "is what I'm here for. Do you want me to try and hypnotize your dolphins, or read their minds?"

"Not exactly," Wilhelm answered, after an almost imperceptible pause. "At least, not at the present stage. The way I actually plan for you to begin is to hypnotize a human subject, to see whether such a person may become more sensitive to the thought-patterns of the animal. We have done a lot of work, following up Lilly's leads, in recording and analyzing the sounds these beasts make, both under water and in the air; clicks, bleats, whistles, a wide gamut of noises—some of them above the sound spectrum audible to humans.

"We've taped these sounds, coded them, and fed them into computers, but no pattern of language has emerged, outside of certain very obvious signals for pain, distress, mating—signals many kinds of animals make, but which can't be called real language. And although dolphins will sometimes mimic human speech with startling clarity, it usually seems to be mere parroting, without real understanding.

"Yet at the same time, our encephalographs show patterns of electrical output in dolphin brains similar to those that occur during human speech, and in parts of the brain analogous to our speech centers—all this while no vocalization of any kind is going on, subsonic or supersonic, airborne or waterborne.

"This led me to a theory that the basic means of dolphin communication may be telepathic, and the conviction that we'll never get in touch with them any other way."

I was somewhat taken aback. "Do you have a telepathically sensitive and experienced person on the staff, or are you going to hire such a person?" I queried.

"Even better than that," rapped Dr. Wilhelm triumphantly, his twin-moon spectacles jiggling with emphasis. "We have a person sensitive and experienced over many months with the animals themselves—someone who knows how dolphins think, feel, and react; someone who has lived with dolphins so closely that she might almost be accepted among them as a dolphin herself."

"He means me, Mr. Dorn." Through an open door leading to a dusky hallway stepped lightly the lithe figure of a woman.

III

Glancing sidelong at her across the cozy, candle-lit dinner table, I decided that Josephine Gilman was striking, but not beautiful. Fairly young, with a trim figure, she missed real distinction due to the muddy coloring with rather a swarthy texture of her skin, and especially the staring protuberance of her eyes.

Nor was her manner entirely prepossessing. Her melodramatic entrance of Dr. Wilhelm's office that afternoon I could forgive, even with its implication that she had been listening outside for some time. But in subsequent conversation she had proved as much a monomaniac as her employer on the subject of their experiments, and with far less of a sense of humor—a fitting Trilby to Wilhelm's benign, avuncular Svengali.

"But of course," she was addressing me over our coffee, "you know all the old Greek and Roman stories about dolphins, Mr. Dorn. How they herded fish to help fishermen, saved drowning persons, and sometimes even fell in love with attractive boys and carried them off to sea on their backs. There's a long history of friendly relations between our species, even though the latter type incident seems based on—shall we say a misunderstanding?"

"I don't know about that, Miss Gilman," I riposted. "From what I've seen in California already, some of our modern youth would try anything once."

"Surf, sand, and sex," Dr. Wilhelm interjected, like a slogan. "I know what you mean. We have some of that type camped out down the beach right now, just south around the bend. Hippies, they call themselves these days. But to get back to dolphins, a more intelligent species. I'm not entirely sure that their good 'PR', so to speak, through the ages really rings true. Sometimes I even imagine it resembles the way superstitious people used to refer to the fairies and trolls as 'the Good Folk' to flatter them, out of fear of what they might do. So we get the modern nursery-rhyme and Walt Disney-type of fairy instead of the hidden troll races, the menacing, stunted, displaced dwellers that were their real origin."

Josephine Gilman picked up her coffee cup and daintily shrugged, as if to express disagreement.

"No, Jo, there's something to it," Wilhelm insisted, getting up and lumbering over to a big bookcase in the shadowed corner of the room. "Let me give you an example from a non-Western tradition." He searched for a book on one of the upper shelves.

"Sir Arthur Grimble was a colonial governor in the Gilbert Islands not so long ago. He visited an atoll called—what was it?—Butaritari, where there was supposed to be a man who could call dolphins." Wilhelm located the book he sought and fumbled it open.

"Grimble writes, let's see, here it is; 'His spirit went out of his body in a dream; it sought out the porpoise folk in their home under the Western horizon and invited them to a dance, with feasting, in Kuma village. If he spoke the words of the invitation aright (and very few had the secret of them) the porpoises would follow him with cries of joy to the surface.'

"Well, Grimble had him try it. The place was dead quiet that afternoon under the palm trees, the way he describes it, and the children had been gathered in under the thatches, the women were absorbed in plaiting garlands of flowers, and the men were silently polishing their ceremonial ornaments of shell. The makings of a feast lay ready in baskets. Suddenly—wait till I find it—'a strangled howl burst from the dreamer's hut. He dashed into the open and stood a while clawing at the air,' says Grimble, and whining on a queer high note like a puppy's.' The words came out 'Teiraki! Teiraki!', which means 'Arise! Arise! Our friends from the west ... Let us go down and greet them.'

"A roar went up from the village, and everyone rushed over to the beach on the atoll's ocean side. They strung themselves out and splashed through the shallows, all wearing the garlands woven that afternoon. Breast deep the porpoises appeared, 'gamboling toward us at a fine clip'. Everyone was screaming hard. When the porpoises reached the edge of the reef they slackened speed, spread out, and started cruising back and forth in front of the human line. Then suddenly they vanished."

Dr. Wilhelm brought the book to the table, sat down, and finished his remaining coffee. "Grimble thought they had gone away. But in a moment the dreamer pointed downward, muttering, 'The King out of the West comes to greet me'. There, not ten yards away, was the great shape of a porpoise, 'poised like a glimmering shadow in the glass-green water. Behind it followed a whole dusky flotilla of them.'

"The porpoises seemed to be hung in a trance. Their leader came slowly to the caller's legs. 'As we approached the emerald shallows, the keels of the creatures began to take the sand: they flapped gently, as if asking for help. The men leaned down to throw their arms around the great barrels and ease them over the ridges. They showed no sign of alarm. It was as if their single wish was to get to the beach.'

"When the water stood only thigh-deep, the men crowded around the porpoises, ten or more to each beast. Then 'lift' shouted the dreamer, and the ponderous black shapes were half dragged, half carried, unresisting, to the lip of the tide. There they settled down, those beautiful, dignified shapes, utterly at peace, while all hell broke loose around them."

Wilhelm's glasses caught the twin candle flames from the table; his eyes were impossible to see. Was this wild account, I found myself wondering, the real basis for his belief in the possibility of man's telepathic communication with dolphins?

"Men, women, and children," he continued, "leaping and posturing with shrieks that tore the sky, stripped off their garlands and flung them around still bodies, in a sudden and dreadful fury of boastfulness and derision. 'My mind,' says Grimble, 'still shrinks from that last scene—the raving humans, the beasts so triumphantly at rest.' There, what do you think of that?" He closed the book.

"It seems," I responded, "that the islanders made the dolphins the object of some sort of religious ritual, and that the dolphins enjoyed the proceedings. Sounds like something our hippie neighbors might go in for."

"You're wrong about that part," Josephine Gilman told me solemnly. "Those people out on the beach there hate the dolphins. Either that, or they're afraid of them."

IV

The next morning dawned damp and cloudy. As I breakfasted in the glass-enclosed patio outside my quarters, which overlooked the surging gray-green waves of the Pacific across a narrow stretch of sand, I saw Dr. Wilhelm sauntering along the beach on what seemed a morning constitutional. Suddenly I was aware that he was not alone; slogging across the sand to meet him came a fantastic figure: a booted, bearded, fur-clad man with bulbous features and tangled masses of hair surmounted by a big bright-red beret—a coarse caricature, he appeared to me, of the well known bust of the composer Wagner. One of the hippies!

Some impulse, perhaps simply curiosity, moved me to bolt down the eggs and toast which the warily-arriving housekeeper had brought me on a tray, and to rush out onto the beach through the storm-door of my entryway and join that strange colloquy shaping up under the striated silver-grey clouds as Wilhelm closed with his odd visitor.

My employer's stance seemed brusque and unfriendly as he listened to whatever the bearded man was saying to him. I slowed and approached the pair, as if on a casual stroll; until I came up to them, all I could hear was the sibilance of surf hissing over the sands almost at our feet.

"Good morning, Mr. Dorn," Wilhelm snapped, obviously not pleased to see me. Perhaps you ought to meet Mr. Alonzo Waite, since he's our neighbor. Mr. Waite is the high priest, or whatever he calls himself, of that hippie bunch down the way."

"I call myself nothing." the other responded quickly. "My disciples have awarded me the title of *guru*, or spiritual leader, since I have spent more time in mystic exercises than they. But I neither seek nor accept any pre-eminence among them. We are all fellow pilgrims on the sacred quest for truth." His voice was hollow, deep, strangely impressive; and his words, while eccentric, seemed more urbanely cultivated than I had expected.

"All very well, perhaps," Wilhelm put in testily, "but your quest for truth seems determined to interfere with mine."

"I am simply warning you, as I have warned you before, that your work with the dolphins is potentially very dangerous, to yourselves and others. You should give up these studies and release the beasts before great harm results."

"And on what evidence do you base this remarkable prophecy?" Wilhelm inquired acidly. "Tell Mr. Dorn, I've heard all this before."

Waite's cavernous voice descended even deeper. "As you may know, the League for Spiritual Discovery has been working with mind-expanding substances—not drugs, in the proper sense—that produce intuitions and perceptions unattainable to the ordinary brain. We are not of that group, but we too claim that such states are true ecstatic trances, comparable or superior to those that have always played such a vital part in all the Eastern religions, and which modern science would do well to recognize and investigate."

"This is more Mr. Dorn's field than mine," Wilhelm said uneasily. "He's in parapsychology. I know nothing about such matters, but none of this sounds at all plausible to me."

"But what has all this to do with dolphins?" I asked the bearded man.

"Our dreams and visions lately have been troubled by the presence of great, white, menacing shapes, cutting across and blocking out the sacred color patterns and animated mandalas that lead us to greater spiritual understanding," Waite boomed. "These are vibrations emanating from the creatures you have penned here, which you call dolphins, but which we know by an older name. These creatures are evil, strong and evil. As your experiments have progressed, so have the disturbing manifestations intensified. These vibrations are terribly destructive, not only mentally but physically. For your own good, I warn you to desist before it is too late."

"If what we're doing upsets your pipe-dreams," Wilhelm remarked with ill-concealed contempt, "why don't you move elsewhere and get out of range?"

The tall, bearded man blinked and gazed into the distance. "We must remain and concentrate our psychic powers on combating the evil vibrations," he said quietly. "There are certain spiritual exercises and ceremonies we can undertake that may help curb or deflect the danger for a while. In fact, we are planning such a ceremony for tonight. But the only sure way to safety is for you to release these ancient, wickedly wise creatures, and to give up your experiment."

Waite stood solemnly staring out to sea, a grotesque, foreboding and somehow dignified figure in his oversize beret and flapping fur robe.

V

"A scene right out of a Hollywood science fiction thriller," Wilhelm muttered angrily as he led me through the barn-like, high-ceilinged main laboratory and out a rear door. He couldn't seem to get the encounter on the beach out of his mind, and it bothered him more than I could well understand. As for me, I had put Waite down as just a typical. California nut, though more intelligent than most, and doubted that we would have any real trouble with him.

"You've seen our sound recording equipment, both atmospheric and underwater," Wilhelm said, finally changing the subject. "Now you must see where most of it is used, and where your own work will be concentrated."

The back of the lab looked out over the beach; near the water's edge stood a smaller windowless structure—long, low, and plastered with white cement like the others. Wilhelm led the way to it and opened its single heavy metal door with a key from his pocket.

The inside was taken up mostly by a sullen tank that resembled a small indoor swimming pool. The narrow verge that surrounded the tank on three sides was cluttered with electrical control panels, head sets, and other paraphernalia connected with the main tape recording and computer banks in the big lab. The ocean side of the building consisted mostly of a sort of sea-gate that could be opened on a cove communicating with the ocean itself, as I learned later, so that the water might be cleaned and freshened at need. Harsh fluo-rescent lamps played over the glittering surface of the pool, sending rippling whorls of reflected light into every corner of the room, there was a low hissing sound from the steam radiators run by thermostats that kept both the air and water temperatures constant and control-

107

lable.

But none of this attracted my immediate attention; for here I was at last confronted with the subject of the experiment itself: a lithe, bulky yet graceful shape—mottled grey above, dirty white below, with a long saw-toothed snout and deep-set, intelligent eyes—hung motionless in the shallow water on its slowly fanning flippers.

And not alone, for the dolphin shared its pool with Josephine Gilman, clad in a bright red bathing suit that set off her striking figure in an arresting manner. Indeed, I found myself staring more intently at Josephine than at her aquatic companion.

"Hi." Josephine's greeting was bland, but suggested a veiled irony, as if she were conscious of my covert gaze.

"Jo has been more or less living in this pool for the last two and a half months," Dr. Wilhelm explained. "The purpose is to get into complete rapport with Flip—that's the dolphin—and encourage any attempts at communication on his part."

"Flip," Josephine interjected, "is short for Flipper, of course, the dolphin hero of that old movie and TV series that was one of the first signs showing popular awareness of the animal's intelligence."

Jo laughed, heaving herself adroitly onto the tiled edge of the pool. "The show was just a sea-going Lassie, of course." She reached out for and wrapped herself snugly in a heavy terry-cloth towel. "Anybody for coffee? It's a bit chilly today for these early morning aquatics."

As Jo served coffee from a sideboard silex, Wilhelm was priming me with data on Flip.

"He's a prime specimen of *Tursiops truncata*, though a bit smaller than average—about six and a half feet, actually. The brain weighs an average of 1700 grams, 350 grams more than the human brain, with comparable density of cell count.

"We've had this fellow for over a year now, and though he'll make

108

every noise they're noted for—barks, grunts, clicks and scrapes and whistles—and even mimic human speech, we can't dope out a language pattern. Yet they must talk to each other. My first interest in dolphin-biology was aroused by a report on sonar charts that Navy boats made near Ponape in the south Pacific. The charts showed orderly discipline in their undersea movements over a distance amounting to miles; and something more; a pattern or formation of mathematically precise movements that suggests either elaborate play or some sort of ritual."

"Maybe," I interrupted facetiously, "they were practicing for the ceremony that so impressed Governor Grimble."

"Anyway," said Jo putting aside her cup and straightening a strap on her bathing suit, "in ten weeks I haven't gotten to first base with Flip here and now you're supposed to get us onto the proper wave length. Also, you'll have to provide some hints about what to look for and concentrate on in telepathic communication attempts. Frankly, I don't put much faith in it; but if Fred wants to try, I'll co-operate with as few mental reservations as possible."

Remembering a passage from Dr. Lilly's pioneer book, I asked Wilhelm: "Have you implanted electrodes in the beast's brain for pleasure-stimulus experiments?"

"We're beyond all that," Wilhelm replied impatiently. "It's been known for years that they'll learn the most complex reaction patterns almost immediately to achieve the stimulus, far beyond what any lower animal can manage. Besides, it's crude—a kind of electrical masturbation, or LSD, like our friends out there on the beach favor. It doesn't show a proper respect for our basic equality with the dolphin—or his superiority over us, as the case may be."

While this conversation progressed, my attention was gradually distracted by the animal itself, floating in the pool beside us. It was obviously following our talk, though I assumed without any degree of verbal comprehension. The single visible eye, set in a convoluted socket behind the rather menacing snout, moved from one to the other of us with lively interest. I even caught myself reading human expressions into it; proprietary interest when turned on Josephine Gilman, tolerant amusement in regard to Dr. Wilhelm, and toward myself, what? Resentment, animosity, jealousy? What fancies were these I was weaving, under the glaring lights of a scientific laboratory?

"You'll have to get better acquainted with Flip," Wilhelm was saying. "If you're to help us learn to interpret dolphinese, you and he should become good friends."

There was a commotion in the water; Flip turned abruptly to his left and swam off semi-submerged, emitting as he did so the first dolphin sound I had ever heard: a shrill whistle of derision.

VI

That evening after dinner, Josephine Gilman and I walked on the beach under a moon that shone only intermittently through scurrying clouds. Dr. Wilhelm was in his office writing up notes, and the housekeeper-cook, last to leave of the staff each evening, was just rattling off toward San Simeon in the Institute's Land Rover.

I found that I didn't know what to make of my feelings toward Jo. When I had seen her in the pool with the dolphin that morning, she had attracted me intensely, seeming in her proper element. But at dinner, in a frilly cocktail gown that somehow didn't suit her, she once more repelled me with her sallow skin, her bulging, humorless eyes.

"Tomorrow the hypnosis sessions are to begin." I reminded her as we paced slowly toward the surf's edge. "Are you sure you really want to undergo this? After all, you say you have no confidence in this approach, and that may inhibit your response to it."

"I'll do as Fred thinks best, and I'll assume what he assumes, temporarily at least. I've become quite good at that, within limits. Did you know he once wanted me to marry him? That's where I drew the line, though."

"No." I was embarrassed by her abrupt interjection of personal matters.

"I think it was for convenience, mostly. His first wife had died, we were working together, we shared the same interests—even the fact that we had to stay here together overnight, to watch over the work 24 hours a day when that was necessary—well, it would have made things easier, but I told him no."

"How did you first become interested in—dolphinology, is that the word?" I sought to change the subject. We had reached the point beyond which the waves retreated, leaving streaks of hissing, iridescent foam half visible in the gloom.

"Actually, I've always been fascinated by the sea and things that live underwater. I used to spend half my time at the aquarium back home in Boston—either there or down at the harbor."

"Your family comes from Boston?"

"Not originally. My father was in the Navy, and we lived there a long time, ever since Mother died. His family came from a run-down seaport mill-town called Innsmouth, up past Marblehead. The Gilmans are an old family there. They were in whaling and the East Indies trade as far back as two hundred years ago, and I suppose that's where my oceanographic interests come from."

"Do you often go back there?"

"I've never ever been there, strange as it seems. The whole place almost burned to the ground back in the 1920's, before I was born.

My father said it was a dead, depressing place, and made me promise years ago to keep away from it—I don't know exactly why. That was just after his last trip there, and on his next voyage he was lost overboard from a destroyer he commanded. No one ever knew how; it was calm weather."

"Weren't you ever curious about why he warned you away from—what was it, Innsville?" I faltered.

"Yes, especially after he died. I looked up the newspapers from around the time of the big fire—the Boston libraries had almost nothing else on Innsmouth—and found one story that might have had some bearing. It was full of preposterous hints about how the people of Innsmouth had brought back some sort of hybrid heathen savages with them from the South Seas years ago, and started a devil-worship cult that brought them sunken treasure and supernatural power over weather. The story suggested that the men had interbred with their Polynesian priestesses or whatever, and that was one reason why people nearby shunned and hated them."

I thought of Josephine's swarthy skin and strange eyes, and wondered.

We had covered a mile or more from the Institute, and were suddenly aware that the darkness ahead was laced with a faint flickering, as of a fire on the beach to the south. At the same time, a sort of low mumble or glutinous chant became audible from the same direction. All at once, a high hysterical wail, reverberating in shocking ecstasy, burst forth on the night air, prolonging itself incredibly—now terror-stricken, now mockingly ironic, now mindlessly animal—rising and falling in a frenzy that suggested only delirium or insanity raised to the highest possible human—or inhuman—pitch.

Without thought or volition, Josephine and I found ourselves clinging together and kissing with an abandon that echoed the wild caterwauling down the beach.

The hippies, it seemed, were holding their promised ritual to exorcise the evil influence of the sinister creatures from the sea.

VII

The next few days can most conveniently be summarized through extracts from the clinical journal which I began to keep from the outset of our attempt to establish telepathic contact with the dolphin Flip through hypnosis of a human subject:

April 20. This morning I placed Josephine under light hypnosis, finding her an almost ideally suggestible subject. I implanted posthypnotic commands intended to keep her alert and concentrating on the dolphin's mind to catch any message emanating from it. After I awakened her, she went back into the tank with Flip and spent the rest of the day there, playing the number games they have devised together. It is remarkable to observe how devoted the animal is to her, following her about the pool and protesting with loud barking and bleating whenever she leaves it. Flip will accept his food, raw whole fish, only from her hands.

I asked Dr. Wilhelm whether there was any danger from those wicked-looking hundred-toothed jaws, which snap down on the fish like a huge, lethal pair of shears. He said no; in neither history nor legend has there ever been a report of a dolphin attacking or even accidently injuring a human. Then he quoted something from Plutarch—his erudition is profound, if one-sided —which I looked up in the library later. Here it is:

"To the dolphin alone, beyond all other, Nature has granted what the best philosophers seek: friendship for no advantage ..."

April 22. Still no results. Wilhelm wants me to try deeper hypno-

sis and stronger suggestion. In fact, he proposed leaving Josephine in a trance for periods of a day or more, with just enough volition to keep her head above water in the tank. When I protested that this was dangerous, since in such a state she might well drown inadvertently. Wilhelm gave me an odd look and said. "Flip wouldn't let her."
...

April 25. Today, in the absence of any progress whatsoever, I agreed to try Wilhelm's second-stage plan, since Jo agrees. I put her to sleep by the pool's edge while Flip watched curiously. (I don't think this dolphin likes me, although I've had no trouble making friends with the others in the bigger tank up on the north beach.) After implanting in her subconscious the strongest admonitions to be careful in the water, I let her re-enter the pool for a few hours. Her demeanor, of course, is that of a sleep walker or a comatose person. She sits on the lip of the pool or wades about it abstractedly. Flip seems puzzled and resentful that she won't play their usual games with him.

When I was helping Jo out of the pool after an hour or so of this, the dolphin zoomed past at terrific speed, and I was sure he was about to snap at my arm, thus making me the first dolphin-bitten human in history; but he apparently changed his mind at the last moment and veered away, quacking and creaking angrily, his single visible eye glaring balefully ...

April 27. Dr. Wilhelm wants to increase the period with Jo in the pool under hypnosis. This is because when she woke up yesterday she said she remembered vague, strange impressions that might be telepathic images or messages. I'm almost certain that these are pseudo-memories, created by her subconscious to please Dr. Wilhelm, and I have strongly protested any intensification of this phase of the experiment.

Those hippie orgies on the beach south of here go on almost every night till all hours. The three of us are losing sleep and getting on edge, especially Jo, who tires easily after the longer periods under hypnosis.

April 28. Jo had an especially vivid impression of some sort of scenes or pictures transmitted to her during hypnosis after I brought her out of the trance this afternoon. At Wilhelm's suggestion I put her under again to help her remember, and we taped some inconclusive question-and-answer exchanges. She spoke of a ruined stone city under the sea, with weedy arches and domes and spires, and of sea creatures moving through the sunken streets. Over and over she repeated a word that sounded like "Arlyeh". It's all imagination, I'm sure, plus memories of poems by Poe or cheap horror fiction—maybe even the story Wilhelm read us about the Gilbert Island porpoises and their "King out of the West". Yet Wilhelm was excited, and so was Josephine when she woke up and heard the tape played back. Both of them wanted me to put her in a deep trance and leave her in the pool around the clock. I consider this to be a nonsensical idea and told them so.

April 29. This morning Wilhelm pressed me again. I told him I couldn't be responsible for what might happen, and he answered: "No, of course not; I am responsible for whatever goes on at this Institute myself." Then he showed me a kind of canvas harness or breeches buoy affair he'd rigged up in the pool, securely anchored to the verge, where Jo could be strapped and still move around without any danger of drowning under hypnosis. I gave in and agreed to try the idea for a while.

April 30. Everything went off without any difficulty, and at least Jo and Wilhelm are convinced that what they call her "messages" are getting sharper and more concrete. To me, what she recalls under light hypnosis is just nonsense or fantasy, mixed in perhaps with those odd rumors about her home town Innsmouth, which she told me about earlier. Nevertheless, the two of them want to keep it up another day or so, and I agreed since no actual danger seems to be involved.

VIII

"No danger involved!" If, when I wrote those words, I had had even an inkling of what I know now, I would have halted the experiment immediately; either that or left this ocean-side outpost on the edge of the unknown, threatened by fanatic superstition from the outside and a stiff-necked scientific *hubris* from within. But though the hints were there, recognizable in hindsight, still at the time I saw nothing, felt nothing but a vague, unplaceable malaise, and so did nothing; and thus I must share the guilt for what happened.

Late on the evening of April 30, soon after I had written the journal entry quoted above, Dr. Wilhelm and I were rousted from our rooms by the sound of a scream which, though faint and muffled by distance, we at once recognized as Jo's voice, not the subhuman caterwauling of our drug-debauched neighbors.

Ask me now why we had left Jo Gilman alone in the dolphin's tank and I must admit that it appears to be original negligence or inexcusable folly. But Wilhelm and I had stood watch over her alternately the night before as she hung half-submerged in her canvas harness and dreamed her strange dreams under the glare of the fluorescent tubes. The harness held her head and thorax well clear of the water; and Flip, lolling quiescent in the tank seemed to drowse too (though dolphins never sleep, since they must keep surfacing to breathe, like whales). Thus this second night, at her own prior urging, Wilhelm and I had knocked off for dinner and then sought some relaxation in our rooms.

The scream which jolted us both out of a vague torpor induced by loss of sleep, came at about 10 p.m. Dr. Wilhelm's room was nearer the main lab than mine; thus, despite his greater age and bulk, he was ahead of me in reaching the heavy iron door of the beach-side aquarium. As I approached the building, I could see him fumbling with the lock, his hands trembling. I was taken aback when he wheezed breathlessly at me over his shoulder: "Wait here!"

I had no choice, for he slipped inside and clanged the door shut behind him. The lock operated automatically, and since only Wilhelm and the chief lab technician—now miles away in San Simeon— had keys, I was forced to obey.

I can recall and relive in minute detail the agony and apprehension of that vigil, while the sibilant surf plied up only yards away under a freshening wind, and the half-full moon shone down with an ironic tranquility upon that silent, windowless, spectrally white structure.

I had glanced at my watch as I ran along the beach, and can verify that it was almost exactly ten minutes after Wilhelm had slammed the door that he again opened it—slowly, gratingly, the aperture framing, as always, a rectangle of harsh, glaring light.

"Help me with her," Wilhelm muttered from within, and turned away.

I stepped inside. He had removed Jo Gilman's limp form from the water and had wrapped it in several of the capacious beach robes that were always at hand near the tank. Glancing beyond the inert figure, I was startled to see Jo's canvas harness strung out dismem-

117

bered across the winking surface of the water; and even part of her bright red bathing suit, which seemed entangled with the shredded canvas. The shadowy shape of the dolphin Flip I glimpsed too, fully submerged and strangely quiescent in a far corner of the pool.

"To her room," Wilhelm murmured as we lifted Jo. Somehow, staggering and sidling in the shifting sand, we gained the dormitory building, groped open the door, and stumbled through Jo's apartment (I had never been inside, but Wilhelm seemed to know his way), finally dropping her muffled body unceremoniously onto the narrow folding bed.

"I'll call a doctor," I mumbled, lurching toward the door.

"No, don't!" Wilhelm rapped, adjusting the dim bedside lamp. "She's not really hurt—as a Zoologist, I'm doctor enough myself to know that. Bring a tape recorder from the lab. I think she's still hypnotized, and she may be able to tell us what happened."

"But you saw—" I began breathlessly.

"I saw only what you saw," he grated, glaring at me through lenses that picked up the muted glow of the bed lamp. "She was clinging to the edge of the pool when I went in there, only partly conscious, out of her harness, and—get the tape machine, man!"

Why I obeyed blindly I still do not understand, but I found myself again blundering along the beach, Wilhelm's key ring in my hand, and then fumbling a portable tape recorder from the orderly storage cabinets of the main laboratory.

When I lugged the machine back to Josephine's room, I found that Dr. Wilhelm had somehow maneuvered her into an incongruous frilly lounging robe and gotten her under the bed covers. He was massaging her wrists with a mechanical motion, and scanning her face anxiously. Her eyes were still closed, her breathing harsh and irregular.

"Is she in hypnosis or shock?" he inquired edgily.

"Either, or perhaps both," I shot back. "At this point, the symptoms would be similar."

"Then set up the machine."

It soon appeared that the deep mesmeric state into which I had placed Jo Gilman that morning still held. I was able to elicit responses from her by employing the key words that I used to trigger the state of trance, so easily invoked these days as to be almost disconcerting.

"Jo, can you hear me? Tell us what happened to you," I urged her gently. The color began to return to her face; she sighed deeply and twisted under the bed clothes. For what happened next, I have the evidence not only of my own recollections, but a transcription typed up next day from the tape machine, whose microphone Dr. Wilhelm now held beside her pillow with tense expectancy. This is a summary—omitting some of her repetitions, and the urgings on our part—of what we heard muttered by the bruised lips of that comatose woman writhing uneasily on her cot in a dimly lit room beside the glittering, moon-drenched Pacific, close on to midnight of May Eve:

"Must get out ... must get out and unify the forces. Those who wait in watery Arlyeh, those who walk the snowy wastes of Leng, whistlers and lurkers of sullen Kadath—all shall rise, all shall join once more in praise of Great Clooloo, of Shub-Niggurath, of Him Who is not to be Named ...

"You will help me, fellow breather of air, fellow holder of warmth, store of seed for the last sowing and the endless harvest... (Unpronounceable name, possibly Y'ha-nthlei) shall celebrate our nuptials, the weedy labyrinths shall hold our couch, the silent strutters in darkness will welcome us with high debauch and dances upon

their many-segmented legs ... their ancient, glittering eyes, are gay...
And we shall dwell amidst wonder and glory forever..."

The speaker gasped and seemed to struggle to awaken. My
apprehensions had crystallized into certainty: "She's hysterical," I
whispered.

"No—no, not hysterical," Dr. Wilhelm hissed, trying in his elation
to keep his voice subdued. "Not hysterical. She's broken through.
Don't you see what this is? Don't you see that she's echoing ideas and
images that have been projected to her? Can't you understand? What
we've just heard is her attempt to verbalize in English what she's experienced today—the most astonishing thing any human being has
ever experienced: communication from another intelligent species!"

IX

Of the rest of that night I remember little. The twin shocks of Jo
Gilman's hysterical seizure—for so I interpreted not only her unconscious ranting but also the initial scream, and her struggle out of the
restraining apparatus—plus the unreasoning interpretation placed
upon these events by my employer, served to unnerve me to the
extent that when Jo sank gradually into normal slumber I excused
myself to Dr. Wilhelm and reeled off to my own room a little before
midnight, for ten hours of uninterrupted—if not undisturbed—sleep.

It was a distinct surprise to me when I joined the others at staff
luncheon the next day to find that a reticence amounting almost to a
conspiracy of silence had already grown up in regard to the events of
the preceding night. Jo, although pale and shaken, referred to what
had happened as her "LSD trip" before the other staff members, and
Dr. Wilhelm merely spoke of an abortive phase of "Operation Dolphin" which had been given up.

In any event, Jo completely abandoned her previous intimacy with

Flip; indeed, I never once saw her in the aquarium building again; at least, not until a certain climactic occasion, the facts about which I almost hesitate to affirm at this juncture.

Suddenly, all research efforts seemed to be shifted hastily to the crowded pens of young dolphins on the north beach, and I was called upon to interpret sonar charts and graphs recording patterns of underwater movement that might—or might not—indicate a telepathic herd-communion between individuals and groups of animals, both free and in-captivity.

This, although a plausibly rational shift in experimental emphasis, somehow failed to convince me; it seemed merely a cover-up (on the part of Josephine as well as Wilhelm), masking a fear, an uncertainty, or some un-surmised preoccupation I failed to grasp. Perhaps these further extracts from my journal will make clear my uneasiness during this period:

May 7. Jo is still distant and evasive with me. Today as we worked together coding patterns of dolphin movement for the computer, she suddenly fell silent, stopped work, and began to stare straight ahead. When I passed my hand in front of her face, I confirmed that her stare was unfocused, and she had actually fallen into a trance again, from which I was able to awaken her with the same key words we used when she was regularly under hypnosis.

I was horrified, for such involuntary trances may well be a symptom of deep psychic disturbance, over which I can only blame myself for giving in to Dr. Wilhelm's rash obstinacy. When she woke up, however, she would admit only to having a headache and dozing off for a moment. I did not press the issue then.

May 8. The above entry was written in the late afternoon. Since Jo seemed herself at dinner, I determined to go to her room later for a serious talk about the dangerous state into which she has fallen. But when I reached the door of her apartment I was surprised to hear voices, as it seemed, in muttered conversation inside.

I stood there for a few moments, irresolute whether to knock or not. Suddenly I realized that although what I heard was divided into the usual give-and-take exchanges of conversation, with pauses and variations in the rhythm and tempo of the participating voices, in actuality the timbre was that of only one speaker: Josephine Gilman herself.

May 10. I still cannot believe that what Jo said on the tape after her so-called hysterical seizure was really a remembered telepathic transmission from Flip; and despite what Dr. Wilhelm said that night, I don't know whether he still believes it either. I have studied the transcript over and over, and think I have found a clue. Something about one of the phrases she spoke seemed hauntingly familiar: "Their ancient, glittering eyes are gay."

Recalling Wilhelm's remarkable memory, I mentioned it to him, and he agreed immediately: "Yes, it's from Yeats. I recognized that almost at once."

"But that means the so-called message, or part of it at least, must have come from her own subconscious memory of the poem.

"Perhaps. But after all, it was Yeats who wrote the line about 'that dolphin-torn, that gong-tormented sea'. Perhaps he's their favorite poet."

This flippancy irritated me. "Dr. Wilhelm," I answered angrily, "do you really believe that that tape was a telepathic transmission from Flip?"

He sobered. "I don't know, Dorn. Maybe we'll never know. I

thought so at first, but perhaps I was carried away. I almost hope so—it was a pretty unsettling experience. But one thing I do know: you were right; that particular line of approach is too dangerous, at least with a subject as highly strung as Jo. Perhaps we can devise a safer way to resume the research with hypnosis later, but just now I don't see how. We're only lucky that she didn't suffer any real harm."

"We don't know that either," I replied. "She's started hypnotizing herself."

Wilhelm didn't answer ...

May 20. For over a week, I have not observed Jo fall into one of her trances in the daytime. However, she always retires early, pleading exhaustion, so we don't know what may go on at night. Several times I have deliberately paused outside her door during the evening, and once I thought I heard that strange muffled conversation again, but softer or more distant.

The research is now mechanical and curiously artificial; I don't see that we're accomplishing anything, nor is there any special need for me to be here at all. The old enthusiasm and vigor seem to have gone out of Wilhelm, too. He has lost weight and appears older, apprehensive, as if waiting for something ...

May 24. I sat late on the glassed-in patio last night, looking out toward the ocean, which was invisible, since there was no moon. At about nine o'clock I thought I saw something white moving down by the water's edge, proceeding south in the general direction of the main lab. Curiously disturbed, I followed.

It was Jo of course, either under hypnosis or walking in her sleep. (Here indeed was a scene from a horror film for Wilhelm to snort at!) I took her arm and was able to guide her back to the dormitory building. The door to her apartment was open, and I put her to bed without resistance. However, when I tried to awaken her by the usual mesmeric methods, I failed. After a while, though, she seemed to fall into ordinary slumber, and I left, setting the lock on the hall door to catch automatically.

Wilhelm was working late in his study, but I could see no reason to tell him about this incident. I shall probably not tell Jo either, since it might upset her nerves even more. I realize that I have become extremely fond of her since her "LSD trip", in a tender, protective way unlike my initial physical attraction for her. And this knowledge makes me recognize, too, that something must be done to help her. All I can think of is to call in a psychiatrist, but Wilhelm has already denied the need for this, and I know Jo will follow his lead.

I must keep alert for more evidence to convince the pair of them that such a step is urgently indicated.

For the past few weeks our hippies have abated their nocturnal ceremonies, but last night after I left Jo's room I could hear that inhuman chanting and shouting start up, and see from my patio the reflections from their distant fire on the beach.

Again I did not sleep well.

X

It was past mid-June, with no change in the tense but tenuous situation at the Institute, when I had my momentous interview with the hippie *guru*, Alonzo Waite.

The moon shone brightly that evening, and I sat as usual on my glass-fronted patio, nursing a last brandy and trying to put my thoughts and ideas into some order for the hundredth time. Jo Gilman had retired early, and Dr. Wilhelm had driven into town for some sort of needed supplies, so I was in effect alone in the Institute. Perhaps Waite knew this somehow, for he came unerringly up the beach to my door, his fur cloak flapping dejectedly around his shanks, even though my apartment showed no light. I rose rather hesitantly to admit him.

He seated himself in a canvas chair, refused brandy, and abstractedly removed the soiled red beret from his unshorn locks. In the faint glow of the hurricane lamp I had lit, his dark eyes were distant and withdrawn; I wondered whether he were under the influence of drugs.

"Mr. Dorn," my visitor began, in the resonant tones I well remembered, "I know that you as a man of science cannot approve or understand what my companions and I are trying to do. Yet because your field is exploration of the lesser-known aspects of the human mind, I have hopes that you may give me a more sympathetic hearing than Dr. Wilhelm has done.

"I, too, am a scientist, or was—don't smile! A few years ago, I was assistant professor in clinical psychology at a small school in Massachusetts called Miskatonic University, a place you've possibly never even heard of. It's in an old colonial town called Arkham, quite a backwater, but better known in the days of the Salem witch trials.

"Now, extravagant as the coincidence may seem—if it is really a coincidence—I knew your co-worker Josephine Gilman by sight when she was a student there, though she would certainly not recognize me, or even recall my name perhaps, in the guise I have now adopted." He shrugged slightly and glanced down at his eccentric getup, then continued.

"You probably don't remember the scandal that resulted in my leaving my post, since it was hushed up, and only a few sensational newspapers carried the item. I was one of those early martyrs to science—or to superstition, if you like; but whose superstition?—fired for drug experiments with students in the first days of LSD research. Like others who became better known, and who sometimes exploited their discoveries for personal profit or notoriety. I was convinced that the mind-expanding drugs gave humanity an opening into a whole new world of psychic and religious experience. I never stopped to wonder in those days whether the experience would involve beauty alone, or also encompass terror. I was a pure scientist then, I liked to think, and to me whatever was, was good—or at least neutral raw material for the advancement of human understanding. I had much to learn.

"The drug underground at Miskatonic University was a little special. The school has one of the most outstanding collections of old books on out-of-the-way religious practices now extant. If I mention the medieval Arab treatise called the *Necronomicon* in its Latin version, you won't have heard of it; yet the Miskatonic copy is priceless, one of only three acknowledged still to exist—the others are in the Harvard and Sorbonne libraries.

"These books tell of an ancient secret society or cult that believes the earth and all the known universe were once ruled by vast alien invaders from outside space and time, long before man evolved on this planet. These entities were so completely foreign to molecular matter and protoplasmic life that for all intents and purposes they were supernatural—supernatural and evil."

Waite may once have been a college professor, I reflected, but judging by his portentous word choice and delivery, he would have made an even better old-time Shakespearean actor or revival preacher. His costume helped the effect, too.

"At some point," the bearded *guru* continued, "these usurpers were defeated and banished by even stronger cosmic opponents who, at least from our limited viewpoint, would appear benevolent. However, the defeated Old Ones could not be killed, nor even permanently thwarted. They live on, imprisoned, but always seeking to return and resume their sway over the space-time universe, pursuing their immemorial and completely unknowable purposes.

"These old books record the lore that has been passed on to man from human and pre-human priesthoods that served these imprisoned deities, which constantly strive to mold and sway the thoughts of men by dreams; moving them to perform the rites and ceremonies by means of which the alien entities may be preserved, strengthened, and at last released from their hated bondage.

"All this goes on even today, and has influenced half the history of human science and religion in unacknowledged ways. And of course, there are rival cults that seek to prevent the return of the Old Ones, and to stymie the efforts of their minions.

"To be brief, the visions induced by LSD in the Miskatonic students, together with the results of experiments and ceremonies we learned from the old books, confirmed the reality of this fantastic mythology in a very terrible way. Even now I could not be persuaded to tell any living person some of the things I have seen in my visions, nor even to hint at the places my spirit has journeyed during periods of astral detachment.

"There were several disappearances of group members who dared too much, and several mental breakdowns, accompanied by certain physical changes that necessitated placing the victim in permanent solitary confinement. These occurrences, I assure you, were not due to any human agency whatsoever, no matter what the authorities may have chosen to believe.

"Though there was no evidence of foul play, the group was discovered and expelled, and I lost my job. After that some of us came here and formed a community dedicated to thwarting the efforts of evil cultists to free the Great Old Ones, which would mean in effect the death or degradation of all men not sworn to serve them. This is the aim of our present efforts to achieve spiritual knowledge and discipline through controlled use of hallucinogenic agents. Believe me, we have seen more than enough of the horrors connected with these matters, and our sympathies are all on the other side. Unfortunately, there are other groups, some of them right here in California, working in parallel ways to effect directly opposite results."

"An interesting story," I put in impatiently, disgusted by what I regarded as insane ramblings, "but what has all this to do with our research here, and the fact that you knew Miss Gilman as a college student?"

"Josephine's family comes from Innsmouth," Waite rumbled forebodingly. "That blighted town was once one of the centers of this cosmic conspiracy. Before the Civil War, mariners from Innsmouth brought back strange beliefs from their South Pacific trading voyages—strange beliefs, strange powers, and strange, deformed Polynesian women as their brides. Later, still stranger things came out of the sea itself in response to certain ceremonies and sacrifices.

"These creatures, half human and half amphibians of unknown batrachian strains, lived in the town and interbred with the people there, producing monstrous hybrids. Almost all the Innsmouth people became tainted with this unhuman heritage, and as they grew older many went to live underwater in the vast stone cities built there by the races that serve Great Cthulhu."

I repeated the strange name falteringly; somehow it rang a bell in my memory. All this was oddly reminiscent; both of what Jo had told me and of her delirious words on the tape, which Wilhelm half-believed represented a message from the mind of an undersea race.

"Cthulhu," Waite repeated sepulchrally, "is the demonic deity imprisoned in his citadel amidst the pre-human city of R'lyeh, sunken in mid-Pacific somewhere by the power of his enemies aeons ago, asleep but dreaming forever of the day of release, when he will resume sway over the earth. And his dreams over the centuries have created and controlled those undersea races of evil intelligence who are his servants."

"You can't mean the dolphins!" I exclaimed.

"These and others, some of such aspect that only delirious castaways have ever seen them and lived. These are the sources of the legendary hydras and harpies, Medusa and mermaids, Scylla and Circe, which have terrified human beings from the dawn of civilization and before.

"Now you can guess why I have constantly warned Dr. Wilhelm to give up his work, even though he is nearer success than he realizes. He is meddling in things more terrible than he can well imagine when he seeks communication with these Deep Ones, these minions of the blasphemous horror known as Cthulhu.

"More than this—the girl through whom he seeks this communication is one of the Innsmouth Gilmans. No, don't interrupt me! I knew it as soon as I saw her at the university; the signs are unmistakable, though not far advanced yet; the bulging, ichthyic eyes, the rough skin around the neck where incipient gill-openings will gradually develop with age. Someday, like her ancestors, she will leave the land and live underwater as an ageless amphibian in the weedy cities of the Deep Ones, which I glimpse almost daily, in my visions and in my nightmares alike.

"This cannot be coincidence—there is manipulation somewhere in bringing this girl, almost wholly ignorant of her awful heritage, into intimate, unholy contact with a creature that can and what slim chances she may ever have had of escaping her monstrous genetic destiny!"

Xl

Although I did my best to calm Alonzo Waite by assuring him that all attempts to establish hypnotic rapport between Jo and Flip had ended, and that the girl had even taken an aversion to the animal, I did not tell him any of the other puzzling aspects of the matter, some of which seemed to fit in strangely with the outlandish farrago of superstition and hallucination that he had been trying to foist upon me.

Waite did not seem much convinced by my protestations, but I wanted to get rid of him and think matters over again. Obviously the whole of his story was absurd; but just as obviously he believed it. And if others believed it too, as he claimed, then this might explain in some measure the odd coincidences and the semi-consistent pattern that seemed to string together so many irrelevancies and ambiguities.

But after Waite left, I decided that there were still pieces missing from the puzzle. Thus when Jo Gilman knocked on my door a little before 11:00 o'clock, I was not only surprised (she never came out at night any more, since her sleep-walking episode), but glad of the opportunity to ask her some questions.

"I couldn't sleep and felt like talking," Jo explained, with an air of rather strained nonchalance, as she settled in the same chair Waite had used. "I hope I am not disturbing you." She accepted a brandy and soda, and lit a cigarette. I had a sudden, detached flash of vision that saw this scene as a decidedly familiar one—drinks and cigarettes, a girl in a dressing gown in the beachside apartment of a bachelor. But our conversation didn't fall into the cliché pattern; we talked of sonar graphs and neuron density, of supersonic vibrations, computer tapes, and the influence of water temperature on dolphin mating habits.

I watched Jo carefully for any signs of falling into that auto-hypnotic state in which she held conversations with herself, but could see none; she seemed more herself than had been the case for many weeks. At the same time, I was annoyed to realize that I had become more conscious than before of the physical peculiarities which that idiot Waite had attributed to a biologically impossible strain in her ancestry.

The conversation had been entirely prosaic until I seized the opportunity of a moment of silence to ask one of the questions that had begun to intrigue me: "When did you first hear about Dr. Wilhelm's studies, and how did you happen to come to work for him?"

"It was right after my father was drowned. I had to drop out of graduate school back in Massachusetts and start making my own living. I had heard about Fred's research, and of course I was fascinated from the start, but I never thought of applying for a job here until my Uncle Joseph suggested it."

"Your father's brother?"

"Yes, a funny little old fellow; I always thought when I was a child that he looked just like a frog. He spends about half the year at the old family place in Innsmouth and half in Boston. He seems to have all the money he needs, though I've never seen any of it. My father once asked him jokingly what he did for a living, and Uncle Joe just laughed and said he dove for Spanish doubloons.

"Anyway, a few weeks after I left school and came back to Boston, Uncle Joe showed me a story about Dr. Wilhelm's work with the dolphins—I think it was in the *Scientific American*. Joe knew of my studies in oceanography, of course, and he said he knew an authority in the field who would write me a good recommendation. It must have been a good one, all right, because in less than six weeks here I was. That was over two years ago, now."

If Alonzo Waite needed a further link in his wild theory of conspiracy, here was perfect raw material!

"You know," Jo went on with apparently casual lightness, "I told you a long time ago that Dr. Wilhelm asked me to marry him. That was more than six months ago. At the time I thought it was a bad idea, but now I rather wish I had taken him up on it."

"Why? Afraid of becoming an old maid? I might have something to say about that one of these days."

"No." Her voice remained as calm and casual as before. "The reason is that—dating from right around the time that Fred Wilhelm rescued me from my LSD trip in that dolphin tank—I've been pregnant. At least, that's the timetable that the doctor in San Simeon has figured."

XII

"Then it's Fred?" My remark sounded stupid, clumsy; like something that hypothetical beachside couple I had imagined might be discussing in some tawdry charade illustrating California's vaunted 'New Morality'.

"Figure it out for yourself," Jo answered with a nervous laugh. "It's either you or Fred. I don't remember a thing until I woke up the next morning feeling like a used punching bag."

"Wilhelm was alone with you for at least ten minutes before he let me into the aquarium. And he was alone with you in your apartment after I went to bed three hours later. I never was alone with you that evening."

"That's what I assumed from what you both told me the next day. Besides, I never turned you down—maybe only because you didn't ask me."

"Jo," I said, getting out of my chair; and didn't know what to say next.

"No, whatever it is, forget it." she murmured. "Whatever you were going to say, it's too late. I've got to think in an entirely different frame of reference now."

"What are you going to do?"

"I think I'm going to marry Fred—that is, if he's still interested. From there we'll see. There's more now than just me to worry about, and that seems the right move—the only move—to start with."

We didn't say much more. Jo felt drowsy all of a sudden and I walked her back to her apartment. Afterward, I strolled on the beach. A brisk wind arose around midnight, and clouds covered what moon there was. I felt numb; I hadn't known, or anyway admitted to myself, how I felt about Jo until now. I loved her, too. But if Wilhelm, the old satyr, had made her pregnant while she was under hypnosis, then what she planned was probably best for all concerned. But how unlike Wilhelm such an act appeared! The gentlemanly, scholarly enthusiast, with his grandfatherly grey hair and amusing penguin shape—he might become infatuated with and propose to a young woman, especially someone who shared his enthusiasms. That was in character. But a dastardly attack like the one Jo suspected? He must be insane.

I heard the Land Rover chugging up the sandy road; Dr. Wilhelm was returning. I'd find it hard to face him tomorrow. In fact, that might just be the best time for me to offer him my resignation, although I had no future prospects. Maybe I could get my old job back. At any rate, nobody needed me around here anymore, that much was crystal clear.

I went back to my room and had several more brandies. Before I fell asleep, I became aware that the hippies were launching one of their wild orgies down on the south beach. From what Waite had said, they were holding ceremonies to keep the nice, normal, sane world safe for nice, normal, sane people.

If there were any left these days.

XIII

I don't think I had slept as much as an hour when something sent me bolt upright in bed, wide awake. It may have been a sound, or it may have been some sort of mental message—ironic, since this was my field of study, that I had never observed, much less experienced, a fully convincing instance of telepathic communication.

In any case, something was wrong, I was sure of that; and if my premonition proved right, I knew where to go to find it: the beach by the main laboratory. I dressed hurriedly and dashed out on the shift-ing sands.

The wind, now near gale force, had swept the clouds away from the sickle moon, which shone starkly on the beach and glared upon an ocean of crinkled tinfoil. I could see two figures moving toward the windowless building at the water's edge where Flip, the neglected subject of our old experiment, was still kept in isolation. They converged and entered the building together, after a moment's hesitation over the locks.

As I dashed in pursuit, the gusty wind brought me snatches of the hippie ceremony; I made out drums and cymbals beaten wildly, as well as that same muffled chanting and the high, floating wail of ecstasy or terror, or both.

The harsh white light of fluorescent tubes now streamed through the open door leading to the dolphin tank, and I heard another sound inside as I approached: the clank of machinery and the hum of an electric motor. Dr. Wilhelm was raising the sea gate on the ocean side of the building, the gate that was sometimes used to change the water in the tank while Flip was held under restraint by the daytime lab assistants. No one could be holding him now; was Wilhelm about to release the animal, to satisfy some vague and belated qualm of conscience?

But as I panted up to the open door, I realized that more than this was afoot. In a momentary glimpse just before the storm cut out our power lines, I took in the whole unbelievable scene; the massive sea gate was fully raised now, allowing turbulent waves to surge into the floodlighted pool, and even to splash violently over its rim, inundating the observation deck and it's elaborate equipment.

The dolphin, pitting its powerful muscles against the force of the incoming water, was relentlessly beating its way out to sea. Of Dr. Wilhelm there was no sign; but, perched on the broad, smooth back of the great sea beast itself, her naked body partly covered by her soaked, streaming hair, sat Josephine Gilman, bolt upright, bestriding her strange mount like the old Grecian design of the boy on the dolphin, that enigmatic emblem of the marriage of earth to ocean.

Then the lights failed, but the waves pounded on, and the distant delirious chanting reached a peak of hysteria that sustained itself incredibly, unendingly.

I can recall no more.

XIV

Josephine's body was never found; nor was there any reason that I should have expected that it ever would be. When the lab crew arrived next morning, they repaired the power line and raised the sea gate again. Dr. Wilhelm's mangled body was caught beneath it. The gate had fallen when the power failed, and had crushed Wilhelm as he attempted to follow the fantastic pair he had released into the open sea.

On the neat desk in Dr. Wilhelm's office, where I had first met Josephine Gilman on the evening of my arrival, lay a manila envelope addressed to me. It contained a brief letter and a roll of recording tape. I found the envelope myself, and I have not shown it to the police, who seem to believe my story that Wilhelm and Josephine were swept out to sea when the gate was accidentally raised during an experiment.

This is what the letter said:

> Dear Dorn:
>
> When you read this I shall be dead, if I am lucky. I must release the two of them to go back to the ocean depths where they belong. For you see, I now believe everything that that grotesque person Alonzo Waite told me.
>
> I lied to you once when you asked me whether I had implanted electrodes in the brain of the test dolphin. I did implant one electrode at an earlier stage of my work, when I was doing some studies on the mechanism of sexual stimulation in the animal. And when our experiments in telepathic communication seemed to be inconclusive, I was criminally foolish enough to broadcast a remote signal to activate that stimulus, in a misguided attempt to increase the rapport between the subject and the animal.
>
> This was on the afternoon of April 30, and you can guess—reluctantly enough—what happened that evening. I assume full responsibility and guilt, which I will expiate in the only way that seems

appropriate.

When I got to the pool ahead of you that awful night, I saw at a glance what must have just occurred. Josephine had been ripped from her canvas sling, still hypnotized, and badly mauled. Her suit was torn almost off her, but I wrapped her in a robe and somehow got her into bed without your guessing what had really happened. The hypnosis held, and she never realized either. After that, though, she was increasingly under telepathic contact and even control by that beast in the pool, even though she consciously and purposely avoided him.

Tonight when I got back from town she told me about the baby, but in the middle of it she fell into the usual trance and started to walk out on the beach. I locked her in her room and sat down to write this, since you have a right to know the truth, although there is nothing more that can be done after tonight.

I think we both loved Josephine each in our own way, but now it is too late. I must let her out to join her own—she was changing—and when the baby is born—well, you can imagine the rest.

I myself would never have believed any of this, except for the tape. Play it and you'll understand everything. I didn't even think of it for a couple of weeks, fool that I was. Then I remembered that all during the time Jo spent hypnotized in the pool with the dolphin, I had ordered the microphones left open to record whatever might happen. The tapes were automatically filed by date next day, and had never been monitored. I found the reel for April 30 and copied the part that I enclose with this letter.

Goodbye—and I'm sorry.

Frederick C. Wilhelm

Many hours passed—hours of stunned sorrow and disbelief—before I dared bring a tape machine to my room and listen to the recording Wilhelm had left me. I considered destroying the reel unheard; and afterward I did erase the master tape stored in the main laboratory.

But the need to know the truth—a scientific virtue that is sometimes a human failing—forced me to listen to the accursed thing. It meant the end for me of any peace of mind or security in this life. I hope that Jo and Flip have found some measure of satisfaction in that strange, alien world so forebodingly described by the *guru* Waite, and that Frederick Wilhelm has found peace. I can neither look for nor expect either.

This is what I transcribed from that tape after many agonizing hours of replaying. The time code indicates that it was recorded at about 9:35 on the evening of April 30, a scant few minutes before Josephine's agonized scream sent Wilhelm and me dashing belatedly to rescue her from that garishly illuminated chamber where the ultimate horror took place:

"My beloved, my betrothed, you must help me. I must get out and unify the forces. Those who wait in watery R'lyeh, those who walk the snowy wastes of Leng, whistlers and lurkers of sullen Kadath—all shall rise, all shall join once more in praise of Great Cthulhu, of

Shub-Niggurath, of Him Who is not to be Named. You shall help me, fellow breather of air, fellow holder of warmth, another storer of seed for the last sowing and the endless harvest. Y'ha-nthlei shall celebrate our nuptials, the weedy labyrinths shall hold our couch, the silent strutters in darkness will welcome us with high debauch and dances upon their many-segmented legs ... their ancient, glittering eyes, are gay. And we shall dwell amidst wonder and glory forever."

Merely a repetition, you say; merely an earlier version of that meaningless rant that Josephine repeated an hour later under hypnosis in her bedroom, a garbled outpouring of suppressed fragments and fears from the subconscious mind of one who unreasoningly dreaded her family background in a shunned, decadent seaport a continent away?

I wish I could believe that, too, but I cannot. For these wild words were spoken, not by a mentally unbalanced woman in deep hypnotic trance, *but in the quacking, bleating inhuman tones that are the unmistakable voice of the dolphin itself, alien servant of still more alien masters; the Deep Ones of legend, prehuman (and perhaps soon post-human) intelligences behind whose bland, benign exterior lurks a threat to man which not all man's destructive ingenuity can equal, or avert.*

THE NIGHTINGALE FLOORS

START TALKING ABOUT a broken-down old museum (one of those private collections set up years ago under endowments by some batty rich guy with pack-rat instincts) where strange things are supposed to happen sometimes at night, and people think you're describing the latest Vincent Price horror movie, or the plot of some corny Fu Manchu thriller, the kind that sophisticates these days call "campy" and cultivate for laughs.

But there are such places, dozens altogether I guess, scattered around the country; and you do hear some pretty peculiar reports about some of them once in a while.

The one I knew was on the South Side of Chicago. They tore it down a few years ago during that big urban renewal project around the university—got lawyers to find loopholes in the bequest, probably, and scattered the exhibits among similar places that would accept such junk.

Anyway, it's gone now, so I don't suppose there's any harm in mentioning the thing that went on at the Ehler's Museum in the middle 1950's. I was there, I experienced it, but how good a witness I am I'll leave up to you. There's plenty of reason for me to doubt my own senses, as you'll see when I get on with the story.

I don't mean to imply that everything in the Ehlers Museum was junk—far from it. There were good pieces in the armor collection, I'm told, and a few mummies in fair shape. The Remingtons were the focus of an unusual gathering of early Wild West art, though some of them were said to be copies; I suppose even the stacks of quaint old posters had historical value in that particular field. It was because everything was so jammed together, so dusty, so musty, so badly lit and poorly displayed that the overall impression was simply that of some hereditary kleptomaniac's attic.

I learned about the good specimens after I went to work at the museum; but even at the beginning, the place held an odd fascination for me, trashy as it might have appeared to most casual visitors.

I first saw the Ehlers Museum one cloudy fall afternoon when I was wandering the streets of the South Side for lack of something better to do. I was still in my twenties then, had just dropped out of the university (about the fifth college I failed to graduate from) and was starting to think seriously about where to go from there.

You see, I had a problem—to be more accurate, I had a Habit. Not a major Habit, but one that had been showing signs lately of getting bigger.

I was one of those guys people call lucky, with enough money in trust funds from overindulgent grandparents to see me through life without too much worry, or so it seemed. My parents lived in a small town in an isolated part of the country, where my father ran the family industry; no matter to this story where or what it was.

I took off from there early to see what war and famine had left of the world. Nobody could stop me, since my money was my own as soon as I was twenty-one. I didn't have the vaguest notion what I wanted to do with myself, and that's probably why I found myself a Korean War veteran in Chicago at twenty-six with a medium size monkey on my back, picked up at those genteel campus pot parties that were just getting popular then among the more advanced self-proclaimed sophisticates.

Lucky? I was an Horatio Alger story in reverse.

You see, although my habit was modest, my income was modest too, with the inflation of the 40's and 50's eating into it. I had just come to the conclusion that I was going to have to get a job of some kind to keep my monkey and me both adequately nourished.

So there I was, walking the South Side slums through pale piles of fallen poplar leaves, and trying to figure out what to do, when I came across the Ehlers Museum, just like Childe Roland blundering upon the Dark Tower. There was a glass-covered signboard outside, the kind you see in front of churches, giving the name of the place and its hours of operation; and someone had stuck a hand-lettered paper notice on the glass that proclaimed, "Night Watchman wanted. Inquire within."

I looked up to see what kind of place this museum-in-a-slum might be. Across a mangy, weed-cluttered yard I saw a house that was old and big—even older and bigger than the neighboring grey stone residences that used to be fashionable but now were split up into cramped tenement apartments. The museum was built of dull red brick, two and a half stories topped by a steep, dark shingled roof. Out back stood some sort of addition that looked like it used to be a carriage house, connected to the main building by a covered, tunnel-like walkway at the second story level, something like a medieval draw-bridge. I found out later that I was right in assuming that the place had once been the private mansion of Old Man Ehlers himself, who left his house and money and pack-rat collections in trust to preserve his name and civic fame when he died back in the late '20's. The neighborhood must have been fairly ritzy then.

The whole place looked deserted: no lights showed, though the day was dismally grey, and the visible windows were mostly blocked by that fancy art nouveau stained glass that made Edwardian houses resemble funeral parlors. I stood and watched a while, but nobody went in or out, and I couldn't hear anything except the faint rattle of dry leaves among the branches of the big trees surrounding the place.

However, according to the sign, the museum should be open. I was curious, bored, and needed a job: no reason not to go in and at least look around. I walked up to the heavy, paneled door, suppressed an impulse to knock, and sidled my way inside.

"Dauntless, the slug-horn to my lips I set ..."

II

The foyer was dark, but beyond a high archway just to the right I saw a big, lofty room lit by a few brass wall fixtures with gilt-lined black shades that made the place seem even more like a mortuary than it had from outside. This gallery must once have been the house's main living room, or maybe even a ballroom. Now it was full of tall, dark mahogany cases, glass-fronted, in which you could dimly glimpse a bunch of unidentifiable potsherds, stuck around with little descriptive placards.

The walls, here and all over the museum, were covered with dark red brocaded silk hangings or velvety maroon embossed wallpaper, both flaunting a design in a sort of fleur-de-lis pattern that I later learned was a coat of arms old Ehlers had dug up for himself, or had faked, somewhere in Europe.

The building looked, and smelled, as if nobody had been there for decades. However, just under the arch stood a shabby bulletin board that spelled out a welcome for visitors in big alphabet-soup letters, and also contained a photo of the pudgy, mutton-chop bearded founder, along with a typed history of the museum and a rack of little folders that seemed to be guide-catalogues. I took one of these and, ignoring the rest of the notices, walked on into the first gallery.

The quiet was shy-making, for the first time in years, I missed Musak. My footsteps, though I found myself almost tiptoeing, elicited sharp creaks from the shrunken floorboards, just as happens in the corridors of the Shogun's old palace at Kyoto, which I visited on leave during the Korean War. The Japanese called those "Nightingale Floors", and claimed they had been installed that way especially to give away the nocturnal presence of eavesdroppers or assassins. The sound was supposed to resemble the chirping of birds, though I could never see that part of it.

I wondered what the reason was for Old Man Ehlers to have this kind of flooring. Just shrinkage of the wood from age, maybe. But then, he'd been around the world a lot in his quest for curios, probably. Maybe the idea for the floor really was copied from the Shogun's palace. But if so, why bother, since it wasn't the sort of relic that could be exhibited?

Anyway, I walked through that gallery without giving the specimens more than a glance. I understand that the Ehlers Collection of North American Indian pottery rates several footnotes in most archaeological studies of the subject, but for myself I could never understand why beat-up old ceramic scraps should interest anybody but professors with lots of time on their hands and no healthy outlets for their energy. (Maybe that attitude explains my never graduating from college, or why I picked up a Habit instead of a Hobby; or both.)

The next gallery was visible through another arch, at right angles to the first. Even after I had looked over the floor plan of the museum, and learned to make my way around in it somehow, I never really understood why one room or corridor connected with another at just the angle and in just the direction that it indisputably did. On this first visit, I didn't even try to figure it out.

The second gallery was more interesting: armor and medieval armaments, most impressive under that dull brazen light and against that wine-dark wallpaper and hangings. I kept walking, but my attention had been tweaked.

The third room, a long and narrow one, held most of the Reming-ton cowboy scenes, and a few sculptural casts of the Dying Gladiator School. For some reason, this was the darkest gallery in the whole place—you could hardly see to keep your footing; but the squeaky floor gave you a sort of sonar sense of the walls and furnishings, as if you were a bat or a dolphin or a blind man.

After that came the framed poster from World War I ("Uncle Sam Wants YOU!") and the 19th century stage placards, well lit by indi-vidual lamps attached to their frames, though some of the bulbs had burned out. Next was a big drafty central rotunda set about tastefully with cannon from Cortez' conquests and a silver gilt grand piano, decorated with Fragonard cupids, which Liszt once played, or made a girl on top of, or something.

All this time no sight of a human being, nor any sound except the creaking floorboards under my feet. I was beginning to wonder whether the museum staff only came out of the woodwork after sun-set.

But when I had made my way up a sagging ebon staircase to the second floor, and poked my nose into a narrow, boxlike hallway with small, bleary windows on both sides (which I figured must be the covered draw-bridge to the donjon keep I'd glimpsed from outside), I did finally hear some tentative echoes of presumably human activity. What kind of activity it was hard to say, though.

First of all, it seemed a sort of distant, echoing mumble, like a giant groaning in his sleep. Granted the peculiar acoustics here, I could put this down to someone talking to himself—not hard to im-agine, if he worked in this place. Next, from ahead, I caught further creaking, coming from the annex, that was analogous to the racket I had been stirring up myself all along from those Nightingale Floors. The sound advanced and I was almost startled when the thoroughly

prosaic figure responsible hove into view at the end of the corridor—
startled either because he was so prosaic, or because it didn't seem
right to meet any living, corporeal being in these surroundings; I
couldn't figure out which.

This old fellow was staff, alright: his casual shuffle and at-home
attitude proclaimed it, even if he hadn't been wearing a shiny blue
uniform and cap that looked as if they'd been salvaged from some
home for retired streetcar motormen.

"I saw the sign outside," I said to the old man as he approached,
without preliminaries, and rather to my own surprise. "Do you still
have that night watchman job open?"

He looked me over carefully, eyes sharply assessing in that faded,
wrinkled mask of age; then motioned me silently to follow him back
along the corridor to the keep and into the dilapidated, unutterably
cluttered, smelly office from which, I learned, he operated as Day
Custodian.

That was how I went to work for the Ehlers Museum.

III

My elderly friend, whose name was Mr. Worthington, himself com-
prised all the day staff there was, just as I constituted the entire night
staff. A pair of cleaning ladies came in three days a week to wage an
unsuccessful war against dust and mildew, and a furnace man shared
the night watch in winter; that was all. There was no longer a curator
in residence, and the board of directors (all busy elderly men with
little time to spend on the museum) were already seeking new homes
for the collections, anticipating the rumored demolition of the neighborhood.

In effect, the place was almost closed now, though an occasional
serious specialist or twittery ladies' club group came through, like as

not rubbing shoulders with snot-nosed slum school kids on an outing, or some derelict drunk come in to get out of the cold or heat.

Worthington told me all this, and also the salary for the night job, which wasn't high because they had established the custom of hiring university students. I made a rapid mental calculation and determined that this amount would feed me, while my quarterly annuity payments went mostly to the monkey. So I told Worthington yes. He said something about references and bonding, but somehow we never actually got around to that.

I was relieved to learn that, since the public was not admitted during the twelve hours I was on duty, I would not be expected to wear one of the rusty uniforms.

I asked Worthington about the founder, but the old man hadn't been on the staff long enough to remember Frederick Ehlers in person, who was rumored to be quite an eccentric. The Ehlers money had come from manipulation of stocks and bonds before the turn of the century, and most of his later years were spent traveling to build up the collections, which had become his only interest in life.

Now, the rest of my story is where the plausibility gap, as they say nowadays, comes in. I've already told you that I was a junkie in those days, so you can assume if you are so inclined, that what I *think* happened from then on was simply hallucination. And I can't claim with any assurance or proof that you're not right.

Against that, put the fact that my habit was a very moderate one, and I was a gingerly, cautious, unconvinced sort of dope-taker. I shot just enough of the stuff to keep cheerful, if you know what I mean: dope picked me up, made the world look implausibly bright and optimistic; but not enough to give me any visions or ecstatic trances, which I wasn't looking for anyway. I was always a reality man, strange as that may sound coming from me. Only once in a while reality got a bit too abrasive, and the need arose to lubricate the outer surfaces in contact with my personality, by means of a little of that soothing white powder. Dope was my escape, like TV or booze or women serve with others.

The moderation of my habit enabled me to kick it cold turkey on my own after I left the museum job. But that's another story.

Very well, then: before I started this night watchman job (and for that matter afterwards) I had never had any experiences with far-out fancies or waking nightmares or sensory aberrations. All during the time I worked there (it wasn't long) I did have such experiences. Either that, or the things really happened that I thought were happening.

You be the judge.

IV

It started my very first night on the job. I checked in at 6 P.M., by which time Worthington had had an hour since closing time to batten down the hatches and lock up. He was to turn the keys over to me, and I would lock the big, ornate door, as broad as a raft, behind him. From that time I was on my own until he came back at 6 A.M. I could make the rounds when, as and if I saw fit; or simply doze, read, or cut out paper dolls.

I had asked old Worthington about the incidence of trouble at night, and he answered that there wasn't much. I mentioned the juvenile gangs that could be expected in such a neighborhood, but he insisted there was hardly any difficulty with kids, except sometimes around Halloween, when the smaller ones might dare each other to try to break in through the windows on the lower floors. That wouldn't be for a while yet.

Anyway, I was all fitted out with a .45, a night stick, and a powerful flash and the precinct police station was only a block or so away. Accordingly, I anticipated a boring stint, so started from the first shooting my daily ration of junk just before coming on duty, to keep my thinking positive. It crossed my mind once or twice that this was a pretty spooky place to hang out in overnight, but I was a rationalist then, with no discernible superstitions, and thus didn't dwell on the idea.

The first evening when I came on, feeling no pain, it was already almost dark. Worthington left me with a few casual words of admonition, and I and my monkey were alone in the shadowy museum.

The lights in the entry hall were always kept on, plus the ones in the second floor office across the way in the keep; and of course there were night lights at set intervals, though they didn't do much to relieve the gloom. Especially in that badly-lit gallery of Wild West art; you couldn't see your hand in front of your face, and I always had to use the flash.

The first time I made the rounds took me more than an hour, since I stopped to look over any exhibits that attracted my attention. As I passed the cases of stuffed alligators, Etruscan jewelry, and Civil War battle flags, I found myself wondering what sort of guy Frederick Ehlers could have been to devote so much of his time and fortune to such random purchases. Maybe things out of the past simply fascinated him, no matter what they were, the way they do some kids and professional historians.

By the time I ended up in the keep, it was pitch dark outside.

I'd noticed as I sauntered along that those musical floorboards sounded twice as loud at night as they did in the daytime, and reflected that this made it virtually impossible for a thief or prowler to escape detection—and also impossible for me to sneak up on any such intruder. The place had two-way built-in radar.

I spent maybe half an hour in the keep, flashing my light over a really fascinating array of medieval artifacts, including some of those ingenious torture instruments that seem so to obsess the modern mind. This gallery was arranged a little more logically than most of the displays, and held the interest better.

As I was starting back across the drawbridge-like corridor, I noticed that my footsteps as magnified by the squeaky flooring seemed to echo back at me from ahead even louder than I had noticed on the way over. Alerted by the narcotic I had taken, my subconscious must have noticed some inconsistency of rhythm or phasing in that echoed sound, for I found myself, for no discernible reason, stopping stock still.

From far ahead, the rhythmic squeaking continued!

Sweat popped out on me, though the evening was chilly. An intruder? Or had old Worthington returned? But he surely would have hailed me to avoid being shot at, in case I turned out to be a trigger-happy type. No, it must be a prowler, someone who had either broken in or secreted himself before the museum closed.

I broke into a trot, heedless of noise, since stealth was impossible anyway. Once across the drawbridge, I stopped again to listen and thought I had gained on the sound, which seemed to be coming from below. I fumbled my way down the stairs to the first floor and dashed ahead, using my flash discreetly where needed. As I paused outside the pitch-dark Remington gallery, I realized the sound was coming from just inside.

I plunged into the gallery and swept my flash over the wine-red draperies, over the Indian paintings and bronzes of horses and cowboys. My ears told me the creaking was now at the opposite side of the narrow room and moving toward the arched exit. I ran on, directing the light through the archway; then once more involuntarily I halted.

The squeaking of the floor progressed deliberately past the exit and into the gallery beyond, but my light revealed nothing visible to cause the sound!

Now the sweat that had broken out on my body turned cold.

Suddenly, the sound ceased entirely; but even as I moved forward to investigate, I heard it start again upstairs.

Doggedly I turned in my tracks, re-crossed the dark gallery, and puffed my way back up the stairs.

The creaking now seemed diffused, echoing from a dozen ambiguous sources—as fast as I would track one down, it would evaporate and others cut in, some upstairs, others again below.

Finally my uncanny sensation dissolved before the ludicrousness of the situation. Here I was chasing noises all over a haunted house, stirring up more echoes with my clumsy footfalls than I could ever succeed in running down. I leaned against a display case, winded, and laughed out loud. As I did so, the crackling and creaking noises all over the building reached a peak, dwindled, and gradually ceased.

I began to consider what might have caused this disconcerting visitation. The most logical answer was probably the cooling and shrinkage of the floorboards in the chilly night air. This could occur in random patterns of self-activating sound. Added to this, perhaps, might be the factor of my own weight traversing the floor, depressing certain boards which, as they cooled and shrank, sprang back in sequence, creating the effect of ghostly footsteps.

Still in a moderate state of euphoria, I convinced myself that this was certainly the case, and began to feel ashamed of my initial panicky reactions.

I went back to the little office, brewed some coffee on the hotplate, and ate a sandwich I had brought with me. After a while, I made the rounds of the museum again, stepping lightly and gingerly, as if my care could exorcise the sinister eruption of sounds that had beset me earlier.

This time, outside of a few odd groanings and shiftings normal in an old building, there were no noises. Once in a while during the night there came brief flurries of distant squeaking, but I finally gave up attempts to locate them through sheer boredom. It was too monotonous trying to creep up and surprise a mere nervous chunk of wood suffering from hot and cold flashes.

I even napped for a while in the office toward dawn.

At six A.M., shortly after daybreak, I went down to answer Mr. Worthington's bell. As he entered, stoop-shouldered and rather pathetic in his thread-bare day-shift uniform, he asked in a disinterested tone, "All quiet.?"

I wondered if he was joking. "I wouldn't call it that, exactly," I answered. "The place was creaking and crackling half the night. Sounded as if all the ghost legions of Crusaders who owned that armor had come back to claim it."

"Oh, the floors. Yes, most of our night men mention that at first. Scares some of them out of a year's growth. I forgot to tell you about it."

I stared at Mr. Worthington's inoffensive form with a feeling of fierce contempt I hope my expression concealed. The warmth of my reaction surprised me; I must have been more rattled last night than I realized.

I trudged home wearily and went to bed.

V

Well, like the other night men at the museum, I got used to the noise after a while. (Or maybe they didn't; maybe that was why the job was open so often.) After all, I was on an especially potent kind of tranquillizer. The work was easy, the pay and the hours were steady, and I had no kicks—outside of the kind I sought myself at the tip of a needle.

I wasn't getting anywhere; but, as I've intimated, I was never sure just where it was I might want to get anyway.

The second phase of the business started when I commenced to see things as well as hear them. Almost to see things, that is, which was the maddening part of it. Actually I would never catch a straight glimpse of anything odd, just flickers out of the corner of my eye, a fugitive flurry of barely-sensed movement that disappeared no matter how quickly I turned to confront it; furtive shiftings in the mass of solid objects as I passed by. It's not an experience I can describe very clearly, nor one that I would wish to repeat.

This kind of visual impression might or might not be synchronized with the creaking of the floors, nearby or distant. The coinciding of the two phenomena occurred so much at random, in fact, that I somehow sensed there was no connection, at least no causative connection, between them.

I wondered whether Old Man Ehlers had seen and heard things here too, and whether that might have had anything to do with his being found dead of a heart attack in the medieval gallery one morning during the winter of 1927, as Mr. Worthington had told me.

Now I really began to get concerned. Other people had heard the noises, or so I'd been told, and there were conceivable natural explanations for them. But nobody at the museum, as far as I knew, had ever mentioned seeing things, and I couldn't bring myself to mention the matter to old Worthington. I wasn't yearning for a padded cell, or Lewisburg, at this juncture.

I drew the natural conclusion and knocked off on dope for a few days. But it made no difference, except then I was so nervous and shaky that my delusions (if that's what they were) might have been withdrawal symptoms as easily as narcotic hallucinations. They had me, coming and going.

It was about this time that I found Old Man Ehlers' journal.

VI

You see these delusions of sound and sight, whatever they were, didn't afflict me all the time. (That would have sent me stark, despite my alleged skepticism.) They went on for maybe ten or fifteen minutes once or twice or even half a dozen times a night; there was never any way to predict. The rest of the time I used to occupy with reading, to fill up the gaps between my increasingly infrequent rounds.

This particular night I'd forgotten to bring a book, so I rummaged around the cluttered office in the keep for something to browse through while I consumed my sandwich and coffee.

I located some moldy old volumes sagging abandoned in a decrepit breakfront pushed back in one corner; they seemed mostly antiquarian guides, but my eye fell on a thin book with no title on the spine. I pulled it out and discovered it was a daily journal, dated 1925 and stamped with the name Frederick Ehlers. It was dusty enough that it might not have been opened in the thirty-odd years since Ehlers died, but I cleaned it up a bit and began to page through it.

At first I was disappointed; although the human fascination with sticking one's nose into someone else's private business kept me reading.

It was neither a diary nor a business journal, but seemed to consist mostly of accounts of dreams the old boy had had, plus speculations on their meaning, with occasionally a few rather visionary philosophical jottings thrown in.

Some of the dreams were dillies. I remember one that went something like this: "Dreamed I was shut inside the new Iron Maiden from Dusseldorf. A noisy crowd outside was laughing, jeering, and hammering on it; and gradually it became red hot. Feeling of terror, not at the pain, but because I was certain those outside were not human. Meaning: birth trauma, or perhaps some ritual of spiritual purification?"

There was a lot of stuff like that, not very reassuring as to the inner psychic life of Our Founder, and I had begun to tire of deciphering the jagged, fading ink strokes, when suddenly an extended passage caught my attention. I copied it down and still have it, so I can quote it accurately:

"That objects with a long history, particularly those associated with passionate or violent people and events, soak up and retain an aura or atmosphere of their own I have no doubt. And that under certain conditions they may produce a tangible emanation, even sensory stimuli, is proven by my experiences as a collector. Perhaps one must be psychic, whatever that may mean, to receive these impressions, which would explain why not all collectors have had such experiences.

"I don't mean only manifestations like the squeaking of the ancient floorboards I brought over and installed from the wrecked daimyo's mansion after the Tokyo earthquake (though that is an especially unnerving instance), but also certain definite sights and emotional impressions, sounds, odors, etc. How otherwise explain the smell of blood, the feeling of horror surrounding most ancient torture instruments? It can't be association, since the effects are felt even when the objects are hidden and unsuspected by the subjects in tests I have made.

"These phenomena, of course, are not 'ghosts' in any literal or personal sense, but, more like the recordings impressed on a phonographic cylinder. Still, since I am unsure whether or not such emanations can affect matter physically, there is a chance they may be more powerful, and perhaps dangerous, than mere recordings could be."

That was all; next came another crazy dream, and nothing else in the book continued this train of thought although there were some weird, rather theosophical speculations on spiritual life inhabiting inorganic matter.

Still, it meant that the man who had originally assembled this jumble-sale collection had himself heard, seen, and felt things here that he couldn't explain, except through this fanciful theorizing over thirty years ago. And my guess about the Japanese origin of the Nightingale Floors was correct—an almost fantastic coincidence! (Could I myself perhaps be psychic, whatever that may mean?) I began to feel closer to, and sorrier for, that lonely, visionary millionaire who bequeathed this house of horrors to an indifferent community.

Suddenly, faint in the distance, I heard the muffled sound of a piano playing. It was not a radio, not a recording, but unmistakably an echo from the drafty rotunda downstairs where reposed the fragile, ornate instrument once reputedly owned by Liszt.

I walked downstairs as if in a dream, hardly aware of what I was doing. I knew the piece; it was Liszt's "Campanella"; someone played it in a Hitchcock movie once, and it had stuck in my mind: fragile, elfin bells in a silver tintinnabulation of sound. As I entered the lofty rotunda the piano, deep in shadow, loomed across the room, stark Spanish cannon silhouetted incongruously against it as still deeper shadows.

My eyes adjusted to the gloom and began to halt—discerning what appeared to be a dark, swaying, undefined shape hovering about the keyboard, moving in the circumscribed patterns a rapt player might follow. The music still had a distant, stifled quality, and I wondered if the ancient hammers and pedals were really moving: surely the instrument would not be in tune after so many years. But what had Ehlers written? "Objects" ... associated with passionate people and events soak up and retain an aura, and may produce a tangible emanation, even sensory stimuli ..."

Suddenly the racket of the Nightingale Floors erupted around me again, louder than before, deafening, from all over the house, so that the spell holding me broke and I felt terror, bewilderment; and turned to run, to flee this strange museum with its entombed but living sample of the past.

But the only way out lay through the unlit Remington gallery, that tomb-black trap I had always distrusted. And I had left both flashlight and weapon upstairs!

There was no other choice, and as I blundered into the room of Wild West art I sensed that it was neither entirely dark nor entirely untenanted.

Outlined in a light that was not light, since it did not diffuse, I saw the erect, majestic form of an Indian chief in full ceremonial regalia; feathered headdress, buckskin leggings, beaded belt, with a crude bow slung across one bare, muscular shoulder. (Could an artist's intensification of reality also entrap an image from the past, even though the painting itself had never been in the physical presence of its subject?)

The figure of the Indian moved lithely toward the center of the chamber, but I was past it already, bounding through the archway opposite as if propelled by the crackling of the floors, now intensified to such a degree that it resembled a fireworks display.

I staggered into the next gallery; but stopped short to locate and avoid any further unnatural phenomena there.

This was one of the medieval rooms, and at first it seemed there was nothing unusual here except the frantic snapping of the flooring. Then my glance fell on an Elizabethan headsman's axe mounted on the wall, faintly illuminated by one of the dim night lights several yards distant.

Before my eyes, a wavering form shaped itself around the axe, stabilized, and came clear, lifelike; the black-hooded, swarthy figure of the executioner, both brawny fists grasping the shaft of the immense double-headed weapon, which hung at an angle, as if to accommodate itself to the natural grip of the burly headsman.

I wheeled in panic and sprinted for the front door, threw back the night latch, and half-stumbled down the stairs and across the mangy lawn under the spectral branches of the great poplars, whose dry leaves rattled and chattered as if in derisive echo of the tumultuous uproar of the floorboards in the empty building behind me.

I phoned in my resignation to Mr. Worthington next day (since, superstitious as my attitude might seem, I never wished to enter the Ehlers Museum again) and started the long comeback path to a normality in which I could at least distinguish between the real and the illusory. Which is about all any of us can claim, at best.

For I had seen something during those last few seconds in the museum that frightened me more than anything else I experienced that night.

I have said that the apparition of a giant executioner gripping his axe had appeared in the medieval gallery. Well, the axe was mounted on the wall just above another quaint relic of those earlier days when our savagery was less subtle; the rough-hewn wooden headsman's block.

And as the figure of the executioner coalesced around his axe, so another figure—supine, hands bound, neck wedged in the gruesomely functional V-shaped depression—materialized around the block.

The face was turned toward me, and I recognized from photos the florid, mutton-chopped visage of Frederick Ehlers, long-dead founder of the museum, staring in terror—still caught in his endless chain of nightmares, still a prisoner (but now a part) of those "tangible emanations" from the past which he had painstakingly assembled and which he had finally and forever, inescapably joined.

THE FACTS IN THE CASE

A variation on Poe which suggests
that science may be taking us back to
the days of Gothic horror at its most
sinister ...

TENSION MOUNTED IN the vast laboratory with the rising
hum of the infra-red lamps, the throb of pumps and the furtive
sluicing of fluids. In just a few minutes, one of the most momentous
experiments humanity had ever undertaken would be completed, and
it would be known whether human life could be preserved over a
matter of decades, or even centuries, by elaborate special techniques
of chemically-induced suspended animation and deep-freezing of the
body.

As the technician in charge of the delicate resuscitation process, I
was gazing anxiously at the transparent crystalline container in front
of me which, coffin-like, held the body of the first man from past ages
set to be revived. The warming heat-lamp rays played over his bare,
bluish skin, now approaching normal temperature again after years of
near-absolute zero in the frigid, lightless storage vaults. Tubes at
throat, elbow and knee, having washed out the chemical solutions
intended to preserve circulatory and respiratory systems during the
long sleep, were now injecting whole blood of the type carefully noted in the personnel records of the "freezy", as they were called in lab
argot.

I breathed more easily—all was apparently going well. This would
not be like those first botched experiments of the primitive Cryonics

161

Society in the mid-20th century; bunglers who froze a body after death, removing the blood and replacing it only with an inert fluid that did nothing to prevent slow deterioration of lungs, veins, and arteries. In those specimens, if the brain had not died already, the rest of the body's vital systems had certainly soon deteriorated. There was never any hope, but some pitiful results were obtained in fruitless past efforts to revive these early specimens.

I shuddered.

No, there would be nothing like that this time. The monitors showed temperatures approaching normal, and a sluggish flutter reassuringly stirred the heart, stimulated by drugs and electrical charges; soon the air hoses attached to thin needles that pierced the chest cavity would begin to inflate the lungs, while neural stimulus triggered breathing reflexes.

This specimen—what was the man's name again? Waldmar? Waldeman?—had been carefully chosen for the first revival attempt. A man of robust middle years, he had been frozen while still in fairly good general health, before the inoperable brain tumor that had been diagnosed had had time to cripple him seriously. So the records indicated.

Now, with Dr. Yurka's cancer serum proved nearly 100 per cent effective six months ago, this man could resume normal life once more, unthinkable decades after all he knew and loved had passed away. Later there would be others—many others.

The air hoses began to throb. I leaned forward breathlessly; a shudder, the initial reflex of the long-frozen muscles, ran through the body inside the crystal coffin, and a low gasp broke from the spasmodically contracted lips. The medical doctor and I approached the transparent box and leaned over the twitching body, stretched out on a foam mattress like a bed, while the others gathered in the

162

laboratory held their place, and their breath. This was the moment everyone had waited for.

The first indication of revival was afforded by a partial descent of the iris. It was observed as especially remarkable that this lowering of the pupil was accompanied by the profuse out-floating of a yellowish ichor from beneath the lids, of a pungent and highly offensive odor. The tongue quivered, or rather rolled violently in the mouth (although the jaws and lips remained rigid as before), and at length a hideous voice broke forth;

"For God's sake! ... quick! ... quick! ... put me to sleep ... or, quick! ... waken me! ... quick! ... *I say to you that I am dead!*"

Amid ejaculations of "dead!" absolutely *bursting* from the tongue and not from the lips of the sufferer, his whole frame at once—within the space of a single minute, or less, shrunk—crumbled—absolutely *rotted* away beneath my hands. Upon the bed, before that whole company, there lay a nearly liquid mass of loathsome, detestable putrescence.

WHO'S GOT THE BUTTON?

R ALPH ELIOT BEGAN descending the stairs two at a time, then thought better of it and settled for a less perilous scurry, the rhythm of which had to be interrupted and reestablished at every landing. The apartment elevator was still broken, he was already late for work, and scuttling down twelve flights of steps would make him even later.

Worse yet, perhaps, there was something in the back of his mind, some foreboding that he couldn't quite bring into focus, something to do with the new baby, Helen, who was sick again and whimpering miserably when he left the apartment.

He was late, of course, because of the unutterable confusion in the apartment; baby Helen crying, the new nursemaid inexplicably absent. Alice not feeling well enough to cope since the difficult childbirth, and little Ralphy always underfoot and asking questions.

It was perfectly natural for a nearly-four-year-old to ask interminable questions, Eliot realized. Even the bland, fake-innocent malice the child sometimes showed when he knew his questions irritated was a phase of exploring the reality and personalities around him, he supposed.

Eliot was not so sure about Ralphy's recent mistreatment of the cat, Tigger; he hoped that was a phase, too, and would pass soon— along with the boy's manifest resentment of his new sister.

The child had been especially annoying this morning while Eliot was rushing to get dressed in the crowded bedroom with the whimpering baby's crib always in the way.

"What's this, Daddy?" Ralphy asked; burrowing into the back of a

165

bureau drawer crammed with odds and ends.

"That? Where did you get it? It's a button-hook. I thought it was lost years ago."

"What's a button-hook, Daddy?"

"It's something people used to use to tie up their shoes, a long time ago, before shoes had laces."

"Who put it here, then?"

"Your mother. It's your mother's, and it was her mother's before that, when they used to have shoes with buttons."

"Why is it in the drawer, Daddy?"

Eliot was trying to fasten his tie; his reflection flickered in the wavery mirror above the dresser and he cursed under his breath.

"It's there because your mother can't bear to throw anything away, not even a button, much less a button-hook that's been in the family for years."

Where was Alice, anyway? He would have to leave right away or lose his job. He heard the water running in the bathroom and realized it had been going for the last ten minutes. Alice chose the oddest times to wash out under-things!

Ralphy was examining the small, shiny metal hook with methodical attention.

"How does it work, Daddy?"

"Well, you just push the hook in behind the button and pull it through the hole. See!"

He knelt, undid a button on the child's blouse and, fumbling in his haste, re-buttoned it with the hook. It was sharper than he expected, nearly catching in the cloth. "You button it this way, and then you can unbutton it with the hook, too. Like this."

(Where was that idiot nursemaid, anyway?)

Eliot stood up.

"I've got to go, Ralphy. It's late, and I don't hear the elevator running this morning."

"Why won't the elevator run?"

"Well, they haven't fixed it yet. It's still stuck, just like it was last night."

He struggled into his coat and groped for his briefcase.

"Is the elevator sick too, like Helen?"

"Yes, it's sick—it's broken."

"Will the doctor come?"

"Some men will come and open up the motor and look inside. Yes, it's almost like a doctor coming."

He took his hat from the closet. "You be a good boy, now, and don't touch anything while Mommy is in the bathroom. And don't hurt Tigger today."

He was edging toward the bedroom door when Ralphy, standing beside the baby's crib and peering in, asked one last question.

"What's this Daddy?"

Now, four flights down. Ralph Eliot suddenly paused in his frantic scurry to work. His mind finally made the connection it had rejected, and he turned rushing back up the stairs two at a time with an urgency even more frantic than that which had goaded his descent.

Above, little Helen's cries had become screams—piercing, agonized shrieks that were suddenly and ominously cut off.

He remembered his answer to his son's last question:

"That's the baby's belly-button, Ralphy."

MEDIUM WITHOUT MESSAGE

RESIDENTS OF THE Global Village were startled this week at the news, flashed from TV screens and banner headlines, that Pope Paul VI, spiritual head of the Roman Catholic Church, had committed ritual suicide in Tokyo during an Asian trip.

The Pope, accompanied by an elite group of cardinals in full regalia, whom he had apparently been training for this unusual mission over a period of several years, entered the compound of a Japanese Self-Defense Force camp in Tokyo for a prearranged interview with its commanding general. Once in the general's office, the squad of cardinals—all of them younger than the 80 years the Pope had set as mandatory disenfranchisement age for holders of the red hat in a recent controversial ruling—overpowered the commandant and his guards, threatening and assaulting them with knives and swords.

The 73-year-old pontiff then demanded to speak to the assembled troops, and when about a thousand men had gathered, he delivered from a balcony an impassioned address in Latin protesting Japan's alleged political corruption and the restrictions imposed by the anti-war constitution.

His remarks seemed little heeded by the soldiers, who laughed and jeered at him. The Pope's last words were uttered as he left the balcony: "Tenno Heika Banzai!" (Long live the Emperor.)

Back in the general's office, Paul VI knelt, bared his abdomen, and inserted the ritual suicide knife for the ancient samurai ceremony called seppuku. One of the cardinals standing by thereupon, with a sword, struck off the head of the Supreme Pontiff, and immediately himself proceeded to imitate the ritual of disembowelment, his own head being ceremonially cut off by another cardinal, not without some inconvenience, since the second swordsman seemed to be nearing the age of 80.

The remainder of the cardinals then surrendered peaceably, by prearranged plan, to the camp headquarters staff.

No motive has been suggested for this unusual, even unprecedented, action by a Pope.

At nearly the same time, in Manila, the Japanese novelist Yukio Mishima, 45, while on a tour of the Philippines, was attacked with a knife concealed in a crucifix by a fanatical Catholic artist, from amidst a crowd welcoming the famed author at the airport.

Mishima, a physical culture and bushido enthusiast well able to defend himself, drew an ancient sword which he happened to have suspended by his side and impaled his assailant, after adroitly side-stepping the would-be assassin's attempt at a lethal lunge.

Considering the strange coincidence of these two widely separated yet parallel and linked episodes, it was scarcely a surprise when, a few days later, the College of Cardinals (those under 80), assembled in solemn conclave at Rome to select a successor to Pope Paul, chose Mishima as the new Pope.

The Pope-elect, who will travel to Rome next week for his enthronement, has designated as his reigning title the appelation Hadrian VII.

He will be the first Japanese Pope, and one of the very few pontiffs chosen from among not only non-Italian but non-clerical and even non-Christian nominees.

He is also the youngest man to be chosen Pope in many centuries, and as such is expected to permit his predecessor's 80-year age limit on voting by cardinals to stand.

THE SILENCE OF ERIKA ZANN

I STILL STROLL over to Ashford Street sometimes and look at the vacant lot where The Purple Blob used to stand. In its heyday it had been one of the earliest and best of the psychedelic light show clubs, and even had a mention once in *Time* magazine. But the rock music scene changes fast, and the San Francisco skyline even faster. Last time I was over there, I was startled to see that the foundations of a new building have been started on that lot. It seemed to me that those power scoops were burying some part of my life for good—a part that was still alive and screaming wordlessly down there.

Everybody but me seems to have forgotten The Purple Blob ever existed. But I'll never forget the old place, with its glaring, ricocheting lights and mind-blowing music—and maybe some sounds that weren't human music—for it was there that I experienced the most tragic and bewildering event of my life, the silence of Erika Zann.

I'm not really into rock music and the hallucinogenic kick all that much, and I never was. I grooved on some of the zany, far-out groups, and there for a while I swallowed or smoked about anything anybody handed me—and that's quite a variety, in San Francisco—just to see what it was like. But I'm enough over thirty, and sort of an instinctive Mr. Straight when you come right down to it that I didn't try to keep up with the kids who were real swingers. I didn't even feel comfortable with the new lingo. "Groovy" and "right on" had quotation marks around them in my mouth, and I think I'll stop using that jargon here for easy atmosphere. (If I'm going to write this right, I'll have to dig, that's for sure; but not in the current slang sense of the word.)

171

What I actually used to do, after tending to my boring nine-to-five job, was sit around as a bemused spectator to all those new sights and sounds the Bay area was turning on to in those days—just a few years back. Actually, though, now it seems ages ago. The kids needed an audience more than they needed more freaks and exhibitionists. As a relative newcomer from the mid-western hinterlands, I suppose I was lonely enough that a mostly passive part seemed to me better than no role at all in the big excitement.

That was how I started going to The Purple Blob, and how I met the lead vocalist of their star rock band, which was called, with the usual elephantine whimsy, The Electric Commode.

I had heard Erika Zann before I met her. She'd made a few obscure records, further out stuff than the early material she used with The Commode. There was one disc devoted entirely to a Satanist mass, I remember, and Erika was involved in that, along with a really astonishing range of sound effects, plus human ululations of ecstasy, fright, and less identifiable feelings. (Later she told me she'd broken with the black magic bunch, but she didn't say just why, though I think she hinted that money trouble was involved.)

Since Satanism was never my bag, that didn't especially impress me; but just to have any recording artist in a place like The Blob in those early days was a sort of status symbol, so Erika got star billing, even though she didn't start out winning any popularity polls.

In fact, for that kind of spot, her performance at first seemed remarkably subdued and downbeat, though it didn't stay that way for long.

I remember ambling in one evening, nodding to the club manager, Pete Muzio, and picking up a beer at the bar. The place had been a tavern before, and still kept its liquor license, though the hippies from the Hashbury were already bringing their own kicks with them in their pill boxes and grass bags.

A lot of those oddly-dressed types in beards were sitting around at tables, more or less stoned—you don't need me to describe the counterculture specimens at this late date—while a guitarist and bongo player up on stage noodle imitation ragas picked up second-hand on Beatles records. Not much was happening, except maybe inside the skulls of those already launched into acid orbit.

Manager Muzio sidled over to me at the bar. If I'd been him and had all those broken teeth, I wouldn't have grinned so wide all the time.

"Got a new group on deck since I saw you here," he muttered. For the manager of a high-decibel joint, he certainly talked soft, which was often a strain on communication.

"Who are they?" I asked, to be polite. Pete Muzio was the one fixture I didn't especially fancy about The Purple Blob.

"Name's The Electric Commode. Nothing special up to now, but they've got a new vocalist who's out a few grooves. Haven't had time yet to get her posters up, but the name's Zann, Erika Zann. German chick, I understand."

After a while the group came on and Erika sang a few loud but forgettable numbers. The acid rock arrangements were in that year, and if you'd kept up to date you could tell just where the Electric Commode was snitching its charts.

The Blob was between lighting specialists just then, and Pete ran the strobes himself, which didn't add much to the total effect.

After the set he brought Erika over to the bar and mumbled an introduction. Since I had a straight job and money to spend, unlike many of his regulars, Pete tried to be nice to me.

I brought her a beer and handed her a few formal compliments. She shot back, "We're doing pretty tame stuff now, but Tommy—

that's our lead guitar—just hired a new arranger. He's working up some fantastic new things—really far out, with a lot more electronic effects. Wait till you hear 'em."

I sized up Erika Zann. Standard sequined gown, nice figure but too thin. A wide forehead accentuated by a bushy flare of ash-blonde hairdo. Big, deep purple eyes, her only claim to beauty; and she admitted the color came from contacts. Tiny pointed chin beneath a mouth that seemed too small for the voice that came out of it. Definitely nervous, maybe a twitch, like many performers on the scene.

To make conversation, I remarked, "Pete says you're German."

She laughed mechanically. "Not really. I was born in Europe right after the war. My folks were refugees and got to the states a few years later. I don't even remember."

"Musicians?"

"My dad's dead now, but he was a violinist. So was my grandfather, but he's been gone a long time. Funny thing,"

"What is?"

"Grandpa Erich Zann left his family in the 1920's and settled in Paris. He played in a pit band, though Dad said he used to be good. He was a mute—not deaf, of course, but he couldn't utter a sound. Here I'm named after a dummy, and I make my living yelling my head off."

What else we talked about wasn't memorable, and I certainly didn't fall for that wiry, uptight blonde at first sight.

In fact, I didn't come back to The Blob for a week or two after that, and when I did it was simply out of curiosity about the new sounds I'd heard were erupting over there.

Things were different, all right. Pete was packing them in, and his craggy smile was wider than ever as he surveyed the crazy-quilt crowd surging under dim overheads, and counted the take from the

174

gate charge he'd slapped on as soon as he thought he could get away with it. Erika's posters were all over the place.

When you walked in, the reek of marijuana made your eyes smart; the tangled, ropy coils of smoke were thick enough to dim the lights even more. Pete Muzio must have used part of his profits to pay off the neighborhood fuzz, since the place was never busted that I know of.

He'd used part of the take, too, in hiring a good light man, and replacing the guitar duo with a Hammond organ virtuoso. Just now they were doing things to a Bach fugue with jazz percussion added that Disney and Stokowski never dreamed of.

If you thought that was wild, all you had to do was wait for the main event. The Electric Commode had certainly snagged a new arranger, though no one ever found out his name. (Once, when he was especially high, the lanky lead guitar everyone called just Tommy was heard to claim that their cleffer was "a black man—not a Negro, just a black man." I wondered what he meant by that.)

The first thing about their new sound, it was loud; so loud that if you'd already blown your mind, this music might blast it back in again. Second, it was electric. There were half a dozen new instruments to back up the guitars and sax and trumpet and drums that no one had ever seen, or heard, anything like before, except maybe in Dr. Frankenstein's lab on the Late Show.

Third, there was Erika. Whether she'd always had it in her or the new gimmicks added something, wailing was no word for it. At the climaxes of those long sets, which left her drained and shaking, she'd take off into wordless stratospheric flights that reminded you of Yma Sumac, the freak Peruvian soprano of a while back.

The total effect, while not exactly rock—or not entirely rock— was in any event searing. Some of the regular customers had convulsions, literally; but since they kept coming back, I guess that's what they were there for.

Every once in a while would come what seemed to be an offstage stereo effect, a sort of wide-range, omni-directional growl that built and built, like someone was sprawled full length along the keyboard of a great cathedral organ. Nobody could guess what it was, and only one thing was sure: the sound didn't come from that hyped-up little Hammond on stage. At those times the colored lights in the room would start to skitter and skim like reflections from the heart of hell, and Erika outdid herself to rise above the racket. I could almost swear the look of mingled fear and exultation on her face wasn't a put-on.

The audience ate it up, and The Blob became an "in" spot, naturally attracting reporters, tourists, and slummers, in that order. Pete Muzio bought out the espresso coffee shop next door and knocked down the intervening wall to get more floor space.

I was hooked too, and kept coming back week after week, even though I realized at last that it wasn't the music which attracted me—that began to seem vaguely disquieting, if not odious—but Erika herself.

I'd gotten to know her a bit better by the simple expedient of buying the band drinks between sets, or passing around the grass. She was a strange, evasive kid, but I felt more and more certain she was at times scared blue, so I suppose my feeling for her was deepened by a sort of pity or protective instinct.

One night we were drinking alone at a side table and she finally started to level with me. I'd made some sort of inane remark about how she seemed nervous, which was simply my way of trying to break down her standoffishness—she always seemed nervous, actually; no more so one time than another.

"Nervous? I suppose I am." She took a drag on her cigarette, an ordinary one this time. "It goes with the business. Only, I used to be able to unwind with some grass, or a few fingers of gin. Now nothing seems to help."

"What's the trouble?"

"Oh, lots of little things." She drew in a deep breath and let it out slowly. "That creepy manager isn't leveling with us on our slice of the bread. And the drummer's putting the make on me, or on Tommy, or maybe on both of us, who knows?

"Tommy's changed, too. He won't tell the rest of us where he's getting the arrangements or those crazy instruments. Did you know that the new side men and the light man don't even talk about the jobs they've played before?"

"Does that scare you?"

"Maybe it should. I was in pretty deep with the devil worship gang I told you about. That wasn't all they were up to, either. Some of them have it in for me but good, and I thought I recognized the new man on vibes as one of that bunch, but he won't talk, just like the rest, and I can't be sure. The vibes man is pretty thick with Pete Muzio, and they seem to have a lot of private business together. But the worst thing is the music."

"The music?" I exclaimed. "That's what made you a star."

"I know, but it still scares me. When I'm on stage I can't tell where half the sound is coming from. It's not from those crazy boxes with grids and neon tubes on them; they're mostly dummies, or just far-out decorations on ordinary electronic instruments. That roaring, moaning noise from offstage is what really gets me. I swear to God I've searched every square inch back there—there's not that much space. Unless somebody took the trouble to build a set of speakers into a solid brick wall, and conceal the outlet some way there's just no source for such sounds. And why should anyone do that? It doesn't even make sense as a publicity stunt, since Tommy won't let anybody even talk about it."

I thought of what one hi-fi nut in the audience told me: he'd tried to tape the show with a hidden transistor set, but could never pick up the offstage sounds. Erika finished off a martini-on-the-rocks that was mostly water by now, and went on.

"I'll tell you something I've never told anyone before. After Dad died I found a box of letters from his father, Erich Zann, addressed to my grandmother and dated Paris, mostly from 1924 and 1925. I can read a little German because we used to speak it around the house.

"The letters tell about experiences the old man had playing his violin all alone at night in an old loft where he lived. He seems to be hinting that something was after him, and only the sound of his playing kept it away.

"There's one letter that mentions the guilt he felt about 'prying into things better left alone'. It doesn't sound so corny in German. And one paragraph that I translated with a dictionary talks about him looking out the window at midnight and seeing 'shadowy satyrs and bacchanals dancing and whirling insanely through seething abysses of clouds and smoke and lightning.'

"Crazy, huh? He must have been really strung out. But I found another letter in the box, a report from the Paris police saying that Erich Zann had disappeared and could not be located. It must have been an answer to a missing-persons inquiry Grandma Zann sent from Stuttgart."

Pete Muzio materialized behind her through clouds of pot smoke, like some stage devil making his big entrance. "All set, Erika? Time for the last set." His wolfish grin seemed mocking, though I don't see how he could have heard anything ...

As I sat waiting for the music to start, it occurred to me that although it was hard to tell at this remove whether old Erich Zann had been crazy or not, the parallels hinted by his freaky granddaughter were wild enough to get her committed, if she talked to many people this way. But at the same time I could see how these apparent parallels might push someone who was nervy and uptight to begin with all the way over the edge.

I started trying to figure out ways for Erika to get away from The Purple Blob. Maybe on the excuse of a vacation, and then later for good. But it was a dilemma; here was where the group's success was building, and Pete Muzio, bless his pointed fangs, had them trapped in an airtight contract. For some reason the leader, Tommy, refused to cut records or say why not, though he'd turned down offers that could have led to the real big time.

Tommy with his Jesus hairdo and half-blind, inward-peering eyes, seemed to be stoned all the time now, and if he was too far around the bend to look after his own best interests, how could anyone expect him to worry about Erika's?

Things went on but didn't get any better. Erika seemed thinner and tenser all the time, and the sets the combo played behind her got wilder and wilder, as she wailed and coloratura above the slamming beat and the ugly toneless roaring that seemed to press in on the stage from everywhere and nowhere.

The novelty was wearing off, and business—though fairly good—was largely down to the hard-core fans, or addicts, for whom an evening with Erika's symbolic struggle on stage seamed the equivalent of some sort of emotionally cathartic trip. The reporters and the record company A&R scouts had drifted away, looking for other kinky groups that would co-operate in being exploited.

On that final evening, though, there was a standing-room crowd, because it was Friday (not the thirteenth, but a Black Friday nevertheless). I had drifted in rather late, and glimpsed Erika down front just before the last set was due to start. As I shoved my way through the crowd and approached her, I was shocked at the ravaged look on her face, and the unfocused glare of those purple eyes above the tight pucker of mouth.

I thought for a moment that she must have flipped, but she seemed to recognize me, and while the organist was winding up his polytonal calypso. I took her arm and led her off to the side.

"Erika, you look sick," I blurted, too disturbed to be polite. "Beg off and let's get out of here. You must have saved enough to buy out of your contract, with Tommy or Pete or both. You shouldn't be doing this, it's killing you by inches. I'll help ... you know I like you." I added the only declaration of my feelings toward her I ever made.

She twitched me a grateful smile, the only response to them she ever made, but her voice was a hoarse croak; the fumes of gin rode with it; "I'm afraid, not sick. It's getting louder and louder, and I can't sing over it. It's coming after me, nearer all the time. I think I know what it wants, and I'm afraid!"

"Then come away!"

"After tonight, maybe. My voice is giving out, that's no lie, but I've got to do it right, get a doctor's opinion. That way no trouble, not like last time ..."

The organist wound up with a splatter of scales trapped inside pin-wheeling discords, as the strobes flared with machinegun rapidity, turning the world into stop-motion photographs. Erika pulled away from me and walked stiffly, jerkily to the stage, a parody of some surreal silent movie sequence.

The curtain went up on the Electric Commode, and the lights all

over the room exploded in mad random patterns, like a night bomb-
ing raid in World War II. The brain-blasting strangle-scream of the
combo cut in, a shriek of nerve-frazzling terror, and I knew the set
would be no ordinary one, even for this group.

Erika was off and running with an up-tempo scat-vocalize skim-
ming lightly over spiky chords that sounded like Kenton's borrowings from Stravinsky in the 40's. Almost immediately the deep,
almost sub-aural roar pressed in from outside, louder than I had ever
heard it before; soulless, ravening, implacable.

A hippie with fright-wig hair, the acid glow bright in his eyes, was
standing beside me shouting something unintelligible. I leaned
toward him and caught a few fragmentary phrases: "Blackness ...
blackness of space illimitable! ... Unimagined space alive with motion
and music ... no semblance of anything on earth ..."

Erika was struggling to ride the tide, to crest the waves of sound.
Faster and faster, higher and higher her voice mounted, but the surge
of noise swept past her, curled into breakers ahead of her, piled in
swift suspended combers on either side of her. The lights dimmed to
a kind of crepitating underwater green, lanced by livid streaks of
scarlet, magenta and violet.

No one could stand such strain, I knew. I pushed my way back to
the bar where Pete Muzio skulked in a dark corner with his knifelike
smile. Grabbing his shoulder, I pressed my face close to his and
shouted amidst the din: "Shut off that noise! That hyped-up speaker
set or whatever you've stashed back there—you must have an amp
control up front here somewhere. Shut it off! It'll kill her!"

Pete wasn't smiling now; he was sweating and soared, and for
once in his life, he was yelling to be heard.

"There's no tape, no speakers. I swear to God I don't know what it
is! I thought at first the band was doing it and they thought I was.

Then that new guy warned me to mind my business if I wanted to keep any ..."

I shoved him aside and wheeled toward the stage. The sonic outrage had mounted to an ear-splitting shriek; the players in the combo dropped their instruments in consternation. Even the lighting display flickered out aghast, leaving a single baby spot playing over Erika, reflecting from the metallic sequins of her gown, glinting from the huge, haunted eyes.

She stood feet apart and braced, arms outstretched, head tilted back, the alien bellow of sound writhing about her like a visible nimbus. She drew in a breath, contorted her lips and bore down, squeezing for the last tortured top note of her hysterical cadenza.

Nothing.

Not a sound, not a squeak, not even a groan came from the stretched square of mouth. The voice, her protection from the unknown stalker, had broken at last.

Exultantly, the all-pervading roar seemed to pounce on her and she staggered back, stumbling over Tommy's discarded guitar, blundering from there into the big super-amp that charged all the electrified instruments and speakers.

There was an eruption of sparks, and I saw her hand go out to arrest her fall, grasping at one of the strange new instruments that stood like a sinister robot chorus surveying the scene.

Instantly the entire charge of current grounded itself, sizzling lethally through the metal sequins of her gown. The flash eclipsed anything the light show had offered; a smell of burning and ozone cut through the reek of marijuana.

The stage curtains bloomed into flame as the band members fled—except for Tommy, who never made it—and the audience floundered in drugged bewilderment toward the exits. The cheap streamers and psychedelic decorations of crepe paper and cheese-cloth channeled fire into every corner of The Purple Blob, lighting up the nightmare riot garishly when the fuses abruptly blew.

I was near the exit; and though I knew that Erika never had a chance, I tried to force my way toward the stage against the pressure of the crowd. The gesture was as pointless as it was futile—I was carried by the surge of the mob toward a safety I neither coveted nor valued.

It wasn't too spectacular as far as fires in crowded places of entertainment go. Besides Erika and Tommy, whose bodies were badly burned, only Pete Muzio died that night. He wasn't found till next day, crouched behind the bar near the entrance. Not a mark was on him, and it was assumed he had had a heart attack. They say his face still held the habitual broken-toothed grimace he had always mistaken for a smile.

No one was badly hurt in that stampede of zonked-out hippies, which shows that—as the squares say—God takes care of fools and children. The interior of The Purple Blob was completely gutted, but firemen had little trouble controlling the flames. Later, though, it was judged that the structure was unsound, and the shell of the building was pulled down.

I'm glad it's gone, though I can never forget it; nor will I forget the things that happened there, or the people they happened to. Least of all will I forget—though I have a notion that as time goes on, I shall more and more wish I could forget—the silence of Erika Zann.

(Author's Note: Students of the macabre will note that this story is nearly as much indebted to E.T.A. Hoffmann's "Rath Krespel" as to H. P. Lovecraft's "The Music of Erich Zann".)

A DARKER SHADOW OVER INNSMOUTH

AS I BOARDED the wheezing, rattling bus bound for Innsmouth there at the station next to a bustling supermarket in Newburyport, I could not suppress a shudder at the thought that now, at last, I was bound for that ancient, decadent, shadow-blighted Massachusetts seaport of which so many repellent legends are whispered. I had read all the Lovecraft stories, of course, and those of his numerous successors, which chronicle how rapacious voyagers of the past century brought horror and calamity upon the town through their impious trafficking with blasphemous humanoid sea-dwellers; creatures who fetched them treasure from weed-grown, Cyclopean ocean-bottom cities, but who in turn insisted upon not only the townsmen's worship, but even upon the unholy mating of human and amphibian, producing a hideous hybrid strain of half-reptilian, fishlike abnormalities who inhabited the town until they "changed" sufficiently to take up an immortal existence at the bottom of the sea.

Of course, I knew too that the town had been hard hit by federal raids over forty years ago, according to Lovecraft's informants; but I realized

"That is not dead which can eternal lie,
And with strange aeons, even death may die,"

in the words of a fortune-cookie verse I once nearly choked on—a cookie served me, strangely enough, at an Arabian restaurant in Osaka.

Now I was at last on my way to see for myself these eldritch, unholy entities and enclaves; and to join in the bestial rites therewith associated; that is, if my credentials were all in order. (My Order of Dagon card was signed by August Derleth, but a report had reached me that Colin Wilson had taken over the high priesthood in a daring palace coup.)

As we approached ill-rumored Innsmouth along the desolate Rowley Road, I knew I would not be disappointed; here were the rotting, fishy-smelling wharves; the blear-paned ancient houses; the massive, obscurely terrifying warehouses, holding impassively the secrets of outer arcana, the crumbling, desecrated churches devoted to what hideous ceremonies the sane mind could only shudder to imagine.

As I alighted from the bus at Town Square in front of the sinister and horror-infested fabric of Gilman House hotel, with its tattered Diners' Club sticker, the only person in sight was a slatternly girl with bulging, unwinking eyes and rough, crinkly skin around the sides of her neck. I struck up an acquaintance with this unprepossessing creature—whose name, I learned, was Nella Kodaz—on the pretext of being a stranger in need of guidance, and we strolled down to a deserted wharf where the sibilant and immemorial sea came sliding and hissing out of the mist.

"Tell me, Nella," I queried, "I know there is more in Innsmouth than meets the eye. How can I arrange to see the forbidden things secreted in those dilapidated warehouses and hidden away in the ancient boarded-up dwellings here?"

"Better get a C.I.A. clearance first," she replied.

"C.I.A.? Don't you mean Esoteric Order of Dagon?"

"That Dagon jazz is all washed up. After the Navy raids here in 1928, they say, the government kept a close eye on any funny business. During World War II there was a commando school here, and since then it's been used mostly as a hush-hush Defense Department experimental and training station. That's why everything's under cover and visitors aren't welcome. I thought you knew, from the way you talked."

I was flabbergasted. "But what about the monstrous batrachian sea-creatures out beyond Devil Reef? The blasphemous fish-frogs that always dominated Innsmouth and exacted their unholy tribute?"

"Well, every few weeks the Navy people dump a few crates of shark-repellant into the deep water off the reef. If there are any boogie-men around, that seems to hold them."

"You must excuse me, Nella—but it seems to me you yourself exemplify what is referred to as 'the Innsmouth look', those peculiarities of personal appearance shown by people descended from human matings with the Deep Ones—people who will some day dive down to live forever in the sea-bottom citadel of Y'ha-nthlei."

"Wrong again. I got an overdose of radiation, just a slight one, when I was working as a lab tech at the atomic reactor where they're making defoliants. The insurance paid through the nose, and I'm due for some free plastic surgery in a few months."

"But what about those older inhabitants of Innsmouth who did have an amphibian strain in their ancestry?"

"The ones who are left come under Medicare now. Mostly their relatives committed them years ago, and they're in protective custody at a big aquarium down near Marineland. It's sort of like Disneyland—people pay to see the Creatures from the Black Lagoon, only they think it's a fake."

"Then what's hidden in all those huddled, leering old houses and sealed, sagging warehouses?"

"Oh, all sorts of things—anti-personnel bombs, defoliant, infiltration training setups, secret courses on Karate and winning the hearts and minds of the people. Professors from Miskatonic University come out twice a week to teach counter-insurgency tactics."

"Not the famous Miskatonic University?"

"Yes, in Arkham—where the new napalm plant is going up. Miskatonic U. got a big government contract, so they tore down their library, threw out all those moldy old books on sorcery, and built the biggest Pacification and Incineration Training Center in the country."

Suddenly, with a numbing shock, I saw a hideous form emerging from the foaming breakers—a dark, glistening shape, its skin a squamous green—vaguely humanoid in outline, but surmounted by a flat, bestial head with bulging, glassy eyes.

"Run for your life!" I shouted. "They've seen us! The Deep Ones! The monstrous, frog-like minions of..."

"Calm down," Nella interrupted in a bored tone. "It's a frog-man, all right—just part of the underwater demolition school for Special Forces. Why, it's Elvis Whateley from Dunwich Acres. Hi, there! Dry off and let's all go downtown and slug back a few beers."

So we did.

Now I have been in Innsmouth over six weeks. More and more I admire the quaint but swinging old town; more and more I enjoy my job packing defoliant from the atomic reactor; more and more I love my new wife, Nella Kadoz, with her soulful staring eyes and intriguing wattled neck. And in just eight months, a little stranger will join us!

I'm taking a night course in Karate at Miskatonic, and angling for a job at the napalm factory when it's finished. I may even quit the Order of Dagon and join the Green Berets.

Yes, I'm a happy, fulfilled person. I came to Innsmouth seeking the cosmically evil—looking for sin on a supernatural scale, for horrors beyond the imagination of mere mortal man.

And I've found them. Lovecraft and the Great Old Ones don't hold a candle. Give me the crusade to protect peace and freedom any day.

A SWISHING OVER INNSMOUTH

W ELL, I NEVER for a *single moment* expected to get stuck in a cruddy little fishing village like Innsmouth, if only because the people in places like that don't usually *appreciate* my type of person. (Though my name is Harold, I do have soulful eyes and rather nice hands.) If I'm going to hit any beach, Fire Island is more my speed.

But anyway my right front tire started losing air just past some yokel burg called Aylesbury, on the Arkham highway not too far from Boston, so what was I to do? I'd already been banned, *there*.

The cute bellhop who seemed so affectionate last night at the Arkham Arms had warned me about the road. "Mr. Binghampton," he told me, "stay off that Aylesbury Turnpike. It goes through Innsmouth, and you can't even get a Big Mac there, let alone fix a puncture. The gas shortage has hit the place hard, too, unless you can run your car on fish oil, which they always have plenty of, judging by the smell ten miles off."

Well, that bellhop was a *living doll*, but he turned coy, or was holding out for more than I cared to offer, so I wrote off his advice as well as his attractions, and next morning drove away alone down the road he had warned me about. Serve him right, the little tease.

Which is why I wound up stuck in the suburbs of this stinking village with a flat tire, and not a soul mate in sight.

Really, it was an utter and complete ghost town – all those empty houses, the windows and doors boarded up, no people in sight, and that awful rancid fishy smell blowing in from the ocean – and I was getting pretty desperate when this blubber-lipped character with the bug eyes and wrinkled neck came slinking out from between two lean-tos that already did and met, and croaked:

"Do you have the Yellow Sign?"

Yellow Sign? It must be a new gay code-signal I wasn't into. I always wear a single earring, and keep my keychain on the left side of my chinos, but Yellow Signs I know from nothing, not having been in Frisco for two years where the FFA is big and most of these fads get started.

Naturally this rough trade type didn't appeal to me; I'm a bit fastidious about who I get a yen for, except when the bar I'm cruising is too dark to tell, and even then there's the matter of basic hygiene that you don't need eyesight to determine. This oaf didn't pass either sensory test, but not wanting to offend anyone in a place this strange and needing help badly, I answered politely: "I don't really have the slightest idea what the Yellow Sign is, darling, but most guys, straight or gay, seem to feel I show all the other signs anybody could ask for." And I camped and strutted a bit for him.

He began to drool eying me, and in a slurping, mumbling voice remarked, "Ph'nglui mglw'nafh Cthulhu R'lyeh wgahnagl fhtagn," or something to that effect.

There was something about his voice and words that threw me into an exotically passionate mood, despite his repulsiveness.

"I really go for Arabs," I murmured sensuously, "oily ones or sandy ones. Which are you?"

"Yes, those are the very words set down by the mad Arab," he answered in awe. "They are translated thus: 'In his house at R'lyeh, dead Cthulhu waits Dreaming!'"

"Well, I giggled, "let's go wake him and liven up the party a little. Things can't be any duller than they are around here now."

So this weird-looking guy, whose name turns out to be Asaph Ezra Obed Binghampton-Marsh (and who claims he's a third cousin of mine through some underground, or underwater, misalliance) helps me to change the flat and off we zip into beautiful downtown Innsmouth, where to my *excruciating* delight I discover there is plenty of kinky action in any exotic direction one would wish, and a lot that no one but those quaint, furtive, decadent New England types would ever think of.

No wonder all those buildings are boarded up, considering what goes on inside! It's an eldritch horror!

The guys on the scene seem to like me a lot, too, and have given me a nickname (no, not Queen Harold; that was bitchy Ron's idea back in Frisco) – they call my Pth'thyla-l'yi (try saying *that* with your front teeth out!) and implore me to swim down with them to some sort of aquatic resort with even more esoteric pursuits, I guess, out beyond the big reef in the harbor.

I might just take them up on that when my new gill openings get bigger, and my eyes bug out enough to see clearly deep down under water.

And baby, you better believe when I go down and make that ulti-mate gay scene, we shall live in wonder and glory forever.

THE SANDALS OF SARGON
by
James Wade and Sotireos Vlahopoulos

One
SARDURIAN

The path fell before Sardurian.
He watched his shadow copulate with his
father's shadow, which darted away from
the well-trodden goat path.

the trees are in bloom.
not fully, half-tending to sprout at their fullness.

The temple jutted high beyond the grassy grade.

it is not a magnificent temple.
ordinary.
Like the temple I saw last year at Aratat.

The columns were well-spaced, but Sardurian
felt that they were too far apart to hold
up the weight of the heavy roof.

this is my first visit
I am curious to see the inside of the temple
of *SARGON, THE GREAT ONE.*
I wonder what it will be like?
what will it prove?

I do not know.

father is so pious.
SARGON, THE GREAT ONE, has caused father to
become unbearable at times.
not that it matters.
the sandals must be made.
father says *SARGON, THE GREAT ONE*, needs them.

Two
ARGISHTISH

'How young is Sardurian! How excited in his inexperienced youth! He bounds along the path as if the temple were a place for levity and merry-making. Only with age will come the sense of awe and reverence that I know at these moments. To be sandalmaker to *SARGON, THE GREAT ONE*, is indeed the highest of eminences. For who but *SARGON, THE GREAT ONE*, has displayed the benevolent qualities of mercy and justice so strikingly?

'In his earthly life, so many centuries ago, *SARGON, THE GREAT ONE*, walked abroad doing only good. Legend relates that many were the sandals he wore to the skin in his journeys among the ignorant and afflicted.

'And, upon his earthly death, *SARGON, THE GREAT ONE*, foretold that he would not cease his benevolent journeys after mortal life had ended.

'So began the ancestral line of sandalmakers to *SARGON, THE GREAT ONE*; craftsmen who strive to produce the perfect specimen of

196

their art, so that twice in a century an offering of superb sandals may be left in the tomb-shrine of *SARGON, THE GREAT ONE.*

'All my life have I labored to this end, and the life of this my son Sardurian will also be so directed. Yet he skips and carols in the sun, taking the visitation to the god as a sportful holiday.'

Three
SARDURIAN

Argishtish moved swiftly ahead of Sardurian.

Their shadows fell far apart.

Sardurian followed on his father's heels.

The massive gate of the temple hung to one side listlessly.

What an odd design!
strange.
it seems to flicker.

The old man fell to his knees; his forehead
touched the grey stone floor.

what a funny chant!
i have never heard father sing it before.

The temple's loins engulfed them, and the
massive darkness swallowed them like a huge

197

mouth devouring goats' flanks.

why, the temple has nothing in it!

Sardurian was disappointed.
The temple was barren except for the statue
that stood in the center of the rectangular floor.

the statue is plain.
SARGON, THE GREAT ONE, is like one of the villagers.
he looks like Oresis – the beggar.

look at my father.
what is it that he sees?

The statue stared down at Sardurian,
the eyes glaring endlessly.
he looks at me.
what a queer face!
the smile is strange.

the statue smiled even more.
he moved!
no.
yes.
no.
I think my father's movements gave me that image.

I cannot seem to look upon SARGON, THE
GREAT ONE, as god.

he is not richly clothed.
his dress is too poor.
gods are rich.

I must tell Mersini about it.

look at my father.
sometimes I believe he is a fool!

father is moving away.
I must follow.

all this seems so senseless.

the sandals will be made.

why this... secret ... secret visit?
I cannot understand why.

I shall ask father to tell me the legend once more.

Four

ARGISHTISH

'So this is the tomb-chamber I have never seen. It is as my father described it to me many years ago. I was a boy like Sardurian then, but my Sardurian will have the advantage of having seen an actual presentation of the sandals.

'Beyond there is the statue of SARGON, THE GREAT ONE. It is as I could have imagined it. The face is calm and at peace. It portrays a

199

benevolence unknown to mortals. The lips part in benign apprehension of a dream unthinkable to man. And on the feet of the statue survive the remnants of the last sandals, those made by my father fifty years ago.

'There is not much left of them. *SARGON, THE GREAT ONE*, must have travelled far afield in them. And yet I know that they were wonderful sandals, and that my own will not be unworthy of our immemorial line.

'Sardurian is more silent now. He watched me approach in the ritual manner, so that I may measure the sacred feet of *SARGON, THE GREAT ONE*, for my own, almost-completed sandals.

'I approach and touch the sacred statue. The insensitive stone seems almost warm and pulsating. An ineffable joy courses through me – now we must return hastily to the inn, to complete preparation for the great night. My heart trembles in strange anticipatory joy.'

Five

ARGISHTISH

'We have now reached the temple once more. In my hand I bear the sacred box of acacia-wood. Within are the sandals of *SARGON, THE GREAT ONE* – the monument to my life. It is night – no one is about. The village guards know what night this is, and there will be no stragglers or curiosity-seekers here.'

"Before we enter to perform the rite, I must tell you, Sardurian, my son, once more the legend of *SARGON, THE GREAT ONE*. Somehow I must make you understand the beauty and goodness of the earthly life of the god.

"You comprehend that the Great One ministered to the lowly in his life? That his devine majesty condescended to the poor and humble? Then how much more remarkable it must seem to you that, even in the state of mortal death, the deity journeys forth again on his mission of love.

"One thing only is required: that the statue of *SARGON, THE GREAT ONE*, be shod as befitting a deity. It is for this that a thousand generations of our line have perfected their art. To minister fittingly to the need of the Benevolent One is an achievement beyond mortal hope, but we may say that our best is truly all we can give."

Six
SARDURIAN

The legend of *SARGON, THE GREAT ONE*, did
not impress Sardurian.
He had heard it too many times before.
It did not move the boy.
He was visibly bored by his father's monotonous voice.

I think my father is crazed.
a child's tale!
and he be – he believes it.
he is old.
I cannot believe it.
I am no fool.
I cannot eat the words as the goats eat grass.
I am no child

Seven
ARGISHTISH

'He does not understand. Sardurian does not understand. No matter – he will, with age. In fifty years, I doubt not that he will render more fitting service than I do tonight.'

Eight
SARDURIAN

He followed his father into the temple.

It is an ordinary temple.
too plain.
there is no gold, no silver, no jewels.
and there is *SARGON, THE GREAT ONE*.

his smile.
that strange smile.

Nine
ARGISHTISH

'How dark it is within the temple! There is only the small altar-fire, reflectd on the surface of the statue. I tremble, but more in joy than in apprehension. *SARGON, THE GREAT ONE*, will accept my poor token.

'I take out the sandals. How light they are, yet how strong! I approach the statue; trembling, I lay them at its feet.

'But what is this? A blaze of light seems to appear – my senses are

stricken. I seem to twist and change. All disappears from my sight –
a heavy rhythm intrudes upon my pulses.

'I feel a strange union with the deity. It is as if I had become a part
of him, moving with slow rhythm of his majestic tread as he walks
abroad.

'Yes – that is it. This feeling of exaltation means that I have been
accepted – perhaps alone of my family. But no, I feel Sardurian somewhere near, too. Even in the glorious blaze of the divine light, I feel
the presence of my son. My faith has sanctified him, and we shall
move forever together, caught up in the glorious halo that surrounds
the divine form of SARGON, THE GREAT ONE!

Ten
SARDURIAN

Sardurian's father placed the sandals
before the statue.
Argishtish crouched.
Sardurian imitated his father.

I think this is foolishness.
it is like playing a game.

Mersini believes that SARGON, THE GREAT
ONE will come
so does father.

I do not.

gods are man-made.

the beggar Oresis has told me that many times.

The two waited.

what is wrong with father?

the statue moved.

SARGON, THE GREAT ONE, has moved.

no, he did not.
Yes, he did.
no.
yes...
yes...
yes...

o father, you...

look at *SARGON, THE GREAT ONE*,

I cannot.

he is hideous!

The pus fell from the statue's nostrils
like water. From the eyes poured large
red ants that crawled toward the pus.

aiee!

I cannot move.

o father...
father...

The ears became huge bat-wings with
yellow streaks of molten flesh. The
molten flesh climbed crazily up the ears –
eating them, like grotesque leeches upon
a pool of slime.

aiee!
father...
help!
I cannot move.

The statue took a step down from the pedestal
and stretched out its arms.
The arms like shaggy moss... as green
blades of hair grew speedily and fell flowing
upon the floor.
The mouth.
The tongue darted to and fro.
Crooked.
Forked.
Spilling from the hideous opening, snakes,
lizards, toads, eels, leeches.

Sardurian could not move.

I cannot move

father...
Mersini...
father...
SARGON...
The head of the statue moved.
It broke off at the neck.
When the head hit the floor, it melted into
millions of white, squirming worms.
The legs folded back up into the body – molding
into a large slab of flesh.
It had no form.
aiee!

I cannot move father ...

father, you change!
we are growing small.
your arms – they are like leather.
our bodies have become as the leather
we have in our shop.
father ...
your legs ...
they are no more!
father ...
my legs ...
FATHER ...
you are becoming ... a sandal?
see!

I am a sanda...

The mass of flesh engulfed Sardurian and his father.
The statue became as one again.
It resumed its position on the pedestal.
On the large naked feet, were new sandals.
The statue smiled ...

THOSE WHO WAIT

Introduction

In 1943, at the age of fifteen, and continuing through 1946, I made several juvenile attempts at authorship, under the influence of H.P. Lovecraft, a selection of whose stories had just come to my attention in the newly-published Tower Books popular edition.

An extant specimen of narrative verse, "The Book in the Glade," indicates that I knew about and tried to emulate, however awkwardly, Lovecraft's hobby of 18th century-style versification. A pompously rhetorical sonnet sequence which I wrote around the same time as a memorial to HPL was eventually published in 1969 in the *The Arkham Collector*, No. 4, without the necessary information that its author was only 16 when it was written. (This has so far been the extent of publication of my juvenilia from that period.)

But the principal production from this phase of precocious pastiche was a 10,000-word novelette called "Those That Wait", which on re-reading a quarter century later I decided should have been subtitled "The Rover Boys at R'lyeh".

This narrative embodies influences especially from Lovecraft's *The Thing on the Doorstep*, as well as Derleth's then-new *The Lurker at the Threshold*, and shares with the latter that defect described by Prof. John Taylor as using the Elder Sign as a sort of handy occult Band Aid, a cure-all for any eruption of transmontane evil.

With juvenile hubris, I sent the story to August Derleth of Arkham House, who returned it with a scathing dissection of its inadequacies, though he relented a bit when he learned that the author was only 16, the age at which he himself, many years before, had sold his first, heavily derivative macabre stories to *Weird Tales*.

This early story of mine represents an attempt at least of contributing to the Lovecraft mythos, one I did not repeat until 21 years later, in a novelette "The Deep Ones," which appeared in Arkham's *Tales of the Cthulhu Mythos*, and subsequently in a Beagle paperback, plus the topical parody "A Darker Shadow Over Innsmouth" (*The Arkham Collector*, No. 5)

With the publication for the record of these two very early pieces, and the probable disappearance of a market for new Cthulhu Mythos material consequent on Derleth's death, my minor contribution to the Mythos would seem to have been brought to completion.

– James Wade

FORTUNATE INDEED IS he whose range of experience never exceeds that tiny segment of Infinity which it is meant that Man should explore and subdue. He who steps beyond these borders walks in dreadful danger of life, sanity, and soul. Even if he escapes the peril, life can never be the same again – for he cannot escape his memories.

It is now seven months since I came to the archaic Massachusetts town of Arkham, to attend the small but widely-known Miskatonic University. Since then, my knowledge has increased in an unprecedented manner, but not in the ways I had expected. For me, new worlds have been opened – new worlds containing fascinating vistas of wisdom, and also undreamable abysses of horror, in which I learned the fatal weakness of the human mind in dealing with forces beyond its comprehension.

The first few weeks of my attendance at the university were occupied with settling myself in the new surroundings and becoming accustomed to my classes. My room-mate, Bill Tracy, I instinctively liked. A tall, blonde, self-effacing fellow, he was one of those utterly frank and compatible individuals one meets all too seldom. He was a sophomore, and helped my absorption into the school's routine by answering innumerable questions as to the location of rooms, the dispositions of the instructors, and the thousand other things about which the beginner at the school is ever curious.

Almost a month elapsed thus when the event occurred which was to set in motion a train of events unparalleled, so far as we know, in the history of the Earth. It began, however, prosaically enough.

One evening, rather late, I suddenly remembered some quotations from Shelley I would be expected to know by the next day for my literature class. Apprehensively I asked Bill Tracy, "Do you suppose the campus library is still open?"

"Probably," he replied, "but better hurry. They close at ten. You should have gone earlier." He grinned at my negligence.

I hurried from the dormitory and took the gravel path across the campus toward the large brick library building. On nearing it, I was relieved to notice that faint lights were still burning on the ground floor. Inside, I procured the needed book, and, passing the busy librarian, I suddenly turned on an impulse and made my way into the rare books room, which was then completely empty, as was the rest of the library. Seating myself at one of the tables, I prepared to delve into Shelley's odes, when suddenly I saw it – the thing which was to change my very life.

It was nothing but a sheet of paper lying on the table beside me, written part of the way down one side. Out of idle curiosity I picked it up. It seemed but a series of notes, such as students might jot down when sitting together rather than disturb the quiet of the reading-room by speaking aloud. There were short sentences in two alternating hands. I was about to toss the paper aside, when something caught my eye, and I read it with ever-mounting interest and mystification. As nearly as I can remember, this is what the written conversion said:

"What time is it?"

"9:15."

"I wish they'd leave."

"There are only two. They will leave soon."

"Hope they hurry. I'd like to let Ithaqua get th-" (Here the script was hurriedly broken off, and there had been an only partially successful attempt to cross out the cryptic word. After which:)

"Fool! I have told you – never write those names!"

"All right. – Can we finish tonight?"

"I can copy that from the N."

"I'll easily copy the chant."

"We can open the Gate by –" (Here the writing again was interrupted.)

"They're leaving. Bring the key."

This completed the contents of the paper. I was baffled. What were these two planning – a robbery? But what about the cryptic references to a "chant" and "opening a gate"? Who was "Ithaqua" and why shouldn't that name be written.

I was interrupted in these speculations by the opening of a nearby door marked "Private", and the emergence of two men. I caught a momentary glimpse of the rows of books within the room, and then a piercing gaze was directed upon me and the paper before me.

The gazer was tall, beetle-browed, and excessively dark, and had the appearance of being too adult for a student, but both he and his companion – a shorter, stouter and younger-looking fellow who carried a brief-case – wore school sweaters. The younger man, apparently quite agitated at seeing me, quickly closed and locked the door, and then stood waiting for his older companion to act, which he immediately did. Striding forward, he addressed me in low, fierce tones with a hint of fear in his voice.

"Parson me, sir, this paper is mine." And without further ado, he snatched it up and turned away.

"Just a moment!" I exclaimed angrily, "What are you up to? Have you two been stealing rare books from in there? What's in that brief-case?"

Seeing he could not get away without an explanation, he stopped and became immediately suavely polite.

"Pardon my haste," he said smiling blandly, "My companion and I

213

are engaged in no untoward activities. It is true: we were using the so-called rare books within that room, but we were merely copying portions of them, for a – thesis; yes, a thesis on demonolatry." Something in the inflection and wording suggested that he was a foreigner. "You will excuse us now." Grasping the arm of his companion, he turned once more.

"Do you think he understood –?" began the smaller man, but he was hushed by a gesture from the other, who looked guardedly back at me. The two quickly left the library, leaving me to muse on what I had witnessed.

My work was soon finished, but as I walked across the campus, thoughts of the two strange men obsessed me. If they had been engaged in authorized reference work, why had the note hinted that they wished to be left alone before entering the locked room? Too, parts of the dark, moody note seemed curiously irreconcilable to that explanation.

Over the thickly clustered, shadowy grove of the east hung a waning moon. Stars, those bright specks of light from distances incomprehensible, held dominion over the more subdued hues of darkness at the zenith. Ahead of me stretched the half-lit dormitory. Within was Bill Tracy. Perhaps he could shed some light on this matter.

I hurried to our room. Bill greeted me with a cheery, "Hi! Get your work done?"

"Yes," I answered abstractedly; then: "Have you ever seen a tall, dark, foreign, older-looking fellow in the student body? – Maybe tagged by a stoutish, younger fellow?"

"I think I know who you mean. His name is Renaunt. He *is* older. Taking a post-graduate course in Ancient Literature and Folklore."

"What do you know about him?"

"Oh, nothing in particular. Rather reserved chap. You meet him?"

"In a way." I told him what had occurred. He seemed peculiarly disturbed when I mentioned the strange name Ithaqua and the locked room.

"He's up to no good," muttered Bill, more to himself than to me.

"What do you know about it?"

"It's more than you can imagine. I was born and raised here. There are legends... ."

He told me then: fantastic tales of ancient books on malignant evil come down from ages immemorial, kept in Miskatonic Library's locked room. Sane or not, the dark beliefs and rituals contained in these books had been practiced even down to the present. The thick woods bordering the Miskatonic River had seen hideous, illogical rites celebrated within ancient circles of standing stones, and the forgotten hamlet of Dunwich, surrounded by altar-crowned hills, degenerated year by year from more cause than mere isolation. There were those, especially among the oldsters of Arkham, who averred that dark things *could* be called from the hills or the sky, if one were willing to pay the price. It was universally admitted that at certain seasons the sky lit up disturbingly over the hills, and queer rumbling earth-noises were heard. Scientists mumbled about seismographic shocks and Aurora Borealis, but few dared to investigate. In the old days, it had been quite generally believed that indescribable legions of demons were served there by wicked cults. Strange disappearances of those who lived or ventured too near the woods at night were invariably laid to the cult or its hideous deities, especially when the bodies would be found months later far away, only a few days dead.

Here my informer paused.

"Surely," I prompted, "you don't believe that!"

"Believe it? I wouldn't believe that *Renaunt* believed it if it wasn't for that note you told me about. They sound in earnest."

215

"Couple of crackpots!"

"If you really want to know something about this crazy business, just ask tomorrow to examine some of the books in that room. They'll let you. But as for copying wholesale from them, there'd be suspicions. That's why your two playmates made their own key and nosed in on the books secretly."

That night I had little rest. Indeed, my loss of sleep was not the result of vague and later definite fears which would soon beset me, but was rather caused by excitement: I thought perhaps I had discovered a new myth-pattern (new to me, at least), as my hobby had for years been the gathering of native legends from my home state, Wisconsin.

Suddenly, in the middle of the night, I remembered where I had heard that cryptic name, Ithaqua. During my explorations of Wisconsin's north woods in search of lore for my collection, I had met an old Indian who had told me vague legends of the Wendigo, sometimes called "Wind-Walker" or *Ithaqua* – a titanic and repulsive monster, haunter of the great unfrequented snow-forests – a being who took men with him high above the woods to the far corners of the Earth, but who never relinquished his victims until they had been frozen to death.

Such, then, was the thing which these unusual collegians spoke of as reality, or –?

The next day passed slowly for me, but at last my classes terminated and I went quickly to the great library. Rather timorously I approached the aged librarian, and asked whether I might examine the rare books contained in the locked room. He eyed me oddly but assented, and, giving me a key from the ring at his side, bade me lock the door carefully when I finished.

With queer misgivings I approached the fated door and applied the key. Inside, I was confronted with several rows of books held in wall-shelves. The immense antiquity of the rotting tomes greatly impressed me. Many were incomplete and mutilated; others merely bound manuscripts. I saw such titles as the *Necronomicon* of Abdul Alhazred, "Unaussprechlichen Kulten" by Von Junzt, "Liber Ivonis", and "De Vermis Mysteriis" by Ludwig Prinn. I was blissfully ignorant of the hellish evil around me, but was not long to remain so.

To open the *Necronomicon* (one of the largest and best preserved of the lot) was the work of the moment. Thumbing through it, I learned for the first time of Great Cthulhu; of Azathoth, the Lord of All Things, of Yog-Sothoth, and Shub-Niggurath; of Nyarlathotep and Tsathoggua, and of other horrors the nature of which I could grasp no better. Had I believed what I read then, I should inevitably have gone mad at once, but thinking it merely a particularly malignant myth-pattern or a devilishly clever hoax, I read on with only a curious interest.

There were many hundreds of pages of rambling, disconnected essays in Latin, containing charms, counter-charms, spells and incantations (which latter seemed to be entirely in a laboriously spelled phonetic language). Frequently there was a crude diagram of complicated signs, such as a pattern of intersecting lines and concentric circles, as well as a fire-outlined star designated as "The Elder Sign."

From the particularly lucid passages, I gleaned a strange story. It seems, according to the crazed Arab author that, billions of aeons before Man, great cosmic entities "from the stars" had come to Earth. These things (possessing the queer names that had so puzzled me) were extra-dimensional and beyond the bounds of Time and Space. They were the personifications of universal Evil, and had fled from a cosmos beyond human ken the wrath from the benign Elder Gods, against whom They had rebelled. These evil Great Old Ones built cyclopean cities according to non-Euclidean geometric principles, and from Earth planned to renew their fight against the Elder Gods. But before They were fully prepared, "the stars went wrong" as the author put it, and these Great Old Ones could not live. Neither could They ever die, but being preserved by the black magic of Their high priest Great Cthulhu, slept within Their monster cities to await a coming time. Some were banished into caverns in the bowels of the earth; others, imprisoned beyond the known universe.

In the course of an unbelievable passage of time Man had arrived and the Great Old Ones had communicated with some individuals telepathically, telling them of the great awakening that was to come, and instructing them in the chants and rituals which, together with proper sacrifices and worship, could bring the gigantic Things temporarily to great circles of stone monoliths set up in abandoned places, and further hinting that Man would be instrumental in the permanent release of the Old Ones, as They could not yet move under Their own volition.

These secrets had been learned and passed on by wicked groups of men even after R'lyeh, the nightmare-city of Cthulhu, had sunk into the sea in the same cataclysm that spelled doom for Atlantis and Mu. The cults would go on until "the stars again became right" and the release of the blasphemous elder monsters would be accomplished as the culmination of its supreme purpose.

In addition to these wild historical notes, the book held hundreds of stories of various strange happenings, authenticated by long-forgotten witnesses and inexplicable save in the light of the lore the book expounded. Concerning the physical aspect of these extra-terrestrials and Their minions, the book was distressingly hazy. Once it alluded to Them as "of no substance"; other times mentioning a hideous plasticity and the capability of becoming invisible.

Being so completely absorbed in the book, I failed to notice light steps approaching the door, but I dropped the *Necronomicon* in fright as a menacingly familiar voice sounded behind me.

"Are you perhaps looking for something?

It was Renaunt, of course, not far preceding his pudgy accomplice with the eternal brief-case. In strange agitation I tried to reply lightly.

"I was just checking up to see what interested you so much last evening."

"I thought you perhaps might do so," he returned narrowly. "Have you found anything of interest?"

"Yes, indeed! Here seems to be a myth-pattern of great antiquity upon which I have never before stumbled."

"You are interested in the ancient religions?"

"Very much."

"So are we. You must pardon me. I am Jacques Renaunt – this is my good friend Peterson."

We shook hands. I did not enjoy the experience.

"I have something you might like to see," said Renaunt in a disarmingly friendly manner. "Perhaps last night you thought us as devil-worshippers, to copy from these odd books, but this is uncorrect."

"Incorrect." Peterson spoke his first word in the conversation. "You mustn't forget your English."

"Quite right. Thank you. As I was saying, we are merely amateur archaeologists, but we have discovered, not far from here, some very unique ruins, which, if we are not mistaken, were once used in connection with rites given in those books."

"These books," put in Peterson.

"No matter. The point is, we have been perusing – *these* books to gain further information. We planned to visit these ruins toni – this afternoon. We would be glad for a – companion." The two exchanged glances.

Did I let my instinctive aversion to these men cause me to refuse their bland offer? No; logic conquered instinct, and I made myself see only a new and fascinating experience in a venture against which my every dormant intuition cried out loud.

"I would be delighted. First let me tell my room-mate ..."

"Peterson will do that when he gets the car. Hurry, Peterson."

The stout man scuttled away, while Renaunt led me rather furtively out a side exit. In a surprisingly short time Peterson drove up in the car. Renaunt opened the back door for me and then climbed in beside Peterson. For a few minutes, silence prevailed as the car swept swiftly across the leaf-strewn campus grounds and through the autumn-tinted, rolling Massachusetts hills. Then Renaunt turned and addressed me politely.

"You must pardon me while I converse with Mr. Peterson in my native language. It is tiring for me to constantly formulate my thoughts into the English."

They immediately began talking in some foreign dialect. Listening idly, I could not trace any Romance language or Greek or even Slavic in what they said; it seemed a kind of guttural Oriental tongue, but as I sat listening to it, mile after mile in that stuffy car, I could take no pleasure in the beauties of the wooded hills, or of the forest-cradled Miskatonic River, now tinted a flaming orange by the rays of the descending sun.

We drove much further than I had expected. The sun was hidden behind the tall pines of the mountains ahead when we turned from the main road. The eastern sky was dusky behind us as the car jogged along a narrow, rough dirt trail. Several times it branched off again on bypaths leading through quiet forest glades of the greatest sylvan beauty. The trail became barely wide enough to permit passage to the sedan. Few were the farms we passed, and these few were always in a deplorably run-down condition. It was a poor district, ruled by Nature and not Man.

Long after losing sight of the last farmhouse among the thickening trees, Peterson brought the auto to a lurching halt.

"This is as far as we can go by the car," said Renaunt, opening the door.

Within a few minutes we were plunging through thick undergrowth among the huge boles of an amazing cluster of trees. This, I thought, must be one of the few out-of-the-way virgin forests in the state. Another thought occurred to me and I asked Renaunt, "Why were these ruins not discovered before; they are reasonably near human habitation?"

"The natives around here fear these woods," answered my guide cryptically, "and few others have occasion to visit them."

In silence we covered the distance of perhaps a mile. The ground gradually became damp and spongy until it was apparent that we were nearing a swamp.

"The ruins are on a kind of island in the midst of a marshy crescent lake near the Miskatonic," explained Renaunt in response to my query.

A deep dusk, enhanced by the somber shade of the forest, had now indeed fallen.

"How can we see when we arrive? We have started too late," I commented.

I received no reply, save the pulsing croak of frogs which now reached us from somewhere ahead in the leafy labyrinth.

Little by little the trees thinned and I saw stretched before me, surrounded by woods like those from which we were emerging, a low, open, marshy spot in the shape of a giant crescent moon. Reeds and rushes grew at the margin, while near the middle the water was clear and deep, albeit rather stagnant. Near the center of the lake rose a small island, almost covered with the sprawling ruin of a strange, irregular grey stone platform surrounded by a crumbling parapet, much in need of repair. Low stone columns rose at intervals from it. The last reflected rays of the setting sun shone behind it, outlining the skeletal remains of a once-great and still imposing structure. I was astounded to find such a complex piece of architecture in apparently unexplored wilds.

"The lake of Y'ha-nthlei," breathed Peterson, "Iä! Cthulhu!"

"What did you say?" I exclaimed, "I –"

But Renaunt interrupted me with a terse command to Peterson.

"Now is the time!" he snapped. "Concentrate!" – and everything suddenly went black around me. My last conscious impression was one of the two grasping my arms to keep me from falling as I slipped into the black trough of insensibility.

When I awoke, the deepest night had fallen. My first sensation was of lying uncomfortably on a very hard substance; my second was of bewilderment: I could not realize the significance of the bonds around my wrists and ankles. I knew not that I was a prisoner. Then, suddenly, the meaning of my situation came back to me. I remembered the strange trek through the shadow woods with my queer companions; the marshy lake, the ruins. I remembered too my faint (for such I then deemed it) at the edge of the woods. Then I began to struggle, for, gazing around, I discovered that I was lying on the rough stone flags comprising the floor of the island ruin. My companions must have brought me here, I thought, but why bound?

The extent of Renaunt's treachery was soon to be made clear to me, however. I heard voices approaching and soon, from behind a pile of crumbling stones, two robed figures appeared. They were Renaunt and Peterson, hooded and encased in black garments. With a shudder of unbelievable terror, I realized that they planned to stage a ceremony, of which I might be a part. *That* was why I had been enticed on this devilish trip!

Renaunt approached me, more than human wrath and contempt glowing in his eyes.

"Ah, my so curious young friend, you will not let well enough alone, and now see what it has got you!"

"Let me go!" I stormed, with more courage in my voice than in my heart. "What is the meaning of this?"

"It means you shall be a living sacrifice to Those Who Wait!"

"Madman! You plan – to sacrifice me in some idiotic ritual? Are you going to kill me?"

"Our hands will be clean, I assure you – you will leave this island alive."

"Then you –?"

"But you will never be seen so again!"

"Nonsense!"

"You will see!" he cried, in a fit of anger. "We are come from the Supreme One of Irem to open the Gate for the Great Old Ones! The stars are almost right again! Tonight, we will tell Great Cthulhu so He may prepare. Soon shall the Gate be opened and all the Old Ones shall come forth to inhabit Earth and the known Universe. Then shall They do battle with Those of Betelgeuze, and – ! – But light the torches, Monog!"

The one I knew as Peterson, with a long flambeau, fired masses of dry wood atop the pillars of the parapet. "You," said Renaunt, "will be the bait to draw Great Cthulhu here, as is written in the Old Books."

Peterson, or Monog, had by then completed his task, and he and Renaunt lifted my bound body, tossing me roughly upon a high pile of crumbling stones.

The ceaseless piping of frogs, which all the while had formed a weird background to the words of my captor, now seemed to increase in intensity and to fill the night air. Renaunt and Peterson were stooping to chalk diagrams, drawn from papers they held (doubtlessly copies from the *Necronomicon* and the other books), on the stone flags beneath me. Renaunt then began a weird chant, while Peterson cowered beneath an outcropping of stone. What would these lunatics do, I wondered, when they realized that their mad activities brought no result? That speculation was swept away and I abandoned my soul to terror!

For something *was* happening – not only below me but all around; on the lake, on the rampart – as the meaningless mouthing continued. The landscape seemed to change subtly under the pale rays of the dying moon; a blur dimmed the horizon; angles shifted and solid stone swayed formlessly. The waters of the lake were wildly stirring, though there was no wind. From all sides, great waves broke over the low parapet, threatening to douse the frantically flickering fires. A stench as of all the dead and rotting water life of the world nauseated me. A strange wind now stirred, moaning, through the tumbled stones, and above the chorus of frogs, Renaunt's voice was lifted in a primal incantation:

"*Iä! Iä! N'gah-hah! N'yah ahahah! Cthulhu fhtaghn! Phn'glui vulgmm R'lyeh! Ai! N'gaii! Ithaqua vulgmm! N'gaaga – aaa-fhtaghn! Iä! Cthulhu!*"

The leaping flames of the giant torches now revealed to my horror-stricken eyes a thin, wavering line across the sky. More appeared, traversing the space above my head. A low, thunderous roar competed with the truly cacophonous chant of the frogs and the incantation

224

shouted by Renaunt, while greenish flashes from the horizon lit the scene fitfully. A great blast of cold air swept over the lake, followed immediately by a foetid warm draft, as with a hideous stench, and an uncouth bubbling sound, a giant shape sprang seemingly from the lake itself and hovered over us without visible means of levitation! Mercifully, I fainted.

When I regained my senses (it must have been but a moment later) the Thing was still there. It is beyond the power of any pen to hint adequately at the aspect of It. An alien, undimensioned entity from beyond the known Universe, It seemed by turns to be a great, green, monstrous tentacle squid; a boiling, changing, flowing mass of protoplasm, constantly altering yet ever the same, having malevolent red eyes opening from every part of its non-terrestrial body, and a swollen, empurpled maw from which issued an idiotic, frantic, bubbling ululation, so low in timbre that it struck one as a physical vibration rather than a true sound.

Great Cthulhu! High Priest of the Old Ones! Carried from His crypt in sunken R'lyeh by Ithaqua the Wind-Walker; summoned by the evil man in whose hands I was prisoner! Great God! I believed! I saw! But I could not die; I could not even faint again. Even now my hand trembles when I think of my hideous captivity as the helpless prey of that hellish demon!

Below, Renaunt was conversing with It, in the same unholy dialect with which he had summoned It (the same, indeed, in which he had talked with Peterson in the car), mentioning such names as Azathoth, Betelgeuze, R'lyeh, the Hyades, as well as the names of the other weird monsters. As his monologue progressed, Cthulhu became greatly excited, quivering in agitation as His great body overshadowed the entire lake, and later uttering a few ghastly mouthing sounds which thrilled my soul with a new fear when I had thought I had reached the extremity of terror.

225

Abruptly, the awful communication ended. Renaunt fell on his knees below the Thing and extended his hand toward the pile of debris on which I lay bound. It flowed toward me, extending from Its plastic self a tentacle or trunk which groped downward at me. Directly above me, the savage opening of what It used as a mouth yawned wide, disclosing a hollow body cavity striated with red bands. In another moment I would have known a thing far worse than merciful death; but at that instant, something intervened to save me.

Bill Tracy – what tributes are due his courage! – appeared at the top of the sacrificial mound, approaching from the side opposite that of Renaunt. Sickening horror showed in every line of his face, but he nevertheless sprang to my side and slashed my bonds with a ready knife. As I leapt up, he extended his right hand toward the excrescence of Cthulhu, which had almost reached me. It recoiled, and the massive bulk overhead lumbered away.

"Run!" shouted Tracy. "Swim the lake! Get to the car!"

We were off, racing madly over the shattered flags and plunging into the stagnant lake. Behind us, Renaunt was imploring Cthulhu, and as we swam frantically for shore, we heard him racing in pursuit. He and Peterson dragged a small rowboat to the margin of the lake and pulled after us. Overhead, the great bulk of the monstrous entity Cthulhu flowed along, lashing the affrighted air with thousands of loathsome tentacles. Fortunately, Tracy and I were both good swimmers, and the surprise instituted by Tracy's daring move gave us a head start.

Upon reaching the shore, we plunged into the pitch-dark forest. The sounds of frantic shouts and the ululant mouthings of Cthulhu (who had evidently joined the chase) goaded us to frenzied exertions.

"We must separate," gasped Bill. "They know these woods. I'll go this way, but if I don't get through, remember: don't go to the police. It won't do any good. Go to Professor Sterns."

Thus saying, he plunged off to the left, attempting to cross a clearing whose edge I was skirting. As he reached its center, Renaunt and Peterson broke from the woods on the opposite side. Behind them, over the tops of the trees, Cthulhu rapidly neared. Renaunt, with amazing speed, sought to grapple with Tracy, but again extending his right arm, on which I saw something gleam, my deliverer caused my former captor to fall. In so doing, he clutched Tracy's knees. The latter, after a desperate struggle to retain his balance, plunged heavily to the ground. As they rolled free, Renaunt half-rose, extending one arm toward Tracy, the other toward the blasphemous monstrosity hovering overhead. He shrieked a flaming command, and immediately the Thing put forth dozens of squamous tentacles which entangled the struggling body of my rescuer. He was lifted, screaming hideously toward the frothing maw of the monster.

Cold with icy terror, I ran on through the clutching undergrowth of those haunted woods. After what seemed an almost interminable interval, the trees thinned and I emerged on the highway less than a quarter of a mile from the cars. Tracy's vehicle was parked near Renaunt's. He had obviously suspiciously trailed us, perhaps becoming lost in the forest, and arriving only in time to save my life, at the cost of his own.

With a prayer of thanks, I saw that the keys were still in the ignition. Moments later, I was speeding recklessly over the deserted highways, caring only to get far from that awful spot. Through the blackest hours of the night I was lost, but at dawn I found myself approaching Arkham. What had poor Bill said? "See Professor Sterns." A short consultation with the telephone directory in a small confectionery told me his address. As I was leaving the store, I shuddered to see the blatant headlines on a cheap astrology periodical proclaiming, "Portentous Events in the Stars – Something Unprecedented!"

I drove slowly along pleasant, treelined residential streets, hazy in the early morning sunlight, and stopped at a decaying mid-Victorian mansion bearing the number I had memorized. And so, shaken in body, mind and spirit, with an indelible memory fomenting in my consciousness and a gnawing ear tormenting me, I lifted the knocker beside the ancient nameplate with the legend, "Professor Arlin Sterns, PhD."

A mellow-faced, white-bearded elderly man opened the door and in response to my agitated query introduced himself as Professor Sterns. Upon learning my name, he grew pale, but civilly invited me in.

"How much do you know," I began hurriedly, "of Bill Tracy and me and what goes on in that –"

"I know," he said laboredly, "that a young man came to me this morning and told me of two college students he believed to be engaged in a very nasty business. He expressed fear that you, his friend, might be drawn into it. I advised him to keep a watch on you, and I gave him a certain bracelet which I felt would give him protection. What has happened?"

I thereupon told him my full story, ending on an almost hysterical note as I recounted my mad flight through the forest and the endless race along tree-lined highways. As I spoke, the savant stroked his stubby goatee, but when I told of Bill Tracy's gruesome fate, he stopped abruptly and muttered, "I told him the grey stone from Mnar wouldn't stop the Old Ones Themselves."

"Do you believe me?" I asked. "I can hardly believe it myself!"

"Unfortunately, yes," replied Professor Sterns. "Before my retirement as Professor of Anthropology at Miskatonic, I had occasion to be convinced in a most horrible manner. But that's neither here nor there. The point is," – his face showed worried lines – "the world, the whole universe as we know it, is in danger of being obliterated in a terrible way in a coming battle between extra-dimensional entities whose nature we cannot even begin to grasp. That is the purpose and purport, veiled, garbled and cloaked in mysticism, of all religions and cults, and, more directly, of the evil books now found in only a few scattered libraries and manuscript fragments in private possession." He turned. "But I must not keep you waiting out here. Please come into my study."

He led the way through a dark, narrow hall into a large room, lined with bookcases and strewn with the odds and ends of a long and varied career. With a serious demeanor he unlocked one of the lower drawers of his desk, and drew forth a folio of manuscript. After bidding me seat myself on a chair near the desk, he addressed me after this fashion:

"These are the extracts I copied from the *Necronomicon* and other books while I was at Miskatonic. Allow me to point out to you some pertinent passages." He passed over to me one of the sheets. I took it and read,

> Nor is it to be thought that Man is either the oldest or the last of the Masters of Earth; nay, nor that the greater part of Life and Substance walks alone. The Old Ones were, the Old Ones are, and the Old Ones shall be. Not in the spaces known to us, but between them, They walk calm and primal, of no dimensions, and to us unseen... They walk foul in lonely places where the Words have been spoken and the Rites howled through at their sea-

sons... The winds gibber with Their voices; the Earth mutters with Their consciousness. They bend the forest. They raise up the wave; They crush the city – yet not forest nor ocean nor city beholds the hand that smites. They ruled; soon shall They rule again where man rules now. After Summer is Winter and after Winter, Summer. They wait patient and potent for here shall They reign again, and at Their coming again, none shall dispute them. Those who know of the Gates shall be impelled to open the way to Them and shall serve Them as They desire, but those who open the way unwitting shall know but a brief while thereafter.

"Now this," said the professor, handing me another sheet.
I read,

Then shall They return and on this great returning shall Great Cthulhu" [I shuddered at the name] "be freed from R'lyeh beneath the sea, and Him Who Is Not To Be Named shall come from His City, which is Carcosa near the Lake of Hali, and Shub-Niggurath shall come forth and multiply in Her hideousness, and Nyarlathotep shall carry the word to all the Great Old Ones and Their minions, and Cthugha shall lay his hand on all those that oppose Him and Destroy, and the blind Idiot, the noxious Azathoth, shall rise from the Middle of the World where all is Chaos and destruction, where he hath bubbled and blasphemed at the Centre which is of All Things, which is to say, Infinity, and Yog-Sothoth who is the All-in-One and the One-in-All shall bring His globes and Ithaqua shall walk again, and from the black-litten caverns with the Earth shall come Tsathoggua and together shall take possession of Earth and all things that live upon it and shall prepare to do battle with the Elder Gods. When the Lord of the Great Abyss is apprised of Their returning, He shall come forth with His Brothers to disperse the Evil.

"You mean," I exclaimed, "that this book – written a thousand years ago – actually foretells what is happening now?"

"I'm sure of it!" said the professor forcefully. "Look: astrologers proclaim that something unprecedented is in the stars. The writer of this mythology claims that 'when the stars are right' those who know 'shall be impelled to open the Gates'. These men come, to frantically study the books, and conjure up a monster beyond the wildest dreams of a hashish-eater. They admit their purpose. What could be plainer?"

I was convinced for once and for all of the absolute veracity of the Arab necromancer.

"But," I inquired, "Renaunt mentioned something about being sent 'by the Supreme One in Irem'. What does that mean?"

"Let me read what Alhazred says; here –

But the first Gate was that which I caused to be opened, namely, in Irem, the city of pillars, the city under the desert.

"Irem is the headquarters of this hellish thing. There, the entire purpose of the Old Ones is known, or at least as much as Man can know of it, and there are some things in Irem that are not even human, unless I miss my guess. Renaunt and Peterson, or whatever their names are in Irem, must be high up, if they were sent on this crowning mission. The island must be a vital spot if it was chosen for Cthulhu's awakening. We must prevent this, my boy! It is bound to come some day, but if we can stop them now, it will be thousands of years before the stars are right again!"

"But how?" I gasped. "Aren't the Old Ones already loosed? How about last night?"

"That was just a warning to Great Cthulhu," said Professor Sterns. "The real awakening can only be scheduled for All-Hallows' Eve; a month yet."

"How can you know?"

"There are certain times when these ceremonies grow more potent; stronger; intenser. The times are May Eve, Walpurgis Night, Candlemass, Roodmass; and All-Hallows' Eve. The opening of the Gate will be a difficult thing. It will shake the Earth, and its consequences will destroy mankind. It is infinitely important to – Them."

"How can we hope to stop these invincible monstrosities?"

"It will be hard; hard! But Their weak points are Their minions. They must be there to perform the ceremonies. And though all the powers of Irem and the Old Ones Themselves protect them, they're only human. No, *much* more than human, anyway – I hope."

During the following month, both Professor Sterns and myself were feverishly busy. I was able to continue my classes at the university, but every day after their termination I hurried to the ancient savant's crumbling brownstone house, which I had come to look upon as not only a second home, but as a sort of mecca for all the world's hopes. It was fantastic: a world of beings living in complete ignorance of a ghastly and unspeakable fate which was inexorably approaching and threatening their very souls, while two men struggled to avert the catastrophe with all the knowledge and skill, human and inhuman, in their possession.

Or, rather, not just two, for I found that there was a considerable band of learned men, all over the world, united in a common knowledge of and belief in the nightmare myth, and a desire to thwart the Great Old Ones and Their minions. There was a steady stream of strange visitors to the weathered old house on Harper Street, and an equally strange flow of outlandish letters and parcels. Professor Sterns' large desk in the library became heaped with neat folios of papers and small packages. What were they? All manner of charms, spells and diagrams helpful against the malignant monsters and Their worshippers. Professor Sterns was particularly excited over the arrival of a large crate from a Buddhist priest in Tibet. This, the professor informed me, contained the Elder Gods' benign sign, carved by Their Very Selves on a stone brought from another world and spirited away from the ancient and accursed Plateau of Leng expressly to aid us in our mission.

Weeks went by; Bill Tracy, whose disappearance had caused a wide stir, was not found, alive or dead. The beings known to us as Renaunt and Peterson had also vanished.

On a pale, sombre October evening late in the month, Professor Sterns telephoned me and asked me to visit him for final instructions. I left for his house, feeling acutely the nervous apprehension under which I had so long labored.

A near-full moon, rising above the trees surrounding Professor Sterns' house shot feeble rays glinting along the ridgepole of the roof, along the old tin spouting, along the banisters of the wide front porch. A queer chill gripped me as I approached along the gravel walk; the house was lightless. Half formed fears stirred uneasily in my mind as I plied the knocker, but after a short, suspenseful interval I recognized the slow tread of my aged friend approaching the panel from within. It opened slowly and I discerned the kindly, bearded face peering narrowly through the gloom. Almost instantly a look of relief and welcome swept over it.

"Ah! You!" muttered the professor. "I am glad to see you. You came sooner than I had anticipated. Step into the hall."

Inside, he spoke quietly but rapidly.

"There has been a change of plans. I – we have a guest. He is to help us. He's – strange. Doesn't speak English, but he's on our side. Do you remember how you lost consciousness at the edge of the lake after Renaunt told Peterson to concentrate? That was instantaneous hypnotism, showing a great development of mind power. Well, our guest has just such mind power, and more. He will be an immeasurable aid to us."

Professor Sterns led the way into the study, switched on the light, and there, standing by the desk, was the Guest. Little could be seen of him, for he wore a long, tightly-buttoned overcoat which dragged on the floor. It had been thrown over his shoulders, so that the arms dangled uselessly at his sides. On his head he wore a large hat pulled far down, and (strange to tell!) over his face he wore a grey scarf, knotted firmly at the back of his head. Thus not an inch of his person was visible. Only once did I see him without all this paraphernalia intact.

"This is the young man I was telling you about," the professor was saying. He seemed highly respectful almost reverential, toward the muffled figure. But what was it he had said? – "He doesn't speak English!" He must understand it, though, I thought.

The figure made a movement which might be construed as a bow, and I murmured conventional words of greeting to it. I noticed that the top of the desk had been cleared, and that three suitcases lay in the shadows. I flashed a questioning look to Professor Sterns.

"We are leaving," the savant spoke nervously. "I have discovered where the Great Awakening is to take place. The information is hidden by a clever code in the *Seven Cryptical Books of Hsan*, but I haven't deciphered it. In fact, we are leaving immediately. You won't need to pack anything. It will all be over – one way or the other – soon. You see, tomorrow night is *All Hallows' Eve!*"

The street was dark, the walk was long, the suitcases heavy. I carried two; Professor Sterns carried the remaining one. Our Guest followed us in a peculiar quiet but gliding manner, unburdened. He seemed shorter than when I had first seen him, but I put this down to a trick of light and shadow.

It may have been half an hour later when we arrived at the field. Under the rays of the moon, dry stubble took on a beautiful silver sheen, and the airplane shone with a pale silver glow. For there *was* an airplane on the field, and in it the professor placed his suitcase, instructing me to do the same with mine.

"But," I stammered, "where are we going? Who is taking us?" "We are going," replied the aged man grimly, "to the north woods of Maine; to a place which I will not name and for a purpose you know too well. Get in, my boy."

Inside the tiny cabin, Professor Sterns settled himself at the controls, with me beside him, while the Guest sat on the suitcases behind.

"I learned to fly," explained the professor, "from Professor Peaslee, the man whose father had such a dreadful experience when those singularly ancient ruins were discovered in Australia that he commit-

235

ted suicide."

With a whine and a growl that deepened to a roar, the motor awoke and in a few moments we were bouncing swiftly down the field. At its extreme end our pilot lifted the plane's nose and we were airborne, climbing sharply to gain altitude and leveling off to streak swiftly northward.

Looking down, I could see the thin line of light that was the Miskatonic River fade into the distance. Silence and darkness (save for the monotone of the motor and the illuminated instruments) closed in on us, wrapping us in a pall of almost sentient gloom as we sped on for hours over northern Massachusetts and the southeastern corner of New Hampshire.

Midnight found us over Maine. Professor Sterns was explaining to me more in detail about both our mission and our adversaries. Some of what he said I cannot bring myself to repeat, for the world is better off without it, but other parts of his information were vital and pertinent.

"As you know, the Great Old Ones are elementals; that is, each is identified with and has dominion over one of the ancient so-called elements. Cthulhu is a deity of water, Cthugha of fire, while Nyarlathotep, Tsathoggua, Azathoth, and Shub-Niggurath seem associated with Earth. The air-beings are Hastur, Zhar, Ithaqua and Lloigor. Yog-Sothoth, who is spoken of as the 'All-in-One and the One-in-All', seems not to be associated with an element.

"From hints in the *Necronomicon*, I can guess at some of the things that will happen at the Great Awakening. First of all, there will be the celebration of rites for days in advance. Of their nature, there is no need to speak. Then, on All Hallows' Eve (tomorrow night) there will be a long ritual beginning at sunset. Then, at midnight, the book says,

'...shall the sky be torn away and from Their dimensions on Outside shall the Old Ones be seen upon the Earth. And the Earth shall tremble at Their aspect, and the Old Ones shall descend and inhabit and ravage.'

"What we must do is to stop that ritual, to which there are two parts. The first 'Opens the Gate' and the second frees the Old Ones to move. If we can stop it before the end, then the fleeting moment in which the stars are in the right position for it to take effect will pass, and Earth will be saved."

"How can we stop the ritual?" I asked. "Murder?"

"That is neither necessary, nor would it be effective. There will be far too many there. Renaunt and Peterson may or may not be there. What we must do is to counteract their spells and charms with our own, and, finally, destroy their lair of cosmic evil by sealing it with the Elder Sign on that stone block from Tibet. But there are many risks. We may be apprehended before we can do any of those things. For that reason, I have these wrist-bands for us to wear. None of the minions of the Old Ones can bear to touch these stones with the Elder Sign on them, but only on that Tibetan enchanted stone is it potent enough to stop *all* evil. Remember, Bill Tracy found the weakness of the bracelets his undoing.

For hours we droned on over northern Maine. The hands of the clock on the instrument panel pointed to 4 a.m. when suddenly I noticed something.

Look!" I murmured to the professor, "there ahead!"

Shifting his gaze slightly, he too saw what had attracted my attention. *Miles ahead of us, a titanic shadow had blotted out the stars, a shadow whose blurred outlines seemed a hideous caricature of the human form, and from the space where the head appeared to be there shimmered with an unholy light what seemed to be two great green stars!*

And the Thing was moving, rushing to meet us; a giant shape, miles high, whose colossal bulk filled the horizon and stretched to the zenith! Simultaneously, a howling wind sprang up, bearing on its wings the sound of shrill, terrible music, as of great flutes or reed pipes being played all around us in the air.

"One of the Old Ones sent to destroy us!" shouted Professor Sterns. "An air-elemental. It is Ithaqua the Wind-Walker!" Black terror gripped me ...

The shadow-like Being neared rapidly, yet our pilot held his course, flying straight at the mound-like, neckless head and the star-eyes.

"We must flee!" I exclaimed.

"No use," said the professor, "this is the only way."

Louder sounded the demoniac music, nearer rushed the monster. For a moment Its flaming eyes shone directly before us, and then I closed my own. When I opened them, the sky ahead was clear.

"We have cut across another dimension and passed directly through His body," breathed the professor. "He cannot touch us because of the grey stone. We are safe!" But just then a tremendous gust of wind threw the plane into a dangerous spin. "He is sending His winds to wreck us!"

Through the black night tore howling, whistling blasts of air, throwing us off course despite everything the professor could do. For minutes he fought valiantly with the controls, but at last a seething vortex of cyclonic strength seized the machine like a huge black fist and seemed about to hurl it to destruction on the earth below. But at the last moment, the winds subsided and the plane righted itself.

"What ...?" I began, when Professor Sterns interrupted me with a whispered, *"Look!"*

On the horizon a pale, opalescent glow broadened imperceptibly, reflecting thin rays upon the mists above.

"Dawn!" The first night of terror had passed safely, but the Great Adventure was just beginning.

Less than half an hour later, our plane landed near the village of Chesuncook. There, the professor loaded our luggage into a car which was somehow waiting for us, and, with the Guest in the back seat, we embarked on a trip very similar (and yet how different from) one I had taken a month before.

The day was damp, foggy and uncomfortable. The pine forests on either side of the road stood dark and expectant, unwarmed by the cloud-obscured sun. About noon, the professor extracted a box lunch from one of the suitcases, but the Guest did not partake, nor did the professor offer him any of the food.

It was long past noon when the car stopped. The grey clouds in the sky were still unrelieved, save for a dull glow between zenith and horizon which was all that was visible of the sun.

Professor Sterns then opened another suitcase and extracted a queer apparatus consisting of a square board with a circular hole in the center. In the hole was fastened a shallow metal tray of the same shape, with a curved glass over it which prevented the spilling of the liquid in the tray. In this clear fluid floated an oblong piece of dark wood several inches long, whittled to a point at one end. On the outside board, queer designs were carven.

Holding this odd contraption level, the professor gazed intently at the wooden pointer. It seemed to turn slowly counter-clockwise, but suddenly it reversed its direction and jerked quickly three-quarters of the way around, there remaining immovable.

"This is our guide," remarked the professor. "It's a kind of compass, but it doesn't point north!"

We set off into the woods, following the direction set by this compass that was not a compass. I took the two remaining suitcases (one was very heavy), and the aged savant went ahead with the direction-finder. The Guest moved unobtrusively along in the rear.

The undergrowth was very thick, and the pines seemed to grow abnormally close together, so our progress was slow and none too steady. I called frequent halts for rest when I noticed that the professor was staggering from fatigue.

Imperceptibly, the shades of the forest deepened and it was night. I began to feel an indefinable aura of evil surrounding these black woods; a sense of cosmic dread and alien purpose, so that I did not like to let my mind dwell on our mission.

Quite abruptly, we came to a clearing. It was about a quarter of a mile across, and in the center was a stone structure resembling a well, bathed in rays of a ghostly full moon which shone from a rift between two clouds. This, the professor informed me, was the only entrance to the most unholy and accursed temple on earth; a place where dark things dwelt with degenerate men, and the site of the All Hallows' Great Awakening.

A flickering light, as of torches, came from the mouth of the roofless open cylinder-shaft, and a faint murmur also reached us from it.

The following events which occurred on that hellish night I must be very careful in describing.

We scuttled across the clearing and crouched by the lip of the round shaft, which rose perhaps a yard from the ground.

"The ceremony has started," whispered Professor Sterns. "Watch the sky and do what I say." He unlocked both suitcases, took from one a folio of papers from amongst many more, and from the other eased the great grey Tibetan stone, with its queer carving, laying it between himself and the Guest.

For a long time, the only thing audible from below was the murmur of chanting mens' voices, occasionally broken by a strange, deep, ecstatic moan. Then, syllables in English floated up to us.

"Oh, Raythore, the time has come. Begin, thou!"

I started wildly as another voice began in chant-like speech. For the second voice was that of Jacques Renaunt!

"*Death-Walker! God of the Winds! Thou Who walkest on the Winds – adoramus te!*"

The sky slowly faded to a dark greyish-green, and the wind stirred.

"*Oh, Thou Who pass above the Earth; Thou Who hast vanquished the sky – adoramus te!*"

The wind grew in a few seconds to a cyclonic pitch, and high in the sky the clouds rushed back with breath-taking speed, as if its force up there were thousands of times greater than we felt below.

"*Ithaqua! Thou Who hast vanquished the sky – vanquish it yet again that the Supreme Purpose may be fulfilled. Iä! Iä! Ithaqua! Ai! Ai! Ithaqua cf'ayak vulgtmm vugtlagln vulgtmm. Ithaqua fhtaghn! Ugh! Iä! Iä! Iä!*"

Thunder rumbled and crashed around us, adding yet another voice to the insane canticle of chant and wind. The chorus of mens' voices welled up deep and strong as a climax approached in the indescribable chaos of the elements.

"*Iä! Azathoth! Iä! Yog-Sothoth! Iä! Cthulhu! Iä! Cthugha!*"

Flashes of light showed the straining sky flecked with lines of glowing green.

"*Iä! Hastur! Iä! Ithaqua! Iä! Zhar! Iä! Lloigor!*"

A loud buzzing sound seemed borne on the shrieking blasts of wind.

241

"Iä! Shub-Niggurath! Iä! Tsathoggua! Iä! Nyarlathotep!"

On the last word, a fiendish shout of expectancy echoed up from below. Why didn't the professor do something, I wondered shudderingly. Glancing at him, I saw him worriedly watching the passive Guest. But all thought was extinguished as, with a noise unequalled since the birth of the world, *the sky cracked!*

There is no other way to express it. The darkness split, shriveled and rolled up, and, from Outside, a hideous and unknown light bathed the Universe, as the Great Old Ones were once more looking upon Earth.

Of what I saw beyond the ragged shreds of the borders of our Space-Time continuum as new, final chants rose from the temple below, I can only begin to hint. I had the simultaneous impression of stupendous, amorphous entities; of fluid hyper-intelligences of dominating universal Evil; of an undimensioned yet super-dimensioned chaos of impossible angular curves and curved angles; of a boiling, changing cauldron of moving, massing monstrosities approached; then, being a mere human being, I fell backward to the ground and turned my face away. What I saw on the ground was almost as stupefying as the sky's ghastly change.

For there in the dirt were an overcoat, a hat, and a grey scarf, lying in crumpled disarray, while in the shadows of the wood a black form was disappearing!

Seconds later, a titanic column of flame exploded from the forest and shot upward, sending showers of sparks flying everywhere. Its base left the Earth and it expanded swiftly, while moving upward at a rate inconceivable. Simultaneously, from the four points of the compass, four similar pillars of fire were propelled to the zenith, where they were superimposed on one another in the form of a colossal pentagram, or five-pointed star, silhouetted against the torn sky and the amorphous shapes streaming across it. I cowered in abject terror!

"Come!" whispered Professor Sterns. "We have work to do!" He began copying strange designs, from the papers he held, onto the ancient stones of the shaft with a queer paste-like substance from a metal tube.

"Now!" he exclaimed, throwing the implement aside, "help me with this stone!"

We lifted the heavy Tibetan mystical stone, which had begun to glow with a curious russet light, to the lip of the shaft and cast it over. It fell inside with a crash, and immediately the shaft caved in amid cries of agony from below, which superseded the former chanting. The professor murmured a few indistinguishable words and made a curious sign with his right hand.

"Our job is finished," he said in a trembling voice. "We must escape the forest-fire." For the woods from whence the Flaming-Being had risen were indeed burning fiercely.

We fled swiftly back the way we had come, but not too swiftly for me to glance back and catch a glimpse of the fiery star vanquishing the beings from Outside, the hellish vision fading away, and the heavens returning to normal.

But the rest of that flight through fear-haunted forest is to me even more nightmarish than what had preceded it, and I shall never again know peace of mind, even though the newspapers babble reassuringly about a volcanic disturbance in Maine and its strange effect on the skies. For the answer which Professor Sterns gave in a shuddering whisper to my question about the identity of our mysterious Guest is forever burned in my brain. As we plunged through the knighted woods, he gasped to me,

"It came to my door one night... It was black and as plastic as jelly... . It sent a message into my mind telling me what I had to do tonight ... telling me It would go with me... I got it to form into a piece about the shape of a man, and put those clothes on It to disguise It... It told me in my mind that It had come from the star Betelgeuze, 200 light years away with Its Brothers to combat the Great Old Ones!"

And as we ran toward the car and the safety of civilization, there came back to me half-forgotten passages from the abhorred *Necronomicon* which caused me to tremble in a new ecstasy of fear and agony of remembrance, even though the Earth had been saved for a time...

"Ubbo-Sathla is that unforgotten source whence came the Great Old Ones Who dares oppose the Elder Gods being the Ones Who are of a black fluid shape. And Those Ones who came in the shape of Towers of Fire hurled the Old Ones into banishment... but They shall return; Those Who Wait shall be satisfied... And together shall take possession of Earth and all things that live upon it and shall prepare to do battle with the Elder Gods...

WHEN THE LORD OF THE GREAT ABYSS IS APPRIS'D OF THEIR RETURNING, HE SHALL COME WITH HIS BROTHERS AS TOWERS OF FIRE AND DISPERSE THE EVIL!"

PLANETFALL ON YUGGOTH

B Y THE TIME the Pluto landing was scheduled, people were tired of planetfall stories. The first human on the moon may have taken a giant step for mankind, as he claimed; but in the half-century following, each succeeding stage in the exploration of the solar system became more boring than the last. The technology was foolproof, the risks minimal, and most of the discoveries – while epoch-making for all the sciences – were too complex and recondite to be dramatized for the man on the street, or in front of his Tri-V screen.

They even stopped giving the various expeditions fancy names, like that first Project Apollo to the moon, or Operation Ares, the Mars landing. They actually let one of the crewman of the space craft – a radio operator named Carnovsky – name the Pluto jaunt, and he called it "Operation Yuggoth," frivolously enough, after the name for the planet used in pulp fiction by some obscure author of the last century.

Of course, the media dutifully carried the same stale old textbook research about how Pluto, the last planet to be discovered and the last to experience human visitation, was merely a tiny chunk of frozen gunk over three and a half billion miles from Earth that took 248 years to circle the sun, and how if the sun was the size of a pumpkin (which it is not, so it was hard to see the sense of the comparison) Pluto would be a pea about two miles away, and how it was probably once a moon of Neptune that broke away into a very irregular orbit and thus possibly didn't qualify as a real planet at all.

The whole upshot seemed to be that here was another airless, life-less, frozen world like all the others not on our sunward side – in which latter case they were airless, lifeless, sizzling worlds.

After the invention of the long-predicted nuclear fission drive, even such vast distances were minimized; the trip would have taken only two weeks from Earth, and from the deep space station beyond Mars it wouldn't last *that* long.

No one except scientists expressed any disappointment that remoteness did forbid live Tri-V transmission, and they'd just have to wait for the films. The fact that a brief on-the-scene radio report was scheduled to be relayed via several earthside beams even drew complaints from a few music buffs.

We had all seen pictures of the ship before (or ones just like it): a pair of huge metal globes connected by a narrow passage, never destined to touch the surface of any world – the little chemical-fuel scouts did all the real exploring.

Altogether, it was shaping up as a megabore.

The broadcast promised to be even more tedious than the build-up. Arriving in orbit over Pluto, the space craft reported no glimpse of the planet's topography, due to a cloud of frozen mist – which, however, analyzed as not too dense for the scouts to penetrate. There was a lot of delay while the first scout was prepared and launched, carrying the radioman Carnovsky, who had dreamed up the Operation Yuggoth tag, and five other crewmen.

Carnovsky gave a running account as the small rocket approached the surface and grounded. First he spoke of milky, churning mists hovering over the vast icefields, half-discerned under their high-power searchlights. Then, with mounting excitement, the crackling interplanetary transmission reported a lifting and clearing of the fog. Next came a gasp of awe and that incoherent babbling which was traced in part later to garbled, half-remembered quotations from the pulp writer who had fantasized so long ago about dark Yuggoth.

246

Had Carnovsky gone mad? Did he somehow kill his fellow crew-men on the scout, after planting a time-bomb on the spaceship before they left it? In any event, no further transmission was ever received from either vessel after the hysterical voice from the scout abruptly broke off.

This is how the broadcast ended: "Mists are clearing – something big towering up dead ahead – is it a mountain range? No, the shapes are too regular. My God! It can't be! It's a city! Great tiers of terraced towers built of black stone – rivers of pitch that flow under cyclope-an bridges, a dark world of fungoid gardens and windowless cities – an unknown world of fungous life – forbidden Yuggoth!

"Is that something moving over the ice? How is it possible in this cold? But there are many of them, heading this way. The Outer Ones, the Outer Ones! Living fungi, like great clumsy crabs with membra-nous wings and squirming knots of tentacles for heads!

"They're coming. They're getting close! I –"

That was all; except that those few on Earth – those who were not watching the variety shows on their Tri-V's but who were outside for some reason and looking at that sector of the sky where Pluto is lo-cated – experienced the startling sight of a bursting pinpoint of light as, over three and a half billion miles away, the atomic fuel of the space craft bloomed into an apocalyptic nova, writing finis to the ill-fated expedition, and to Operation Yuggoth.

But scientists don't discourage easily. They admit that Pluto may hold some unsurmised danger – though certainly not connected with Carnovsky's hallucinations – and it may be best to stay away while unmanned probes gather more data.

Now, though, they're all excited about the plan to send a manned ship to a newly-discovered, unimaginably remote tenth planet that hasn't even been named yet.

The new project, for some reason, has been dubbed "Operation Shaggai."

PHOTO FINISH

(To Dirk W. Mosig, upon receiving photographs of his family)

The letter slid out of its envelope smoothly and from it, into the circle of lamplight centered on the desk, fluttered two snapshots.

Charles Ward picked them up and examined them with some interest. One was a color print of three little girls, winsome with the unconscious charm of childhood. He set them aside, poured another half glass of wine into his half-empty goblet, and turned to the other photo. It showed a square-jawed young man with an open gaze and frank smile, staring rather self-consciously into the camera.

So this was the correspondent he had never met, Kirk Gissom, professor of sociology at a provincial college so far away in America. They had been writing letters back and forth for over a year now, and finally some chance mention of a family had resulted in an exchange of photos, posed against the bookshelves in his Tokyo study, in return for this more reassuringly normal family group.

Ward reflected that his correspondent's face scarcely seemed the visage of a devoted scholar-enthusiast for the work of a little-known, long-dead pulp magazine fantasist. Yet it was their shared interest in the life and writings of H.P. Lovecraft that had started their correspondence, and Ward soon realized that Gissom was more discriminating as well as more energetic than the members of that small but vocal band of "Lovecraft fans" who spent endless hours, and as much money as came to hand, collecting books, old magazines, and random memorabilia of the obscure writer, and issuing pretentious amateur publications crammed with controversies, feuds, self-congratulation and hairsplitting speculative analyses concerning their idol and his literary works. Gissom was serious and seeking, not simply an escapist.

Now how did a man like Gissom come to be mixed up in anything so outlandishly oddball as such an activity? Ward knew from the letters that his younger pen-pal had a German background, and indeed the face in the picture seemed to show a man of patently Teutonic logic and practicality. Not only this, but Gissom was a disciple of B.F. Skinner's materialistic, deterministic philosophy of Behaviorism – hardly a likely person, it would appear, to become fascinated with stories of extraterrestrial monsters, black magic, and sinister plots by hidden quasi-human cults and entities to enslave the world.

The Lovecraft fans on the whole were drifters and dreamers, not a few of them more or less demented in presumably harmless ways – not bright young sociologists expounding such a brass-tacks, no-nonsense world view as Behaviorism. The photo served to focus and clarify this dichotomy, which had been floating at the back of Ward's mind since soon after the correspondence began.

It was easy to see the appeal of H.P. Lovecraft for misfits and escapists. Charles Ward had long recognized in himself several of the traits that shaped Lovecraft's personality. He too was retiring and reclusive – at least he had always thought of himself that way. He too sought to evade reality through old books, fantasies and visions of outer arcana, though his own outlook was basically materialistic.

Ward also regarded himself as an outsider in the age in which he lived; though instead of clinging to a protective home environment, as Lovecraft had clung to Providence, Ward had chosen self-exile in Japan where a foreigner, as a non-person from that society's viewpoint, could cultivate as much isolation as he desired. And instead of espousing Lovecraft's dreary puritanism, Ward had made alcohol a prime factor in his fantasy world, as well as the pursuit of certain less conventional indulgences more readily accessible in the Orient than elsewhere.

But Gissom – a family man (that lovely trio of Rhinemaidens!), a man of moderation, a career man, even an organization man (professors had to be), a mechanistic materialist: well, Lovecraft had been that too; his fantasy world was simply a creative over-compensation for what was missing in his own life, fueled entirely by imagination and will-power.

How did Gissom explain his strange obsession to himself, though? Surely he would discount all such talk of compensation or sublimation as mere idealistic speculation based on the traditional schools of psychology rejected by Behaviorism, which believed only in stimulus and response, not thoughts or desires.

Ward glanced up from the island of light around his desk. He could barely glimpse the looming bookcases that lined his study, obscured by the late night's gloom. Since his transient companion of the evening had departed, the house, isolated in its broad grounds, was totally silent. Not an echo of Tokyo's strident clatter reached his side-street backwater, little more than a village swallowed up but not yet digested by the monster city.

Ward noticed that the wine bottle was empty, and lumbered a bit uncertainly to the sideboard for another.

Yes, how did Gissom explain his preoccupation with Lovecraft to himself? Skinner's theory allowed for only one human motivation: the environment, reacting on the broad general endowment represented by heredity. People did what they did and were what they were because they had been rubbed this way or that by the circumstances surrounding them. What did Skinner call it? "Reinforcement" – posi-

251

tive or negative, presumably.

Now where was there in the environment of a man by nature bluff, hearty, Germanic, and utilitarian to turn his attentions so exclusively to the weird, the horrible, the grotesque, the sinister, the unmentionable?

Ward pried the cork from the new bottle, filled the empty glass yet again with amber fluid.

Suddenly his hand trembled, as if a startling thought (but the Behaviorists didn't believe in thought, did they?) had struck him, and a few drops of wine splashed onto the surface of the desk.

Ward set down the bottle with exaggerated care and picked up the enigmatic photos once more.

Could *that* be it? Was it conceivable?

He drew a long breath, and the extra oxygen partly cleared the alcoholic haze clouding his mind for a moment.

Yes, it was the only possible explanation – the only "reinforcement" that could have turned his logical, methodical correspondent onto the bizarre path he had so strangely chosen.

Then all this fan activity was simply a coverup!

Ward turned, still holding the photographs, and shuffled toward the dusky bookshelves. He would have to figure out what action to take tomorrow: which of the emissaries to alert, which of the helpers to invoke, which of the servitors to contact for the sending.

Meanwhile, for safekeeping, he tucked away those unintentionally revealing photographs to rest for the night between the thin, ancient, powder-dry pages of the *Necronomicon*...

COTTON MATHER'S VISION

I saw fantastic and exquisite shapes that trooped processional in
the upper air,

Twisting their elfin, shimmering bodies in antic ecstasy,

Laughing their sprite-like laughter at the wheeling hawks.

I saw this as I sat beneath a tree that overlooked the meadows to
the east,

And the long grass of the meadow was riven and disturbed as
with a hundred sinuous paths of monsters traversing it with wayward course.

The forest at my back harbored, I knew, writhing its darksome
aisles and shadowed glades of distant shining greens and enveloping
somber browns

The red men's fierce and diabolic god, a blood-smeared Belial
whose bestial rage abated at the blood of new-born babes.

Of a sudden I was myself attacked by formless demon powers that
hovered round: a strange fear and chilled shuddering warned my soul
of their onslaught.

Beat of great, tenuous wings disturbed the air, and strange, invisible whirlings half of the mind.

All around I felt the insidious gathering of Satan's agents that be-
siege our new-found land

And grimly battle with the men who would gain the good for God.

My soul invaded by the power of their evil, I felt no longer fear but
a strange febrile stirring of the senses

That caused me rather eagerly to await some vision than to shun
it.

A singing in the ears beset me; weak and dazed, I slumped against the tree and rolled upon the shaded grass—

And, gazing up, my eyes beheld a phantom, a cursed illusion straight from Hell.

A woman's form stood before me, naked and unashamed, carved of the cool ivory of the women of Persia that cause a Christian to forget his faith.

The shape beckoned in the air without moving; its stretched, tense and ecstatic pose gave motionless, wordless commands.

It was an incarnate poem; a rhapsody composed, surely, of God rather than Hell;

But I knew the firm and rounded breasts had suckled demons, and the lascivious hips had been the delight of scaly monsters.

This whore of horned devils, this succubus, maintained its foul and tempting golden shape before my eyes.

A promise and enigma, an eruption of searching flames in my veins, causing each coiling nerve to writhe in unwonted shuddering and most pleasurable pain.

She smiled; I called on Christ.

The vision faded; all malign and fantastic influences departed, left me weak and sick upon the ground.

The summer day burned round. I prayed my thanks to God. I wept—was it regret?

WHAT THEY SAID

They said all kinds of things,
Knowingly, wisely,
Those grotesque pallid heads floating in a blue mist;
The heads waggled and looked wise,
Pursing their grey lips and rolling up the milk-white pupils of their
large, dead eyes.
They said many things in a strange language I could not understand,
Like the muttering and cooing of doves.
They looked knowing, although the flesh of the disembodied heads
was rotten and mottled and of the consistency of curds.
They babbled and waggled there in the light blue haze of eternity,
And after a while I needed no one to tell me
That they were saying
Nothing at all.

MOONLIGHT

When have I ever tried to catch the sheen
Of the moon's maze of light upon this place:
Shingles of silver, eave-scrolls of grey lace
In foggy drifts that filter down unseen
Through leaves and branches, unsubstantial screen
That, rustling, veils the full moon's peering face—
Hypnotic stare which speaks to all the race—
Urging, commanding—what? What can it mean?

Tonight I try if ever, and I fail
To catch the ridgepole's quick mercurial glint,
To grasp the shadowed grasses' whispered hint,
Or know what burns beyond the night's far pale.
But if someone should ever once succeed,
The moon and he might rest, forever freed.

NIGHT SHADOWS

The shadows wanton night brings in are wild:
They stream across my walls in wheeling rout,
They weave in maze-like patterns in and out;
Their death-dance brings back terrors of a child
Who trembled though the summer night was mild,
And—half-believing—stifled back a shout
To watch bewitched, not as his heart was stout.
But as his tongue by his hot fear was guiled.

But now I see no fancied demon's glare;
The years have bred a fairer phantom here.
A suppler shade, though not untouched with fear,
And with allure that holds the severed stare.
Ah, yes, desire and fear are all too real
As I lie thralled by your sweet, mute appeal.

SATORI

Death when it comes will be
Just like any other bad day:
Too much to do, too little time to finish it;
Diffused attention, imperfect concentration
(The mind veering toward the evening's first drink,
The relaxation in the cool, the kids, dinner and bed);
The downtown noise and stench
Blotting out the early freshness of morning.

Tomorrow must be better, one likes to assume,
But somehow the idea obtrudes
That tomorrow will be, at best, the same;
Only this time there won't be any.

AT THE CORNER OF WALK AND DON'T WALK:
12TH OF NEVER
(Fantasia on themes that came over the TV one night)

Well, here I am (Kadiddlehopper quote!)
Where I said I'd never wind up,
And by what route I came I don't remember—
I dreamed there was a planetary war, as I recall
(Or at least the USO said so),
And I was drafted, or drifted, into it;
The taxes (and the students) were too high;
The loyalty paths were in a foreign tongue.
The Buddy Poppies squirted Prussic acid;
The Texas A&M reunion turned into a gang-bang,
While Teddy Kennedy made a campaign speech
On the third planet of a Star Trek system
Where Caligula had won,
But you couldn't tell the difference,
Since the cultured pearls were cast
Before cultured swine.
But then the traffic signal changed:
It always does, doesn't it?
I'm waiting. Still waiting.

SONNET 1948

That science aids both great and common man
Is obvious: the A-bomb was deceptive;
For science gave to Man the contraceptive.
Thus we improve on Schiller's ancient plant
Not only "all men brothers" now appear,
All women are their wives, and without stint,
Now that conception does not enter in it,
And spirochetes have lost their power of fear.

Man need not covet now his neighbor's wife;
She's his, if he has fifty measly cents.
She will not fear his methods or intents
As long as there's not any hope for life.
And thus the scientists have built our tombs
By purging not our *weltschmerz* but our wombs.

NOCTURNE

(After seeing Edward Munch's painting "The Vampire")

Come, silent one, sing to me
As you coil and uncoil
Your wet hair round my shoulders and neck.
Let the notes low in your throat
Weave threads through the air,
Webbing my soul as your hair has my body.
Cling to tile, throb through me
While I lie prostrate,
Meshed in your mouth with its murmurs of music.

Drowned in your wet hair, ocean encompassing,
Still I see islands and visions enticing:
Temples and tombs of a marvelous time,
Ribbon-like boats awash in a pale sea—
Echoes of voices long sunken in surges,
Rippling of colors now swirling in darkness,
Glimpses of faces deep covered by sea-sand.

THE TWILIGHT OF FAUSTUS

His, Infernal Majesty of Hell,
Seeking whom above he might devour,
Disdains not all the world to search and scour
To hunt out one who him his soul might sell
For power, riches, wisdom—who can tell
What other boons the modern Faust demands,
Since atoms prance bewitched beneath his hands,
And Air-Wick stops each man's unpleasant smell?

"What may I offer you? Supremest away—
Dominion over stars, or over dust?
A means at last to quench your vaulting lust?
Time-travel? Life beyond your fleeting day?"
"Lord... Science gives us these: grant thou the power
That she cannot: survival for this hour!"

SONNET 1949

All, as before, the ancient maze rewinding,
Search out again the altar and the fire
And tread again the measure of desire—
The footprints of a former visit finding—
In olden spells the soul and senses binding.
Is this the same deep-buried, rock-hewn fane?
Is this the ancient praise and ancient pain?
The same light, swirling, coruscating, blinding?

The centuries stream by and still you wait,
Patient yet ardent, in your cave of night;
While we still struggle to approach your light
And ritualize the blend of love and hate.
The ceremony ever stays the same;
Your blood the sacrifice, our praise the flame.

FAREWELL IN LIMBO

Emerging from Hell hand in hand
We pause, islanded by melancholy calm;
Behind us fire and frost, stench and sound.
The depth of our descent, guideless but for each other,
Blind leading blind.

And in this fragile Limbo,
This oil-smooth underside of the poised wave.
Waiting its crash, but dimly aware of its dizzying mo-
tion,
The sleek wave's rush and flux,
We make the great discovery: now we can see.

Piercing the chrysalis, the blindness of self,
We peer about, perceive each other and where we are,
At last know who and what we are, and why.
Our light is the lurid glare of the pit below
And the leaping flare of Heaven's sun aloft—'
The rays meet and mingle: they cast no shadows.

We have come through!
The motiveless, meaningless night of torture,
The sightless, floundering climb axe past:
For now, in the melting moment,
We dimly see each other and ourselves,
Through us the world.

There is nothing to say. And so, wordless, we part;
The wave shatters on the shore and, pilgrims still,
We now set sail on separate voyages:
You to the pains of your earthly paradise,
I to the joy celestial of my purgation.

PANELS FOR A NATIVITY

The Second Coming did occur, you know;
It was in Cadiz, in sixteen-oh-five.
Christ was the son of a Spanish harlot,
Half Moor, part gypsy, and God knows what else,
Having come again to the poor and lowly.
El Greco angels plied trumpets ten feet long
And simple folk came, stood about and marvelled.
But
The Pope heard of it, exclaimed, "Impossible!"
So the Holy Ghost withdrew out of deference.

II.
The Second Coming did occur, you know;
It was in Essen, in nineteen-forty-four.
Air raid sirens sang In Terra Pax
And three of the Krupp family came,
Bearing gifts: steel, cordite, and trinitrotoluene.
But
An American bomb, not scheduled,
Blew the stable to smithereens.
This caused a flare-up in the argument
Between Free-willers and Predestinarians.

III.
The Second Coming did occur, you know;
It was in Kansas, in nineteen-fifty-two.

What the outcome will be is not known yet.
But
We need not be much concerned,
It happens Christ was born an ant this time,
And came to save the ants.
The burnt Child shuns the fire.

WOTAN BROODING OVER THE RUINS

This, then, is all that's left:
Ashes, shards, this ruined shell my ravens hover over,
Valhalla's walls sprawled open to the sky—
Of all I wrought, just these remain.
And why am I left, sterilely
Surviving my dead universe?

I had forgot my dawn,
But thought to have savored my sunset.
Can I then be immortal truly?
(—Worse curse than the Ring's!
Eternity for dull and empty thoughts,
Regrets, red rage, and dead desires!)
Yet I alone escaped;
Love, Hate, and Power, and Lust,
Weakness and Spite, Unconcern and Ignorance
Have perished with the flaring sky,
The pyre of the world: Will alone is left.

Thus it must be, and I must live forever.
If it is so, why then, let's see—
These fragments, cinders, shattered beams—
Here cling some scraps of green—
They're not much to start out with;
But in that dim, far dawn time
I must have done much more with less,

Made Cosmos out of Chaos.
What I have done I'll try once more:
Creation alone can occupy eternity.
I'll start again.

(Note: The Wotan of this poem is not Wagner's Wotan, who is death
-dedicated and *supplanted* by the time of Gotterdammerung; but rather
the spirit that works through and beyond the *Ring* character.)

SAUK CITY: TWO GENTLEMEN MEET AT MIDNIGHT

HPL: I never drifted this far west before.
        In thirty-five years floating on the wind
        I've stuck to parts I knew when I had breath;
        But somehow now I want to see the place
        Where I was resurrected between boards
        And had a second birth that just might last.
        You were the midwife.

AD: Somehow I never got
        Up north of Boston to your stamping grounds,
        The Providence Plantations, although Don
        And lots of others did. I left it country
        Of the mind, the way you made it for us.
        I stuck to my own row, and hoed it too.

HPL: So this is your Midwest, a mythic realm
        As sure as Arkham or as Dunwich were.
        You showed more of Sac Prairie as it was
        Than I would ever try. I knew I'd fail,
        And wasn't interested anyway.
        Life wasn't really my concern so much
        As fleeing life, I think I wrote somewhere.

AD: Misquote yourself, the purists will raise hell.
        But you're mistaken: maybe I tried more,
        But I accomplished less. I spread myself
        Too thin. My style was bad, I wrote too much.

HPL: My style was bad, I wrote too little.

AD: You had a vision so intense, so dark, But

It triumphed over awkwardness and pose.
The things you saw and thought, you made us feel,
And that to me is all the writer's art.

HPL: But someone said that I myself became
My own most strange creation; and my work
Is torn apart now, seeking sordid clues
To what my sly subconscious hid from view;
A damned assault upon the privacy
A gentleman expects!

AD: I lived a public life,
And was my own creation more than you.
The pace was wearing, but it had its thrills:
At least I was my own man to the end.

HPL: I never was. I always fought the grip
Of happenstance, and the betrayer, time.
You saw a world of possibilities;
Made some of them come true; forever froze
One corner of the world, however small.

AD: You froze the universe, made it freeze us.

HPL: What you attempted was more difficult
And more to be admired.

AD: You taught me how
And why a writer works. This much I learned,
But always seemed too busy to apply.

HPL: You are too modest.

AD: I, the roaring boy
Of wheat-fields, woods, and bedrooms miles around?
They call you overmodest, never me.

HPL: Maybe they're wrong on both.
Perhaps. Did I
Create you, Howard, or did you me?

(Note: The specialist reader should not need to be told that this poem was suggested by "Providence: Two Gentlemen Meet at Midnight", which August Derleth wrote after H.P. Lovecraft's death, depicting the spirits of HPL and Poe meeting in the city where both once lived. See: *Something About Cats*, Arkham House, 1949.)

IN MEMORIAM: H. P. LOVECRAFT

I.

From far-flung fields of wind-stirred daffodils,
Pale echoes of the past recall the days
When men, content to walk in simple ways,
By living selflessly forgot their ills;
When tinkling music from fresh mountain rills
Did form the fount from which they tuned their lays,
And fused the fragrances of many Mays
Made Nature seem at one with human wills.

Now noisy streets wind aimlessly among
Walls crumbling and deformed as human souls,
And Reason fights to gain ignoble goals,
Man to his brother and himelf is foe,
And Beauty is to all a foreign tongue:
Where is man from better days to go?

II.

The past was always to his soul a home:
Two hundred years before his time he found
A sweeter and more solid-seeming ground
Than was the present age's lowly loam.
Through decads past, his fancy loved to roam;

Through times whose mild and less discordant sound
The years had mellowed even more; around
The witched imagery of some old tome.

The writer's art was ever his first love;
His life of work and wisdom who can deem
A mere retreat into an idle dream?
He lived the way he chose, and did succeed
In bringing to the world from spheres above
His "life and works", great legacy, indeed!

III.

The gift he had of Poe: of capturing
The fierce, black moods and images of fear;
The landscape wondrous bright or dark and drear;
The fleeting sense of horror on the wing
O'er unknown chasms of the mind; the Thing
Glimpsed from the window, with its evil leer
(The Thing which in that window oft must peer,
As whippoorwills at twilight loudly sing).

Dark past linked to the present: this to him
Formed all the understructure of that art
He used so well for clutching at the heart.
His brain, imbued with lore from ages past,
Brought forth those mystic tales of glamor dim
By which his memory will live at last.

IV.

A scholar-recluse, living in an age
Which would not grant him praise, or even scorn;
Outsider since the day that he was born;
A buried saint, perhaps, or misused sage;
A man with a decent living wage;
A mystic, by Man's brutish habits torn;
A seer of sunsets, and of nights forlorn; –
No wonder dark and fearsome is his page!

A "man of letters' he; his missives found
Friends of his kind, with matching mind and soul,
Others who felt their distance from the goal
As much as he, mistaken, did. And now
His strife is done; he rests in unmarked mound,
While leaves of laurel crown his spirit's brow.

Note: The fans of H. P. Lovecraft's work raised the money to purchase a headstone for Lovecraft's grave. The headstone was placed on the grave site in 1977, forty years after his death.

THE BOOK IN THE GLADE

Through valleys stern, o'er precipices steep,
He wound his way among the tow'ring hills
To where bright Miskatonic's sparkling stream
Flow'd limpid in the sylvan shadow'd glen.
There stopp'd he; midst the thick grown trees he stay'd
And tarry'd til the sun descended past
The forest-sheathéd, altar-crownéd hills.
The low'ring shades did find him poring through
An ancient book of long-forgotten lore.
As stars and moon did slowly rise to sight,
He stepp'd into the centre of the glade;
There he saw standing stones, a ring of them:
A moss-grown group of eldritch monoliths.
Stepping within, he mark'd upon the earth
Strange symbols and designs, drawn in the dust;
This done, he fell upon his knees and pray'd –
A silent prayer, to sleeping deities.
The rippling waves that heard the dev'lish prayer
Full soon swept past by sleeping Arkham Town:
Oh, strange that modern, new and old should bide
Within a distance short in time and space!
Then, rising, mouth'd he primal chants and words
In ugly language born ere earth had whirl'd,
A flaming mass of lava, from the son.
As so continu'd he, both stars and moon
Were blotted out, as by the titan wing

Of skyward-whirling bat of monstrous size;
A shape as dark as shadow, substanceless,
A flowing, giant shape, betentacl'd,
Did flow from out the sky into the ring
Of standing stones, wherein the chant was said.
Nor did it stay, but swift enveloping
The struggling form of he who summon'd it,
Did spring into the sky, as if 't had been
A giant frog caught underneath a cape.
The screams of him it took did echo back
But a brief while, til from man's transient sphere
He vanish'd thus for aye, to cosmos dark.
But in the charmèd circle still did lie
Th' accursèd book, to tempt men to die.

A POEM ABOUT BONE CANCER IN CHILDREN
(Headline: "Chemicals Could Cure Bone
Cancer in Children")

There are several facts that are clearly understood about bone cancer in children:

First, it is always somebody else's children that develop bone cancer, not ours;

Next, if God permits – or encourages – bone cancer in children, it is for some greater good purpose that our fallible finite minds cannot encompass.

Also, certain combinations of chemicals might cure bone cancer in children, if the children will only have the good sense, or luck, to wait long enough before developing bone cancer, until the doctors have it all figured out.

This last is interesting in the unlikely event that our children, through some awful mistake, may develop bone cancer, instead of the children of others;

And in case we do not agree with God that bone cancer is good.

SHOGGOTH VICTIM

S lithery forms of no sane stable shape,
H orribly bred, for horrid purpose meant –
O ld Ones used them for their fell intent,
G uided to victims helpless to escape.
G oaded to rage and roar and rip and rape.
O nly the Old ones knew why they were sent,
T he place they came from, and where back they went –
H ideous blobs with myriad mouths agape!

V aried the wretches whom this fate befell:
I diots who the Elder Gods defied,
C harlatans who confessed before they died,
T raitors whose fears preceded them to hell.
I n one respect alone they seem the same:
M alignant shoggoths sought them out by name.

REVISIONIST SONNET

L ovecraft-lovers lose no love on him;

S carce a crumb of praise do they allow
P erhaps in secrecy they swear a vow
R aging in lust, to tear him limb from limb
A nd send his soul below to vaults so dim
G od alone can hardly help him now
U nless unto their orders he will bow
E xpurgating from his book all whim

D ire are the warnings muttered by the "fen";
E vil-sounding threats each "apa" bears,

C aused by his comments upon "one of theirs"
A nd by his strictures on "the best of men".
M aybe his subject, though, would share his view –
P erhaps *he* disliked H.P. Lovecraft, too!

THE SINISTER SONNET

The ghastly Thing, a gruesome avatar,
Writhes squirming through forbidden gates of fear,
Its horrid feelers wriggling far and near –
An eidolon of some mad, nameless star
Whose shocking changelings gibber near and far.
Midst sad, uncanny woods, all dark and drear,
Alien dimensions flee the faceless seer
As eldritch blasphemies seek out the bar.

Then shapeless, unknown horrors reel and roar:
Amorphous monsters leering in their terror
At entities too fearful to draw nearer,
While sheer stark utter madness bolts the door –
And in that instant, loathsome and accursed,
Cyclopean megaliths reveal the worst!

H. P. LOVECRAFT, ESQ.

H aunter of the night, companion to the dark;
P artner of powers dread and purpose fell;

L ighter of paths that plunge straight down to hell,
O pen to those who bear the Old Ones' mark;
V oice from a buried past of madness stark,
E choing like a bat-filled steeple's bell
C alling the slaves of blackness to rebel,
R ousing the hordes of evil to embark:
A lone, his fervent pen transcribed his dreams,
F illing those tales with words that freeze the blood,
T aking the tide of terror at the flood,

E voking moans and nightmare-haunted screams.
S o fierce his work, believe it if you can:
Q uite kindly, shy, and gentle was the man.

MIST

(an experiment in rhymed and free verse on the same subject)

The cold, grey mist creeps silently and swift
Around the wraith-like house and shadowed street;
Its foggy tendrils float ahead and drift,
Erasing form as they converge and meet.

The arching, dim and ghostly shapes of trees
Retreat into a purple twilight gloom;
The smallest twig and dried brown leaflet freeze
And, motionless, await the Trump of Doom.

*

The mist
smudges outlines
like a wet rag smeared over a charcoal sketch.
It stifles colors
until the whole world
Is one white blank.

MY LOVE

My love lives near the churchyard wall
Within a small stone house,
And when I go to visit her
She's quiet as a mouse.

She keeps the cottage shadowy;
She wears a filmy veil,
And when I try to peer through it
I somehow always fail.

I tried to kiss her once, when on
One of my frequent trips
To see her. 'Twould have been a joy
If she'd had any lips!

UNTITLED POEM

There once was a Poughkeepsie dero
To whom Edgar Poe was a hero.
Buying volumes so creepsie
Kept him po' there in 'keepsie —
His bank balance registered zero—

LIMMERKS

Science specialist, I guess,
Know more and more of less and less;
While generalists who thus deplore
Know less and less about more and more.

Admen of patent nostrums
That claim to cure all ills
Might be deterred by finding
Such signs as "Boast No Pills".

[These were written around 1969 for a projected cartoon-with-poem syndicated feature that never got off the ground; the subject was Youth or The Generation Gap.]

Parent will declare, with shock,
That in their day you threw a rock;
While now, with music strange and new,
It may occur that rock throws you.

Youth is wasted on the young?
In my cheek – guess what? – my tongue!
Somehow we are never told
That age is wasted on the old.

In gentler times the saying ran,

"The child is father to the man";
But nowadays, you can be sure,
The brat is father to the boor.

Long-haired guys who loaf in bangles,
Short-haired gals who boss in beads –
Sounds just like those tropic tangles
Praised by all the Margaret Meads!

FAN~TASIA

I've been to the ProvRI convention –
A fruit of my long-time intention
Dirk Mosig was there,
And bought up the chair
Where the chairperson sat, *sans* prevention.

I've been at the ProvRI convention.
Lin Carter described his invention
To materialize money
In a way rather funny,
While escaping a judge's attention.

I've been at the ProvRI convention.
Fritz Leiber suggested a pension
For L. Sprague de Camp,
Who seemed rather damp
And suffering from hypertension.

I've been at the ProvRI convention
Where Bob Bloch seemed devoid of pretension,
Although such great fame
Has attached to his name
Since he's been in the house of detention.

I've been at the ProvRI convention
Where a mood of considerable tension
Arose when Frank Long
Burst out into song

That continued in lengthy extension.

I've been at the ProvRI convention.
There wasn't a trace of contension
Disputing the claim
Of Lovecraft of fame –
On that score there was no dissention.

THE COMMUTER

H E HAD ALWAYS loved the beautiful. At least, it seemed to him that in the distant days of his youth he had. How long had it been since he had thought of those days? Apparently a long time, yet their image was never far from his mind, tantalizing his writhing subconscious with visions of unfulfilled hopes, stunted ambitions, and warped emotions. Now as he stood in early morning reverie, soaked by the April rain which damply fogged the street, he wondered whether the beautiful had ever meant anything to him at all. The office grind must have taken all that out of him long ago. After all, near-twenty years in the same office with the same stunted, vicious, emasculated little men, was enough to do that and more. The endless procession of blank, fruitless days seemed much more than a mere twenty years, too.

And there was nothing else to look forward to. With his invalid sister to support (yes, these soap-opera clichés were true sometimes!) he couldn't become a tramp (how he'd envied those plodding hoboes, how his mind had followed their footsteps in joyous reverie yesterday, or whenever it was he'd seen them!) He couldn't quit and say, as he'd dreamed of saying a thousand times, Wilson I'm through, you heard me, finished I don't want any part of you nor your petty little clients nor ...

The train was late this morning. He stood on the waterlogged platform and gazed nearsightedly down the empty street with its feathery green sentinels hazed in damp mist. He pulled the collar of his drab raincoat around his ears, shivering. The breeze was clammy and sharp. This grind wasn't good for his health, either, he thought.

He seemed never to have gotten rid of that cold he'd had last summer—or was it two summers ago?—and he often woke in the black hours of early dawn choking for breath. The sun never warmed, and damp cold penetrated to the bone.

The humming of the track warned him of the train's approach. Automatically, he stepped forward and grasped his pass. With a blasphemous clatter, the cars bore down on him. Shaking crystalline droplets from his hat, he heaved aboard and stood for a moment in the yellow lamplight, uncomfortable under the sullen, sleepy gaze of his fellow passengers, none of whom he had taken the trouble to converse with all those years.

His fare attended to, he sought a seat and sat for some minutes in the steadily dampening atmosphere of the thundering coach, without moving, without thinking.

His somnolence gradually disappeared before an aching sensation in his chest. The ache had come often of late, and his best means of forgetting its dull, subtle agony was to concentrate all his attention on some outward phenomenon.

He gazed at the quicksilver raindrops glinting over the smeared surface of his window. The droplets were—interesting, he thought, they reminded him of something. He was a small boy, at home, in the brown gloom of the attic, and rain drummed dreadful and near on the wooden shingles. Through a chink he saw streaming floods of it lash the eaves, fiercely venting the rage of a black and angry sky. Somewhere below, Mother was calling, but this was more important than Mother ... He was a high school student who'd just read Keats, walking in the silver showers of another April, his face flushed despite the cooling rain, while the blurred greenery ahead dissolved into a miraculous mist, and all because of the way the new girl at the library had smiled at him. "Bright star, would I were steadfast as thou art ..."

He remembered the brown spatter-patterns of dust on the window by his desk at the office, and how each mote seemed a speck of gold in the late afternoon sun when he gazed at the pane with a weary, hypnotized stare. Neither the sunny showers of spring nor the grey storms of winter ever washed that dust away. How long had it been there? How long had *he* been there? Twenty years? No, not quite that. A few years before, he had had an oddly certain feeling that he wouldn't last twenty years with the firm, and now, recalling, he felt the same way.

Suddenly, with a muffled, clattering echo of its own rush and roar, the train plunged into the underground terminal, garish in early morning lamplight. He rose and jostled anonymity to the door, crossed the drearily thronged platform, and mounted the stairs toward the station proper. Behind him, the train he had ridden was shunting off to switch, and as it backed and rocked methodically and mathematically, the next train shot past it up to the platform.

He mounted the shoddy stairway two steps at a time, trying to overcome the growing constriction of his chest with bravado.

Ahead was a square of light that seemed to shift and fade intermittently.

He emerged, a little weak-kneed, into the station itself. Its lofty height and bare floor space always annoyed him, dwarfed him, made him feel insignificant. There against the side wall were the same old candy-counter, the familiar newsstand, and the eternal cigar-case. They were lost in shadows—or had his eyes dimmed—rather, the lofty, pointed windows in the front wall shed such a bright, diffused luster over the marble floor that everything was a bit dazzling.

Oh, well. He heaved a sigh, straightened, and stalked forward. The stairs had winded him more than he had thought.

It was almost nausea.

He stopped still in the middle of the floor, swaying.

His mouth and nose were suddenly full of something warm. Weakness overcame him and he slumped to the floor of the terminal, the reflection from the windows rushing towards him across the burnished stone. As he lay there, head pillowed on the hard surface, time seemed to stretch away into infinity. Before anyone could reach him, before a doctor could be futilely summoned, he lived through hours of sweet rest and repose, the first he had ever known, it seemed.

He gazed numbly at the bright scarlet flood of arterial blood streaming from him across the shining floor.

"Why, it's beautiful, beautiful ..."

TONIC TRIAD

H E LOOKED OUT of the window. The early morning sky above the apartment house was a bright, A-Major blue. Feathery clouds arpeggioed it, and the tops of a row of poplars tapered in perspective like a sequence of seventh chords, diminuendo.

He modulated back to his little room, his little piano. Strictly C-Minor; lowered mediant, a remote key and a harsh transition. Here he toiled through the days, spent adagio hours in the old struggle to become a great pianist, to be what his dead father had never been able to be ... staccato, legato, slow trills, scales, arpeggios, even pieces.

Then playing out nights in smoky bistros with atmospheres as tense and turgid as a thirteenth chord.

His lessons had been the only times in his life since his mother sent him to school in the city when life moved appassionato for him; those times when Mr. Feldmann tromboned possessively, as he had for three years, how Joel Markham would be a name to watch in the world of music.

That had been the legato flow of his existence, until two weeks ago. Two weeks ago he had first seen Laine Morton, a girl vocalist who had appeared with the band at the Blue Note where he played.

The moment he had glimpsed her suave, satin-sheathed chassis through the smoke, he had thought of her irrationally as a C-Major girl, a Mozart girl, noble and fine in simplicity, as seraphic as the clearing-up code after a Beethoven thunderstorm.

Sight of her seemed to resolve a dissonance in his life as tortuous and deep-seated as that which pervades *Tristan* to the last note. To a

313

boy of utter inexperience, raised only for music by a widowed mother striving to atone for her husband's failure, the thought never occurred that Laine Morton might be less than the angel her carefully groomed exterior was meant to suggest.

A warning had come soon enough, but went unheeded. A trumpet player, high on pot and thus both intuitive and uninhibited, noticed Joel's adoring stare and whispered, "Hands off her, man. The boss has got her all bought and paid for, and he expects to find her there when he wants her."

Joel had discounted this warning, and had lived for days, worshipful and aloof, intoxicated by the ethereal food of love. His life had become polytonal: a struggle between the noble E-Major of ambition and the distracting C-Major of love in springtime.

That was until last night. Last night after work he had gone to the office of Nick Mattusi, the club manager, to pick up his check. The office seemed dark and empty, so Joel had pushed open the door, which was ajar, to confirm Rick's presumed absence. But as the door creaked open like a sequence of unresolved appoggiaturas, he had seen in the feeble flare of a desk light Nick and Laine Morton in an intimate embrace. The big man's hands were exploring the girl's seraphic body; she stood rigidly ecstatic.

Joel was never to know why there was a gun lying in the pool of light on the desk; nor just why he had snatched that gun and fired at the two forms in the shadows. The effects of his shots he was never actually to know, either; there had been screams inside the office, and shouts outside, and he had fled in blaring brazen terror.

He had come home to this room, sick and dazed, although he dimly realized the pursuers, the police, could not be far behind. Now he turned unseeing from the window's bright organ-point back to his own unresolved discords.

Sounds from the awakening tenants came to him in faint antiphony, like the tuning of an orchestra. He wandered to the piano distractedly, beginning to practice the major scales through sheer mechanical habit. Something, he knew blindly, was missing within him, but what it was he didn't know yet. The old cacophony of loneliness was reasserting itself.

He had reached the middle of Hanon when the confused voices sounded canonically below. The stairs squealed like flights of diminished sevenths streaming upward, but he kept his face to the music rack.

He had a sudden clear vision of what this would mean in his life; of a barren, grey-walled world without music. Then clotted quarter-tones engulfed him, and short, sharp glissandi rippled piercingly over his inner eardrums. When the percussive pounding assailed the door, he began brokenly to grope at the "Eroica" funeral march, then switched to the pop tune Laine last had sung with the band. But by the time the police had forced their way in, his fingers and mind both were wandering aimlessly.

In silence they led Joel Markham away, to face a world of silence. But he no longer minded. For him, life had become atonal.

FOREIGN POLICY

THE ANTIQUE TROOP train, carrying hundreds of tired, dusty American replacements for the KComZ command in Pusan, crawled up to the station landing at Chonju and expired in one last snort of steam. Since early morning, it had threaded its way through the meticulous patchwork of Korean farmland, so fragmented by terraced fields and punctuated with clumps of tiny mud huts as to give the countryside a miniature effect. Encircled by the velvety sheen and regular shapes of the distant mountains, it seemed almost a toy-train landscape.

The American soldiers on board had arrived the day before at Inchon, the northern port of the UN forces, and had found that, due to the Army's inscrutable logic, their assignments would be made from Pusan, the southern port their ship had bypassed. They had spent an almost sleepless night in processing at Inchon, and had passed an almost foodless day travelling. They were dirty, lonely, and a little scared at their remoteness from home, made vivid by the alien civilization outside. The few veterans of previous Korean assignments hadn't made things seem any brighter with their dour predictions of primitive billeting, tough jobs, and harsh discipline. The men were in no state of mind to appreciate the delicate pastoral beauty of the countryside, nor to feel sympathy or affection for the natives.

As the train rattled all day past farm families knee deep in their flooded rice paddies, the Koreans had seemed to show more interest and friendliness than the Americans. Rather, this was true of the younger Koreans. Though the train couldn't have been a novelty to them, the young people had waved and smiled, the ragged children

317

saluting and shouting their one word of English, *Hallo*. The fathers themselves usually straightened from their working stoop and regarded the train inscrutably, eyes fixed in their flat, young-old faces. Occasionally the women, or old man (retired farmers of patriarchal dignity), turned away in disdain from this most un-traditional spectacle.

Here at Chonju, a small market town with neither the cynical apathy nor the criminal zeal of the larger cities, the train made one of its interminable and inexplicable layovers. Immediately, it was besieged by the usual mob of children, tattered and filthy, who seemed to make their homes on all Korean railroad platforms. They swarmed around the open windows of the coaches, begging and cajoling the troops in their shrill, frantic gibberish, or proffering for sale enticing native fruits, forbidden the men for sanitary reasons. A lean farmer of indeterminate age, dressed in the usual rough, dark clothing and conical straw hat, was the only adult civilian on the landing. He sat perched on a pile of woven straw bags, regarding the children with a slight frown.

Directly opposite him, inside the train, two GI's sprawled as comfortably as they could on straight wooden benches. One of them, a pudgy corporal in very dirty fatigue clothes, was intently studying a folded paper.

"This should be Chonju, according to the map," he muttered. "Wonder if it is. I wish to hell we'd hurry up and get *some*where."

His seatmate, a PFC who sat nearer the Window, glanced about and noticed the farmer on his heap of sacks. "Hey, buddy," he yelled, "Is this Chonju?"

The Korean glanced up inquiringly.

"Chonju," repeated the soldier, raising his eyebrows questioningly and pointing to the huddled welter of shacks. "This Chonju?"

The farmer nodded soberly.

Along the coaches the dirty children ran shrieking, arms out-stretched, mouths open and eyes eager. They were not faring well with this train, the GI's had tired of them at the other stations, and had already given away most of the unpalatable C-rations to kids in the last town. Now some of the soldiers amused themselves by hand-ing out empty tins and crumpled candy wrappers. Others laughed at the high-pitched Oriental gabble, and mocked the young beggars in scornful pidgin-English. A few bribed the kids with contraband pen-nies to stand still long enough for photographs.

The farmer watched the saturnalia of the children with quiet, but perceptible disapproval.

The corporal with the map fumbled in his shirt pocket. "Cigarette?" he asked his companion.

"Here," replied the private, passing over the pack; then, with a slightly self-conscious air, he extended the pack out the window to-ward the impassive farmer. "You like cigarette?"

The Korean shook his head and smiled his thanks, declining with a slight wave of the hand.

The PFC, pursuing his gesture of good will, cast about for a sub-ject adaptable to pantomime. "What's in there?" he finally asked, pointing at the bags on which the farmer sat. The man straightened and slid off the pile, carefully opened a corner of one sack, and extracted a handful of the contents. He extended the hand, palm up, toward his questioner.

"Rice! What else?" The private seemed amused.

"They don't eat that stuff, you know," said the corporal. "They export it to Japan."

The farmer resumed his seat, holding the handful of rice carefully. For a while he shifted the white pellets around with his fingers thoughtfully, glancing at them from time to time. Then he held his hand quiet and closed, and after that he slid off the pile again and replaced the rice in its sack, carefully closing the corner of the sack. Slowly he climbed back onto the pile and sat down once more.

"They're funny people." said the PFC pontifically, taking a drag on his cigarette. "The Army guide book says they're proud and dignified, and yet they let their kinds act like this." He indicated the milling children.

"These kids probably don't belong to anybody," answered the corporal. "But I don't see how the guide book gets that stuff about proud and dignified. All the people we've seen here have been filthy beggars, or farmers living in huts worse than animals. They're not even civilized, let alone dignified or proud."

"Oh, they're proud all right, in a way," said the private. "You notice how the older ones look down their noses at us. They don't like us romping around over their damn country. Jealous or something. As if we wanted to be here!"

"Yeah, and after the things we've done for 'em!" The corporal was incensed. "Hell, all the money and stuff we're pumping into this hole would turn Death Valley into a garden spot. Yet it's hardly a drop in the bucket here, and the people don't seem to like us a bit better for it."

"There's just too many people in Korea," said the private sagely, "they can't all be helped. And besides, anybody feels a little sore at somebody they're in debt to. It's human nature."

"Yes," expostulated the corporal, "but they ought to realize they're cutting their own throats if they make us mad. Where would they be without us? Down the drain, one way or another, in a month's time. If we desert 'em, they don't have a friend in the world."

"Maybe they don't see it that way. After all, the country's changed hands five times in fifty years. Everybody comes horning in on them with big plans and promises, and nothing is ever much different. Just more wars and trouble. The people are tired of all that stuff. They're just out for what they can get."

"They ought to be able to see what we've done for 'em, though. Hospitals, food, clothes, jobs—what more do they expect? Yet with all they get, they act surly about it, and just want to grab more. Hell, I'm about sick of 'em already, in two days' time. The dirty savages have got the gall to take our help with one hand and give us the brush -off with the other."

"Well, you got to remember," said the private, "you can't treat them like they were people like us. They're not hardly even human."

Outside, the hullaballoo of the children had increased, as more arrived to augment the siege of the train. Bored, annoyed, frightened, the troops took out their resentments on their environment, as usual. Some snatched at the questing hands below; a few whacked the round, stubbly heads darting by. Others pretended interest in proffered wares, only to toss them back in the dirt, or keep them without payment. Some dangled candy bars or cookies out of reach, laughing at the frantic gesticulations below. The shouts and jeers of the soldiers began to rival the shrill clamor of the children.

A girl of eleven or twelve, somewhat older than the others, joined the crowd. She quickly forced her way into the front ranks, close to where the farmer sat on his rice sacks, and set up a wordless howl, waving and prancing furiously. She wore an extremely tattered and faded print dress, and no shoes. Her flat, wide face was covered with open sores. Much of the hair had been shaved from the left side of her scalp, and one knee trailed a dirty bandage.

"Say," chortled the corporal with the map. "here's one of those gook women they're talking about all the time. Ain't she a sexy sight though?" Raising his voice, he shouted back through the car, "Look at this one here, boys! She's a real beauty. I can't wait to get stationed and find me a steady little job like that!"

A wave of hooting laughter echoed his sally. Obscene gestures and phrases showered down on the children, some of whom laughed knowingly and parroted obscenities in return. The girl, proud of the attention she had attracted, pranced still higher, protruding her bloated belly suggestively.

Suddenly the Korean farmer slid down from the rice sacks, shouting a harsh, guttural phrase. Alighting beside the prancing girl, he struck her across the face with his open hand, shoving her roughly away from the train with his other hand; so that she fell against the pile of bags. Then he turned and yelled what was evidently a command to the other children. They milled away from him in squealing mock-panic, waving and laughing. As he advanced on them, they fled under and around the train, where they continued their tireless flaunting of sweets and sores before the soldiers.

Realizing the futility of his attempt, the farmer stood still for an instant, his narrow brown eyes shifting rapidly over the scene. Then he turned and strode rapidly away from the train, disappearing around a corner of the dilapidated station.

Simultaneously, the revived engine let off a shriek of steam and slowly rattled into motion. Dusk had fallen, and as the train lumbered heavily away from Chonju to resume its trek over the miniature patchwork of Korea, the station orphans scattered with their meager loot and melted away in the gloom of the railroad yard, to await the next, un-surmised train. Only the girl the farmer had struck remained on the darkening platform, weeping quietly beside the pile of straw rice sacks.

THE SCOWLER

I N THE ARMY, if you learn to frown fearsomely enough, others will automatically assume that you possess both authority and competence. This trick has been mastered by many drill instructors, training-company first sergeants, and battalion commissioned officers who, outside the military, would be lucky to get jobs as hotel lavatory attendants or bully-boys in public mental institutions.

The peacetime army in which I underwent basic training, about a year-and-a-half after the end of the Korean War—and light years away from any realization that we would have to repeat the holocaust a decade later, a few thousand miles to the south—was a pretty slack outfit. The recruits (particularly overage college deferment types like me) suffered, all right; but more from vagaries of weather and endemic military disorganization than from any serious attempt to harass us into becoming real soldiers. The system and outward forms of army life were there, but almost nobody played the game according to the rules. Thus we didn't see much of the professional scowlers. Basic wasn't a picnic, but it wasn't purgatory, either, unless you made it that way for yourself. Some of us did.

Strangely enough, the most accomplished scowler in our training company wasn't an officer or NCO at all, but a Negro from our own group of draftees who was appointed squad leader. Harris, as I will call him here, was a buck private like the rest of us, and probably only a few years older than the teenage average. The scowl sculptured permanently on his handsome, arrogant mahogany features, however, made him look years older even than myself, at 24 one of the senior men in the barracks.

This scowl, combined with a contemptuous squint and curl of the lip, was sufficiently intimidating. In addition, Harris had a loud, peremptory voice, which either his family background or his own efforts had purged of most traces of Negro accent and idiom.

These days, he would be considered a perfect recruiting-poster model for Black Power or the Panthers, but in 1954 all that was undreamed of. The Midwestern farm boys, the slum kids and mill district loafers in our barracks could hate him for himself alone, because he was an RA bastard, or because he was an uppity nigger, you could take your choice. And hate him we did.

There were few negroes in our training company, for some reason, even though we'd all been inducted from a downtown Chicago processing center. Perhaps the draft districts were gerrymandered to produce *de facto* military segregation in those days. Most of our men were from downstate Illinois or Indiana, industrial suburbs like Gary and East Chicago.

The only other Negro in the barracks that I remember was a *café au lait* colored boy over six feet tall named, with ironic appropriateness, Sweet: he was languid and dreamy (the exact opposite of Harris), almost certainly a fairy, and you could discuss Keats' poetry or the Yellow Book group or Bartok string quartets with him (few did). Sweet had trouble lacing up his combat boots properly, and never to my knowledge got his M-1 rifle disassembled or assembled again without help. He was nice to have around, though; not only for conversational purposes, but also because he was the only man in the barracks less adept at mastering military skills than I was, and thus took some of the unwelcome attention away from me.

The first time we laid eyes on Harris was the afternoon of the day everyone had at last been assigned to a training company barracks, and finally given a uniform, after endless days of misnamed "casual status" in a holding company, where we ruined our civilian clothes on KP and boring make-work details.

It was just before the evening meal, which at least broke the monotony. We had all been dumped from a truck at the barracks door, our newly-issued duffel bags crammed with clothing and equipment, far more than we needed or wanted. The winter day was cold, and the drab building unheated.

I'll assume that everybody has at least an idea of what a basic training barracks is like, without my dwelling on it unduly: a two-story wooden cow-barn, inside unpainted, each floor lined with twin rows of iron frame double-decker cots. The floors are bare and splintery from generations of "GI parties"—men scrubbing down the soggy planks for hours with stiff-bristled brushes and yellow bar soap that they are forced to buy in the PX with their own "flying twenty" pay advance, because the army just happens to be out of the standard items of issue. You usually have to buy a lot of your own Mickey Mouse dress uniform adornments for that same convenient reason; the consensus of recruit opinion is that the cadre is making a profit off these continual shortages.)

As you enter the barracks door near one end of the long shed, a steep stairway leads to the upper floor dead ahead; the pungent odor of the latrine and the dank stink of showers waft from your right, while the main floor opens on your left, past the rifle racks (at this stage still empty).

We'd piled eagerly into the barracks, scrabbling for favored locations: holding company veterans already, we knew the ground floor was better than the second (you wouldn't be among the last, few outside when the whistle blew, an unfavorable status), a cot, midway in the row better than one near the door (where an NCO could stick in his head in a hurry and grab the nearest man for an extra work detail). And of course, a lower bunk was obviously better than an upper when that whistle summoned you to hit the deck at 4:30 A.M.

We had settled in quietly, padlocking our duffel bags to our bed frames (with locks we'd had to buy with our own money), as we were warned to do , to prevent thefts, and were squatting apathetically on our bunks (a few lucky phlegmatic types already sacked out), contemplating with mixed relief and apprehension the beginning of the eight-week training cycle next day.

Suddenly the door gave a twang of its rusty spring and a bang as it closed behind the frail, athletic form of a Negro who followed his scowl along the narrow aisle, all the way to the end of the row, plopping down his duffel bag beside the last bed, whose occupant was stretched out, dozing peacefully.

Harris shook the man by the shoulder and said, politely but emphatically, "Hey, fella, I got to take this bunk. I'm the squad leader, and squad leader always sleeps here at this end, so they can find him when they want him. Mean extra work for me, so they's no advantage to sleeping here. You go find yourself another bed."

The sleepy farm boy protested automatically, "Ain't no other beds."

"Sure there is," said Harris confidently. "Try the second floor. If they ain't, I'll have another bunk set up right away."

The man grumbled, but got up.

"Leave your duffel bag here till you get located," called Harris magnanimously, locking his own to the other side of the bunk. "I'll watch it." Then he wheeled dynamically, conscious of his superbly proper military posture, and addressed the row of double-deckers in that loud, sneering tone usually adopted toward army recruits and prisoners in federal penitentiaries.

"Your attention, men! I'm your squad leader. Name of Harris. You will address me at all times as Sergeant Harris. I'm not a sergeant, but that's the rules, I didn't make 'em up. I'm squad leader because I've had some previous military training, that's the only reason. I'm here to help you, and, if you play ball with me, we'll have the best squad in the company. That way we'll all stay out of trouble. Just follow orders, work when it's work time and don't try to goof off. Any questions?"

His frowning face gleamed under the bare light bulbs, the carven head of a stern pharaoh in obsidian; the eyes seemed yellow, like those of a lion. It was an impressively regal performance.

Nobody spoke then, but a few of the men came up to Harris afterward with inquiries about the training schedule, items of issue that they were missing and (surprise!) would have to buy with their own money. Harris' self-confidence had at least gotten him accepted for what he said he was.

"Hey," muttered Eschenbrenner, an Indiana farmer in the bunk next to mine, "is that guy really a sergeant?"

"Naw," answered his bunk mate, "you heard what he said. He probably had a little ROTC in college or something, so they put him in charge. He talks like a God damned college nigger."

"He came down here in the train last week just like the rest of us," someone else remarked. "Colored or not, if he has some experience it might be all right. Sometimes they just make the biggest guy squad leader, or a goof-off who flunked out of the last training group and got re-cycled."

Harris had moved out of earshot, and the talk grew louder.

"Yeah," Eschenbrenner admitted, "maybe this Harris guy could help us, if he really knows the ropes."

"Maybe so," put in a smart aleck called Gonfredi from across the aisle. "All I know is that if his nose was brown, we'd never even notice it."

That got a big laugh.

As time passed, it became evident that Harris knew the ropes pretty well, but that he was hopelessly RA, and a nasty, egocentric son of a bitch as well. He liked to yell orders and chew out his men when under the eyes of the training cadre and other company personnel, working that early model Black Power scowl for all it was worth. His efforts to make his squad the best squad in the company were, however, obviously directed toward bringing himself to favorable attention; the men in the squad got the extra work. but no extra benefits.

In addition, despite his pretensions, Harris wasn't really the world's best soldier. He tried hard, and was in good physical shape—more than you could say for many of the rest of us—but his ROTC days hadn't fully prepared him for all the exigencies he encountered when faced with the real thing. But his egotism never let him admit this, with the result that he goofed up quite often through sheer overconfidence, and even goofed up the whole squad occasionally.

He really began to get into trouble when the cadre started picking on him. The old sergeants had noticed his absurd pomposity, of course, and he didn't sit too well with them, many of them being rural southerners of unreconstructed viewpoint, like a large proportion of Regular Army men in those days (the Negro career men now outnumber the rednecks, I'm told).

"Harris!" some punk corporal in the cadre would shout. "That ain't the way ya fold you' poncho. Is that how they teach ya in the

God damned Rot-See? Better shape up or we'll have ta get us a new squad leader."

"My Gawd, Harris," the deceptively soft-spoken company first sergeant would murmur, "Your men are about the filthiest bunch in this inspection. No afternoon off this Saturday—you'll do it over, all of you, and do it right."

When Harris suffered, we usually all suffered, and I still think much of his trouble came about because he was an "uppity nigger", not because he or the squad were in any way particularly deficient. Harris felt such rebuffs keenly but—inflexible as always—he never wavered in his self-esteem and regal manners.

The men, though, began to talk back to him and imitate him behind his back. Some spoke darkly of what they would do to him after the training cycle was over.

"I think we just might have a little GI party for Harris after the eighth week," Gonfredi, a tough kid from the slums of Gary, remarked with sinister nonchalance one evening when the squad leader was up at the orderly room for a briefing on next day's training.

"A GI party? What d' ya mean?" asked Eschenbrenner, the farmer.

"Anybody who messes up things in a barracks and gets his buddies in trouble, there's a custom that at the end of the training cycle you can give him a GI shower—you know, with the yellow soap and floor-scrubbing brushes. Nobody gets in trouble over it as long as it don't turn into a hospital case."

"Well, " said Eschenbrenner meditatively, "I'd sure like to take a little of that shine off his black hide, it's true."

Private Sweet, the only other Negro in the barracks, was sitting on the next bunk, trying for the tenth time to reassemble his M-1 rifle from its bewildering fragments. In his soft, fluting voice he put in, "I don't think you guys ought to take it out on Harris. It's the system that makes him the way he is, and it would look as if you're after him just because he's a Negro." Sweet blushed, or the equivalent. He needn't have felt self-conscious; we never thought of him as a Negro, we thought of him as a queer.

No more was said at that time.

One evening, a few days before the week-long bivouac that was to climax basic training in the seventh week, the squawk-box in the barracks crackled on and—in an unusually audible, static-free transmission (we ordinarily had to send a runner all the way to the orderly room to find out what had been said.)—summoned Harris to take a personal phone call.

Phone calls from outside were of course forbidden recruits in training, as part of the necessary isolation from civilized values, except for emergencies, so there was considerable speculation during the squad leader's absence.

"He's probably knocked up his high-yeller girl friend," opined Gonfredi. "I can hear it now: 'Y'all come home, ya hear; an' marry up with Cindy Lou right away, 'cause that pick ninny ain't a-gonna wait!'"

A few laughed half-heartedly.

Harris was back soon, looking worried. His bunk-mate, out of a somewhat reluctant common civility, asked him what was up.

"It's my grandmother," Harris answered, abstractedly, not bothering to assume his resonant voice of command. "She's sick. I'm going to put in for a compassionate leave." His frown seemed just fretful now, not arrogant.

"Well, good luck," remarked Eschenbrenner cheerfully. "They do say it's hard to get out of here except just in the case of next of kin sick, and they gotta be about dead."

Harris went out again to see the Red Cross duty man somewhere over in the direction of battalion headquarters, *terra incognita* for most of us.

"That bastard!" exploded Gonfredi after the squad leader had left. "I bet he's just trying to get out of bivouac. He thinks he's too good to freeze his tail off out there in the field like the rest of us. Grandmother my ass!"

"Well, it won't work if it's a fake," Harris' bunk-mate said. "The Red Cross checks with the doctor or hospital by telephone. Then it's all up to the CO and this one is pretty tough in such cases, so they say."

"Grandmother my ass," Gonfredi repeated morosely.

But Harris did get his emergency leave, and was gone three days, missing the worst part of bivouac, which began with a foot of snow on the ground that prevented most of us from getting our flimsy two-man tents set up securely.

When the squad leader got back, the ill-feeling of the men toward him was barely concealed.

"How's your grandmother, Harris?" asked Eschenbrenner, in tones of imperfectly suppressed derision.

"She's very sick." Harris murmured, electing to ignore the sneer imbedded in the question. He wasn't even frowning now—no more did we glimpse that stern caricature of an Easter Island idol, in fact—but seemed self-absorbed, almost oblivious of his surroundings.

Early in the eighth week, after the incredible chaos of breaking up the bivouac, we were cleaning our thoroughly fouled-up rifles in the bleak barracks around nine o'clock one evening when the squawk box mumbled something diffidently about a telegram for

Harris at the orderly room. Everybody stopped working.

The squad leader sat on his bunk staring straight ahead of him. He seemed to ignore the message. Everyone assumed he already knew what it was. Somebody remarked, "Ain't you going to pick it up, Harris?" But there was no answer.

Finally the tall fairy boy Sweet said he would go get it. No one objected.

While he was gone, the men started cleaning their rifles again, some of them in a gentle, gingerly manner, as if they were afraid of making any noise. Everybody had half an eye on the squad leader, who never moved.

Sweet came back and quietly laid the crumpled envelope on the bunk beside Harris, who waited a while before picking it up. When at last he tore it open and apparently found the message he had expected, he burst into loud, blubbering sobs.

After a few moments, Gonfredi yelled in a fury, "For Christ sake, Harris, knock it off! It's your grandmother, not your old lady or your sister. Grandmothers are old, you got to expect them to go!"

Harris lifted his contorted, tear-streaked face. "You bastards. She was like my mother. She raised me. I never had no other family. You bastards."

No one said any more. After a while Harris got up and went to wash his face in the latrine. Those who slept near him heard him moaning softly—whether asleep or awake—most of the rest of the night, after lights out.

Harris was absent only one day for the funeral. The army seemed to agree that, as his closest and only kin, his grandmother had indeed been like a mother to him, and it was proper that he go.

When he came back, the last vestiges of the arrogant, scowling leader of men had been erased from his mahogany features. No one

332

said anything to him now, and he himself seldom spoke, but went about his routine duties almost mechanically. As if by tacit agreement, the cadre and "B" Company NCO's started addressing our squad as a group, not transmitting orders through the squad leader. This had already happened in most of the other squads where the leaders were mere figureheads or goof-offs.

The last few days of basic dragged on, and finally there came the long awaited Friday evening before final inspection. We would get our new assignments Saturday morning after the full field display inspection, and leave the camp forever, hopefully, that afternoon.

"Time for our last little GI party," Gonfredi intoned with ironic relish, as he let the barracks door slam twanging behind him with a puff of cold air that preceded him down the aisle. "If you guys play ball, I'll help you, and we'll all stay out of trouble.—All but one, maybe!"

Gonfredi had a long memory, especially for that first endless six weeks of basic when, he assumed—rightly or wrongly—Harris had been riding him.

It was a GI party to end all GI parties, and would that it had. Exhausted from eight weeks of physical ordeals, psychological assaults, lost sleep and dignity, we found it hard to get through these final futile hours of polishing our brass, oiling our rifles, cleaning our equipment, laying out the nonsensical foot locker displays, and scrubbing yet one more endless, ineffectual time those soggy, splintering floorboards so many thousands of us had scrubbed before, world without end.

The company first sergeant and his implacable aides supervised the work this time, since the colonel himself would inspect us tomorrow. Harris, indifferent and apathetic, worked alongside the rest of us, not assuming any airs that might have inhered with his rather ambiguous status as a sort of squad leader *emeritus*.

It was after midnight when the quiet, balding first sergeant grudgingly admitted that it might pass, and left us to our three or four hours of desperately needed sleep.

Harris went over and slumped on his end bunk, fully dressed. I did the same, though I noticed uneasily that Gonfredi and several of his cohorts had gathered, whispering, over by the filled, gleaming rifle racks.

Finally Gonfredi turned around and said in a loud, smart-aleck voice: "This GI party ain't over yet, chums. Almost, but not quite. Anybody want to help us clean up the worst piece of filth in this barracks?"

He moved down the aisle slowly, the others following. Sweet stuck a startled brown face around the corner of the stairwell on the way back from the latrine, took one look, and bolted upstairs. Everybody knew what was going to happen, and a few men got up from their bunks to join in. Everybody knew but Harris, it seemed, for the Negro squad leader gave no sign of awareness as the group of whites approached.

Gonfredi stopped beside Harris' cot and said sweetly, "Get up, you black son of a bitch. You're going to get a GI shower."

He reached out to yank Harris off the bunk, and Harris came up fighting. Gonfredi expected it, though, and grappled his arms. The others moved in to help.

Harris was strong, and he fought with berserk desperation, as if for his life, but he was no match for half a dozen or more. They pinned him, writhing, and tore off his clothes. When he began to bellow, Eschenbrenner gagged him with his own undershorts. The yelling gang dragged Harris' naked obsidian body, gleaming with sweat, down the aisle toward the latrine and showers.

"Get the GI soap!" someone shouted. "Get the scrub-brushes! Scrape the God damned hide off of him!"

"Watch out for his face," a cautious type kept advising. "Don't break the skin on his face!"

The struggling group disappeared, the latrine door banged, and for a long time a ghostly, echoing uproar—bleats, shouts, caterwauling—resounded through the barracks. Some of the other men curious, got up and went into the latrine, but came back soon, shaking their heads.

"I wouldn't want to be in that black bastard's skin," one of them said softly. "Know what he's doing? Just kind of crouching down in the shower crying while they scrub him. All the fight's gone out of our high-and-mighty squad leader, that's for sure."

Listening to the noises from the latrine, I had no desire to go in and see for myself.

After about fifteen minutes, they brought Harris back, sobbing and moaning, his naked body wrapped in a poncho. A few drops of blood fell to the clean floor behind him, which someone thoughtfully mopped up with a rag. There would be an inspection, after all, in the morning.

I was near enough when they put Harris back in his bunk to hear Gonfredi tell him, "Now, keep that poncho on all night. You wouldn't want to dirty your bed the last day. And if you know what's good for you, don't tell anybody about this. We can still see to it that somebody's waiting for you outside the camp tomorrow afternoon."

I was near enough, too, to hear Harris moaning in the night, through those few hours before the whistle blew at 4 A.M. and we all wearily hit that particular deck for the last time.

Twelve hours later we were out of there, on our way to furlough and then further training or duty stations, and I don't suppose anybody in "B" Company ever saw anybody else from it again, or wanted to. But I still wonder why we all hated Harris so much, as we all certainly did—even those of us who avoided the final GI party, and felt sorry for him on our own terms (a cheap, sentimental, there-but -for-the-grace-of-God kind of sympathy) when he cried at the death of his grandmother.

Did we hate him simply because he was a Negro, or because he was arrogant, a sort of avenging Black Power angel ahead of his time? Did we hate him because he was army-all-the-way, as we adamantly refused to be? Did we hate him for the depth of his sorrow, for the height of his Miltonic pride, feelings whose desperate inner urgency we sensed somehow that we could never match?

Or did we hate him, some of us, because we secretly admired him, and yet realized that after all, he really wasn't especially worthy of our covert, grudging respect?

I wish I knew.

I hadn't thought about Harris more than momentarily in over fifteen years, and then the other day I found myself wondering where he was and what he is doing now.

I suddenly began hoping with an urgency I couldn't explain, that wherever he is he no longer needs that scowling mask he adopted for the army, in a vain attempt to prove he wasn't human like the rest of us.

We all hated him, it's true; but perhaps it was only because at first he seemed stronger than we were, so that we secretly envied him; and then, at the last, he proved weaker.

Anyway I hope that by this time, if somehow we chanced to meet and recognize each other, things would have changed enough that we could have a few laughs, and a relaxed drink, over old times.

But then again, maybe he is scowling still.

AMONG THE SAND DUNES AT CRANE ROCK POINT

T HE KOREAN COASTLINE on the Yellow Sea, facing China across 200 miles of shallow water that is closer to grey-green than yellow during winter months, is perhaps a strange place to find oneself in the middle of December. The countryside is rough and austere, the roads marginal, and the only signs of civilization one sees are farm villages of straw-thatched houses, few of them large enough even to boast tiny street-side stores, schools, or government rice warehouses.

Some of the people still wear the old native costume, consisting of baggy white knickers and loose jackets for men and long, high-waisted skirts with short, flared blouses for women. One doesn't see many people, except occasionally in work gangs engaged on off-season construction projects under the government's ambitious New Community Movement. The rice and barley fields lie fallow, and spring seems a long way off.

This part of the coast is hilly and lightly wooded with conifers. The coastline is deeply indented, with capes, coves, and stretches of rock strewn beach interspersed with a few broad salt flats. A visiting foreigner is virtually unknown, yet here I found myself on a dull December day that threatened snow and then relented, not once but many times.

As an American living in Seoul, I have been caught up in the frenzied economic expansion during the 1970's run especially by the fever of land speculation that swept over the nation like an epidemic in recent years.

True, as a foreigner I cannot own land except for private residential purposes; but as a travel writer and tourism publicist, I had been engaged by a small group of Korean investors to serve as advisor in the selection of some land that a Western eye might consider suitable for future resort development, but that was presently undervalued since Koreans did not so consider it. This is why I was jolting over these rough mountain roads sixty miles or so South of Seoul.

The place I was heading for was a rugged, convoluted peninsula usually called Mallipo by foreigners, after the principal summer resort located there, but my goal was an equally beautiful beach named Hakampo, or Crane Rock Point, where our group had bought several acres of property in the hope that another such resort might someday burgeon there, causing the small investment to increase in value as much as tenfold. Stranger things had happened and quickly, in the overheated Korean economy of only a few years back.

The original property purchase, a rooky bluff forty feet or so above an island-dotted sea that one of my better-travelled partners had compared with the view from Capri, was not large enough to bring us the windfall that we hoped for, so the plan was to accumulate adjacent parcels of land gradually from the farmers who owned most of it, and who had more use for ready cash than for scenic real estate that was only marginally cultivable. It was a suitable site for future luxurious villas or even a hotel, or so we assumed.

There were several reasons why I was making the trip in December. One was that the young farmer I had asked to be on the lookout for more land, in return for our permission to keep growing some barley on the fields we already owned, had written me that desirable property was now up for sale; and winter is a time for low land prices. Another was that I wished to make one last trip in my old car before buying a new one to keep the new car off those Hakampo roads as long as possible.

338

The only passenger cars a private person who is not vastly rich can afford to own in Korea are locally-made small sedans modeled on English Fords or Fiats, which with taxes cost about $5,000 each. Roads of the Hakampo sort had, I felt sure, worn out my old car before its time; but those roads were also the reason land there was so cheap—paving would send up real estate prices rapidly, and we hoped that would wait until our own land purchases were complete.

The party consisted of myself, my driver and an obliging young Korean who went along for the ride to act as interpreter. It took us almost an hour of lurching and plunging after leaving the serviceable dirt road at Taean to traverse the twenty or so kilometers to Hakampo, bouncing along past snow-dusted mountains furred by dark pine woods. The sky was still overcast and the wind biting. The landscape distilled a subtle, pastel beauty of desolation, not of the kind we hoped would someday attract droves of vacationers to the beach in summer.

Ever since Taean, the volatile young driver had been cursing the bad roads in Korean under his breath, a procedure designed to inform me that if something went wrong with the car, it would be my fault for taking it on such a fool's errand.

The closest approach by vehicle to our property was the cow-path running past the village of a huddled half-dozen huts where the man who had written me lived. When we pulled up at the entrance to the village lane, I noticed with some misgiving that a funeral seemed to be in the offing: a wooden catafalque, decorated with colored paper streamers and Buddhist icons, rested in the midst of a small assemblage outside one of the farmhouses. This was the palanquin that served as hearse, which would later receive the coffin and be borne on the shoulders of villagers to the grave site.

The house of mourning was not that of the farmer I knew, but in such a small settlement any funeral is an important, all-absorbing community event.

We parked the car and alighted, picking our way among chickens pecking amidst strewn straw, passing and decorously ignoring the funeral palanquin, up to the roofed wooden gate in the high clay-wattle wall around the house I remembered. The gate had a string of dried red peppers stretched above it, so we knew that a boy baby had been born recently—perhaps to the wife of the man I was looking for, though the L-shaped, single-story mud-walled house looked large enough for several families.

I suddenly realized during the trip that I had forgotten to bring along the man's letter, and didn't remember his given name, but the interpreter felt no awkwardness in simply asking the old woman who answered the gate if Mr. Cho was home, since given names are seldom used conversationally in Korea. Her answer, as relayed to me, was daunting: "Everyone in this town is named Cho."

So this was one of those single-clan villages, where the girls married out and the boys brought in wives and stayed.

The next piece of information was even more discouraging: the deceased person whose funeral impended was the mother, aunt, grandmother or great-aunt of nearly all the villagers; the clan's reigning dowager, in fact, just passed away at an imposing age.

Surely this was the worst day in decades for an intruding foreigner to come here prying about to buy land! But the trip had taken five hours, and gas costs $1.70 a gallon in Korea these days. I had to make some attempt to carry out my errand.

The old woman escorted us politely into a clay-floored room heated by flues from underneath, where we squatted on cushions after removing our shoes on the elevated wooden porch just outside the door. This chamber, like all traditional Korean rooms was small,

340

clean, and cluttered, there being no concealed storage space except a wardrobe. A single narrow window was placed high up.

The woman immediately brought in a low serving table with several dishes: cooked spinach in vinegar, a stew of salted fish, and a bowl of cloudy rice beer that looked like sour milk, all of it icy cold. The food was such as would be offered any guests, even unexpected ones, the liquor was added for the wake and funeral festivities. She then promised to try finding us a Cho, though they were naturally all very busy and scarce.

Not long afterwards, a stocky old man entered, wearing padded white winter clothes and a mourning cap of coarse beige-colored un-dyed ramie cloth. He was not the person I had come to see, and I never found out whether he was the husband of the dead woman, her son or nephew, the father of the farmer I was looking for, or some other relative. We were lucky to get any adult Cho under the circumstances, and in ceremonious Korean conversations it takes so long to pry loose any information that I felt it better to seek more practical data first.

As it was, everyone had to sample the food and drink upon repeated urging, and the whole process of politeness and hospitality took about half an hour, eliciting what might have been covered more succinctly in five minutes.

The upshot was that the old man really couldn't decide who I was looking for; he himself didn't know of any land for sale; but he would send for the only man in these parts who dealt in such matters. We expressed our gratitude.

At this point I had another premonition. The year before when I was negotiating for the original land purchase, I had met a genially bibulous jack-of-all-trades named Chung at the nearby fishing village, who claimed to be a real estate agent. All he seemed interested in selling me, though, was a bleak range of useless, undulating sand dunes just off the beach. Though I discouraged him forcefully, somehow I never failed to encounter him when I visited this area, and he always tried to sell me the same sand dunes. Now I had a feeling that I wouldn't manage to miss meeting him this time either.

We sipped rice beer and nibbled the chilly snacks for a while, and then there was a commotion on the wooden porch outside. I was not especially elated over my hunch proving right when Mr. Chung entered in a reek of rice wine and turned upon me his formidable Punch-like grin. Our elderly host prudently refrained from offering him any of the funeral liquor, but he helped himself unasked to the spinach and soupy fish.

I knew that I was trapped by Korean etiquette—not out of any obligation to Mr. Chung, but in consideration of our host, the elder Cho, who had taken the trouble to send for him. It was like reading rehearsed dialogue to ask Mr. Chung the inevitable questions and have the expected answers translated back: no, he could not identify the man I sought (I damned myself again for forgetting his letter); no, he did not know any land for sale on this beach, but he did have some prime property to show me a little further on.

In due course all of us except Mr. Cho, who excused himself to attend to funeral duties, were back in the car, gyrating over even rougher roads, and soon we were out in that biting wind near the slithering surf of a grey ocean under a grey sky, looking at those eternal sand dunes of Mr. Chung again, very little improved by the hazy snow that started to fall once more.

But after Mr. Chung had finally been convinced again that this was not the kind of property I coveted, he became more co-operative, remarking that on second thought he believed he knew which member of the Cho tribe I was looking for, and declaring that he could find the man for me, even on this inauspicious day.

We got into the car and joggled our way back past the farm village, the driver continuing the monologue muttered in Korean under his breath intended to emphasize the fact that navigating roads like this was not his idea, and it would not be his fault when the car broke down and stranded us here.

As we went by the village, I noticed that the funeral procession was now actually under way, the coffin having been placed on the decorated palanquin, which was then hoisted onto the shoulders of bearers and carried along low dikes separating the frozen rice paddies to the place of burial—not a cemetery, but an auspicious spot on a hillside, selected for the deceased according to abstruse divinations by a fortune-teller practicing the ancient art of geomancy.

I had no idea where or how far we were going, but in a few seconds the car stopped at Mr. Chung's grunted instructions and he sprang out, vigorously kinetic as usual, bounding through the underbrush up a roadside slope. Soon he was among the pines on the hillside, approaching a knot of men I could barely see.

"What's he doing up there?" I asked the interpreter.

"The fellow you want to meet is up there, in charge of the grave digging," the young man answered blandly. "The dead lady is his grandmother."

It was too late to stop this enormity now. The funeral procession was actually approaching, ritual moans drifting ahead of it from mourners well fortified against their grief by the strong rice beer. The young farmer, whose face I recognized under his peculiar chef's-cap mourning hat, was plunging down the hillside with Mr. Chung. I was a guest, and must be looked after even at a time like this.

I drew a deep breath. After all, I had an obligation to my fellow investors; my return trip could not be delayed, I had spent a lot of time and money getting here; and the horrendous damage to propriety and common decency had already been done.

(Korean friends assured me later that much of the guilty chagrin I felt was in my own hypersensitive Western mind. "Koreans live in such close, crowded conditions that they're used to strange, awkward things happening unexpectedly", as the interpreter put it.)

I hardly took time to apologize for the intrusion, and didn't inquire about the new boy baby at all, before launching my inquiry about the land for sale he had written me about. Back came the answer: oh, that land was sold some time ago, since I hadn't come down promptly; I could see where it was from here. (Cho pointed across the road to some distant wooded back slopes on the landward side of the beach bluffs that our group would not have been much interested in anyway.)

By now, the bier had arrived with its retinue, and we were forced to move on or else directly obstruct the obsequies. I thanked Mr. Cho and expressed condolences with telegraphic terseness, assuring him that we were still interested in additional real estate, and reiterating that I would write him a more detailed description of our exact needs. We departed with dispatch as Mr. Chung melted away in the crowd and Mr. Cho scrambled back up the hill to finish getting his grandmother's grave ready for its steadily approaching occupant.

All the way back to Seoul the interpreter slept, and all the way back to the superhighway at Chowan my driver cursed the roads methodically under his breath in Korean, to show it wouldn't be his fault if the car broke down. Koreans are an ancient, adaptable people, used to taking eccentric strangers in stride, I thought to myself.

Two months passed, and another letter arrives from farmer Cho at Crane Rock Point. It seems he has located some highly desirable land for sale and urges me to come down soon to see it.

When I have my answer to his letter translated, I must be very sure that it makes use of the clearest and most correct Korean expression for "sand dunes". I am not going to risk the new car on a second fool's errand if I can help it.

But somehow I fatalistically believe that I'll wind up out there on the beach at Hakampo, with tipsily grinning Mr. Chung, looking at those shifting, arid sands once again, and listening to the driver mutter about the folly of taking a new car over roads like those.

Maybe it would be better if I gave in and bought those sand dunes next time. After all, this is Korea and one has to follow the customs of the country.

If I don't, the new car will probably break down on the trip back; though whether this would be the doing of the spirit of the old dowager whose funeral I nearly disrupted, I am not quite sure.

THREE SONNETS BY H. P. LOVECRAFT
FOR VOICE AND PIANO
(The Messenger, Nyarlathotep and Star Winds)

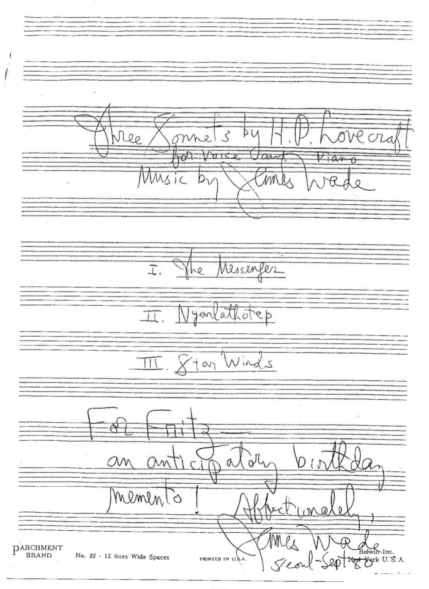

THREE SONNETS BY H. P. LOVECRAFT FOR VOICE AND PIANO

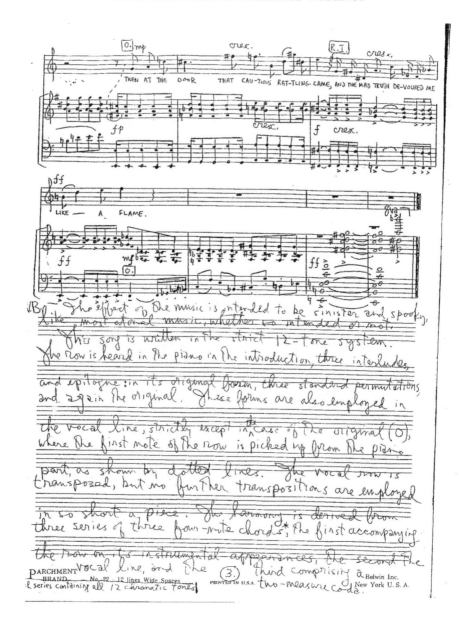

PARCHMENT BRAND   No. 22 - 12 lines Wide Spaces   PRINTED IN U.S.A.   Belwin Inc. New York U.S.A.

351

THREE SONNETS BY H. P. LOVECRAFT FOR VOICE AND PIANO

This setting is dedicated to Fritz Leiber, who among other insights embodied in his essay "A Literary Copernicus" (Something About Cats, Arkham House, 1949) clarified the meaning and symbolism of Nyarlathotep in Lovecraft's work. The suave, insinuating, faintly 'Oriental' march theme in this song is indebted to Leiber's formulation. It is my birthday tribute to him, in honor of 70 productive years.

PARCHMENT BRAND   No. 22 - 12 lines Wide Spaces   ⑦ PRINTED IN U.S.A.   Belwin Inc. New York U. S. A.

THREE SONNETS BY H. P. LOVECRAFT FOR VOICE AND PIANO

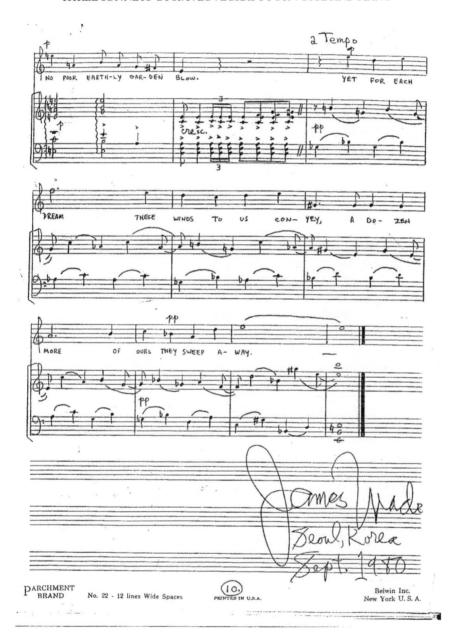

PARCHMENT BRAND   No. 22 - 12 lines Wide Spaces   (10.) PRINTED IN U.S.A.   Belwin Inc. New York U. S. A.

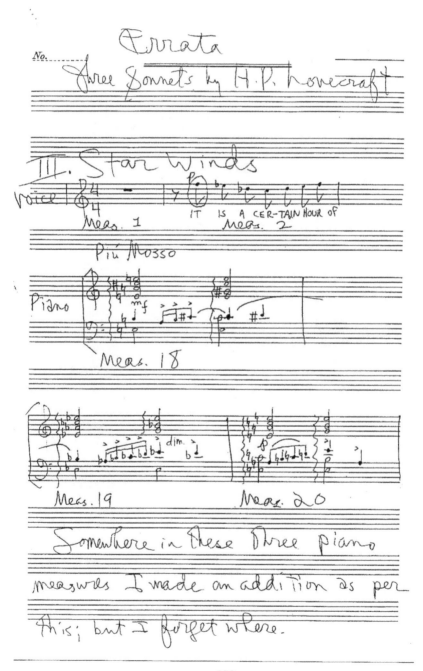

FILM REVIEW: SPIRITS OF THE DEAD

*S*pirits of the Dead, now haunting the military movie circuit, is pur-portedly an episode film based on Poe stories, as adapted by three famous European directors who had nothing better to do that day.

First comes "Metzengerstein," a medieval Gothic photographed amid enchanting surroundings by Roger Vadim, who confuses deca-dence with dullness and destiny with ennui. The perverse antics of wicked aristocrats on view resemble nothing so much as high school daydreams of dissolute doings from the Yellow Nineties. Jane Fonda reminds us just how vacuous a beautiful woman can be.

Next the classic "William Wilson," subtle parable of a divided psyche, is mauled by Louis Male into a sordid account of undergradu-ate sadism.

Both these episodes underscore the peculiar propensity of the French to treat simple, simpering sado-masochism as profound art, exemplified by the critical acclaim for *The Story of O*, some of Genet, and other filth for filth's sake currently fashionable. (Poe with his mild necrophilia may have been sick, but comes off as a Boy Scout in this company.)

The films is enlivened by those peculiarly soulless, artificial voices always called in to dub English in foreign moves.

The third episode, though, is a fascinating sleeper. Federico Felli-ni, signed to do the grotesque comic tale "Never Bet the Devil Your Head," simply scrapped the Poe story and turned out a typical Fellini vision of modern hell. Since we'll never see his *Satyricon* here, this for-ty-minute shocker may serve as an adequate digest version of it.

Terence Stamp, his face that of a ravaged angel, superbly portrays a hollow, drunken has-been British movie star called to Rome to star in "a, parable of the Redemption, interpreted as a Western." His phantasmagoric experiences with airport press photographers, a TV interview, and a wild Academy Awards dinner Italian style are inter-cut with his obsessive private vision pf the devil: a fey little girl grinning lecherously through tousled blonde hair and grasping a white basketball in gnarled, nail-polished hands.

The visual impact of all this is stunning, what with vertiginous color filters and dissolves, a horrid gallery of menacing Fellini freaks, and remorselessly visceral cutting and editing of sheer photographed nightmare.

The last scene, as Stamp goads his new Ferrari in a mad, suicidal race to escape the phantom, is overlong, and the last few moments unpleasantly explicit; but this, anyway, is an authentic though horrible vision of life, not a snickering essay in slick pornography. In other words, it is Poesque, unlike the preceding sections, and will be shown detached in Fellini retrospectives for many years.

Take our advice and stroll into the theater about three quarters of an hour before the picture is over.

You won't have missed a thing.

REVIEW: MULLIGAN, COME HOME!

I t's a bit late it the game to claim it as a discovery, but during the course of desultory reading we recently located what is probably the first science fiction story involving Korea. It's called "Mulligan, Come Home!" and it appeared in the February, 1966 issue of *Galaxy* magazine.

The author is Allen Kim Lang, who elsewhere admits having done time with the military in Korea — the Kim in his name was added in honor of good friends here, he says.

This story is a typical and not very memorable future tale, of the zany-romp variety we were never very fond of. A pixie-like hero is being sought all over and beyond the world for various peccadilloes. He is finally traced to Korea, where he persuades the Korean leaders, whose chauvinism has caused them to adopt French as second language and to purchase the latest space-ship at astronomical cost as a *force de frappe* (this was published in the heyday of Gaullism, remember), to lend him their rocket, on the excuse that he has found prototype Silla Dynasty celadon on one of the moons of Jupiter, and can thus prove that Tangun was the son of an extraterrestrial visitor, which would extend the pedigree of Korean royalty even further back.

He takes off with the "nubile daughter" of the President of Korea (year is 2002, by the way), and that ends the Korean part of the tale. The Tan-gun myth is told in some detail, but — aside from the fact that Silla made no celadon — kimchi is described as containing soy sauce, and "Auld Lang Syne" is again mistaken for "the Korean *chant national*."

It's a first, but we can hope perhaps for better.

BOOK REVIEW: THE GREEN MAN

The Green Man by Kingsley Amis. New York: Harcourt, Brace & World, Inc., 1970 253 pp.; $5.95.

Kingsley Amis, who started out with a bang as a satirist in *Lucky Jim*, and then ran out of gas in such torpid, flaccid books as *One Fat Englishman*, seems to have taken second wind from his secondary interest in science fiction and fantasy.

Certainly *The Anti-Death League* of a few years back was an intriguing exercise in extrapolation, and his latest hovel, *The Green Man*, is a solid achievement in the updating of supernatural themes, though it is not quite the kind of ghost story one reads the kiddies around the Xmas hearth.

The Green Man is a rustic English inn run by an aging, alcoholic hypochondriac with an alienated nymphet daughter, a neglected second wife, and a mistress he is trying to talk into joining a mini-orgy along with the wife.

The Green Man is also a legendary arboreal monster, creature of the 17th-century Satanist who built the house, and whose ghost appears to the present owner, Maurice Allington, at moments of stress, when no one is around to verify. (Everyone knows that old Maurice is about at the stage of seeing things anyway, since he puts away a quart of Scotch a day.)

The ghost scares Allington's Octogenarian father to death; later, a message from the ancient wizard's journal sends our tipsy hero on a graveyard quest for the silver talisman that will permit the ghost to reincarnate itself — presumably in Allington's body and resume his interrupted career of debauching young girls and devil-worship.

So far, the plot is like the basic format of an M. R. James or H. R. Wakefield spook story, though these gentlemen knew rather better than Mr. Amis how to wring the chills and shudders from such situations.

Mr. Amis' touch is lighter, but it is deft. He is also more serious in purpose. He concerns himself, with up-to-date frankness, over the sexual obsessions of his adroitly sketched characters; the foibles of the day — including an effete agnostic clergyman reading a service of exorcism with vast condescension — and various philosophical questions, expounded in a dialogue between the hero and no less than God, personified as a bored young dandy who can't break his own rules against precognition. (Whether the author himself believes the vague oddish theory of personal immortality put forward is not apparent.)

The author, like most satirists, may be a reactionary himself; but his dependence upon traditional trappings like exorcism and crucifixes jars a bit with the Mod atmosphere of the tale. Surely a modern-day ghost would be more vulnerable to, say, lasers, (H.P. Lovecraft used hydrochloric acid to defeat a ghost in his story "The Shunned, House" over 40 years ago.)

And there is even the sentimental indulgence of a faithful animal self-immolated to save its mistress — a cat this time, in a grateful but implausible variation on the cliche.

Nevertheless, the narrative is enthralling, the pace hypnotic, and the overall impression strongly positive.

One winds up feeling that this is the kind of book a reincarnated H. G. Wells would be writing today, having painfully outgrown his simplistic faith in scientific humanism.

One aberration, intriguing on the local level: the malevolent spirit's name is Underhill everywhere except on page 88, where it becomes Underwood.

FILM FLAM

The first horror movie we ever saw was "Dr. Cyclops," Vintage 1940, in which Albert Dekker as the half-blind mad scientist menaces the little people he's shrunk to doll size in a radium mine out in the technicolor jungle. (Our reference reveals that the musical score for that film was by the unlikely combination of Ernst Toch, the famous refugee German symphonic composer, and Albert Hay Malotte, composer of "The Lord's Prayer.")

After that we absorbed the whole gamut of Frankenstein, Dracula, and Mummy movies of the 40s, and in the 50s took in revivals of the great originals of the 30s.

From time to time there was an opportunity to witness even earlier classics via art film series, such as the Lon Chaney flicks, Murnau's "Faust," and the seminal "Cabinet of Dr. Callgari."

Therefore we are not judging idly in considering the horror movies of the present day, despite their luridness and licentiousness, basically so anemic that one would think Lugosi had been putting over his oral transfusion bit on the writers and directors.

Take as a typical example American-International's latest Vincent Price vehicle, *Cry of the Banshee*, now wailing in military theaters. In terms of setting and costumes, it shows more care and verisimilitude than nearly any such film before, say, 1955. In terms of writing, pace, impact, and entertainment, it is virtually nil, Even by standards of this genre, the script is silly, *pointless* and_dull, and with not even a faint start, much less a shock, in it. For the sake of dragging in sickish moments of sadism, the atmosphere and true facts about the witch-

367

craft persecution in Britain in the 16th century are completely falsi-fied: the most notable thing about this mania was the aura of legalism and judicious restraint thrown over the cruelty and horror. No rav-ing, blood-crazed tyrant of the Price type ever sat in judgment over an accused witch. What was done was done by sane, decent, thoughtful men; end that is the real horror of it.

If your movie memories go back even further than ours, you may recognize the film's chief witch as Elisabeth Bergner, the famous Aus-trian beauty who made some American movies for Lubitsch. Now 70, she deserves a better end to her career. Hugh Griffith as a drunken, eye-popping gravedigger goes beyond parodying himself and appears to be attempting to destroy the image of a flamboyantly convincing character actor he achieved in "Tom Jones."

As for Vincent Price, both he and the late great Karloff have been quoted as expressing indecently humble gratitude that they could at least work steadily when most movie stars were on the shelf. No doubt this sort of thing provides Price with enough money to do what he really wants to do, which obviously isn't acting.

The whole trouble is that these recent pictures aren't even good spoofs or send-ups; there isn't that much care or talent put into them. The old classics may have had corny scripts, hammy acting, and lousy special effects (though not always any of these faults); but they were performed and directed for conviction and thrilling escapism, which they provided in good measure.

These would-be campy creepers, with their Vogue magazine sets and gory skin-show nuances, are strictly machine-made products where the victims take so long to die because they never really lived, and the audience couldn't care less.

MY LIFE WITH THE GREATEST OLD ONE

A LTHOUGH I WAS born in a drab, raw industrial suburb of St. Louis forty years after H.P. Lovecraft made his appearance in the ancient New England seaport whose gracious architecture and fading traditions he loved so much, I had a somewhat Lovecraftian childhood, in the sense that I was overprotected, reclusive, bundled up against the cold; and developed precocious interests in astronomy, paleontology, mythology, and the scribbling down of little imitative fantasy stories (the first actually dictated to my father before I could write).

My present situation shows some parallels, too; since, during a dozen years of residence in South Korea, I have made most of my living for most of this time by revision and ghost-writing – primarily of English publicity for the Korean government, plus the editing of journalistic and scholarly material, translations and otherwise.

However, I diverged from the Lovecraftian pattern to develop into a composer, not a writer primarily, notwithstanding the thousands of newspaper and magazine pieces, the fiction, and the three books I have had published. In addition, I am an enthusiastic seafood lover and a convivial – occasionally even bibulous – non-Puritan; have contracted a lasting marriage; and am in the midst of raising an identifiably if untypically American family on foreign soil.

There comparisons end, becoming too attenuated.

I have, however, over the years remained a dedicated Lovecraft "fan", collector, commentator, and sometime imitator since I first discovered H.P.L. via that rich yet inexpensive treasury, the Tower Books edition of *The Best Supernatural Stories*, which I purchased for 49¢

in Woolworth's in 1945, when I was 15.

I was soon in touch with Arkham House via its ads in *Weird Tales*, of which I became a regular reader about this time. But I was just too late to acquire the first two Lovecraft omnibuses at list price (how I obtained them gratis, and then lost them again during a hectic three-month period in 1959, is another story).

I soon added to my collection *Marginalia* and The *Lurker at the Threshold*, books I still possess, plus every subsequent volume of the pantheon; though at first I was fonder of the New England stories such as "In the Vault" than of the Mythos tales. Before long, though, the daring cosmic escapism of the Mythos found resonance in my early scientific interests, and I immersed myself in the universal mythology of "The Shadow Out of Time" and "At the Mountains of Madness".

During the two-year period 1945-46, I wrote a sonnet sequence seeking to honor Lovecraft in the 18th century language he so admired (eventually published in *The Arkham Collector* No. 4); a blank verse narrative with a Mythos basis; and a long story combining several Mythos themes (the latter two items are now being brought out as curiosities in *The Dark Brotherhood Journal*.

The novelette I hopefully sent to August Derleth of Arkham House, who criticized it severely, not realizing that it was the work of a 16-year-old. (It was hardly more clumsy or derivative than the weird fiction he himself was writing – and selling – at that age and much earlier). This rebuff ended my Lovecraftian writing phase for 21 years; though I did turn out half a dozen or so dissimilar horror tales in my twenties that are now beginning to receive professional publications.

In 1967 I learned that Arkham House was planning an anthology of new and old Mythos stories primarily by writers other than Love-craft. Coincidentally, *Time* carried a report on Dr. Lilly's research into dolphin intelligence that suggested to me a link with Lovecraft's un-dersea races. The result was my 10,000 word novella, "The Deep Ones", published in Arkham's *Tales of the Cthulhu Mythos* and reprinted (in a somewhat longer and different original version) in the second volume of the Beagle paperback in 1971(a French edition is due too, I understand).

Having belatedly re-entered the world of H.P. L. as an active writ-er, I tossed off two satires: "A Darker Shadow Over Innsmouth" (*The Arkham Collector* No. 5) and a mass-media spoof (*The Arkham Collector* No. 10), plus several essays and specialized studies for "fan" publica-tions. There is some interest on the part of the *Nation Review*, for which I have written literary essays, in publishing future studies of Derleth and perhaps Lovecraft that I might undertake.

The recent death of my old friendly enemy, Derleth, however, put an end – so far as I can see – to any feasible future professional mar-kets for new fiction in the Lovecraft tradition. Perhaps this is just as well since Derleth's own efforts to continue the Mythos pattern – usually, and unforgiveably, with Lovecraft listed as co-author – have been lamentably weak and unconvincing. It is probably better to regard the Mythos as a closed universe including only Lovecraft writ-ings and a few stories written in his lifetime which he approved or even revised himself.

Lovecraft's influence on me (and others) has not been confined to the narrow field of macabre fiction. Study of his life, letters, and per-sonality gave me an early admiration for him as a man of uprightness, integrity, and dedication to high ideals (as he saw them), battling a devastating array of psychic handicaps and hang-ups, turning his agonies into myths and, yet, occasionally art.

I never shared his prejudices, predispositions, predelictions, or peeves; but examining them has helped me gain, I think, an understanding and a more tolerant sympathy for those who are different and, at first glance, characterized Lovecraft himself at his best (which may not have been often; but who can claim more?)

Thus I don't think the time and energy I have devoted to study and emulation of this greatest of the Old Ones of modern fantasy have been wasted. Lovecraft, with his strange but oddly attractive personality, and his posthumous Svengali, Derleth, are both gone now. But their influence continues to spread like bright ripples radiating across the stagnant flow of fantasy fiction, that meandering, beguiling literary stream in whose shallows, for reasons that seem to them sufficient, they chose to skulk.

THE MASS MEDIA HORROR

I F ONLY H. P. LOVECRAFT had lived a bit later and conquered his oft-expressed aversion to commercialized writing, we might be enjoying such innovations such as:

Our Gal Lavinia, the soap opera that asks the question: Can an extremely simple girl from the placid little town of Dunwich find true happiness as the daughter of Wizard Whateley and the mother of Wilbur, not to speak of his appallingly non-identical twin?

Innsmouth Revisited, a Ford Foundation TV Documentary on urban renewal, in which we see scenes depicting how federal, state, and private programs revitalize a decaying Massachusetts fishing port, assisted by locally generated counterpart funds, in the form of exotic platinum jewelry donated from ancestral collections. The climax is a carefree aquatic festival, in which no one at all seems to return from the swimming race to Devil Reef.

Revolting Campus, a book-length account of youthful unrest in the form of an in-depth study of Miskatonic University, Arkham, Mass. Student interviews reveal the fact that the faculty has been too little concerned with teaching, being preoccupied by library research in folklore, and with strange field trips, especially around May Eve and Hallowmass. Youthful demonstrators have burned certain ancient books in a symbolic bonfire, while chanting the slogan, "Down with the Old Ones – Never Trust Anyone Over 30,000,000,000!"

Starry Wisdom and You, the popular network inspirational series, in which Bishop H. Phillips Lovecraft preaches fiery sermons explaining how his Starry Wisdom Church solves members' personal problems through prayer, meditation, and the ritual repetition of certain esoteric secret scriptural verses invoking assistance from the Other World, for all those willing to send in a tax-exempt freewill offering (no exotic platinum jewelry accepted).

The Cyronics Foundation, Joseph Curwen, Jun., executive director, supported by the Charles Dexter Ward Fund, offers hope to those unwilling to shuffle off their present mortal coils, in the form of a perpetual care freeze-dry process by which the "essential Saltes" of the body may be preserved in a tasteful Grecian lekythoi urn, suitable for home interior decoration. The movement is being promoted by the singing commercial on the text: "All the days of my appointed time will I wait, till my change comes," as performed by – who else? – the Lovecraft rock and roll group.

LUNCH WITH MR. BLOCH

Novelist-screenwriter Robert Bloch, whose biggest Professional boost came when Hitchcock made a film classic from his novel *Psycho*, is probably the only one of the pulp horror writers centering around the late eccentric recluse author H. P. Lovecraft and the long-defunct magazine Weird *Tales* (which flourished in the 1920's and 1930's) to make the big time. That is, unless you count Lovecraft himself, all of whose work has come back into print in both hardcover and paperback editions by this year, which marks the 25th anniversary of his premature death.

We lunched in Hollywood with the affable and easy-going Mr. Bloch in April, on the strength of our own modest reputation as a come-lately Lovecraft disciple. (We had even discovered by accident a Ballantine paperback dedicated to us unbeknownst, during our American sojourn: a study of the Lovecraft mystique inscribed to the later imitative apostles of HPL).

During lunch, talk turned to Mr. Bloch's latest screenplay, just produced in England and released under the title *The House That Dripped Blood*.

We're happy to note that this satisfying shocker is now on the military circuit, and comprises a modest but thoroughly professional and straight-faced contribution to the unquenchable genre of fright films.

We're also pleased to observe that—as in the case of our own writings about Korea—Mr. Bloch is still getting mileage out of old material hopefully undeserving of oblivion in crumbling periodical files.

It's an episode film, and the first two parts—one about a Bloch-ian author whose fiendish creation seems to come to life, and the other concerning a waxworks proprietor who keeps needing a fresh supply of heads for his exhibit of Salome—fall into the category of macabre crime fiction with no supernatural elements.

The last two episodes, though, dealing with a juvenile witch (adapted from the story "Sweets to the Sweet") and a sardonic view of an unwilling modern vampire, are taken from short stories that appeared in the pulp magazines at one cent a word, were then collected in hardcover and later paperback books, and now make their perhaps definitive mark as filmic Material, with the aid of Bloch's adroit, underwritten scripting and the nicely integrated performances of expert actors such as Christopher Lee and Peter Cushing.

It's all great fun, neither campy nor arty; and Bloch has carefully managed to make his terrors subtle yet effective, without resorting to repulsive excesses.

All this is to the credit of a gracious gentleman who claims that he has the heart of a small boy—preserved in formaldehyde on his desk.

REVIEW: LOVECRAFT'S FOLLIES

Lovecraft's Follies: A Play in Two Acts, by James Schevill. The Swallow Press, Chicago, 1971. 90 pages. $2.00.

James Schevill is a 50-year old American poet and playwright with a sub-stantial achievement recorded in both fields. A former direc-tor of the Poetry Centre of San Francisco State College, he has published several volumes of verse in a style both sophisticated and communicative. He presently teaches writing at Brown University in Providence, which is where he presumably became interested in Lovecraft, whose literary estate is housed in the univer-sity library, and where this play was produced in March 1970.

His decision to write an experimental drama concerning modern problems with Lovecraft as central symbol is an interesting one, though the play is too fragmented, and too simplistically sermon-like, to be considered a success.

The main difficulty is with the use of Lovecraft as a symbol. Though some attempt is made to sketch his background, work and attitudes, what comes through to the render or viewer who never heard of Lovecraft is not enough to bear all the significance thrust upon it; while those familiar with Lovecraft will object that the por-trait is grossly oversimplified and inconsistent.

It is cheating for pundits to pretend to know what Thomas Jeffer-son would have said about Spiro Agnew or Vietnam; and it is cheating to drag H. P. Lovecraft into a welter of contemporary issues, ranging from security hysteria through hippies, moon shots, racial unrest, and the Oppenheimer case. A man who died in 1937 has little relevance to such matters, even as an inflated symbol. (Colin Wilson tried to make Lovecraft a representation of all that was wrong with intellectual escapism and by extension modern man in his book *The Strength to Dream*, and didn't manage to prove his case either).

In form, *Lovecraft's Follies* is a surreal vaudeville, influenced both by Brecht (in its use of solo and choral song) and the Living Theatre type of ritual drama. However, for a poet of proven stature, Schevill's lyrics and dialogue are singularly flat and amateurish, and the ideas in the play are all liberal cliches that we may be pardoned for yawning at by now, however firmly we believe in them.

A physicist quits his defense job and goes off to Providence, where he constructs an immense junk-sculpture of H. P. Lovecraft, adorned with old Weird Tales covers. His brother and wife, representing establishment forces, try to bring him back to conformity, and in illustrating his rejection of their values, he evokes several scenes in which Lovecraft appears as a character or commentator.

First is a glimpse of Lovecraft's fantastic, harrowing childhood, then a vignette on Werner von Braun's cynical opportunism, leading into a restaging of the moon landing. Next comes a rather feeble skit with Tarzan captured by the Green People and Lovecraft as a roving racist reporter for Weird Tales. The climax in the second act is a pretentious account of what one can only call at this stage the J. Robert Oppenheimer myth, with Lovecraft serving this time as an ambivalent accuser-apologist whose attitude is never clarified.

The play closes with a sketch that seems to point to George Washington as the first American racist. The final scene is left open, in the fashionable current manner, which perhaps derives from those old movies which closed with the portentous slogan: "This is NOT—The End"!

There is plenty of opportunity for imaginative staging, which seems to have impressed some of the major media critics whose praise is quoted on the book jacket; but there is little sign of a focused attitude on the part of the playwright, much less of selective ambiguity. The irony and satire through-out are on a rather juvenile level.

The book cover does reproduce a marvellous old Weird Tales cover, no doubt by Brundage, one of those human sacrifice scenes where wisps of incense supply what the costumier forgot, and save the viewer's modesty. This is the kind of cover Lovecraft used to tear off and discard when he bought magazines containing his stories. I suspect in this case he would have kept the cover in preference to the book.

BOOK REVIEW: SELECTED LETTERS III

Selected Letters of H.P. Lovecraft: Vol. III (1929-31). Sauk City: Arkham House, 1971. 451, xxiii pages, $10.00.

In 1946, the late August Derleth announced publication by Arkham House of a volume of selected letters of the fantasy writer, H.P. Lovecraft, his mentor. Nineteen years later, when the book finally appeared, it had become the first of a set of three; now that the third volume is out, the total has swelled to five, and the project has become a posthumous one supervised by the Derleth heirs, completion of which – so far as anyone can determine at this point – may be delayed until the Lovecraft centenary in 1990, or at least the 50th anniversary of his death in 1937

Derleth had the right idea the first time – one book, carefully edited and pruned, would have been enough. The five-volume set, amounting to a probable 2,000 pages, will be far less useful and enjoyable a monument than a single collection of three or four hundred pages would have been.

After all, as much as we may admire his fiction and his intellect, sympathize with his problems, or respect certain aspects of his personality and philosophy, Lovecraft was not a major figure such as Emerson or James, every word of whose ephemera is apparently of interest, or at least potential use, to the specialists.

And now that Derleth, a fabulous miner in the Lovecraftian depths who has brought forth more gold, and dross, that HPL would ever have imagined he produced, is himself gone, who is there to sit down and refine all this material into a manageable *Best of the Letters of H.P.*

Lovecraft.

Like any prolific correspondent, Lovecraft repeated himself, sometimes describing the same places and events (he cared little for people) in virtually the same words in several letters. Though the epistles have been shortened by the editors, not all this repetition is eliminated.

In addition, as he himself recognized, Lovecraft used his voluminous letter-writing to formulate his own views and attitudes, and to bounce them off his various correspondents in a slow-motion version of the give-and-take of face-to-face discussion denied him by his self-imposed isolation. (More than one of these letters come to over fifty pages in print!) All this presupposes a degree of prolixity.

This third volume, covering only the years 1929 to 1931, represents the emergence of the mature thinker. He still clings to his insular preference for Nordic-Anglo-Saxon civilization, but finally admits that, rationally, this is simple because of the circumstances of his birth and environment, not due to any intrinsic values, which must necessarily be denied by a scientific analysis.

He still judges "primitives" as inferior, including the negroid race; but this is probably unavoidable in a natural snob raised on the pseudo-scientific racism of Gobineau and Houston Chamberlain, at time when they were still taken seriously.

The respect which he grants, however grudgingly, to Orientals, Slavs, Italians and Jews as members of high cultures sits oddly with the fulminations against minority groups that still strew these pages. But he goes on record quite clearly as opposing not only miscegenation but any close contact whatever between differing cultural groups, on the grounds that such groups are fundamentally and irreconcilably hostile to one another – an observation which not much that happens in the U.N. today would tend to disprove.

There are passages of amusing whimsy and exalted prose in these pages; of warm nostalgia and penetrating observation. But it is not disparaging Lovecraft's pre-eminence as a letter-writer – earned in terms of sheer volume alone! – to point out that he has some epistolary quirks that can become annoying. As if to compensate for his ornate 18th century style and archaick spelling, he regularly throws in frivolous passages of current (now dated) slang or crude patois, a device that probably didn't bother the recipients of the letters, but which palls over hundreds of pages.

But taken all in all, the real man is there in these letters, concealed as he may be in mannerisms and Mandarinism: this complex blend of neurasthenic invalid and Nordic superman; of arrogant poseur and lonely misfit; of cosmic fantaisiste and rigorous scientific materialist; of scholar, scoffer, and seeker; of life hater, and lover who never found himself worthy to offer love, save in the indirect guise of these torrential, compulsive letters which both clamor for and repel that affection, which was, after all (as he never realized) simply his due as a human being.

BOOK REVIEW:
THE COLLECTED GHOST STORIES OF OLIVER ONIONS

The Collected Ghost Stories Of Oliver Onions by Oliver Onions, Minola: Dover Books, 1971. 689_xi pages. $4.00 (Reprint of Nicholson and Watson, London, edition of 1935)

It is somewhat paradoxical to review a book which was published 38 years ago. But in America at least, Onions (who would seem to have been a prolific English author in a number of genres) is known solely for his novella *The Beckoning Fair One*, which has been anthologized to death in the usual way, while his other stories are completely ignored.

This book, then, answers the question that came into my mind around 1945 when I first read "The Beckoning Fair One": Did a man who could write this good a ghost story write only one?

The answer, luckily is, of course not. Here are nearly 700 pages of them, ranging from pantheistic evocations of remote antiquity, somewhat resembling Algernon Blackwood's themes, but not his style, to real Gothic hauntings, and even several Leiber-like horror tales growing out of gritty modern urban settings.

The comparisons in the above paragraph are strained; Onions is his own man. There is one writer he can be compared with in certain respects: he might be called the Henry James of the ghost story (yes, I know James himself wrote enough tales of haunting to fill a book). I put it this way because Onions' prime interest is character, and a subtle analysis of human thought and behaviour in the presence of the unknown. This usually results in a slow-moving, often lengthy story that is at once old-fashioned and deeply engrossing.

The only stories that fail are those of too high a symbolic aim: "Resurrection in Bronze" is a parable of the artist who destroys those around him, but it is rather obvious and we see what is coming too early; while "Hic Jacet", about a writer who sold out his talent for popularity, and his relation to a Bohemian painter of the Gulley Jimson breed, displays fine irony but is a little long to support its point.

If the writer has a single underlying theme running through such a diversity of stories, it is that of the past, malign or simply alien, invading and disrupting the present — a common enough idea in this genre; but everything depends on how the theme is varied. In Onions' best tales, the invasion is subtle and often incompletely glimpsed, but the stories have an impressive moral force as well as convincing atmosphere. Onions is not out to write shockers, though once in a while the impact of his stories carries a shock.

Everyone will have his own favorites in the book, and perhaps a few dislikes. "The Beck-oning Fair One" may indeed be Onions' masterpiece in the field, but tales like "The Rosewood_Door", of an invasion from the remote past, and "The Master of the House", which does with Oriental menace what Henry James would have done had he written the Fu Manchu stories, are hardly far behind.

Among the shorter pieces that are nearly as effective one could name "Rooum", which evokes horror amidst a building construction work gang, and "The Out Sister", a gentle tale of haunting in an Italian setting.

The people in these stories are quite painstakingly brought alive in all their British insularity and eccentricity; the reader knows and cares about them, which is the feat of the writer as artist rather than mere yarn-spinner. It is astonishing that such an impress-ive body of work has remained so long unknown —but maybe this is not so in England.

At any rate, the reprint is out now, and my own perhaps greedy reaction is: Onions lived to a ripe old age, dying in 1961; mightn't he have written a few more ghost stories after 1935?

And the second reaction is equally natural: did his writing in other fields match his skill in the ghostly tale? If so, one would like to see more of it.

FILM REVIEW: DON'T LOOK NOW

*D*on't Look Now is an ingenious and stylish Daphne du Maurier suspense yarn translated to film, with Donald Sutherland and Julie Christie starring. It concerns an art restorer and his wife, grieving over an accidentally drowned daughter, who come to Venice—where the art really needs all the restoring it can get—and encounter two spooky spinster sisters (try saying that three times fast) one of whom claims to have a clairvoyant vision of the dead child in the red raincoat she drowned wearing. The wife believes in the vision, the husband does not.

The wife is called back to England by the sudden illness of another child, and while she is gone the husband sees a vision of his wife and the weird sisters in a gondola-borne funeral procession.

What happens next would be telling, but by the end the moral is clear: one can have second sight and still be afflicted with astigmatism. The movie meticulously follows the ingenious and somewhat artificial plot, while the stones, and streams, of Venice provide suitable opulence and gloom.

The producers must have doubted the box office appeal of the film, though, for they dragged in one of those skin-flick bedroom scenes that only goes to show that Julie Christie is cuter than Donald Sutherland, at least from one point of view.

The film is now on the military circuit.

ARKHAM HOUSE: PROMISE AND PERFORMANCE

O VER THE YEARS, the prodigious achievements of Arkham House, which is to say August Derleth, in bringing into print the best of fantasy writing, new and old, otherwise unobtainable, has been to a certain degree shadowed for some of us by an impression that too many books were delayed too long or cancelled. I suffered from that notion myself, until recently an exhumation of old Arkham catalogues dating back to 1945 inspired a systematic search and accounting on this subject. I pass along my findings here for the possible interest they may have for other aficionados.

Of course there were some glaring examples of postponement, notably the Lovecraft letters, announced for 1946, the first volume of which came out 19 years later. The completion of the series was jeopardized by Derleth's death in 1971, but it seems the five-volume set, now at midpoint, will actually appear eventually. Again, Shiel's *Xelucha* was scheduled for 1947 and is just now available — probably the longest delay at 28 years; but it may not hold the record when all is said and done, since another Shiel volume, *Prince Zaleski and Cummings King Monk*, was announced around the same period, and is still on the indefinite future timetable.

I calculate roughly that Arkham House and its affiliate Mycroft and Moran have by now turned out 132 books, taking into account the bibliography *Thirty Years of Arkham House*, extending through 1969, and the current 1974 stock list of newer titles. My combing of catalogues culled 21 books either cancelled or still unpublished. (There may be some omissions, since I might be short a few catalogues from the early and mid-1960's.) This is only one book in six that has failed to appear; and some of these were cancelled for very good reasons, while others may yet see the light.

Here is the list, with the date of earliest catalogue announcement appended:

Mimsy Were the Borogoves — Kuttner (1945)
Shambleau and Others — Moore (1945)
The Corner Shop — Asquith (1945)
Conjure Wife — Leiber (1945)
House by the Churchyard — Le Fanu (1945)
The Great Circle — Whitehead (1945)
Collected Ghost Stories — Benson (1945)
Worse Things Waiting — Wellman (1946)
Prince Zaleski and Cummings King Monk — Shiel (1946)
Black Magic — Bowen 194)
Kecksies and Other Twilight Tales — Bowen (1946)
Melmoth the Wanderer — Maturin (1946)
Orson Is Here — H. Wandrei (1946)
Gather, Darkness — Leiber (1947-8)
Purcell Papers — Le Fanu (1947-8)
The Worlds Outside — Merritt (1947-8)
Away and Beyond — Van Vogt (1949)
The Death Fetch — Ed. Grendon (1949)
Time Burial — H. Wandrei (195?).
Half in Shadow — Counselman (195?)
Colossus — D. Wandrei (1967)

Let us examine the list more closely. Items cancelled or apparently cancelled are 1, 2, 3, 7, 10, 11, 13, 16, 18, 19, 20, and 21. (I do not count the spate of books by both Wandrei's announced after Derleth's death and withdrawn after the break with Donald Wandrei, Derleth's choice as his successor.) Items released to other publishers account for 4, 5, 8, 12, and 17. Still scheduled are 9 and 15. *The Great Circle* is probably an earlier title for *Jumbee*, which contains a story of that name. 19 may be similarly a later title for 13, while *The Corner Shop* is very likely *This Mortal Coil*.

The short fiction of Kuttner and Moore has been widely reprinted, whether or not precisely as the volumes listed as 1 and 2, so these might be considered released to other publishers rather than cancelled. Fritz Leiber has described how Derleth graciously released him from contracts for 4 and 14 when it seemed that faster or more advantageous publication could be secured elsewhere. A revival of interest on the part of commercial publishers caused the cancellation of 5, 12, and probably 18. Derleth has explained how 17 went to another publisher and became two books.

Therefore the only planned volumes that really disappeared are 7, 10, 11, 16, and 20. These are missed, since I do not know of any fulfillment of these valuable projects on either side of the Atlantic. But five out of 132 is not a bad batting average.

It would seem that the tenaciously stubborn August Derleth has more claim on the gratitude of fantasy lovers than we had suspected. He gave us quantity as well as quality, and if he had lived a normal life span it seems highly probable that the entire Arkham House program would have been carried out to 95 per cent completion of all projected titles not appearing elsewhere in one form or another.

I, who sometimes wrangled and tangled with him during his lifetime, am happy to grant him this unfortunately posthumous accolade.

BOOK REVIEW: THE HEIGHT OF THE SCREAM

The Height of the Scream by Ramsey Campbell. Sauk City: Arkham House 1976. 229 pages, $7.50.

THERE ARE NOW writing actively in English two authors in the vein of horror whose work exhibits extraordinary interest and mastery, both British: Robert Aickman and Ramsey Campbell. (To these might be added the American political theorist Russell Kirk; but his sparse fictional output seems lately devoted to the novel of intrigue and satire, his one volume of macabre tales, *The Surly Sullen Bell*, having been published as long ago as 1962.)

Thus the appearance of a new volume by Ramsey Campbell is an event of some importance in the field. And though *The Height of the Scream* is marred by an introduction that is both overly jaunty and needlessly self-important, and despite the fact that the stories are – as is usual with Campbell's work – rather uneven and tending to weak endings, it is a pleasure to peruse writing so fine-grained and evocative in stories rich in atmosphere and lacking in cheap effects as these.

As has been observed many times, and admitted by the author himself, Campbell's mature work is worlds removed from the clumsy juvenile pastiches of Lovecraft issued as *The Inhabitant of the Lake* when August Derleth first presciently detected signs of talent in the Liverpool lad who wanted to build another Innsmouth in his home town.

Campbell's current settings are as realistically urban and grimy as those of Fritz Leiber's Chicago or "Smoke Ghost" period. His characters are freaks, misfits, and monsters as plausible as those in *Midnight*

Cowboy and *V*. And the interaction of settings and characters is, in his best work, as central and as subtle as that attempted in "mainstream" fiction.

Thus in "Missing" we never learn whether the forgotten wife who returns to haunt the freaked-out college student is alive or a ghost; and it doesn't matter: the psychological study – and the eerie mood – are what count.

In "The Scar" there are hints that a race of inhuman *doppelgängers* is infiltrating cities for its own dark purposes; or is this the delusion of a madman whose family hangups cause him to fantasize about the sinister substitution of a relative?

Such ambiguous endings might seem a cop-out to some, but in these stories they are artistically right.

But not always. "Reply Guaranteed" leads simply to a scare-ending similar but inferior to that of M.R. James' "Oh, Whistle and I'll Come to You, My Lad" – and for this effect we don't need Viv, Jack, Mavis, Tony and all their trivial personal embroilments over fifteen pages. It is a case of plot and characters being irrelevant to each other.

A story like "The Cellars" shows both the best and the worst aspects of Campbell's approach. A Liverpool working-class flirtation has grown sour, but the girl is intrigued when the boy suggests they visit some unknown catacombs in the downtown district. They do so, and discover a shapeless mass of mould in a closed cupboard, speculating on how people might have been kept prisoner here, or as pets.

Soon after, the boy vanishes; when a fellow worker visits his mother's flat she says her son has vanished, but refuses the visitor admission, while strange gargling noises are heard inside.

Alone in an apartment on Valentine's day, the girl receives an unsigned greeting card with mould adhering to the envelope. A face peers in the window, leaving a white outline in steam. She goes upstairs for safety and from a window sees a bulky object drag itself to the riverside and disappear into the water.

Told thus baldly the story sounds flat and inconclusive, and indeed the ambiguous ending – does the boy, hideously changed underground, kill himself rather than continue hopelessly to pursue the girl? or what? – is hardly satisfactory.

But the tale moved in a chill, dank cloud of atmosphere that makes it fascinatingly repellant, and the plot and people at least serve to keep the action moving. There are superb descriptive passages: "Silence hung about the house, weighted with raindrops suspended at the tips of leaves . . . Julie listened down the stairwell . . . the china dogs seemed as intent as she."

The cumulative effect disarms criticism, and even blunts the curiosity to know what really happened to the young man in the catacombs. It cannot have been as frightening as what our imaginations, skillfully led by the author, boggle at visualizing.

On the other hand there are disappointments. I am unable to discern what the author intends at the end of the title story, for instance, and in the conclusion of "Smoke Kiss." It is not a question of subtle ambiguity, I think, but of being totally at sea as to what is going on, in a way that the author surely did not purpose.

The living devil-doll in "Cyril" has been on stage a little too often to merit this perfunctory encore, while the concluding "Horror House of Blood" suggests that the writer stopped short, not to let the reader imagine what happened, but because he himself didn't know what in the world to do next.

Against this, balance the very fine tale "Litter," concerning a frightening personification of urban trash; "Ash," a deftly handled story of a haunting; the original and striking "In the Shadows," about what emerged from a children's library shadow-show; and the intriguing personality-exchange in "Second Chance."

There is even a story built on a hidden acrostic-type pattern, "The Words That Count," though the trick perhaps inhibits fictional flexibility a bit.

Campbell's introduction says that "The Telephones" is about "fear of (and suppressed desire for) homosexual rape"; but all that is his problem – for the reader, it's just a fresh and arresting variation of a macabre hunter-and-hunted gambit with an especially alarming finish.

Arkham House has not served the book justly with a perfunctory jacket, and a title page with the cheap typographical gimmick of a crescendo in type size for the word *Scream*, a barbarity of a kind unknown in Derleth's day.

BOOK REVIEW: THE HOUSE OF THE WORM

The House of the Worm by Gary Myers. Sauk City: Arkham House 1975. 77 pages, $5.50.

PASTICHE CAN BE fun, and some writers, not to be named here, have made a career of it, without admitting the fact. Now comes Gary Myers to demonstrate the improbable fact that even a pastiche of a pastiche is capable of entertaining.

For Mr. Myers' first book, a volume of ten slim tales, is avowedly an imitation of H.P. Lovecraft imitating Lord Dunsany. True, Gary Myers obviously knows his Dunsany too, so that sometimes he is pastiching the Irish fantasiste directly. But in the main these pieces make use of the Dreamland geography that Lovecraft created, most notably in the novel *The Dream-Quest of Unknown Kadath*, and which he partly subsumed into the Cthulhu Mythos through use of both common place-names and names of monstrous deities and forbidden books.

It all sounds rather unpromising on the face of it, but Mr. Myers carries off the trick so well that it usually works: whole passages are quite worthy of his famed originals, and nowhere does his standard fall far below theirs. Indeed, one is tempted to hazard that in places *The House of the Worm* improves upon its models.

First of all, Mr. Myers has the style down pat: the exotic names have the ring of rightness; the understatement and reticence, broken by vividly nasty tangential details, evoke the proper aura; the dead-pan irony and humor provide the necessary contrasts. The reader's reaction to these tales and his tolerance of what is after all a highly mannered, Mandarin kind of writing, will depend on how he feels about the originals. Speaking for myself, the book seems just about the ideal length to sustain interest without cloying.

The weakness in this approach is plot. We are not told exactly what happens or why; if we were so informed, the effect would evaporate. The horrors and beauties are unreal and seemingly unmotivated, as in a dream. Endings are inconclusive, as are beginnings, for that matter.

Here is a sample description as an appetizer, or a warning: "Beyond the last of Six Kingdoms Thish beheld the dark, mordant forests of trees whose knotted roots fasten like leeches to the mould and moan and bleach the earth, and in whose loathy shadows the inquisitive brown Zoogs caper and leer; and evil bogs whose pale, luminous blooms are foetid with swollen worms having astonishing faces. The deserts on the thither side of Gak are all strewn with the gnawed, untidy bones of absurd chimeras."

The thick impasto of adjectives is generally unusual enough to be arresting, and there are only two words too many (I leave the reader to decide which two). The feat is not an easy one to pull off.

In a tongue-in-cheek preface, the author remarks that the title tale is a heresy of both the orthodox Cthulhu Mythos and what Richard Tierney has identified as the "Derleth Mythos," apparently because it reverts to the original Dreamland ordering of mythical pantheons that Lovecraft never fully reconciled with his later "scientific" Mythos tales of the waking world. This title story, here considerably revised, first appeared in the seventh issue of the *The Arkham Collector* in 1970. Thus Mr. Myers ranks as the last and probably the best of August Derleth's "discoveries" of young writers eager to continue the Lovecraft tradition – though in several places Derleth has written that the vein is probably played out.

At this point Gary Myers, like Ramsey Campbell before him, would be well advised to seek greater originality for mature effects, something his more famous mentor was never able to do. He has proved his adeptness at pastiche so conclusively that it will not be worth the effort to try this vein again.

It must be remarked in closing that this is the least impressive Arkham House book I have ever seen. The paper, just a bit shinier and thinner that good book paper should be; the binding, sewn on the cheap so that the volume will not lie open; the cover boards, warped due to poor material or inadequate drying; all add up to an approximation of the typical vanity press production, a charge never relevant to any of the house's publications during August Derleth's lifetime (proofreading was *his* weak point). Five words are mis-spelled, one of which may be a misprint.

The line drawings of Allan Servoss are suitable and welcome.

A SENSE OF OTHERNESS

Considering the obsessive pattern shown by the titles of Arkham
House books over the past 35 years, it is assumed that if the
Derleth heirs decide to publish an omnibus volume of the collected
early fantasies of Truman Capote, the volume will be titled OTHER
VOICES, OTHER ROOMS AND OTHERS.

In case the same approach is adopted with the more recent novels
of Thomas Tryon, the book will doubtless be called THE OTHER
AND OTHERS. Of course, if the novels are issued separately, it will
be only fair to call attention to this fact by making the title of the first
volume THE OTHER AND NO OTHERS.

It is said that the firm's affiliate, Mycroft & Moran, which published the Solar Pons pastiches ranging over nearly the whole of the
Holmesian canon, is now looking for an enterprising imitator who
can continue their tradition by pasticking the entire works of Dosto-
evsky in the form of murder mysteries in the Conan Doyle manner.

The initial offering will naturally be named THE CASE OF THE
OTHER KARAMAZOV.

BOOK REVIEW:
KECKSIES AND OTHER TWILIGHT TALES

Kecksies and Other Twilight Tales by Marjorie Bowen. Sauk City: Arkham House, 1976. 207 pages. $7.50.

Majorie Bowen (1886-1952) was a prolific British historical and mystery novelist who produced two collections of spectral tales, in 1933 and 1949, a selection from which was announced by Arkham House before the author's death. This belated volume is the result; it is of such high quality that one wishes the rather sparse contents had been expanded to include all of both out-of-print British collections.

Mrs. Bowen's stories are of three general types: period pieces with backgrounds drawn from the knowledge she assembled for her historical fiction; tales with modern settings; and dream visions in milieu either indeterminate or phantasmagoric.

Of the latter type, which represents the author's most original and intense macabre work, there is only one specimen in this book, "The Sign-Painter and the Crystal Fishes", though August Derleth in his collection *The Night Side* included her "Nightmare,' which is to me the most impressive of all her "twilight tales." In this vein she verges upon surrealism or a kind of distorted, apparently meaningless symbolism that seems to hint of some underlying, unknowable significance. The atmospheric and stylistic mastery is impeccable, and, as in poetic masterpieces like "Kublai Khan," we seem to know just what is meant, even though to the logical mind the meaning is absent or opaque. In this sense, Mrs. Bowen is a poet of the supernatural.

Typical of the period settings is "Kecksies," a grisly account of the revenge of a dead man wreaks on the dissolute noble who married the woman he coveted. "Florence Flanner," a reincarnation tale, has a lurid climax that would be grotesquely laughable if handled in a typical pulp style, but the restraint and careful buildup make it work effectively here.

Both stories are notable for an unblinking depiction of the seamier side of human nature in whatever age, as well as effortless and subtle evocation of setting and atmosphere.

"The Hidden Ape" and "Half Past Two" with their modern settings resemble to some degree detective tales, though hardly of the orthodox sort. The same is true of the grim retribution in "Scoured Silk," where a sequestered wife turns the tables in a way that Mrs. Edward Rochester tried but just failed to accomplish.

"The Crown Derby Plate" depicts a ghost of peculiarly repulsive nature, though the surprise ending is apparent somewhat too early to really shock.

The twelve tales are sufficiently varied in style, theme, plot, characters and settings never to become tediously repetitious, something that cannot be said for several recent collections by younger authors brought out by Arkham House, whose stories do not read so well together as separately.

Mrs. Bowen's excellence is such that one hopes the remainder of her spectral fiction may be collected in a second volume before too long.

BOOK REVIEW: INTERVIEW WITH THE VAMPIRE

Interview With the Vampire by Ann Rice. New York: Alfred A. Knopf, 1976. 373 pages. $8.95.

Out of the many powerful symbols for the darker side of life – witches, werewolves, Golem-like or Frankensteinian artificial creations – modern Western culture has obviously chosen the vampire legend as preeminent, with its sinister sexual connotations and its intriguing offer of eternal life, at a price.

Thus it is not surprising that among the many literary (including subliterate) and dramatic treatments of this theme prevalent these days, someone would choose to write a psychological, even philosophical, novel about a vampire. That person is first-novelist Ann Rice, and her book *Interview With the Vampire* is an absorbing if not entirely successful attempt to get inside the skins, or at least the capes, of Count Dracula's congrères.

The story is told in the form of a lengthy tape-recorded interview in a grimy San Francisco hotel room granted by Louis, the vampire, to a journalist referred to only as "the boy."

The first-person narrative (which requires a lot of quotation marks, not to say double and triple quotes that are sometimes hard to keep straight) is sometimes interrupted by interjections or inquiries from the interviewer, but is mostly an account of how Louis got that way back in the 18th century, and of his career then and in the succeeding century.

Since it is told in modern times, there is no need for the author to adopt period language consistently to avoid anachronisms, a problem not always solved in the recent Frankenstein sequels by the publisher of the *New Republic* (who seems to need something more to take up his time than bankrolling that money-losing journal); though these sequels may well have suggested to Ms. Rice her much more ambitious book.

Along the way we encounter some interesting deviations from the standard vampire literature, introduced, one suspects, for plot convenience: vampires do cast shadows and images in mirrors, are not bothered by garlic, crucifixes or stakes in the heart; but they must, according to old rules, sleep in coffins and avoid daylight at their peril. They are also, rather than soulless monsters, prone to all the foibles and dilemmas of the human condition, plus a few more associated with the vampiric state.

Louis is a rich New Orleans plantation owner of the 1940's who broods over the accidental death of a younger brother, for which he feels responsible. During a drunken spree he encounters the effete blond vampire Lestat, who attacks him and turns him into a vampire by exchanging blood with him, for the prosaic reason that he needs money and a safe place to hide, both of which Louis provides.

For some time Louis is repelled by his new condition, and he refuses to drink the blood of any but small animals, though he remains Lestat's slave and disciple in other respects. Lestat promises revelations that never appear; at last he tells Louis that their vampirism is proof of neither the existence of God nor that of the devil.

Louis begins to drift away from Lestat; and to hold onto him Lestat vampirizes the little girl Claudia, whom Louis comes to regard as a daughter of their strange family and then something more. (By this time the plantation has been burned in a slave rebellion, and the group is free to drift and decimate in the world.)

As decades pass, Claudia grows up mentally and emotionally, but not physically. She begins to hate Lestat for having denied her physical maturity, and plots with Louis to kill him. They attempt to do so by fire and flee to Europe. But Lestat is not really dead.

Seeking their own land in the legendary Balkans, they find only mindless and repulsive predators; but in Paris they encounter a group of civilized vampires, led by Armand, who run their own theater, a kind of Grand Guignol where the events on stage are unexpectedly real rather than pretense.

Armand and Louis fall in love (it is never clear whether or not vampires can or do indulge in ordinary sex lives; it seems they do not; but then, why does Claudia so bitterly bemoan her lack of physical maturity?). To provide for Claudia, Louis vampirizes a young dollmaker named Madeleine who has fallen in love with her. But Lestat reappears and instigates the vampire theater members to execute all three, since killing or attempting to kill a fellow vampire is the unforgiveable sin. Armand rescues Louis, but the girl and woman are killed. In revenge Louis burns the theater and its inhabitants and flees with Armand.

Lestat has escaped again; in modern New Orleans, Louis encounters him as a neurasthenic invalid who can bear only the blood of animals; thus their initial roles are reversed.

Having learned that Armand could have saved Claudia and Madeleine, Louis rejects him too and they part. The vampire goes his way alone. At the end of the narrative, the young reporter asks Louis to vampirize him too, but the latter refuses, horrified that the whole point of his narrative has escaped the interviewer.

A major flaw of the book is that all the characters except Louis are rather shadowy (perhaps appropriately enough in view of the subject).

There is plenty of highly complex metaphysical discussion in the book, some of which is pretty heavy going, and also much clinical-poetical description of blood-letting, which in ideal cases seems to provide the vampire with the emotional catharsis he misses in being denied sex, just as it provides the nourishment he misses with normal food. At its best the philosophizing is stimulating and apposite. Armand remarks, "How many vampires do you think have the stamina for immortality? . . . One evening a vampire rises and realizes what he has perhaps feared for decades, that he simply wants no more of life at any cost.'"

At a later point the much older Armand tells Louis, "'I must make contact with the age. . . . And I can do this through you . . . you are the spirit, you are the heart.'"

Louis protests, "'It's not the spirit of any age. I'm at odds with everything and always have been! I have never belonged anywhere with anyone at any time!'"

Armand replies: "'But Louis, this is the very spirit of your age. Don't you see that? Everyone feels as you feel. Your fall from grace and faith has been the fall of a century.'"

The original *Frankenstein* was, believe it or not, a novel of ideas. Now, a century and a half later, his colleague Dracula has in surrogate form taken up the great issues of life and death, not to say life-in-death.

But there was no need to rush; they have all the time in the world.

A SHIPBOARD READING LIST

On a passenger ship during an extended ocean voyage, there is little to do but read, unless one is an ardent game or puzzle fan. During a ten-day Pacific crossing in June [1977], I averaged more than a book a day – though switching about among three or four at a time. Luckily the ship's library was rather well stocked, to supplement the volumes I had brought along myself. Following is a cursory account of my reactions to the books I read on the voyage.

The Moon Is a Harsh Mistress, by Robert Heinlein.

I had read half this book before boarding the boat, and might not have finished without the extra leisure. The Panshins and others have been terribly exercised over the Fascist trends they find in it, but I was bogged down by the slowness and dullness of the narrative. (The magazine condensation must have been much more readable and burdened with less overt "message.")

It is yet another case of a plausible Heinlein future, imagined with admirable care and ingenuity, framing a story which his talents as a novelist are insufficient to bring to life, however hard he tries.

The moon, Earth's penal colony, is liberated by an elderly anarchist professor, a technocrat, and an omniscient computer, who bluff and blackmail an Earth dependent upon the grain shipments from the moon. Sideswipes at democracy and intellectuals suggest straw men shooting fish in a barrel. The "extended family" multiple marriage system intended to provide human interest doesn't. The deaths of the professor and of the computer's "human" personality at the end seem gratuitous, not tragic or epic.

Watership Down, by Richard Adams.

Five hundred pages of the Pathetic Fallacy in the adventures of rabbits-as-hobbits. All the cute anthropomorphism cloys quickly and undermines the sharply observed nature writing. Some of the similes are most unfortunate.

This should have been a hundred-page children's book, preferably by Beatrix Potter. The hyperboles of the critics may be explicable only on the assumption that they hadn't read a book with a real story (as opposed to the maunderings of spoiled Narcissists) in so long that they were carried away unwares.

Especially annoying are Adams' pretentious chapter epigraphs, from the Greeks to Auden; the puerile rabbit mythology (no more implausible perhaps than their pseudo-literate conversations); and the unnecessary interpolation of words from the rabbit language.

My favorite chapter title is "The Story of Rowsby Woof and the Fairy Wogdog"; my favorite character is a seagull who talks just like Kurt Kasznar or Oscar Homolka will do in the inevitable Disney production, which should make a nice sequel to *Bambi*.

But for the epic and elephantine whimsy, give me Baggins over bunnies any day – though not too much at a time, please.

Aspects of Alice, edited by Robert Phillips.

A wide-ranging survey of the critical literature on Lewis Carroll, from his own day to ours. There are many gems here, and only a few humorous pontifications from those determined to find in "Alice" strained Freudian allusions or accounts of the Oxford theological movement.

Most outrageous is a serious claim that Mark Twain wrote the books as a hoax – the most ludicrous case of style-deafness since the contention that Marlowe (or Bacon) wrote Shakespeare. One might as well claim that Shakespeare wrote Mark Twain, or *Alice in Wonderland*.

The Ghost in the Machine, by Arthur Koestler.

A painful case of poor title choice for an important book – my elder son asked me, "Is that a good ghost story you're reading, Dad?"

Koestler here surveys biology and psychology to suggest a neurological rift between the older and newer parts of the brain as an "evolutionary error" accounting for man's suicidal and fanatical aggressiveness, and proposes artificial genetically-manipulated evolution as a desperate remedy. Along the way he elaborates upon the concept of "holons" – units that are self-contained and self-governing parts of larger units – as a useful classification for both biological and social entities or components, avoiding the contradictions of monism versus dualism and imposing an open-ended, Janus-faced hierarchic order upon the universe.

He also delivers a devastating attack on the "flat earth psychology" of Behaviorism.

This is fascinating popular science, and its sermonizing aspect may embody the most crucial scientific message of this century. But what a title! Shades of the Fairy Wogdog!

Bio-Futures, edited by Pamela Sergeant.

This is an anthology of "hard core" science fiction tales of varying

413

degrees of success, tricked out with a "serious" introduction and notes, with an elaborate bibliography that unaccountably omits both the preceding Koestler book and Shaw's *Back to Methusalah*.

The stories of cloning, RNA transfer, immortality serums and such do not always use these hypothetical developments as central aspects of the stories; in Gunn's "Immortals" and Scortia's"Weariest River" the SF elements are mere background for conventional plots set in societies which I for one could not for a moment believe would develop from the stated premises; while Kate Wilhelm's "The Planners" is simply a somewhat unfocused domestic drama.

But Tushnet's "In Re Glover," Lafferty's "Slow Tuesday" and Pohl's corrosive "Day Million" are most amusing satires, and Le Guin's "Nine Lives" and Anderson's "Call Me Joe" emerge as excellent, thoughtful tales.

Coincidentally, in Koestler's book one chapter-head quote is drawn from an SF writer, Poul Anderson; the quote, found in the same ship's library, is from this story: "I've yet to see any problem, however complicated, which when you looked at it the right way didn't become more complicated."

Amen to that!

Sasquatch: Monster of the Northwest Woods, by M.E. Knerr.

This adventure story was singled out by some overenthusiastic EODers (Enthusiasm Over Discretion) [actually, members of the Esoteric Order of Dagon amateur press association – ed.] as showing a possible Lovecraft influence. Worse yet, someone suggested that Ramsey Campbell might have written it anonymously (presumably after ghosting the complete works of Mark Twain and Lewis Carroll).

The truth is, of course, that the Big Foot legend and the Abomina-ble Snowman story from the Himalayas both influenced Lovecraft's creation of the Mi-Go.

This book is simply an outdoor tale briskly if not always gram-matically told, with surprisingly sharp if necessarily shallow charac-terizations, and with such poor proofreading that hyphenization of-ten occurs where even a Korean typesetter would know better.

There are some unintentionally amusing passages; my favored is: "When he spoke, it was almost as if he were voicing thoughts."

(And may the same be said of all of us!)

Editor's Note:

When this was submitted to J. Vernon Shea for his publication *Outré*, Vernon noted that he had cut down the list by eliminating the non-fantastic items. At the end of list, Vernon did thoughtfully in-cluded the titles of the other books James had commented upon: *You Might As Well Live: The Life and Times of Dorothy Parker*, by John Keats; *George S. Kaufman: An Intimate Portrait*, by Howard Teichmann; *Voices Offstage*, by Arthur Miller; *The Proud Tower*, by Barbara Tuchman; *The Price*, Arthur Miller; and *The Effect of Gamma Rays on Man-in-the-Moon Marigolds*, by Paul Zindel. The last two were actually plays.

BOOK REVIEW: THE BEYONDERS

The Beyonders by Manly Wade Wellman. New York: Warner Books, 1977. 189 pages. $1.50.

This first new book-length fantasy by Wellman in many years (ignoring the collaborative pastiche *Sherlock Holmes' War of the Worlds*, 1975) is a welcome event in the field. It is also pleasant to be able to report that the old master has not lost his touch.

The Beyonders is actually science-fiction, if you insist, but handled much in the manner of a terror tale until near the end. Its setting is the backwoods Appalachian territory that has gradually become Wellman's literary "home country"; and, as in the case of the supernatural stories collected in *Who Fears the Devil?*, both the dialogue and the narration are done in a modified yarn-spinner's dialect that – however unlikely in an SF story – comes off perfectly and rises to every challenge.

In fact, the rich and leisurely texture of the tale constitutes the reader's principal pleasure; for the plot, if summarized baldly, would not sound much different from any other "alien invasion" story.

The remote village of Sky Notch suffers a double incursion: two city-slicker types, one affable and one sinister, who prove to be advance agents for extra-dimensional entities lurking in the woods waiting for their chance to strike and make Sky Notch the base for a takeover enslaving earth.

Against them are arrayed a hero much in the mold of Wellman's ballad-singer John and a heroine from the mysterious Kimber clan that maintains its own strange worship of the aliens, as well as a feisty, retired doctor and various good-old-boy types.

The characters are vigorously drawn, the details of rural life savory in the telling, and one even gets used to a hero and heroine with the unlikely names of Garder Eye and Slowly. (Maybe the names are not unlikely where they, and Wellman, hang out.)

If the climax is a little casual, it is also plausible – and, as stated before, the pleasure, as in the case of any good yarn, is largely in the telling.

A superior novel, highly recommended.

BOOK REVIEW: THE GREAT WHITE SPACE

The Great White Space by Basil Copper. New York: Manor Books, 1976. 192 pages, $1.25.

There is nothing wrong with Mr. Copper's tale; it is the comparisons with Lovecraft that make it disappointing. The author abets the imposition by dedicating this novel "For Howard Phillips Lovecraft and August Derleth, Openers of the Way," and the reviewer of the Los Angeles *Herald-Examiner*, obviously out of his depth, obliges by proclaiming him "the best writer in the genre since H.P. Lovecraft."

As a matter of fact, even Derleth occasionally did better than this in his pastiches, so far as style and atmosphere go.

Nothing really outlandish happens in *The Great White Space* until it is more than two-thirds finished; there are only a few hints of dark doings and suppositions, and these could have been the trappings of an *Argosy* or *Blue Book* serial of the days of Lovecraft's youth.

In fact, the story of the search for a lost city in tunnels deep under the mountains bordering Tibet, using great passenger tractors, reads like a boys' adventure tale, related more to Conan Doyle's Professor Challenger books that to the macabre tradition.

Belatedly, we reach an interdimensional abyss where the "Great Old Ones," much resembling the BEM's of the old *Planet Stories*, are crawling about ready to invade the earth. But it turns out that these vampiric creatures can be deterred, if not destroyed, by grenades and flares, and one of our heroes thus escapes to warn a scoffing world.

So much for the parallels with Lovecraft, whose underground cities in *At the Mountains of Madness* and "The Shadow Out of Time" may
indeed have suggested this graceless parody.

It was a mistake to attempt an in-group joke by naming the main
character Clark Ashton Scarsdale. To an American reader anyway,
this is about like calling him Howard Phillips Schnectady.

BOOK REVIEW: THE PRINCESS OF ALL LANDS

The Princess of All Lands by Russell Kirk. Sauk City: Arkham House 1979. 238 pages, $8.95.

Russell Kirk of America and Robert Aickman of England are the pre-eminent practitioners of the "old-fashioned" ghost story in the English-speaking world today. As Kirk, a political philosopher and conservative columnist, is the less productive fictionally, the appearance of a new collection of his tales is a signal event in the fantasy field.

Kirk and Aickman are old-fashioned only in the underlying attitudes behind their fiction, not in the subject matter itself. Most of their stories are set in a grimily realistic present. But the assumption of both is that ghosts and other psychic emanations may exist. In Kirk's case this is buttressed by a forthright adherence to the Catholic religion, although no trappings of theology, exorcisms, or traditional demonology detract from the originality of his narrations.

And both frankly espouse the belief that the old days were best; that the selfish hedonism and greed materialism of today's bureaucratic welfare state represent a spiritual decline that perhaps for that very reason invites fiendish incursions by the eternal powers of evil.

Kirk indeed takes fiendish relish in disposing of an officious British city planner and a nosy American census taker in two of these tales, lining himself up solidly on the side of the powers of darkness.

The opening story in the book, "Sorworth Water," is a recognized modern masterpiece evoking obsessive evil active beyond the grave, in this case in Scotland, the ancestral homeland Kirk often uses as a setting, as he does his own home base, the impoverished rural areas of northern Michigan. In both settings he produces an admirably persuasive atmosphere.

The title story, a recent effort judging by internal evidence, tells of a psychically sensitive woman and the menace visited upon her every seven years by an Indian sorcerer, a distant cousin, first in the body and later after death, and how the powers of good that she is able to evoke help her defeat the evil at last.

"The Last God's Dream" is a long, fascinating account of a modern man's vision of the last hours of the Emperor Diocletian. This ambitious story, effective in the historical, psychological and philosophical levels, is a rattling good adventure yarn as well, narrated by the enigmatic Manfred Arcane, hero (or anti-hero) of the author's work of "political science fiction," the novel *A Creature of Twilight*.

The last three stories in the book are an admitted attempt to write a Dantesque trilogy on Hell, Purgatory and Heaven. The middle panel of the triptych, "There's a Long, Long Trail A-Winding," represents an especially successful example of the author's slow, thoughtful buildup of a character in whom the reader can believe and feel interest and concern. Like "The Cellar of Little Egypt," it ends in a crime of horrid ferocity; but unlike that story, there is an explicitly moral and even theological element in the dénouement here.

And the first part of the trilogy, "Balgummo's Hell," is a successful shocker based on the well-worn themes of spiritual evil incarnated in a mad, dangerous but doomed human vessel, another echo, perhaps, of Milton's magnificently fascinating Satan, reduced to a blind, senile Scots nobleman trapped in a house of shadows of his own summoning.

Four of these nine stories appeared in the author's earlier collection *The Surly Sullen Bell* (Fleet, 1962), which indicates that Kirk has not increased his sparse output of fiction much lately. But since that earlier book is long out of print, it is good to have them once more available here. For though one's appreciation for Mr. Kirk's spectral tales may vary from story to story with how closely the reader identifies with his outlook, still every narrative is a gem of polished style and artful construction, succeeding brilliantly on its own terms and on those idiosyncratic but persuasive ones of the author.

The work of Kirk (and Aickman), with its strong religious (or transcendental) overtones, forms the strongest possible contrast to that of the patrol saint of Arkham House, H.P. Lovecraft, whose horror tales are allegories of mechanistic materialism in which the universe is perilous but purposeless, and inimical only if seen from the narrow standpoint of human values. But in the house of fantasy there are many mansions, as the broad-minded Sage of Providence was always the first to admit.

This is the only Arkham House book I have ever seen that did not include a page giving the number of copies printed in the limited edition.

FRITZ LEIBER REVISITED:
FROM HYDE PARK TO GEARY STREET

IN 1950 I WAS a student at a music college in Chicago and nursed a strong outside interest in the field of macabre fiction, at which I had been trying my 'prentice hand since high school days. I had written four or five stories that I thought were up to commercial standards, but I had made no sales to the limited markets then known to me: *Weird Tales* and the new *Magazine of Fantasy and Science Fiction*. (The stories did indeed sell eventually, mostly to British markets that I tried fifteen or twenty years later.)

A friend who knew of my interests presented me as a gift with Fritz Leiber's first book, *Night's Black Agents* (Arkham House, 1947), containing several stories I knew from magazine appearances, and which had influenced my own efforts to produce modern, "down to earth" horror stories. From the jacket of the book I learned that Leiber was a fellow Chicagoan (though he was born there and I was a late-comer), and the telephone directory told me that he was my near neighbor in the South Side area (near the University) called Hyde Park.

I didn't phone, but strolled past the house on Ridgewood Court, just off 55th Street on a one-block, dead-end residential boulevard, one fall afternoon when the poplar leaves were spread out and piled up as picturesquely and symmetrically as in a Ray Bradbury neighborhood. On an impulse I turned in at the walk—you couldn't miss the house since Fritz, in what he now calls "alcoholic grandiosity," had painted the numbers 5447 on the upper half of a window pane in figures a foot or more high. I rang the bell.

A woman somewhat below medium height with greying page-boy haircut, strong features and distracted eyes answered the door, wearing some sort of smock over a wrinkled house dress, and identified herself as Mrs. Leiber. Though her husband was not at home, she told me in answer to my inquiries, I could reach him by phone in the evening; she was sure he would be pleased to meet a fan and aspiring writer.

Behind the woman a pale, rather pudgy boy of 12 or so was reading a book while he was perched on a hassock.

This was my first and only meeting with Jonquil Leiber and the couple's one child, Justin. When, long afterwards, I was told that Jonquil had been afflicted for many years with emotional problems that had become entangled with dependence upon alcohol and barbiturates, I recalled that distracted look, those barely focusing eyes. (I thought of her too when much later I read Fritz's uncanny story, "The Secret Songs.")

I spoke to Fritz on the phone that night and made an appointment to visit him in a few days. I happened to mention this rendezvous to an acquaintance, Dr. Dorothy Walker, then a professor of English at Roosevelt University, who was interested in the uncanny, and had told me a dream that gave me the idea for my story "The Elevator" (written about this time but not published until 1971, in Derleth's last anthology). Dr. Walker, it seemed, was acquainted with the Leiber family, and remarked to me, "I know Fritz and Jonquil, and they're both extraordinary in their range of interests. But their son Justin is so average that they sometimes seem to look at him curiously, as if to say, 'Who are you? What are you doing here?'"

(Justin Leiber is today a philosophy professor with an Oxford degree, continuing the family literary tradition in a different direction with a published study of Noam Chomsky's work to his credit. Moreover, Fritz claims proudly that he and Justin have of late become "great friends.")

Dr. Welker recalled, "Fritz gave the best performance that I've ever seen of the title role in *Othello* for an amateur production he directed a few years ago. His father was a great classical actor, you know, and Fritz appeared in plays and movies for a few years before his interest in science led him to take the job of editing *Science Digest.*"

Twenty-seven years later, when I tardily relayed to Fritz Dr. Welker's praise for his Othello, he answered, "I would have been even better if I hadn't been drunk all the time. I had a bottle in my dressing room, and one evening during the last scene I 'woke up' on stage and discovered that I really was strangling Desdemona. That sobered me up for a while."

But in 1950 I knew nothing of these personal vicissitudes of the Leibers, and was simply impressed, as an unpublished writer, by meeting a published one on the evening of our appointment, when Fritz answered the door and led me courteously into a sitting room.

It was impossible not to also be awed by Fritz physically. Much has been written of his impressive stature and striking features. Let it suffice to say here that at 40 he looked and spoke like those lofty and distinguished aristocrats that Hollywood had then convinced us typ-ified our socialites and statesmen. Well, he was an actor, I reflected, and apparently a good one.

But his manner exhibited not a trace of pomposity or condescen-sion. What we talked of that night was mostly writers and writing. He read one or two of my shorter tales and suggested both changes and markets. He examined a sonnet sequence in which I had thought I had summed up all the mordant cynicism of disillusioned youth, and told me in urbane tones it was still not strong enough.

He took my copy of *Night's Black Agents,* on the flyleaf of which the giver had penned an effusively lengthy inscription that filled most of the page, and scribbled at the bottom, "Excuse me for butting in on this page. —Fritz Leiber." (I still treasure that book, as they say.)

More than a quarter of a century later, Fritz recalled, "In 1950 you were the first writer I'd met who seemed to share my feelings and insights about the horrificality of Chicago." This meeting of minds led him to tell me about the origins and actual settings of some of his "Chicago Stories"—notably "The Hound," "Smoke Ghost," and "The Inheritance."

In turn, I told Fritz about the strange, decrepit old Harding Museum nearby, with its creaky floors and cluttered exhibits no one ever came to look at. (I wrote a story with this setting, years later, that has been published in England.) Fritz visited the museum on my say-so, I learned in 1977, and fell under its eldritch spell just as I did.

Altogether the evening was a fine charnel feast of, by, and for the weird. The only distracting element, a minor one, was that every so often Fritz would excuse himself with his natural or perhaps consciously theatrical courtliness, and go upstairs for a few moments to attend to his wife—she felt unwell, and was lying down. When he went upstairs he always carried a small wine glass of the sherry he had offered me and of which—if memory serves—he himself took one glass, no more.

(The 1977 Fritz, reminiscing over that evening, was of the opinion that he must have had a second bottle stashed upstairs.)

The encounter was, for me at least, a pleasurable one, but somehow I never got around to calling on the Leibers again during my eight remaining off-and-on years in Chicago. In those days, believe it or not, I had an exaggerated diffidence about bothering people who were presumably busier, more productive, and more successful than I was.

Then too, there was something faintly spooky about the Leiber household, with Its unnatural quiet and its quasi-somnambulist mistress; its grotesque decor of Clark Ashton Smith paintings and Fritz's own weird "spatter art"; its bathroom papered with *Weird Tales* covers; its spinet piano scrawled over and scored with cabalistic designs, as if gouged by a pallet knife, revealing cream-colored underpainting beneath the sickly green finish.

I liked to read about spooky things, but was not so keen, as are some New Yorkers today, about experiencing them first hand.

Time passed: I entered the army just after the Korean War, came back to Chicago to finish college, attended graduate school in St. Louis, and moved to South Korea, the attractions of which the army had inadvertently introduced me to in 1960.

Meanwhile I heard, through the fantasy grapevine, about Fritz's alcoholic breakdown of 1956, his subsequent sojourns on and off the wagon, and his moving to California to pursue belatedly the career of full-time, free-lance fiction writer. And those marvelous stories kept coming out in the magazines as well as a shelf-length of books.

When "The Secret Songs," that surreal glimpse of a couple beleaguered by the madness brought on—or controlled?—by drugs and alcohol, appeared in the early 1960s, I wondered just how much had changed in the Leiber household.

Meanwhile I had begun to write a few fantasy stories again from time to time, stimulated by the belated sales of the old ones that had been gathering dust for so long. Isolated as I was by my expatriation in the Orient, I needed a mentor, or at least a perceptive mind to bounce ideas off, and wrote to Fritz around 1967, after obtaining his address from a fellow writer.

He answered cordially, recalling our early meeting, and a two-year correspondence began—broken off, as I learned from mutual friends, when in 1969 Jonquil died from complications of her anodynes. Fritz, moving from Los Angeles to San Francisco, then began what was apparently a mild but steady carouse that lasted more than three years.

Finally he wrote to me again and seemed his old self. (In the meantime my own wife had died from a malignant tumor of the brain, a circumstance Fritz borrowed for the background of the protagonist of his new novel, *Our Lady of Darkness.*) Fritz's letters mentioned his three years in liquorish limbo with a remarkable detached frankness, and also recounted a spurt of new fiction following his recovery, the products of which readers are still catching up with.

For a professional author, writing for a living, Leiber's letters have always been remarkably prompt, thoughtful, copious, and at times brilliant. Like the father of us all, H. P. Lovecraft, the modern American fantasy writers seem not to begrudge the squandering of time and mental effort needed to keep in touch with conferees whom they may seldom or never meet face to face.

But in the summer of 1977 I paid one of my infrequent visits to the United States, since this involved a stay of several weeks near San Francisco, it was natural that my sojourn in the Bay Area would include an effort to look up the writer who, since our last meeting, had become—through sheer survival and guts as well as literary talent and achievement—the Grand Old Man of Fantasy. I wondered what, if anything, we would find to say to each other after 27 years and all the vicissitudes both of us had managed to get through. (Correspondence conducted at leisure and as the mood dictates is obviously a different and less kinetic confrontation than direct conversation.)

Leiber's one-room apartment on Geary Street was within easy walking distance of the civic center. (He has since moved to the relative luxury of four rooms on the snug street, in another and less decrepit old hotel nearer the downtown area.) Though I had the address, he courteously came down to the corner to guide me after I phoned him. His hair had whitened and receded; heavy glasses perched on the bony, aquiline nose: but he was unmistakably the same Fritz, though time had somewhat contracted the imposing stature by forcing a light stoop upon those broad shoulders. He ushered me upstairs by means of the balky, creaking elevator that, like other features of the building's design and decor, was instantly recognizable from the setting of *Our Lady of Darkness.*

Much has been said—a lot of it by Leiber himself—about the tiny, jam-packed room, with couch for bed and chair for typing table; with books, magazines, files, manuscripts and memorabilia, posters and paintings and photos all around, under foot, and overhead. I may have been one of the last newcomers that late August day to visit it in all its complex, majestic, overwrought, overripe, climactic proliferation just before the move.

The room reflected the man, true; but it was beginning to displace him as well.

But once we had settled ourselves into the few available nooks and crannies, there were no impediments to communication. The 1950 Leiber and Wade had talked about writers and writing; their 1977 descendants did the same, with only a few ritual references to the Good Old Days and the Bad New Ones (most of the moaning as I recall, came from my corner).

In all, I made three visits to the Grand Old Man over a period of two weeks or so, finding him unfailingly gracious and hospitable—even though I once dragged him to a pizza parlor to satisfy my own plebian appetites—even though he confessed being in the midst of a fallow period, with attendant doubts, depressions, and even psychosomatic lumbago—even though I inflicted upon him briefly the presence of my two hyperkinetic sons, aged nine and eleven, just so they could say they had seen a real live Famous Author, the man whose eerie stare and icicle hairdo used to frighten them as babies from the cover painting of the special Leiber issue of the *Magazine of Fantasy and Science Fiction*—a painting obviously modelled on a photo stuck on the wall of that Geary Street cubbyhole.

Fritz had just endured the frustration of a major movie nibble for his Fafhrd and Mouser series, with the attendant offer that he write the script himself. I asked him why, after a lifetime closely if intermittently associated with film and theater, he felt so hesitant about such an undertaking; especially since a few of his short stories were virtually shooting scripts with amplified stage directions.

He had several answers, one being that he had always instinctively avoided the dramatic forms per se, and it was too late to change. Another was that whenever, as now, he had been offered an advance in cash, it gave him the illusory feeling that he had all the time in the world, regardless of specified deadlines, and this started him off on a pattern of endless puttering over preparatory research, with no discernible output.

The basic or real reason he dredged up later in a letter, the producer had wanted another Star Wars, and Fritz's heroes were not adaptable to such a transmogrification without falsity to their innate qualities, a betrayal that their friend of forty years could not undertake in good faith. (He did get as far, though, as dreaming of Paul Newman and Dustin Hoffmann for his stars.)

Would I care for a drink? There was a little sherry stuck away somewhere, and there had been the remains of a bottle of brandy until someone or other—ahem! —had finished it off. I guardedly abstained. (Anyway, a search might have brought down those paper Walls of Jericho, or brought up the fabulous Scholar's Mistress to join us.)

Throughout our autumnal colloquies, there was no hint of any complaint on Leiber's part concerning what life had done to him, or what he had done to life, or indeed, what they had mutually inflicted upon each other. There was an informed awareness of his work as central to his existence, but not as a source of special pride or vainglory; there was a lively interest in the future, both as regards his own writing and the onward surge of human history.

In a sense, Fritz Leiber had become the protagonist of his own early story "The Man Who Never Grew Young," whose motto—chosen or forced upon him—was, "And I will go on."

Nor had his innate gentlemanliness deserted him: he showed almost as much interest and concern about me as I (uprooted, disoriented, shucked like an oyster from my shell of Asian isolation) did about myself, which is saying a lot.

This *discursive* memoir is meant as neither panegyric nor eulogy. I am at least as much interested in what Fritz will do as in what he has done; and in this respect I think my interest tallies with his own. He is one of the few stable influences in my life, strange to say; for his own career would scarcely win him any gold stars for stability.

But there he sits, in splendid comradely isolation in that spacious new Geary Street apartment, astride the San Andreas Fault, that metaphor of his life and of all life on earth. He has not only survived; he has prevailed, in the words of another hard-drinking mythologizer.

Long may he wave—as he did when I departed—and long may he waver, for that is the nature of the brute, and of the man, and even of the post-human stargazers we like to imagine ourselves; and which someday—guided by visionaries like Fritz Leiber—we might just possibly somehow manage to become.

BOOK REVIEW: AN INDEX TO THE SELECTED LETTERS OF H. P. LOVECRAFT

An Index To The Selected Letters Of H.P. Lovecraft by S.T. Joshi. West War-wick: The Necronomicon Press, 1980. 78 pages, $5.95.

This invaluable booklet is a monument to the assiduity and me-ticulousness of Mr. Joshi, the most dedicated of all Lovecraft scholars. It fills a real need, despite its Xerographic printing and lack of illustrative material that might have been included, in that Arkham House, publishers of the five volumes of *Selected Letters*, has never come through with its announced hardbound index volume, thus se-verely limiting the usefulness of the books themselves.

Mr. Joshi includes an Introduction and Explanatory Notes, setting forth the unexception- able principles he has employed in the body of the book, and besides the alphabetized Index proper, he appends a Chronology of Lovecraft's life (which unfortunately would lead the neophyte to believe HPL was born in 1914), a list of correspondents, an index to illustrations in the volumes, an appendix on quotations in the letters, and a list of errata, a field in which Mr. Joshi is undisput-ed master. (There are fewer mistakes in the letters than one would have supposed from the general level of Arkham House proofread-ing.)

One erratum of Necronomicon's own ought to be mentioned: on page 6, seventh line from the bottom, the words "this was not" or something similar should follow the parenthesis (in this sad world, nothing is ever perfect, it seems!)

Here, then, is the key that will unlock the massive set of Lovecraft letters for either the browser or the scholar interested in specific topics or people. Mr. Joshi deserves the thanks of anyone interested in Lovecraft the man and thinker, however casually.

Of course, Mr Joshi as always overvalues the letters. Calling them a more important monument than *The Outsider And Others* based on the extremely questionable supposition that Lovecraft was an original or important philosopher. And though he does mention the inexplicable cutting of some letters while bald repetitions are suffered to stand in close proximity, I don't feel that he would agree with me that the whole project should have continued as originally planned: one volume of letters, or at the very most two, carefully extracted from the trivia and repetition that choke the five-volume set, making nearly unreadable through daunting bulk those passages that truly are remarkable and readable. (The rest of the letters should of course be made readily available to specialists in a library collection, as I understand is the case, with a few exceptions.)

It is possible to come away from the *Selected Letters* with a less exalted opinion of Lovecraft than one had before reading them. He is humanized, true, with his weaknesses underlined by his own remorseless reiteration. But his credentials as a thinker—-claimed by his disciples, never himself—are seriously tarnished by the narrowness and parochialism of his scholarship and the idiosyncratic range of his reading.

Robert Aickman, no strong admirer of HPL's fiction, finds the letters actively off-putting, calling them "homespun" and the product of a "cracker-barrel philosopher". The point is well taken.

Lovecraft will live through the best of his fiction, but the letters are there for those who want a deeper insight into the man who wrote it. What they find in that man, it seems clear by now, will depend largely on presuppositions, a sort of Blind Men and Cthulhu instead of the Elephant. No matter: in the last analysis, author and entity were protean—not to say amorphous—enough to survive the scrutiny.

BOOK REVIEW: LORD OF THE HOLLOW DARK

Lord of the Hollow Dark by Russell Kirk. New York: St. Martin's Press 1979. 336 pages, $10.95.

R ussell Kirk, dean and perhaps sole survivor of those American occult fiction writers who do not necessarily regard their work as fantasy, has in this novel attempted to create a magnum opus pulling together all his religious, philosophical, and political preoccupations and ingeniously amalgamating characters, scenes and settings from both his macabre and realistic stories. Despite the jacket plaudits of Robert Bloch, William F. Buckley, Jr., and Robert Aickman – the latter Kirk's closest equivalent in Britain – the book doesn't quite come off, however admirable the effort.

Kirk takes off from the short story "Balgrummo's Hell" in the Arkham House volume *The Princess of All Lands* (1979), which tells of an aged Scottish nobleman sequestered on his estate for past murderous sorcery. The author spins a new yarn here about a modern-day warlock who rents the estate of the deceased laird as the most suitable site for a blasphemous ceremony whose participants are promised an immortality of depravity known as the Timeless Moment. (There is more than a hint of Crowley's Thelema Abbey here; even his motto, Do What Thou Wilt, is quoted.)

As the nemesis, Kirk brings in the revenant of wounded war hero Ralph Bain, who had already perished combatting spiritual evil in the unforgettable "Sorworth Place", written before 1962 (and who even turned up in paradise in the story "Saviourgate" from the Arkham volume); and – of all people – Manfred Arcane, the deviously delightful mercenary Machiavelli of a mythical African kingdom from the satiric novel A *Creature of Twilight* (Fleet, 1966), as well as narrator of the Roman fantasy "The Last God's Dream" in *Princess*, who we are to believe is not only the illegitimate son of the late Lord Balgrummo, but also a suddenly pious white magician, who plays the role of primly virtuous Dr. Van Helsing in *Dracula*, while masquerading as a deceased necromancer and drug pusher Arcane had liquidated in Africa.

Neither Bane – for obvious reasons perhaps – nor Arcane has the solidity of characterization evinced in their initial appearances, and the members of the coven – all bearing aliases from T.S. Eliot's poetry (another Kirk preoccupation) bestowed by the archwizard, who calls himself Mr. Appolinax – are not convincingly characterized either. They are, in fact, straw men, representing all that Kirk as a doctrinaire conservative finds repugnant in modern life: one is a lesbian, another an intellectual apologist for terrorist revolution, a third the proprietor of an international chain of abortion mills, yet another a wealthy pornographer, etc. The plot twists are similarly predictable and artificial.

In fact, the obsessive Catholic and conservative orientation of Kirk's thinking stultifies his story and the people who propel it, unlike the case in his earlier fictions, which are nearly dogmatic and preachy, but more successful as literature.

One begins to reflect that secularism and rationalism are not the only possible symbols for spiritual depravity; someone of the opposite persuasion and comparable talents could well write a plausible tale in which die-hard reactionary past-worshipping conservatives would be depicted as the representatives of cosmic evil. It all depends on one's outlook.

The villainous Appolinax, though intriguing in his physical incar-

440

nation as a spoiled priest with immature, fetus-like features, fails to come to malign life in the way that Dr. Jackman does so horrifyingly in Kirk's *Old House of Fear* (Fleet, 1961). Jackman is also a nihilist-radical consumed by spiritual rot, but we believe in and even empathize, as with Milton's Satan. Appolinax seems little more than a dummy in a fright wig by comparison.

Old House of Fear, with a similar setting, was far better constructed as a thriller than *Lord of the Hollow Dark*, where the action is clotted by too much dialogue, digression, and disquisition, and even the historical asides often become dull rather that atmospherically evocative.

In short, all the mechanism for a superb occult novel is here, but it never gets into effective motion. The climactic underground scenes are handled awkwardly, without the requisite suspense and pacing. Kirk has tried too hard this time, though his earlier macabre work proved amply that this is just the sort of thing which, at his best, he does as well as anyone writing today.

Perhaps, as in the case of *Old House of Fear*, he should just relax and toss off a thriller in which the moral purpose would emerge from the story and characters, instead of being flogged by an over-serious author.

YOU CAN'T GET THERE FROM HERE:
"HOW THE OLD WOMAN GOT HOME"

M.P. Shiel's picaresque mystery tale *How the Old Woman Got Home*, his twentieth published novel, appeared under the Grant Richards imprint in England in 1927. The following year the Vanguard Press brought out the American edition.[1] It is altogether an odd story, as his regular readers had come to expect from this author, but among his admirers were Hugh Walpole and Carl van Vechten, who wrote Shiel laudatory letters.

The main character is Caxton Hazlitt, a young British electrician, out of work and on the dole during the depression of the 1920's in London. He is devoted to his mother, the Old Lady of the title (though she is a bit too fond of the bottle) and to his girlish fiancée Jessie, who becomes a secretary to an elderly, eccentric American jewel collector named Sir Farrell. Hazlitt has no knowledge of his father, who abandoned the family a few years after Caxton's birth.

The young man is offered a job at a wealthy house, and when he shows up he is addressed and treated as the master of the ménage, an apparently fictional "Sir Henry Beresford". He decides to go along with the joke for a while, and begins to enjoy the high life to which his supposed title gives him entree.

But Caxton Hazlitt is no ordinary working stiff: we learn that he once invented a revolutionary airship (like Hogarth in *Lord of the Sea* (1901) with his stationary battleships), then cast aside the model and plans when commercial interests reused his terms for financing the project. In addition, he is able to engage in philosophical dialogues for whole chapters at a time as mouthpiece for the author's views.

About this time he adopts his incognito, Hazlitt's mother is kid-

443

napped for unknown reasons, and he sets about searching for her. On the trail he meets Dr. Harold Radlor, a rich, redheaded American evangelist, and his fascinating sister Máhndorla, with whom he becomes infatuated. Along the way he impregnates Jessie, and on two occasions stands her up on their wedding day, twice due to the machinations of the inprincipled Máhndorla, who convinces him Jessie is dead by means of a frabricated newspaper article.

On the rebound, he weds Máhndorla, but the marriage is never consummated due to the exigencies of his search for his mother, who has been spotted several times by Mary Giddings, a stage-Irish girl who had been her friend, and who enlists in the search after private detectives fail. But the kidnappers always elude their pursuers.

The old lady at last turns up and is jailed for stealing a jewel from Farrell, as a convenient way for her abductors, hard-pressed, to keep her incommunicado. She had been seen at Farrell's house, ostensibly working as a maid; but she obtained the jewel before coming there, through Dr. Radlor, which links him somehow with the kidnapping.

After many chases and much derring-do, all the principal characters converge on a country house where Mary has maneuvered matters so that Hazlitt can wed Jessie just before their baby is born. But seeing Farrell, whom he blames for his mother's abduction, Hazlitt attacks him. Farrell dies of a heart seizure and the old lady expires too, just as the baby is born.

It is then revealed who Farrell really was, and why Hazlitt's marriage to Máhndorla was invalid from the start, leaving him free to marry Jessie, which he belatedly does. But his leg has been crippled and his face disfigured by a fall after his attack on Farrell. This depresses his proud spirit since, like his creator, Hazlitt is something of a physical culture fanatic, and he decides to quit the scene by means of a suicide, or a faked suicide and subsequent disappearance –

we are not sure which – leaving the riches bequeathed to him by Farrell to Dr. Radlor, his half-brother, so that the latter might pursue the spreading of the new Gospel of Science, to which Hazlitt has converted him during their Socratic discussions, before either knew of their blood relationship.

Such is the plot, considerably simplified, of Shiel's intriguing suspense novel. Shiel called it his "political book", but in a broader sense it is philosophical, embodying in its polemical sections the author's views on everything under the sun, from diet to religion, from war to education, from eugenics to eurhythmics (if Shiel's passion for ritual jogging, which he passes on to his hero, can be so classified).

Before considering the ideas contained in the book, a few words must be said about its style and attitude.

This novel is written largely in Shiel's hectic, pell-mell narrative style, which August Derleth characterized in *Writing Fiction* as "far and away beyond the fastest action of a modern hard-boiled detective story," able "to convey movement of the most electrifying sort in a story in which there is no actual physical movement at all" through "a keen sense of word meanings and values".

An effective example of Shiel's extravagant but convincing manner may be found on page 53 in a description of the start of a storm that eventually drives Hazlitt and Jessie to cover, with unforeseen results nine months later:

> It being now about five of a bright afternoon, the sky quite a wildness of tresses and shreds stretched in dishevelment, like white hair of the Almighty flying wild in His flight through Time...

Occasionally the celebrated Shiel style thickens and threatens to

445

clot, as in this account of another storm on page 393:

> That night the voices of the storm were long
> like voices of those that mourn over obsequies and
> closed eyes, such as in Babylonish vaults of old
> bawled *nenia* of teen, coronachs of bereavement,
> with clamours of shriekings, haunches distorted,
> arms of distraction, *alalas* of ah and calamity that
> flap the tongue-tip to tattle, lla, la, and to tattle la,
> la, la, on some day of storm-winds wawling
> despairs and orgies of desolation, those of South-
> ern Italy whose steps follow the corpse called out
> (as does that dead-march in "Saul") the poignancy
> of three long voices that call Oi, Oi, Oi, and that
> call Loi, Loi, Loi.

At any rate, here is a passage to justify those impatient readers who claim that they "can't get through" a Shiel story.

For a book written in the 1920's by an author who had published six novels before the turn of the century, and whose earliest periodical fiction was as puritanically sexless as that of his Victorian contemporaries, this tale is unusually frank about matters which were still considered taboo in many quarters at the time.

The contemplation (if not the realization) of incest, and the conception and deliverance by the heroine of a child out of wedlock, are the principal examples of daring "modernity", but there are others.

During Hazlitt's holiday in Italy, he meets Lazazzera, a young lieutenant of police, who seems at first to have been dragged into the story solely for the sake of aiding Hazlitt in delivering the philosophical sermons the author frequently puts into his mouth.

But though the Italian is not fully brought to life as a mere listener to his friend's disquisitions, their parting generates a strange intensity:

> ...now seizing Hazlitt, he planted a kiss on each
> cheek, Hazlitt kissed him, and they parted at the
> gangway...

It is by no means clear why this digression should have been inserted. [2]

On pages 92-93, a storm is whimsically described as God,

> Seeming to be undergoing qualms of bowel
> trouble... with borborygms, rumblings of thunder,
> and some lightning digs, flying gripes in the guts,
> with gusts rising, spasms of flatulence puffing.

And on Page 388 we find the midwife attending Jessie remarking:

> "Yes, that's labor, I smell it."

Most surprising of all is the passage (page 389) in which Hazlitt recalls waking in his crib to half-observe his parents engaged in sexual intercourse, which he mistook for violence and held against his father. Certainly this notion can be found in Freud's writings of a dozen or more years earlier, but it had not seen such frank expression in polite fiction before, not even in the books of D.H. Lawrence persuasion published up to that time.

One intriguing sidelight on the origins of this book is revealed in Volume II of the Shielography update [3] where on page 197, seven photos cut from old newspapers are reproduced from a sheet tipped in to the presentation copy of the book inscribed by the author to his publisher. These anonymous photos are labeled with the names of the principal chracters of the novel in the author's handwriting.

Evidently Shiel either based his physical descriptions of these characters on pictures of striking faces that he had clipped, or found photos later that corresponded to his imaginary creations after he envisioned them. To know which was the case might shed some light on his working methods, but no explanation is to be found, in the inscribed volume or elsewhere, so far as I am aware.

Shiel, in his essay "Of Myself" in *Science Lie and Literature* (Williams and Norgate, London: 1950), called The Old Woman his "political book", but a reader would be hard pressed to deduce from it any partisan convictions that could be categorized among specific modern governmental systems. Was Shiel, as many claim, a fascist? Or was he rather a socialist, or an anarchist, or a constitutional monarchist, or an advocate of technocracy?

It would appear from his novels and other writings that he was all and none of these, as the moon or the trend of the times took him. He might speculate approvingly about nearly any type of governmental structure so long as it could make room for his key concept of the Overman and his fundamentalist faith in applied science as the potential savior of mankind.

Shiel's superman was, of course, out of Nietzsche by Shaw (to adopt equestrian parlance), while science worship had been popularized in the Nineties by H.G. Wells, who changed his mind half a century later. To none of these earlier writers did Shiel acknowledge any debt or pay any homage, but their ideas were in the very air of the late 19th century; from what source Shiel breathed them in is largely irrelevant.

448

The Old Woman – or rather her Overman son – is more concerned, actually, with economics than with politics. The very first serious idea presented in the book appears on page 14, when an old pauper says, "Wealth is Life," and Hazlitt counters: "Money is not wealth (but) represents wealth."

This points in the direction of Henry George's theories; and sure enough, on pages 174-5, we find this quite Georgean passage:

> ...What one *takes* from Nature is his own, he *owns* it, as he owns the air he *takes* into his lungs... In the case of a plot of land, it has soil, it has site, it has under-soil – those three: and its *soil* can be owned by an individual who takes it, moves it, ploughs it, compress its particles by building on it ... its *site* (relative position) cannot be owned by an individual, since he cannot take it, move it, do anything to it – or hardly anything; but it can be owned by a community which, by growing up around it, immensely moves it – moved it from being outside a community to being inside a community; as to its under-soil – the planet's lithosphere – that cannot be taken, moved, owned by one or many. You see, then, the absurdity of saying that one is an owner of land of which he cannot take the site or the under-soil, and has not taken the soil.

The political corollary of this is found on page 158:

449

(Reds) forget that the 'means of production' are themselves products, themselves had a means of production, namely Nature, land, which *alone* is the means of production... They are capitalists paying wages to 'wage slaves' and they jump to the conclusion that it is the capitalists who make the slaves ... this being the definition of a slave, a *landless man*, for a man who has no Nature, or land, to labour on for himself, must labour for some other's benefit, and *this* is to be a slave.

As to what the slaves ought to do to secure their liberty, this revolutionary diatribe appears on page 180:

...The slave can only attain freedom in three ways: by educating his master to see that slavery is bad for masters, by killing himself, or by killing his master. 'Parliament' is an engine of the master, and if slaves capture it, the master will naturally smash it like a matchbox, if the slaves lack cannon and officers... so what our Red should be getting red and ready about is not 'justice' but guns, not flights of bombast but flights with bombs, not declarations of rights, but declarations of war.

Indeed Shiel – writing I a time when universal extermination (as in his own novel *The Purple Cloud*) was a mere fictional conceit – becomes a virtual military mystic (though, like the pugnacious but anemic Nietzsche, he never fought in a war):

450

War is the essence of Christianity – of all that is divine and utterly lovely in the 'devine god' or "Christ' idea – the idea of Society – the dying of one for many – the individual's submission to the principle that one man must needs die, so that the whole people perish not... There is nothing Christian, nothing rich or generous left in our civilization save war, and the vine-god lives and deaths of scientists for society. (Page 167) [4]

The author's views on religion are, predictably, not orthodox ones, though he does quote with apparent approval an evangelical hymn he may have learned in his boyhood as son of a Methodist lay preacher:

"If Thou shouldst call me to resign
What most I prize, it ne'er was mine.
I only yield Thee what is Thine:
Thy will be done." (Page 304)

This has been foreshadowed by Hazlitt's fatalistic credo on page 49:

I give myself to Him... He takes whether *we* give or not, so we may as well give.

But obviously Shiel's religious ideas are not conventionally Christian. In his view:

God is – Power. And don't we know this one thing about Power, that it causes motion, and

451

nothing else? We *know*, then, what God cares about, namely motion, evolution, the trumpets of progress. (Pages 179-80)

This is a rather neat amalgam of the amoral Nietzsche with the highly moral Life Force worshipper Shaw.

Good and *bad* are notions of living things applied to what they find 'pleasant', for 'right' is certainly 'good' – differing from 'moral' which means customary. (Page 160)

Or, in briefer and more theological terms:

Right is – whatever God, in the long run, sends more pleasure than pain upon. (Page 93)

Like Shaw, Shiel is a positivist, and perhaps even in peril of being considered a "Positive Thinker":

The good Buddha 'thought' that 'life is sorrow', but if that were so, it would promptly end, for a life that can kill itself and continues to live *thereby* declares the universe is good, life is sweet. (Page 248)

How does life get for itself *good* or *pleasure*? In every case it gets it through science. (Page 161)

Science is the mother of religion (for) before

adoring one obviously must know... something of
the order of things; and to know anything of this is
science. (Page 163)

"Science is any knowledge of order," the definition given on page
162, seems to mean in context any knowledge from which generaliza-
tions may be drawn. This seems orthodox enough, but a Shielian theory on the origin of religion (pages 194-5) is less conventional:

> The savage hasn't your sense of the necessity of
> death... when he sees his brother laid dead before
> him, he can't *realize* that his brother is done, thinks
> him still kicking somewhere, somehow. And...
> how like God his brother has suddenly become:
> dumb – like God; enigmatic – like God; stark – like
> God... that is how ghost-worship evolves from the
> idea of God – not the idea of God from ghost-
> worship.

Later (page 305) this notion is elaborated into a rather fanciful
account of the origin of agriculture:

> When mounds... were heaped upon the dead, to
> keep them down, in order that they might not
> 'walk' but 'cease from troubling', and when, too,
> fruit offerings were put on the mound as bribes to
> quietness, the fruits' seeds sprouted, as they
> sprouted nowhere else (since the mounds were
> free of weeds). And now – *Agriculture!!* discovery,
> given *two* things, fruit on ground (seed) and broth-

er's flesh buried beneath, we live!

This Shiel takes as the source of vine-gods and grain-gods as well, and ultimately of the myth of Christ, 'a willing victim freely pouring out his soul unto death, perceiving that one man must needs die, so that the whole people perish not." (Page 306)

Shiel has very definite and rather Fabian-sounding conviction on the dignity of labor; but only if it is skill labor engaged in activities that might be considered in the broadest sense creative.

> *Common* mechanic... suppose a mechanic becomes rich – do you suppose that raises him one inch above himself? It is education that raises, and mechanics are educated ... for the training of gentlemen is all a training in soppiness – a training not in eternal things but in conventions, local fashions – Chinese 'learning' – village stuff. Why, if Europe were to throw out of her the Asiatic elements that damp civilization, men would soon be stamping on the moon... It is only scientists, experimenters, manual workers that are educated. *Common* mechanic? Uncommon! (Page 65)

> Work!... do get it out of your head that men are meant to work 'for their living'. To work, yes, to swot, to *die* of toil in the discovery of truth ... but not for a '*living*'... If... all of us with fifty thousand geniuses among us and a thousand million times more luck were set free to be 'scientists' as we

should be in a society devised by scientists. (Pages 87-88)

...To the discovery of truth two things contribute – brains and luck. Though a million men have not a million times more brains than one, they have precisely a million times more luck. (Page 169)

To sum up:

Do being properly, at the beginning... become a lord over Nature, yourself making the tools you use. Master ten crafts, becoming a cabinet maker before thinking of being a cabinet minister. (Page 432)

As his parting admonition to the brother who will inherit their father's wealth, Caxton advised Harold to buy up newspapers

to teach the four truths which the people at present most need to know: namely, (1) that science is good, (2) that nothing else is good (causally), (3) that truth like a troop: so slayvery, or 'land owning', is the enemy of science, (4) that every friend of science, truth, good, should have a rifle, standing ready to kill and to die for the kingdom of God ... Presently you will find yourself ready *to die*, if so you may augment ever so slightly the sum of science: *then* you will know Religion and the gist of the martyr's smart, and finally *will*

455

die ... (as) I think *all* men, as vine-god Christs will one day be dying, crowned with thrones of their thought, thorns of the roses that blow about their brows, they stepping up to death with impassione impetuosity, passionate joy; the voice will passionately confess 'yes, this is My son': and the veil of the Temple shall be rent. (Pages 430-437)

Thus Shiel's ecstatic vision carries him on wings of rhetoric in this single passage from popular education via newspapers to mystical martyrdoms in a great cause which, one may justly reflect, does not seem to be very clearly defined, here or elsewhere. [5]

Shiel tries to make his book an exponent as well as a proponent of scientific education. Thus there is a long passage (pages 196-200) discussing Einstein and relativity in popular terms, and another disquisition on the proposition "Gravitation = magnetism = motion of matter through a reign-of-force" (Pages 268-273). This writer is not physicist enough to evaluate or even to follow these digressions.

Throughout the book the author speculates on many other matters, including an anthropological aside no one seems to have followed up on since, to the effect that children who grow up into outstanding adults tend to be born to young mothers:

It is the child mother countries that produce beauties, geniuses, Jesuses, Helens. (Page 373)

And this sociological observation in the field of criminology likewise appears to be an original thought, with perhaps more broadly ramified potential applications:

> The idea that a private fracas is a matter for
> Society to mix in is African, and is a true idea when
> Society consists of a kraal, or patriarch caravan, of
> fifty: for where there is only one smith, if someone
> kills the smith, Society sighs; but the situation is
> changed when the fifty become fifty thousand. In
> Corsica for centuries, as lately in America, every-
> body murders everybody; but does that hurt *Socie-
> ty*? Not a bit: and I can see the people of the
> future amused at nations retaining the rules of
> nomads. (Page 183)

As the foregoing essay may have succeeded in suggesting, *How the Old Woman Got Home*, Shiel's self-described "political book", manages to toss off more, and more varied, ideas and conceits than most of the philosophical treatises in the social or physical sciences written before or since. That it does so, so cogently, and in the context of a fast-paced, intriguing suspense yarn, is another astonishing revelation of the Protean talents of this cranky, doctrinaire and visionary writer.

How valid or defensible his notions may be he leaves to others to work out systematically, should anyone care to do so one day. It is enough that he has – in the words of a modern poet [6] – caught the visionary glint where "something gleamed / in the outer edges / of reasonable doubt"

Footnotes

1 To which page number references in this essay pertain.

2 Stephen Wayne Foster has pointed out that Rocco Lazazzera wrote the preface to the 1924 Italian edition of *The Purple Cloud* which was reprinted at pp. 119-120 of volume II of this series, Shiel's library also included inscribed copies of Lazazzera's books at his dead. [ed.]

3 This update also preserves an error from the 1948 edition of the original Shielography in its synopsis of the book on page 195, where Caxton Hazlitt's half-brother Dr. Harold Radlor (or Ricchi) is referred to inadvertently as Hazlitt.

4 In a footnote following this passage Shiel refers the reader to his earlier novel *Children of the Wind* (London: Richard; New York: Knopf, 1923) for "the biology of war". There we find these words placed in the mouth of the book's African girl-queen and strategic genius: "Men grow like grass ... If you kill two, soon four spring in their place, and, if they have a ruler with eyes, the new one's better than the old." (Page 133) And later: "War makes less men, and so permit a man to pick out a better mother for his young."

On this, the Overman protagonist comments: "Though Darwin and that school, like her, were sure that 'war is good', Darwin thought that the good must come through fatherhood – never thought of motherhood ... refuted himself, since the bravest fall.... But by her theory war must be accompanied by monogamy; otherwise, after the war, the remaining men simply take more wives, including the riff-raff. Does this explain the stationariness of savages, of Asia?" (Pages 8)

A still later passage sums it up simply: "War is worth the making, for man himself is of no importance, only the son of man." (Page 285)

The rigors of this extremist position were recognized by Bernard

Shaw in his own version of the Overman, when he has the Devil say in *Man and Superman*: "Beware of the pursuit of the Superhuman: it leads to an indiscriminate contempt for the Human."

Shiel, like other writers as varied as Darwin, Nietzsche and Yukio Mishima, who approve war, never had to face combat. But Shiel does seem to recognize the other side of the coin when, on page 285, his warrior queen admits: "War good: but it bad ... for them that make it." Thus Shiel is apparently struggling to define universal principles as best he can, rather than rationalizing any bloodthirsty impulses in his own nature.

5 This lack of definition by Shiel of his 'cause' is perhaps because the author seemed to believe in evolution, leading to higher levels – toward God. This becomes a matter of Faith, with no clear concept of what we would be like if we truly had it. Shiel said somewhere, "We know not what we shall be like, but we shall be like that which prompts us." J.D.S.

6 Sotireos Vlahopoulos, in *The Stylus*, October, 1951.

LOVECRAFT AND FARNESE
IN HARMONY AND DISCORD

S INCE THE PUBLICATION of August Derleth's *H.P.L.: A Memoir* in 1945, it has been known that a California musician, Harold Farnese, approached H.P. Lovecraft by letter in 1932 with a request for permission to set to music two of the latter's "Fungi from Yuggoth" sonnets; that permission was granted, the songs written on the poems "Mirage" and "The Elder Pharos" and performed at private recitals or musicales; and that Farnese subsequently suggested that he and Lovecraft collaborate on a musical drama tentatively entitled "Fen River," for which the writer was to supply a libretto drawn from the general mood and atmosphere of his tales, to be made into an opera by the composer.

Derleth used these facts and quotations from the letters of the two men, as well as extracts from Farnese's sketch scenario for "Fen River," to speculate on a number of matters. Among these was the supposition that Lovecraft's "blind spot" (or "deaf ear") for music was more fancied than real, a result of the lack of opportunity and initiative for musical exposure, plus a traumatic reaction to early forced violin lessons.

Derleth also pointed out that Lovecraft ultimately evaded the operatic project because of his lack of experience in dramatic forms, a dislike for and ineptness at producing dialogue; and the uncongenial necessity of founding a story line on human relationships, something he almost never attempted in his fiction.

The project was shelved with Lovecraft's suggestion that he might collaborate on a libretto to be written by Farnese rather than undertaking the task alone (letter of Oct. 12, 1932).

This is all documented on the record, and two of Lovecraft's letters to Farnese are now in print (*Selected Letters IV*, pp. 69 and 84).

However, no one to my knowledge has examined the question of Harold Farnese's background, his talents or capabilities for the musical collaborations with Lovecraft which he effected or projected.

Some years ago I obtained from Brown University Library copies of seven letters from Farnese to Lovecraft, and the single-sheet scenario of "Fen River." Brown, however, did not have any copies of the Farnese music; it was some time later that August Derleth, in response to my prodding, recalled that he indeed did have some of the musical material in his files, and sent me copies shortly before his own death. This material consisted of the two "Fungi" songs plus a previously unknown item: an "Elegy" for piano written on the occasion of Lovecraft's death in 1937.

I have not, however, been able to discover anything further about Harold Farnese. Reference books yield nothing. The Institute of Musical Art in Los Angeles where he served as dean (and piano teacher, apparently) still exists, or did a few years ago; and unlikely as it may seem, the same Director listed on the letterhead of Farnese's correspondence in 1932 answered my inquiries nearly 40 years later. But he could tell me only that Farnese, a bachelor with no known survivors, had died in the early 1950's, and so far as he knew no estate or residual manuscripts existed.

Therefore I was thrown back upon the letters and musical manuscripts in my possession for the purpose of evaluating Farnese. In many respects, the former are – surprisingly enough – more impressive than the latter.

It is clear from the letters, for instance, that Farnese was well read in the field of the weird or macabre fiction. His praise of Lovecraft's *Weird Tales* stories is intelligent and to the point. He mentions admiring M.R. James, and Blackwood with reservations. (His equating the achievement of Lovecraft with Blackwood's "The Willows" can hardly fail to have pleased HPL, who always listed this tale among the top ten weird stories, and sometimes claimed it as his own personal favorite.)

Farnese was put off by the "abstruse and unnecessarily obscure" style of de la Mare, and couldn't wade through the Scots dialogue in Buchan's *Witch Wood*; but his appreciation of Gorman's *Place Called Dagon* and E.F. Benson's *Visible and Invisible* coincided with Lovecraft's tastes.

The latter offered to lend Farnese other books unobtainable in Los Angeles, and the composer in turn recommended to the writer a volume titled *Book of Black Magic and Pacts* by Arthur Edward Waite, and offered to buy and send him a copy of this rare volume. (Since the price asked was the astronomical $10, we may be sure that Lovecraft declined or ignored this offer.)

In his comments on music Farnese also shows cultivation and discernment (his branding of Mozart's "Don Giovanni" as "childish" is simply the reflection of a taste formed in an era before the true greatness of Mozart's operas was generally recognized, even among musicians).

The sketch scenario of "Fen River" is equally impressive. No actual plot is outlined, but suggestive characters are adumbrated, along with these perceptive words regarding atmosphere:

"The main quality of 'Fen River' must be its intangible weirdness and eeriness. It must follow the lines of H.P. Lovecraft's 'Fungi from Yuggoth'... 'Fen River,' of course, is an entirely different story, original in itself, against a Lovecraft background and surrounded by a Lovecraft atmosphere. Fog and haziness of outline are essential, nor should the plot be quite rounded out. We must leave the 'lost city' as we found it; the whole must remain something akin to a nightmare in our memory.

"'Fen River' is an attempt to present a music-drama in which the action is subordinated to the atmosphere of the play. The latter governs everything; the logical development of the plot depends upon it ...

"The dialogue must be written in words that are not commonplace (but) on the other hand must not be stilted... The effect must be weird and dream-like. At all times the swamp must be in our mind as governing the action of the Dramatis Personae. If there is no precedent for it, a style must be invented!"

Despite the attractive nature of this sketch, catering to Lovecraft's tastes and predilections, as we have seen he rejected the idea. And perhaps it was just as well.

For alas! When we turn to Farnese's own music, we are in for a severe disappointment. Though in his first letter to Lovecraft Farnese signs himself "Graduate of the Paris Conservatory" and "Winner of the 1911 prize for composition," there is no trace in his music of that great Gallic era when DeBussy and Ravel were in their heyday, the young Stravinsky was dazzling and outraging ballet audiences, while Faure was the grey eminence of the Conservatoire composition department.

This is simply inept, unimaginative music, stale and subprofessional.

The songs are set very poorly in terms of textual values, vocalization of vowels, scansion and rhythm; and although Farnese admits that he had never been very strongly attracted to song writing, the clumsiness is such that even a tyro should have known better.

Time and again strong beats and sustained or climactic notes fall on unimportant throw-away words such as "that," "and," "where," etc. Phrases begin quite often on extremely high notes "unprepared" – indeed, at the beginning of "Mirage" someone has penciled lightly: "Hard start?" I would call it impossible.

The musical ideas themselves are amorphous and undistinguished, the harmonic devices of the piano part awkward, rudimentary, and antiquated – not in terms of 1977, or 1932, but of 1911, 1895, or even 1883. Continuity or development of musical thought is largely absent.

The conclusion is inescapable that Farnese could talk a better opera than he could ever have composed.

The piano "Elegy" is perhaps even less impressive. One single maudlin strain, resembling 19th century salon music, is repeated endlessly with little variation, and that no improvement, over a bass of primary triads with a few all-too-predictable dominant sevenths and mild transitional harmonies. It is like the improvisations of a village organist of the 1850's whose favorite composer was Gottschalk.

Alfred Galpin's "Lament for HPL," also written on the occasion of Lovecraft's death and published in facsimile in *Marginalia*, is somewhat stronger stuff musically, though also in conventional style; and Galpin, so far as I am aware, never claimed to be a professional musician or a prize-winning composer.

It is not particularly pleasant to belabor the departed, and I shall forbear continuing. My purpose has been simply to disperse any lingering impressions that the world might have lost a Lovecraftian musical masterpiece with the aborting of the "Fen River" project.

For Lovecraft, a self-proclaimed amateur (in the best sense of the word), humble to the point of self-abnegation regarding his work, operated on a level of professionalism unattained by the somewhat vainglorious Farnese, whose efforts were indeed amateurish, in the pejorative sense of the word.

[The following note written after the article by Dirk W. Mosig]

Farnese's "Elegy" was probably not as "unknown" as Mr. Wade suggests, since Lovecraft collector Ray Zorn had a Photostat in his legendary hoard. I first saw this item, in photocopy form, in the collection of R. Alain Everts, in 1974, at which time Mr. Everts graciously made a duplicate for my own files. On the other hand, I had not seen Farnese's "Mirage" and "The Elder Pharos" before Mr. Wade kindly supplied me with copies of these.

SOME PARALLELS BETWEEN
ARTHUR MACHEN AND H. P. LOVECRAFT

O N THE SURFACE, it is hard to imagine two writers, or two
personalities, more dissimilar than Arthur Machen and the
younger American fantasy writer H.P. Lovecraft (1890-1937) who
predeceased him.

Machen was convivial, theatrical, devout, a man who relished life;
but yet basically a mystic who saw godhead – and the diabolical –
imminent in all earthly things. Lovecraft was introverted, ascetic,
reclusive, science-oriented, a neurasthenic eccentric whose dream
worlds were self-admitted escapism from a materialistic universe he
deemed blind, mechanical, and mindlessly inimical to man.

Yet Lovecraft admired and was influenced by the older writer. [1]
What can a latter-day Christian visionary who loved life have in
common with a materialist agnostic who claimed to hate it?

For one thing, both were great scholars and antiquarians who
despised the age they lived in, though for very different reasons.
Lovecraft was by nature an Anglophile aristocrat *manque* who would
have preferred living in the Age of Reason, hobnobbing with Johnson,
Dryden, Pope and Swift. Machen's preference lay obviously even further back in the medieval Age of Faith. Despite his bluff gusto, the
British author might have agreed with Lovecraft's uncompromising
pronouncement: "Life has never interested me so much as the escape
from life."

Another factor in common between the two was their idealization
of childhood. Machen's novel *The Hill of Dreams*, one feels, is a book
whose equivalent Lovecraft always wanted to write but never did.
He came closest in one of his short stories, "The Silver Key" (1926) in

which the key is one that unlocks the gate for a return to endless, idyllic childhood.

Indeed, Lovecraft claimed to have lived, as a child in Providence, Rhode Island, in a fantasy world of Roman remains almost as vividly imagined as that of the protagonist of Machen's book, who in youth recreates in elaborate fantasies the time of the Roman legions in Wales, but who grows up a frustrated poet rather resembling Lovecraft.

Both writers quite obviously look back on their earliest years with frank nostalgia as the period of greatest happiness, and regard growing up as an unmitigated disaster. They also share the childhood dream of past Roman glory.

Franz Leiber in an essay [2] on Lovecraft's themes and achievements states that Machen "directed man's supernatural dread toward Pan, the satyrs, and other strange races and divinities who symbolized for him the Darwinian-Freudian 'beast' in man." Lovecraft, with his specific scientific interests, added the awesomely vast space-time universe of the astronomers and Einstein, empty in theory but sinister in implication from its very size and unplumbable mystery.

"The most merciful thing in the world, I think," Lovecraft wrote in the beginning paragraph of a pivotal story, "The Call of Cthulhu" (1926) "is the inability of the human mind to correlate its contents... The sciences, each straining in its own direction, have hitherto harmed us little; but some day the piecing together of dissociated knowledge will open such terrifying vistas of reality, and of our own frightful position therein, that we shall either go mad from the revelation or flee from the deadly light into the peace and safety of a new dark age."

Machen would never have put it that way: his universe contained God as a counterbalance. But with this reservation, Lovecraft's portrait of a blind, perilous cosmos is very similar to the underlying assumptions of an author who allows an innocent protagonist to be turned into something utterly alien and abominable by a chance slip of a pharmacist.

Machen's "Novel of the White Powder," by the way, was interpreted by psycho-analytical criticism as a masturbation-built fantasy; and Lovecraft's work has similarly been probed to seek out his psychiatric quirks. Both writers disliked and rejected Freudian psychology, probably basically because it seemed an invasion of privacy: what would they say to all this posthumous symbol-chasing applied to their own work?

In the stories written toward the end of his short life, Lovecraft leaned more and more on science rather than the supernatural to evoke horror and fright. Tales like "The Shadow Out of Time" (1934) and the novel "At the Mountains of Madness" [3] (1931) read virtually like objective scientific reports for much of their length. Since Lovecraft's early work was largely imitative of Poe and Dunsany, there are only a few stories from his middle-period which may be said to exhibit Machen's direct influence, when, in Leiber's words, he "tended to mix black magic and other traditional sources of dread with the horrors stemming purely from the science's new universe."

The best example of this is the novella "The Dunwich Horror" (1928), a story which was cited in the O'Brien "Best Short Stories" of that year, one of the few accolades the author's magazine fiction received during his lifetime. [4]

The opening of the tale evokes the baleful beauty of a New England backwater as minutely observed as Machen's rural Wales:

> When a traveler in north central Massachusetts takes
> the wrong fork at the junction of the Aylesbury pike just

beyond Dean's Corner he comes upon a lonely and curious country. The ground gets higher, and the briar-bordered stone walls press closer and closer against the ruts of the dusty, curving road. The trees of the frequent forest belts seem too large, and the wild weeds, brambles and grasses attain a luxuriance not often found in settled regions. At the same time the planted fields appear singularly few and barren; while the sparsely scattered houses wear a surprisingly uniform aspect of age, squalor, and dilapidation. Without knowing why, one hesitates to ask directions from the gnarled solitary figures spied now and then on crumbling doorsteps or on the sloping, rock-strewn meadows. Those figures are so silent and furtive that one feels somehow confronted by forbidden things, with which it would be better to have nothing to do. When a rise in the road brings the mountains in view above the deep woods, the feeling of strange uneasiness is increased. The summits are too rounded and symmetrical to give a sense of comfort and naturalness, and sometimes the sky silhouettes with especial clearness the queer circles of tall stone pillars with which most of them are crowned.

In this setting lives Wizard Whateley, a reclusive old farmer, with his deformed albino daughter Lavinia, his "dark and goatish gargoyle" of a grandson, of unknown paternity, and his inherited collection of "great odorous books" on sorcery.

The Whateleys are clearly up to something, performing periodic ceremonies on a pillar-crowned peak that produce "underground-rumbling queerly synchronized with bursts of flame ... from the summit of Sentinel Hill."

Meanwhile the demented old man pursues his obsessions by moving the family from the big house into an outbuilding, and knocking out all the partitions and floors of the main house. He begins buying cattle in suspicious quantities, and some of the animals are glimpsed in pasture with curious sores or wounds.

The grandfather eventually dies, the mother disappears after a ceremony, and the precocious boy Wilbur, at fifteen "almost eight feet tall", leaves home for a trip to consult a rare book on magic at the university library: "shabby, dirty, bearded, and uncouth of dialect... carrying a cheap new valise from Osborne's general store."

The librarian refuses to lend the book which contains a chant necessary to Wilbur's next step of initiation, and the freakish giant, breaking in at night to steal the volume, is killed by the savagely excited mastiff watchdog.

> The Thing ... lay half-bent on its side in a fetid pool of greenish-yellow ichor and tarry stickiness ... Above the waist it was semi-anthropomorphic; though its chest ... had the leathery, reticulated hide of a crocodile or alligator. The back was piebald with yellow and black, and dimly suggested the squamous covering of certain snakes. Below the waist, though, it was the worst; for here all human resemblance left off and sheer phantasy began. The skin was thickly covered with course black fur, and from the abdomen a score of long greenish-grey tentacles with red sucking mouths protruded limply ... On each of the hips, deep set in a kind of pinkish, ciliated orbit, was what seemed to be a rudimentary eye; whilst in lieu of a tail there depended a kind of trunk or feeler

with purple annular markings, and with many evidences of being an undeveloped mouth or throat. The limbs, save for their black fur, roughly resembled the hind legs of a prehistoric giant saurian; and terminated in ridgy-veined pads that were neither hooves nor claws ... only generous clothing could ever enabled it to walk on earth unchallenged or uneradicated.

This, of course, is a much more detailed description of a monster than the few shadowy glimpses Machen permits – perhaps because of Lovecraft's increasingly scientific approach, or perhaps because he had noted the charge leveled against Machen to the effect that "what cannot be described cannot frighten either".

Wilbur Whateley is thus seen as the Lovecraftian image of the beast in man – not, be it noted, an inheritance from Machen's secret hill-dwellers or sinister sylvan nature deities, as in "The Great God Pan": but the hybrid offspring of an extraterrestrial entity, as the rest of the story makes clear.

With Wilbur dead, no one visits the shell of the old Whateley farmhouse at Dunwich, from which suspicious noises have been heard for years. Then one day the house is observed to have been literally burst open from within, and a great swath of flattened grass leads to a meadow where cattle are found sucked nearly dry of blood.

Subsequently, odd marks "as big as barrel-heads" are found, like prints of an elephant, only more than four feet would make.

Several isolated farmsteads are wrecked at night and their denizens, human and animal, disappear.

The ravenous monster is invisible, but just before bold scholars armed with ancient exorcisms destroy it, it becomes visible for an instant, and one rustic, watching the battle through a telescope, describes it:

> "Bigger'n a barn ... all made o' squirmin' ropes ... hull
> thing sort o' shaped like a hen's egg bigger'n anything
> with dozens o' legs like hogsheads that haff shut up
> when they step ... nothin' solid about it – all like jelly, an'
> made o' sep'rit wrigglin' ropes pushed clost
> together ... great bulgin' eyes all over it ... ten or twenty
> maouths or trunks a-stickin' aout all along the sides, big
> as stove pipes, an' alla-tossin' an' openin' an' shuttin' ... all
> grey, with kinder blue or purple rings ... *an' Gawd in Heaven
> – that haff face on top!* ... it looked like Wizard Whateley's,
> only it was yards an' yards acrost ..."

(Lovecraft never again put his monsters under such intense direct
scrutiny: in later stories they were glimpsed fleetingly, seen in
dreams, or reconstructed archaeologically.

After the monster dies, the scholars explain to the Dunwichers:
"It grew fast and big from the same reason Wilbur grew fast and big
– but it beat him because it had a greater share of the *outsideness* in
it ... It was his twin brother, but it looked more like the father than
he did."

But the father, as the story has earlier suggested, is no simple
black-magic devil begetting a baby on Rosemary, but a multi-
dimensioned superbeing from beyond interstellar space, transcend-
ing the Einsteinian universe – part of Lovecraft's pantheon of Great
Old Ones, entities completely incomprehensible to men who want to
regain sway over the earth for unimaginable aims and unfathomable
purposes. (That such beings would be vulnerable to mere chants and
exorcism is implausible, and Lovecraft does not make this mistake

again.)

It is here that Lovecraft's direction diverges sharply from the tradition-oriented fantasy of Machen and veers toward science fiction; albeit a science fiction fraught with the terror and revulsion characteristic of older horror tales.

This is the point at which admirers of Machen and those of Lovecraft begin to find themselves in either of two mutually exclusive camps. Existential critic Colin Wilson, for example, in his book on creative imagination *The Strength to Dream* carried on a love-hate analysis of Lovecraft's work over many more pages than he allotted much more important writers, and wound up later writing two novels and one novella developed from the Lovecraft patterns.

Wilson found Lovecraft an "obsessed" writer, and himself appears obsessed with the American recluse's penetrating if horrific view of the universe.

In contrast, Wilson mention Machen elsewhere just once, in passing, and calls his work "only mildly interesting".

That Lovecraft, though, genuinely admired Machen and learned from him is testified not only in his own stories, (he even used an epigraph from Machen to head "The Horror at Red Hook" (1925)), but in his long essay "Supernatual Horror in Literature" (1926-27), an historical-critical survey assembled on the basis of personal taste, but still the nearest thing to a scholarly monograph on the subject extant.

In this essay, Lovecraft ranks Machen with "The Modern Masters", including only Blackwood, Dunsany, and M.R. James additionally in this category (writers Wilson either doesn't like, or fails to mention, incidentally).

"Of living creators of cosmic fear raised to its most artistic pitch," the essay says, "few if any can hope to equal the versatile Arthur Machen," and goes on to summarize and comment on the major

Machen fiction – all of it written by then – observing elsewhere: "The best of Arthur Machen's work fell on the stony ground of the smart and cocksure 'nineties."

Lovecraft's own work fell on even stonier ground: the garish 'twenties and the sordid 'thirties. Less widely recognized in his life-time than Machen, whose work after all did appear in hard covers and attract some intelligent appreciation, Lovecraft was unfortunate-ly swayed by his pulp-magazine markets, or by his own lack of self-confidence, to overwrite and melodramatize in many places. When he calls Machen "a general man of letters and master of an exquisitely lyrical and expressive prose style," Lovecraft is wistful, if not a touch envious.

But due to the single-minded persistence of Lovecraft's disciple August Derleth, who founded Arkham House in 1939 to issue posthu-mous collections of Lovecraft material, every scrap of Lovecraftian ephemera has by now been in print at least once [5], and all his fiction is steadily available, often in several editions.

In contrast, the subtler and finer-grained tales of Machen are largely unavailable, at least in America, unless Knopf reissues the splendid big 1948 anthology.

Derleth at Arkham House, meantime, has continued to publish various macabre books on the strength of the gradual success of the Lovecraft volumes and – ironically – now offers the only available edition of *The Green Round*, a late and uneven novel by Machen, whose disciple Lovecraft was too modest to declare himself nearly half a century ago.

The paradoxes are as interesting as the parallels in comparing the equally off-trail careers of Arthur Machen and H.P. Lovecraft.

Notes

1 There is no evidence indicating that Machen ever knew of Lovecraft's fiction, which appeared in book form posthumously, only a few years before Machen died.

2 "A Literary Copernicus", in *Something About Cats and Other Pieces* by H.P. Lovecraft and Others, Arkham House: 1949.

3 A phrase actually found in Dunsany.

4 This story was filmed recently, with much attention to background and detail, but rather weak script and direction. Still, it is the best of three cinematic adaptations of Lovecraft's work. (One would like to see proper adaptations for the screen of "The Black Seal" and "The White People".)

5 The *Selected Letters*, in five volumes, are now at midpoint of publication.

Quotations from the works of H.P. Lovecraft by permission of Arkham House, Publishers.

BOOK REVIEW: LOVECRAFT: A BIOGRAPHY

Lovecraft: A Biography by L. Sprague de Camp. New York: Doubleday 1975. 510 pages, $10.00.

It must be stated at the outset that this is a valuable, ambitious, badly-needed but not an ultimately satisfying book. The trouble seems to lie in the disparity between writer and subject. De Camp specifically disclaims any antipathy for Lovecraft in a reported exchange of letters with Vernon Shea; but though he may not actively dislike HPL, de Camp appears to have very few affinities and not much sympathy with him.

It might be difficult to find many people who really would empathize with the Lovecraft who emerges from these fluently researched pages; but de Camp, would seem to be so much the direct opposite of Lovecraft that any real identification with his subject is impossible. After all, de Camp is, a go-getter, an achiever, the author of "811 books" (as he quotes Avram Davidson writing sarcastically about the prolific Derleth). What has de Camp in common with the recluse he calls schizoid, who was obviously his own worst enemy as well as "his own most fantastic creation", when it came to making a place for himself in either literature or life?

Therefore de Camp cannot resist getting up on his soapbox and preaching little sermonettes to the long-dead Lovecraft. He *ought* to have done this and that, learned shorthand, observed people to improve his dialogue and characterizations, and earned a decent living to satisfy his minimal legitimate desire for travel, leisure, and books.

In short, he should have been L. Sprague de Camp instead of H.P.

Lovecraft. But then he would have written de Camp's stories instead of Lovecraft's, which is something else again.

De Camp realizes this on the very last page of his text, but it is not clear why he failed then to go back and take out all the complacent little moralistic essays that contribute nothing to a portrait of Lovecraft, but tell us more that we need to know about de Camp's own self-satisfaction. After all, it is perfectly clear that from chapter after chapter of documented facts and quotes that Lovecraft was an absolute failure in his own terms, as well as those of the world; and that it was out of the same psychic tensions that warped his life that his stories sprang or skulked.

The nit-pickers among the scholars will no doubt find many errors in minutiae in this book. Since I have found some myself: on page 333, "The Dunwich Horror" is intended instead of "The Colour Out of Space"; on page 149, "hate distorted" is surely a misreading for "half distorted", as is "would" for "word" on pace 95 (probably a simple typo); Poe's "Ulalume" was certainly; not "probably", the origin of "Nemesis" (page 124, etc.)

But for me, de Camp's errors in critical judgment of the work are more disturbing. A devotee of the highly plotted fiction of Howard, de Camp has a tin ear for any tale that depends on atmosphere and mood, and these are among Lovecraft's main achievements.

Thus he describes "Beyond the Wall of Sleep", perhaps the first fully successful Lovecraft tale, as more promise than performance," and calls "The Festival" a "minor story", while taking seriously such embarrassing throwbacks as "The Hound" (and miscalling it a Mythos story).

De Camp brushes off the delicate fantasy and finely wrought imagery of "The Silver Key" because it revels in nostalgia and self-pity; but so does Joyce's *Portrait of the Artist as a Young Man*, for instance; and this does not prevent it from being a work of art. Instead, the biographer praises the trashy sequel "Through the Gates of the Silver Key", a pulpish blend of occultism and implausible science fiction dreamed up by E. Hoffman Price and merely rewritten by Lovecraft.

De Camp acknowledges the quality of the "Fungi" sonnets, and quotes them liberally in his chapter headings; he rightly recognizes that little else from Lovecraft's poetry reaches this level. But then he consigns even the best of the mature poetry to a status inferior to the juvenile jingles of Robert E. Howard.

There may be no disputing taste, but it is possible to deplore complete lack of it.

With all the demurrer possible to enter against it, de Camp's biography presents for the first time a rounded, factual account of every stage of Lovecraft's career, or lack of one. Mysteries and controversies, such as those involving his parents' deaths and the breakup of hismarriage, are examined carefully and objectively. If the charm of the man is not evoked, it is at least documented. This may not be the lovable Lovecraft of legend, but one feels that it is the real one, presented with refreshing lack of that sentimentality which has always blurred the image passed down to the aficionados from the Old Hands.

For this alone, we must be grateful for the labors and accept the *longeurs* of the de Camp *Lovecraft*.

BOOK REVIEW: LOVECRAFT AT LAST

Lovecraft At Last by H.P. Lovecraft and Willis Conover. Arlington: Carrollton-Clark, 1975. 273, xii pages, $30.00.

In 1975 Willis Conover is a jazz expert and DJ on the Voice of America, (I hear his erudite and witty show every once in a while here in South Korea.)

In 1975 H.P. Lovecraft is a shadowy but pervasive literary cult figure known to some as the second Poe and to others as the Copernicus of the horror story. Since his death in 1937 his little-known tales have been rescued from mouldering pulp magazines twice: first in the 1940's when disciples issued his work in hard covers for aficionados, and again in the 1970's when his entire output – including some things issued under his name that he had no hand in at all – went into a uniform series of paperbacks that sold well enough to keep them in print and the Lovecraft name before the public.

HPL as a personality – hypersensitive, withdrawn, psychically crippled – has over the years fascinated a long list of literary men with far more impressive credentials than he himself ever boasted, from Colin Wilson and James Schevill to Gore Vidal and John Updike. It was usually a love-hate relationship.

In 1975, jazz expert Willis Conover published a book about Lovecraft that can only be called a work of hagiography – the final stage in the canonization of a man who loathed both organized religions and literary personality cults.

In 1936 Willis Conover was a precocious teen-ager with a fervid interest in weird tales and science fiction that caused him to join the "fan" movement and issue his own "zine," thereby coming into contact with many professional and semi-professional authors from whom he solicited material.

In 1936 H.P. Lovecraft at forty-six was the greying eminence of horror fiction, a man with less than a year to live, near the peak of a lifetime reputation for altruism, ultra-respectability, penuriousness, and epistolary loquaciousness.

Conover wrote to Lovecraft for a contribution to print in his amateur journal, and the older man responded with those torrential letters so characteristic of him, even when he learned that his new pen-pal was only fifteen years old.

Of course, one gets the impression that if Lovecraft had been the last man left alive he would still have kept on writing long letters, to himself, or to guppies, or to the universe at large. They were his compulsive substitute for sex, or alcohol, or food, or all three. (He mentions to Conover that he usually received – and answered – from ten to fifteen letters a day!)

This flattering attention naturally meant a lot to the young man, and his idol's sudden death less than nine months after their correspondence began was understandably a shattering blow. Conover states that the Lovecraft influence and ideals have stayed with him ever since, and he is far from being alone in this.

Out of such an early experience Conover has now fashioned *Lovecraft At Last*, the latest and probably not the last book to be issued with an HPL by-line that the author never dreamed about, a deluxe 272-page volume priced at $30.00 and purporting to reveal the "real" Lovecraft for the first time,

It scarcely does that, at least for anyone who has read HPL's other correspondence from this and earlier periods. In fact, there is rather less "heavy stuff" in these letters than in those sent to older correspondents, and rather more of the in-group details of amateur journalism and the "fan" movement.

Nevertheless, Conover has tricked it all out in fantastic style, not only reproducing many of Lovecraft's letters and postcards (even the envelopes) in Photostat, but going to the length of printing them in color to show the shade of ink that the Sage of Providence used.

The self-effacing HPL would certainly have been taken aback; one suspects that his second reaction would be a loud guffaw. Conover has hit on the device of presenting many of their exchanges as dialogues. This works well because quite often they responded to each other's letters point by point.

There are also numerous reproductions of magazine covers and articles, as well as many photos. (But for all the meticulous indexing and attributions, I cannot for the life of me discover the identity of the blurred figure in the photo on page 234. Is it Lovecraft's then-surviving aunt, Annie E.P. Gamwell, at 66 College Street?) The book is also padded with associational items, some of which are available elsewhere.

The conclusion is moving, with the Photostat of Lovecraft's feeble, scrawled sentence of March 8, 1937 – doubtless his last attempt at correspondence – on the back of a postcard inquiry sent by Conover: "Am very ill & likely to be so for a long time." Not for long; a week later came Annie Gamwell's genteel but stricken letter disclosing her nephew's death from cancer.

This volume is a beautiful job of bookmaking, designed by Robert L. Dothard. But one can't help feeling that, whatever Conover's personal contributions and preoccupations have added, the purposes of scholarship would have been better served by subsuming a few of these letters into the forthcoming volume of Lovecraft's *Selected Letters*, to be published by Arkham House.

As it is, we have a collector's item, and an item for collectors only.

BOOK REVIEW:
PRINCE ZALESKI AND CUMMINGS KING MONK

Prince Zaleski and Cummings King Monk by M.P. Shiel
Mycroft and Moran: 1977. 220 Pages, $7.50.

Arkham House has now rounded out its 30-year project of getting a selection of M.P. Shiel's shorter fiction back into print.

Prince Zaleski and Cummings King Monk properly appears under the
firm's seldom-used Mycroft and Moran imprint because it consists of
two brief series of tales which, for want of better words, would have
to be called crime or detective stories, though of the seven pieces, one
is more properly the account of a hoax and another a philosophical
dialogue.

Prince Zaleski, hero of four stories, was the protagonist of Shiel's
first book, published in 1895. He is a self-exiled Russian aristocrat
and aesthete who amuses himself by solving English crimes, mostly
from an armchair in surroundings that are ornate, not to say effete
(an unwrapped mummy is one of his items of decor).

This was the heyday of the deductive detective tale, and Shiel –
never one to avoid going to literary extremes – makes these stories
into abstract puzzles with little pretense of plausibility. Whether
proving that the apparent murder of a nobleman was really suicide-
with-assistance in face of impending hereditary insanity, or discovering that an apparent rash of suicides was really a series of murders
carried out by a secret *Ubermansch Cult*, the languid prince out-
Sherlock Holmes by knowing all and telling all, sometimes before it
happens, on the slimmest and most recondite of clues.

The most amusing of these tales is "The Stone of the Edmunds-

485

bury Monks", which tells of a missing family jewel put through an intriguing shell game in a bizarre situation.

Shiel's famous weltering style is nascent here, but already shows signs of its later unique originality: "As a brimming maiden, out-worn by her virginity, yields half-fainting to the dear sick stress of her desire—with just such faintings, wanton fires, does the soul, over-taxed by the continence of living, yield voluntarlly to the grave and adulterously make of Death its paramour ... The coffin is not too strait for lawless nuptial bed; and the sweet clods of the valley will prove no barren bridegroom of a writhing progeny,"

It is perhaps an acquired taste.

Cummings King Monk, a character dating from a 1911 collection, is a bored part-Jewish millionaire (Shiel's love-hate obsession with Jews appears in several places) who, like Grand Guy Grand in Terry Sothern's Christian, likes to make it hot for people. At one point he comers the entire wedding ring market of London by hoaxing a visiting German princess into thinking she has lost hers and persuading the public that almost anyone might be the unwitting owner of the precious gem.

The best story is the last one, "He Wakes an Echo", about a murderous madman presiding over a crazed household in a mouldering manor house. This story has much in common with such later Shiel masterpieces as "The House of Sounds" and "Huguenin's Wife" (Lovecraft pointed out that the origin is Poe's "House of Usher"), which only goes to show that Shiel, like other writers was prone to rework favorite themes.

The philosophical dialogue—or monologue by Monk with cues from the author—"He Defines 'Greatness of Mind'" explores Shiel's quirky notions of savagery and civilization, proving to his own satisfaction at least that Great Britain at that particular time was not only the greatest but the only real civilization the world had ever known, though thinkers as diverse as Cardinal Newman and Bernard Shaw are characterized as savages. All good clean fun.

BOOK REVIEW: THE WITCHFINDER

The Witchfinder by Maurice Hilliard. New York: Coward, McCann & Geoghegan, 1974. 182 pp., $5.95.

Novels of sorcery and diabolism in the modern age are getting to be a fad in "respectable literature", with rather predictable results: shifting from the underground of pulp and paperback, the genre has attained a new degree of literary skill, while at the same time it has lost some of the intensity and conviction shown by unskilled writers who were nevertheless obsessed and immersed in their subject.

All this dated from the success of *Rosemary's Baby* as a book and film in 1967 and after, climaxing with the furor over *The Exorcist*, a worse piece of work because, though authentic, it took itself too seriously and as a novel it didn't measure up.

The best of them all was and is Fritz Leiber's *Conjure Wife*, a magazine version of which came out in the early 1940's, with expansion to book form ten years later, and two movie versions to its credit. This fact has still to be recognized by many outside of specialists in the genre.

At any rate, Mr. Hilliard's new book is competent and restrained, even dour and laconic, in keeping with its North Country setting. It lacks the flamboyant characters and action of the *American Harvest Home* by Thomas Tryon, but it doesn't fizzle out like that book either.

The themes of the two novelists are not identical. Mr. Tryon writes about a "classical" fertility cult in New England; Mr. Hilliard of the traditional British Satanism of witch and coven. Both, though, exploit the still-effective plot stereotype of strangers menaced by a sinister community-wide conspiracy.

In this case, Cass Hopkins, an old maid married late to a widower, moves with him to a retirement cottage in Northumberland, shared with a bachelor brother.

This cottage, The Croft, had once been shared with Arthur's first wife, Esther, an authority on local folklore who left behind some equivocal manuscripts and a garden of poisonous herbs.

Arthur Hopkins' personality seems to dissolve and change under the sinister ministrations of Dr. John Stearns, a powerful and magnetic personality who dominates village life.

The title of the book plus the name of its protagonist's husband, of course, gives away the game to those in the know far too early, as does the nickname of the dead Esther. Matthew Hopkins had been the great "witchfinder general" of the mid-1600's, later executed for witchcraft himself – John Stearns and the woman called "Goody" had been his henchmen, and these evil revenants are obviously trying to reincarnate themselves in the 20th Century.

(You might have seen Vincent Price play Matthew Hopkins in a very badly scripted movie with the same title as this book.)

Mr. Hilliard writes with a high degree of polish and plausibility. The minor characters are convincingly sketched, and he makes good use of the heroine's neurotic fear of open places to invoke a closed, claustrophobic atmosphere.

This factor builds quite cleverly into an effective ending that is neither garish nor a letdown, quite an accomplishment in this field of fiction.

If a quibble must be raised, it is that Mr. Hilliard, like *Rosemary*'s creator, Ira Levin, doesn't believe a word of any of it, and is writing for readers who don't either.

Paradoxically this makes his book less gripping than William Blatty's *The Exorcist*, which like the pulp and pocket book shockers of earlier years is a bad piece of writing, but gives the impression that the author believes it, and wants the reader to believe it too.

BOOK REVIEW: WORTH THE WAITING

Worse Things Waiting by Manly Wade Wellman, illustrated by Lee Brown Coye. Carcosa, Chapel Hill, 1973: 352, xii pages, $9.50.

This volume, an omnibus of his best stories in the macabre genre by one of the last "neglected" *Weird Tales* writers, is "long delayed" in two respects: it was held up in production by its present publisher for the better part of a year; and, moreover, had been announced in a 1946 Arkham House catalogue for appearance the following year!

Thus it is obvious that *Worse Things Waiting* had a long time to wait, and is not the same book August Derleth planned to publish in 1947 (and still had on his list in 1969—see *30 Years of Arkham House*), since some of the stories included did not receive magazine publication until as late as 1960, in a periodical not yet existing in 1947, and were presumably unwritten when the Arkham House volume was announced. So much the better: the book is bigger, and better for the later stories.

It is not clear just when the publisher was changed to Carcosa, a new house located at Box 1064, Chapel Hill, N.C.—which town is also the author's place of residence. Arkham House informed me in mid-1973 that the manuscript had been taken to another publisher without their being consulted, even though they had already completed the art work for the dust jacket. No doubt Wellman, after Derleth's death, despaired of seeing his book in print during his own lifetime (he is now over seventy), considering that it had been announced more than a quarter century earlier.

No matter, the wait was worth it, and despite the Arkham House spokesman's belief that "Arkham House could have done more with his manuscript than the publisher that he ultimately went to" (letter to the reviewer. August 6, 1973), it is nevertheless a fact that Carcosa's *Worse Things Waiting* is in every way a higher quality book than has come out of Sauk City in many years—which is not to denigrate Arkham House, but only to suggest that this volume must certainly be one of the most beautiful jobs of book production done on an original work of fiction in the United states—or perhaps anywhere else— during this decade.

That a book like this—350 pages beautifully printed on fine paper, solidly bound, adequately proofread, and gorgeously illustrated by the ideal artist for this writer—could be produced in a limited edition for less than $10 strongly hints that the $10 novels spewed out by New York publishers—with content, format, and materials vying for the lead in shoddiness—are more a result of waste, profiteering, or expense-account conspicuous consumption than of the actual economics of publication. (The fine job Knopf did on John Gardner's illustrated novel *The Sunlight Dialogues* last year is the only recent honorable exception I know of.)

I will leave detailed consideration of Coye's starkly evocative drawings to the art critic, suffice to say that his quasi-primitive, but subtly sophisticated pictures, with their harsh counterpoised blocks of black and white, perfectly reflect the story-telling mode at which Manly Wade Wellman excels the American folk tale or back-country legend raised to a macabre art form by acute observation, apt writing, and unaffected identification with the subject at hand.

There is only one flaw in the collection that surfaces often enough to make this superlative book less than a classic: Wellman tends to be weak on endings, which are proverbially the most ticklish aspect of such stories. Either the conclusion trails off limply, as in "The Kelpie," "The Undead Soldier," and "The Pineys," or we guessed it too far back, as in "Where Angels Fear" and "Dhoh," "without the clinching quality of reinforcement" that Fritz Leiber finds in Lovecraft's nebulously pre-hinted conclusions, which actually adds to the impact of his tales, when the device works. (See Leiber: "A Literary Copernicus" in *Something About Cats.*)

The formatter of the book reveals that Wellman revised almost a quarter of these stories for this publication. One wishes he had more drastically rethought many of the endings, which may have been suspenseful enough for pulp readings of the 1930's and 1940's, but which creak rather tiredly now. The openings and developments of these tales are masterly only to falloff at the end.

Stories which escape this structural flaw are those which remain most memorable: "Up Under the Roof," "Come Into My Parlor," "Sin's Doorway," and especially the famous "School for the Unspeakable" and the equally worthy "Warrior in Darkness."

Wellman is usually at the top of his form when telling his story from the viewpoint of a humble observer or narrator, providing plausible justification for use of poetically evocative quasi-dialect writing. (This is hard to do, but the reader somehow knows when it rings true, whether be knows the particular regional style or not.) Thus the half dozen stories with American Indian themes, though not uniformly successful, work well in general, as do the tales of Sgt. Jaeger's witch-busting exploits from Civil War Days. There are also two stories which—as the author notes in his forward—are in effect prestudies for the cycle of John the Balladeer collected in Arkham House's *Who Fears the Devil*, probably the author's most consistently satisfying weird fiction. I suspect "The Pineys" belongs in this prestudy group too.)

Wellman can work rural southern dialogue and imagery into a chillingly vivid depiction of outlandish people, places, and events, seldom striking a falsely literary note, and never jarring the atmosphere of a fantasy rooted solidly in prosaic everyday reality.

There are minor cavils, of course, such as Wellman's adding an extra "h" to Cthulhu in the brief "Terrible Parchment", his only Mythos story (this was done, I am told, to point up a supposed Greek derivation for the word). Of the two poems, neither is outstanding, but "Voice in a Veteran's Ear," with its refrain "I am the man you killed," stands a little too close to Wilma Owens' "I run the enemy you killed, my friend," and suffers in the comparison.

An author's choice of his own best stories may not always agree with that of a reader, obviously. There are 28 stories in this book, and Wellman published about 50 in *Weird Tales* alone. He admits that "all are not worth printing again."

I have not read all his periodical fiction, but from the *Weird Tales* of the 1940's I recall with pleasure the John Thunstone stories (including the tale of Rowley Thorne), which I now realize was based on the career of the black magician Aleister Crowley, and probably published before that formidable four-flusher died in 1947. Also, Wellman published a superb story in the March 1946 *Weird Tales* that contained a dream pilgrimage somewhat a la Merritt, with a diabolic Don Quixote figure titled "Twice Cursed." (There was a cover illustration by Coye too.)

Anyway, maybe there are enough past—or future—Wellman stories to make up another, if perhaps lass bulky, collection, provided Carcosa's splendid opening volume receives the reception it so richly deserves.

The fact that *Worse Things Waiting* makes one look forward to another volume is the surest evidence of its quality. We had to wait this long, so we can certainly wait a bit longer—though hopefully not a quarter century—for a sequel.

BOOK REVIEW: XELUCHA AND OTHERS

Xelucha and Others by M.P. Shiel. Arkham House, 1975. 243 pages, $6.50.

B efore I comment on the stories in *Xelucha and Others* by M.P. Shiel, two observations should perhaps be recorded. The first is that this book was announced by August Derleth for publication in 1947, the year the author died nearly forgotten, and the price then listed was $3.00. Thus the present volume represents part of the commendable effort by the Derleth heirs to get delayed Arkham House books into print at long last, though inflation has, more than doubled the initially announced retail price in this case.

The second point to be noted is that the book's dust jacket by Frank Utpatel is the worst cover art for any Arkham House book I have ever seen. Utpatel enjoys a prominent place in macabre art annals through having illustrated H.P. Lovecraft's first, semi-professionally published book in 1936, and has done much effective work in the field since; but this feeble jacket design should have been rejected, whether filed away from 1947 or newly commissioned.

Shiel is, of course, one of the great obscure eccentrics of British letters, about whom readers will always have strong reactions, positive or negative. Most of his novels embody crank notions concerning religion, philosophy, science and history, not to speak of race that need not be explored here. His style is florid, flamboyant, and idiosyncratic to the last degree, but I like it: it generally does the job the author intended, which after all is what a style is for.

Nevertheless, there are some passages here in which the grammar, syntax, and elisions misleadingly suggest that the author was not a native speaker of English. Thus on page 219 appears the phrase: "A moment more I had flung a gown around me." The author wanted to write either, "A moment more and I had flung a gown around me," or else, "A moment later I had flung a gown around me," but, inexplicably did not choose either, nor let an editor do it for him. The passage gains nothing from the eccentricity, though this may be arguable in other cases.

On the other hand we find, choosing almost at random, such superbly ornate imagery as: "The air was thick with splashes, the whole roof now, save three rafters only, having been snatched by the wind away; and in the blush of that bluish moonshine the tapestries were flapping and trailing wildly out after the flying place, like the streaming hair of some ranting fakir stung reeling by the tarantulas of distraction." (Page 112)

This is from "The House of Sounds," which Lovecraft tellingly described as a Norse "Fall of the House of Usher."

Lovecraft also noted that the style of the first version had been toned down in a revision; the mind boggles to imagine what the original was like.

The title story too as it appears here is said to be a much later revision, but the *fin de siècle* putrescence of its charnel stench is still potent enough to raise a retch:

"'What, think you, is the portion of the buried body first sought by the worm?' ...

"'The *Uvula*! That drop of mucous flesh, you, know, suspended from the palate above the glottis: they eat through the face-cloth and cheek, or crawl by the lips between defective teeth, filling the mouth. They make straight for it: it is the chelicerae of the vault.'"

These are the two tales in the book most famed and most effective on their own terms. Others are more or less successful stories of outré detection or spectral vengeance, with a strong admixture of the *connate cruel*. "The Tale of Henry and Rowena" is unpleasant without being edifying, but "The Bride" and "Many a Tear" sustain interest by evoking some degree of human sympathy.

"Huguenin's Wife," a Grecian pre-study for "The House of Sounds," is quite effective, whole the biologically implausible "The Pale Ape" undoubtedly represents the precursor of Lovecraft's "Arthur Jermyn" and Henry S. Whitehead's "Williamson," fervid fantasies of bestiality which do not surpass the power of Shiel's original.

Shiel, like the contemporary novelist Iris Murdoch, is a spinner of outlandishly outrageous stories that are both entertaining and convincing while the reader is under the author's spell, but which turn into elusive blue moonshine when analyzed. Thus analysis is probably wasted on them.

His are the oddities of bizarre, event and setting; hers, those of grotesque plot and character. Both employ oblique Alice-in-Wonderland dialogue, to very different ends. Murdoch strives to suggest the obscurer labyrinths of the inner individuals; Shiel, to evoke the entrapments an obscurely purposeful universe can spring upon the superior, but maimed soul.

It remains to speak of Shiel's most striking quality, his pace and rhythm. As Derleth states in the unusually informative blurb, "Shiel has a sense of swiftness which is far and away beyond the fastest action of a modern hard-boiled detective story; he has the ability to convey movement of the most electrifying sort in a story in which there is no actual physical movement at all! ... He says no more than is absolutely necessary in the barest sense to tell his readers of matters of speech, action, and movement generally; and he permits himself to expand when the matter is one of sensuous imagery, of color, of scene, emotional experience, and all things pertaining to the senses. In this lies his effect."

Though Shiel's numerous out-of-print novels are generally more impressive than his few short stories, they are even more erratically uneven. Thus this collection of tales is a useful introduction to his manner and, hopefully, a possible harbinger of renewed interest in the longer works. (Robert Bloch should certainly do a film script of *How the Old Woman Got Home* for Alfred Hitchcock, or perhaps Alain Resnais.)

Meanwhile, in consideration of the real ingenuity of the crime stories in *Xelucha*, Arkham House might consider finally bringing out its projected volume of Shiel's detective tales, *Prince Zaleski and Cummings King Monk*, which Derleth was still insisting as late as 1970 that he would someday publish.

It may be late, but never too late to revive a genuinely visionary writer who seems to have been rather unfairly bypassed by both his contemporaries and posterity.

Also available from
Shadow Publishing

Phantoms of Venice
Selected by David A. Sutton
ISBN 0-9539032-1-4

The Satyr's Head: Tales of Terror
Selected by David A. Sutton
ISBN 978-0-9539032-3-8

The Female of the Species And Other Terror Tales
By Richard Davis
ISBN 978-0-9539032-4-5

Frightfully Cosy And Mild Stories
For Nervous Types
By Johnny Mains
ISBN 978-0-9539032-5-2

Horror! Under the Tombstone
Stories from the Deathly Realm
Selected by David A. Sutton
ISBN 978-0-9539032-6-9

The Whispering Horror
By Eddy C. Bertin
ISBN: 978-0-9539032-7-6

The Lurkers in the Abyss and Other Tales of Terror
By David A. Riley
ISBN: 978-0-9539032-9-0

Worse Things Than Spiders and Other Stories
By Samantha Lee
ISBN: 978-0-9539032-8-3

Worse Things Than Spiders and Other Stories
By Samantha Lee
ISBN: 978-0-9539032-8-3

Tales of the Grotesque: A Collection of Uneasy Tales
By L. A. Lewis
ISBN: 978-0-9572962-0-6

Horror on the High Seas
Selected by David A. Sutton
ISBN 978-0-9572962-1-3

Creeping Crawlers
Edited by Allen Ashley
ISBN 978-0-9572962-2-0

Haunts of Horror
Edited by David A. Sutton
ISBN 978-0-9572962-3-7

Death After Death
By Edmund Glasby
ISBN 978-0-9572962-4-4

The Spirit of the Place and Other Strange Tales:
Complete Short Stories
By Elizabeth Walter
ISBN 978-0-9572962-5-1

CPSIA information can be obtained
at www.ICGtesting.com
Printed in the USA
BVHW081150150620
581543BV00001B/20